The Wrong Kind of Indian

The Wrong Kind of Indian

Jey Tehya

Wyatt-MacKenzie Publishing

DEADWOOD, OREGON

The Wrong Kind of Indian
Jey Tehya

ISBN: 978-1-942545-47-7

Library of Congress Control Number: 2016936888

Intended for mature audiences.
TW: Graphic; Eating disorders.

Wyatt-MacKenzie Publishing
DEADWOOD, OREGON

Wyatt-MacKenzie Publishing, Inc.
www.WyattMacKenzie.com
Contact us: info@wyattmackenzie.com

For the real C. (Of course).

Acknowledgements

An enormous thank you to my husband, the real C, for putting up (for years!) with my using you as my muse. Sometimes in my writing you're also the scapegoat, occasionally a villain (especially in the early years), but thank you for letting me hang up all our dirty laundry for the world to see. Look at that stain over there. See that rip down the middle, that spot in the corner? We made those—and isn't it lovely? Now. Tell me something nice.

A big thank you to Erin Smith, who showed up at just the right time and has stayed there ever since. Even when oceans have separated us, those waters may as well have been a trickle.

Thank you to Anne Looser. Because you were there, and I know you always will be.

An incredibly heartfelt thank you to my publisher, Nancy Cleary, owner of Wyatt-MacKenzie Publishing, for loving my book like it was her own baby. Faults and all. To have a publisher who genuinely believes in your work, nurtures it, and takes a poet like me on an Oz-like trek into novel territory is a rare and wonderful thing. I will be forever grateful.

To all the nouns—the people, places and things—that inspired this book, thank you. For better or worse. You helped inform who I am, as a writer and beyond, and part of this book is yours. You may never know it … and that's likely for the best.

Finally, thank you to all the readers and to those who relate. To the Native American writers, the women writers, the ones with eating disorders and a littering of abusive upbringings, relationships and scars. There are more of us than you think, so hold on. And there's incredible power in our fold.

PROLOGUE

Kismet isn't a guarantee. The world won't split down the middle and offer up its heart if you don't catch the signs. Destiny, it's just a map—sometimes with too many keys and "x's" to make much sense. It's *our* job to read closely, between the lines, and piece together what we can. If we do, maybe we'll get lucky and calm those rocky waves inside us. Kismet, it's not telling us one person is it. Or one place, or one activity, or any one success. But it screams. Can't you hear it? It's banging against the thin membranes of you right now. *Look! It's here! Right here, this path, this person, this place that will stop that wandering circling inside you.*

But so often, we don't look. We don't see. We skim the messages instead of reading them, letter by letter. We overlook them altogether because we're so stupidly certain of what we're *supposed* to be doing. Should be seeing. We want to get to the end, to check everything off our list. All done! A nice, clean, blank sheet of paper. And in that rush, we miss the whole point.

We miss what's so blatantly, hungrily before us.

This doesn't mean we won't find happiness if kismet gets ignored or only half heard. It doesn't mean we're doomed to loneliness or boredom or always feeling itchy for more. Sometimes it does, but mostly we'll all move on. We'll keep moving forward, and we'll have incredible moments. And shitty ones. And a lot of mediocre ones while we keep our eyes anywhere but at where destiny is pointing. That's some kind of life. Isn't it?

But what if, what if—what if we could have more?

Part 1

One Boy's Trash

FROM BELOW, you can see the nervous scratch marks. The dried snot smeared into delicate doilies, the hasty sketches of penises, bulging grotesquely and flanked by hairy balls. It wasn't that big a deal, finishing first grade. It wasn't even a "finishing," just a long, long break stretching ahead, a summer fat with the same piano lessons on Wednesday nights. Calligraphy classes Saturday mornings in a dusty downtown Medford studio. My father spraying the cold water from the garden hose at my head when my blonde head bobbed up like a sun-bleached apple in our flimsy pop-up pool—the only form of play we'd ever made.

It was 1987 and none of us were graduating Mrs. Koppel's first grade class. She would be our second grade teacher, too. It would be a different classroom in a different hall at Jewitt Elementary. Maybe even one on the inside of the building, where the toilets weren't made for such short, stubby legs.

Like always, I finished first then played busy while the others caught up. Cleaning out our desks, spreading the findings on the scratchy carpet beneath them like confession, it seemed weird even at six years old. *Look at all the garbage! The nubby pencil, the peeled off fingernail entrails!* The pencil case, ruler, compass, markers, sharpener, baby stapler, all anointed with *JT* in my mother's pregnant handwriting.

"Five minutes!" Mrs. Koppel said as she wrote *Happy Summer Vacation* on the chalkboard, the invisible eyes in her bulbous neck watching us with fervor. The lure of summer hooked her hard, too.

I could see John H. watching me. We had been put in "nests" for the past month. Four squat metal desks huddled in a pod at random. For five weeks, he sat across from me, drilling *fucks* and boobs into his desktop with a vengeance. I had escaped his spitfire words the whole year, even as I'd been placed directly in his vision. I was the absolute epitome of helpless prey, complete with an extra tube of fat at my middle for protection. Until now.

Without a word, John took his trash pile, his disgustingly heaping, dirty, chewed-up pile, and pushed it neatly into mine. And smiled.

Words always stuck in my throat. It's like they're made out of peanut butter, creamy Jif, refusing to leave the safety of my mouth. But this was the end of first grade. I wouldn't see these people, John H., Mrs. Koppel, or any of them, for three long months. It may as well have been a lifetime.

Something wild grabbed me inside, and my arms moved without my brain telling them to. I pushed his pile back. Firmly, not toppling his filth mound at all. Success.

"*Jennifer!*" Mrs. Koppel's voice snapped me back. "Go throw that away right now."

"It's not mine." My voice came out of nowhere, doggedly forced its way past the peanut butter words and through my lips. It was the first time I had spoken freely the entire year. Without being forced to read out loud (embarrassing) or take my turn reciting equations (humiliating). "It's J—"

"I don't care *whose* it is. Throw it away *right now*."

The walk to the garbage bin was a mile. Ten. Every pair of eyes in the classroom latched onto me, fast and hungry. They watched the entire trek, from picking my body off the floor to clutching John's mess, mating with mine, close to my heart to keep it from falling.

The summer bell rang while I cascaded his waste into the wire basket.

CHAPTER ONE

I ALWAYS KNEW I'd get married at twenty-seven. It was decided, just like I knew seventeen was going to be one hell of a fucked-up year. And it was. My mother had kicked me out/I ran away (depending on whose story you believed) when I was sixteen. Now *that* was a glorious year. It was before my high school boyfriend, Scott—a dropout three years older than I—went all-in emotionally and verbally abusive. We were losers together. Driving from that stunted southern Oregon town across the California border to Weed in case my mom had called the cops. For six months we lived in his car and on random friends' couches. We pawned what we could, showered in gas station truck stops, and slowly meandered our way up to Portland where his semi-wealthy family reluctantly took us both in. Now, when I tell people I was technically homeless and lived in a car as a teenager, they look at me with that special cocktail of shock and sympathy. I just don't get it. It was every sixteen-year-old's dream to be free.

That was over ten years ago. That was two abortions, my father's death (hepatitis C), one miracle of an undergraduate degree, and a master's degree so brand new, squeaky clean it still didn't seem real, ago. I wasn't supposed to have or do any of that. Then again, my father was a Stoneclad, he wasn't supposed to die. But I was a scholarship committee's wet dream. Considered independent by the government due to "abandonment by both parents," low-income, first-generation college student, female, and with a tribal enrollment card from the Cherokee Nation, I was set. Well, I *would* have been had I figured out the whole

3

scholarship, diversity poster child deal sooner than my junior year. It was too late, and the student loan iron maiden was already inching close by the time I mailed in my first diversity scholarship application.

Yeah. I always knew I'd get married at twenty-seven. I just didn't know I'd get divorced then, too.

"I'm done," I said as soon as Eli opened his eyes. He didn't seem surprised. "I'm moving in with Michelle. You can have everything."

"Okay," he said. And that was it.

We had been married for less than six months, but "together" for six years. The meet cute was spot on. It was freshman year of college. I was in a sorority, which I eventually became president of (that was a laugh). He was in a fraternity, which he eventually became president of (not much of a laugh there). We got together because it made sense; and I was still licking the wounds from the Scott years. He had turned real bad three months prior. I wanted safe, stable, boring, and non-threatening. That was Eli.

We should have broken up years ago. I was never attracted to him (he was barely my height), and I'm sure the feeling was mutual. I got fat in college. Real fat. I was never slender, but my high school weight hovered around 145, and that looked decent on an admittedly curvy 5-foot, 6 and ½-inch frame (gotta count that half). The weight slipped on slowly during freshman year, then I exploded for the rest of undergrad. I stopped weighing myself at 235 pounds and size 20. Eli stayed. In that rush of perfectionism I tend to have, I went hardcore Atkins my junior year and vowed not to weigh myself for one year. No cheating from the diet, no cheating with the scale. One year later, I was down to 155, just in time for Eli's cancer diagnosis.

Hodgkin's lymphoma is one of the easiest cancers to treat when caught early. I didn't know that. All I knew is that my father, who had run away with a woman he met online when I was fifteen, was diagnosed with liver cancer that same June and died in November. Since he was Indian, most people assume it was from drinking. It wasn't (although the once-a-year binges he went on lasted a week and were hardcore). It was from a tattoo.

My parents, they had a crazy love story. It was the 70s, and my mom was a waitress in a Chinese restaurant. She worked with a girl, Alice, who briefly dated my dad before he went to prison in Oklahoma. He'd been there before. He would get drunk, rob people, and get into fights. But this one was bad. He took a pepper shaker, wrapped it in a cloth napkin, and beat some guy at a bar to the ground with it. The story I had always heard was that the guy had a bad concussion, but didn't die. Later I heard he was left a vegetable. Either way, my dad got five years and his second strike.

Alice wasn't into that, not for real. Bad boys aren't fun anymore when they get locked away. But my dad was bored and horny. He wrote her love letters every week. Wanting to show off, Alice let the girls at work read them and my mom fell in love with his words. She began writing him in Alice's place. When my dad was released to a halfway house and ran away, it was my mom he called. "They took my shoes," he said. "I'm leaving. I can either hitchhike to you, or somewhere else. Your choice." She told him to come. He arrived a few days later, barefoot and with a glorious smile set against that NDN brown backdrop.

By then, the Hepatitis C was already settling into him. Did you know liver cancer can be caused by Hep C? It takes years, sometimes decades, but it's true. A lot of people hear Hep C and think shooting up with dirty needles, but my dad could never stomach drugs, not even marijuana. But it was still a dirty needle that did it. In prison, he had a tattoo of a squirrel inked into his arm, all bouffant tail and clutching an acorn. The needle had been used on countless inmates before him. He wasn't diagnosed with Hep C until he was diagnosed with cancer 35 years later.

I never went to see him after the diagnosis. Part of me

was scared, and part knew, in my darkest places, that he wouldn't want me to see him like that. I heard the stories. His waist-length black Cherokee hair, strands falling like drunks in the bathtub. He became emaciated. Skeletal. I heard the stories, but never saw the pictures. *That* was what I knew of cancer, so when Eli got his diagnosis and was still living in the fraternity house—his family 300 miles away in a town of 250 people and no hospital—there was no question about it. He moved in with me, and I spent my senior year taking online classes while tucked next to him in the hospital for eight hours of chemo a day. That's just what you did. You marry the person you stick by while they get the cancer poisoned out of them. That's just what I did.

Now I'm not saying it was all bad. Most of our relationship was mediocre. It was me avoiding sex, because *that's* what you do when you hate your body, yourself, and have no attraction to your only sexual option. But we partied like college kids and I developed a binge-drinking habit that was surprisingly easy to kick later on, even with half my blood coursing thick Indian red. But I'm not saying it was good, either.

Right after Eli was declared cancer-free, we started "play shopping" for engagement rings. Okay, it was real, but neither of us wanted it to be. It was the end of senior year, and we were grasping at what to do next. Grad school was secured, together (I wrote both of our applications and essays). We had internships set up in London for the second half of the year (again, I applied for both of those).

It was our last quarter, and I had forgotten to print an assignment for some asinine class. No big deal, I'd just swing by our house and print it from the Sent folder in my email. My laptop wasn't booting up. I had a penchant for breaking any and all electronics. Still do. Grabbing Eli's laptop, I went directly to the email icon and that's when things started turning.

It was empty. My *entire* inbox was empty. But I didn't have time to worry about that, I had a paper to retrieve. So

I went to the sent folder, and there it was. This wasn't my email. It wasn't even Eli's email, at least not the Eli I knew. He had stayed logged into a phantom account, JeepGuyPNW. He'd taken care to delete, permanently, any incoming mail, but overlooked that Sent folder. Countless Craigslist casual encounter responses were there, all to dominatrices looking to peg guys. "What do you have in mind?" he asked them. Even more curious were the emails he sent to himself. "What do you think of these?" he asked himself, attaching photos of thigh-high pleather boots in his size.

It was an ugly fight, the kind that goes on 'til morning and leaves your chest cavity aching from deep sobs. I don't know what I was sad about. I never even figured out, for sure, if he was a cross-dresser, trans, just liked a different kind of kink than me, or what. Either I didn't want to know, didn't care, or both. But I promised him I'd never bring it up again. Three months later, he proposed in a vapidly transparent show that I saw coming two hours away. I said yes, because what the hell else were we supposed to do at that point? When the guy you've been with for five years turns out to love shopping for slut boots and getting it in the ass *a lot* more than you, you marry him. That's just what you do.

"I'm going to work," Eli said after my big declaration, and I was grateful—so godawful grateful—that I'd never feel required to touch him again. I'm really good at leaving. Even better at leaving stuff behind. I took only what I needed, and my keepsakes from London. It was the easiest divorce anyone had ever seen. It looked totally civil. Still, when we met at the courthouse to sign the final papers, I wore my six-inch heels so that I towered over him like a warrior. We had gotten married on Maui, dragged all his family and our friends to a place that distracted us from reality: We were about to marry someone we didn't love, and didn't particularly like. But, seriously, aren't the palm trees just so enchanting?

It was perfect timing, or maybe I timed it that way. I had known Michelle since sixth grade. I might have been awkward and quiet, still am, but if I see something I want, I barrel full speed ahead. We were all new to middle school, but she was new to the entire district. She was beautiful, sure, half Hawaiian and half white. But her real beauty radiated out from deep inside like a lava chamber. She was loud, always laughed first, and had not a whit of shyness or boundaries. I asked her to sell my Girl Scout cookies with me, and the friendship began to bake.

In high school, she attached herself to Chris, two years older than her and already in his first rehab stint for cocaine. He looked like Devon Sawa in *Casper*, and she lost herself in him entirely. We didn't speak for almost a year as she reinvented herself into Chris' Girlfriend. Eventually we gravitated back towards one another, right in time for me to do my own disappearing act from that suffocating town. In that little pinch of time when we were both antsy to leave, I toyed with the idea of slipping my head between her thighs on one of those nights she was fake-drunk on two beers and I was hungry for that other kind of sweetness. But it was wrong, like fucking my sister, and when I had a sex dream about her and woke up with regrets staining my teeth, I knew we never would.

But she and Chris, they followed me to Portland when she turned eighteen. By twenty she was pregnant, got married in a quickie ceremony nobody was invited to, and had somehow convinced herself that she had a lifetime of housewifing ahead of her. That delusion lasted five years and one more baby before she found Chris high as the Burj Khalifa with his motorcycle crashed in a bush and infected track marks seasoning his arms. Under his toenails. She soon found his second apartment with his equally strung-out girlfriend, too.

Their divorce was a messy one, as those with kids and mortgages tend to be. He was out of the house fast, and I was in. Within a six-month period, both she and I had filed for divorce and we got the party years together we had never had. Oh, yes, I had plenty of those years in college, but none with *her*. None the way it should have been. We did an amazing job of playing catch-up. We were in the bars every night, thighs draped in crepe miniskirts even during one of Portland's rare snowstorms. We did Meet the Fleet, had a "magic dress" (I shiver to imagine the stain combinations on that monstrosity), and were there for her bevy of one-night stands and my meager sprinkling of them. The kids? Her mom was an eager babysitter, sure that Michelle could snag a new, better husband with every one-night stand and syphilis diagnosis. When the bank *really* kicked her out of the house, we packed together and I scrawled the clichéd Robert Frost quote on her wall with permanent marker: *Two roads diverged ...* ,

Yeah. All the difference indeed.

The Rabbit Den

THE BACKYARD was an amusement park, Dad's garage sale finds and auction treasures peppering the acre of land like a warped junkyard. There was the pony exerciser, a big wheel he'd kitted out with benches that could spin so fast it would make my whole class dizzy. The swing set (of course), old tire swing hanging from the walnut tree, and a makeshift zipline that strung together two old pines. Having any kind of pool was a big deal, and the summer I was turning eight Mom and Dad had sprung on a real one. It nestled into the ground so Mom could sunbathe topless and the neighbor kids had to feign more interest in me than usual if they wanted a golden ticket entry.

My eighth birthday, and it was going to be amazing. As any summer birthday kid knows, parties during these months, especially for the weird ones, can be a challenge. I was happy to let my mom take over the social aspect of my life, bribing parents with promises of a full day off and kids with the idea of endless toys, games, and playground equipment. I already had more than one hundred Barbies—way more than anyone else (they were all salvaged bodies from thrift stores, but we were all still too young to care).

"If you don't want anyone staying the night, don't offer," Mom said. She was putting the last of the icing on the cupcakes, licking her fingers and getting her musky smell into the chocolate. "I'm not bailing you out this time."

"*Okay*," I said.

"Go check on the rabbits' water before everyone gets here." The rabbits were the latest addition to her menagerie, including a Holland lop ear that had just had a litter. They burrowed into a handmade pen made with two-by-fours and chicken wire. After the single Shetland pony, twin Pekingese puppies, Persian cats, ducks (that disappeared and nobody really missed), a stint with a goat who ate everything he wasn't supposed to, a turkey (?), and a lamb that was flat-out boring, it was clear: My mom only liked animals that were either miniature or had flat faces, and who did nothing but be cute.

I was indifferent to the rabbits, bordering on annoyed with how much effort they took. "My" animals were seemingly adopted on whims with zero research. It was somehow a surprise when the goat ate the privacy bushes, a shock when the turkey was mean and chased me.

So far that summer, I'd learned that bunnies are really ugly when they're born. They look like rats, but not adorable like my chubby pet rats that consumed the entire twin comforter I used as their cage cover. Bunny-rats have pink skin so bald and soft you can see their organs pulsing beneath them. And they don't do a damn thing.

Their water was half sloshed out, evidence that I was the one who was supposed to fill it last. It was a pain to walk all the way to one of just two garden hoses to fill it back up, so instead I dunked it in the pool, which was closer. If I could swallow chlorine, surely the rabbits could handle it, too.

And besides, today I was eight. I had a mint chocolate sheet cake from Food 4 Less, chocolate and mint cupcakes, mint chocolate chip ice cream and a stash of Andes mints I had been hoarding from the Mexican restaurant we went to where the waiters tried to talk to my dad in Spanish, and he'd just point at himself and say, "Indiano." The rabbits would live.

And they did, rabbits are terribly viable things. "Want to see the rabbits?" I asked my cousin Mandy that afternoon. We were the same age, and she was somehow even quieter than me. Especially here, in my domain. My classmates from the previous year screamed in the pool, showing off cannon balls or smacking each other with water balloons.

"Yes!" she said. She lived with her parents and brother in a small house with no backyard. She didn't have rabbits.

I was allowed to go into the rabbit pen whenever I wanted. The same went for just about anywhere else on the deprecated half-zoo, half-fun park that was Home. Leading the way, I held the door open for Mandy and could already see the mother rabbit cuddled with her litter in the faux den.

"Ew, they're not cute," she said.

"I know." Disappointment. Did she have to call ugly ugly?

"The mom is neat, though," she said. I didn't care if it was a consolation comment, I'd take it.

"Wanna hold her?" I asked.

"Okay."

Do *not* pick up a mother rabbit who is quite likely nursing her babies. I was wearing a two-piece swimsuit, my first. I had begged for it, and even though Mom said it was too grownup and my belly hung out like one of those starving kids in *National Geographic* (okay, she only said the "too grownup" part and the belly part was insinuated when she eyed my middle), when Dad brought home his usual Sunday pile of "clothes that might be the right size for Jennifer" from his day-long garage saling and a ruffled two-piece was included, there was no tearing me away from it.

Mother Rabbit looked at me, really looked at me, with a blend of fear and anger. She was soft and warm in my hands, her furry folds scrunched up against her cheeks. In seconds her back feet were slicing at my belly, cutting out ribbons of red. The pain didn't register, but I dropped her fast.

"*Jennifer*!" suddenly my mom was there, in the pen. Mandy was already crying and blubbering, her eyes stuck to my blossoming tummy. "What the hell are you doing? You're going to *hurt* her!" My mom smacked the back of my head like she always did when I did something wrong.

Stupid. At least daily.

The Mother. She was talking about the Mother. Someone grabbed me, maybe an aunt, maybe a friend's dad. They whisked me away to attend to my hot, slick stomach as my mom dropped to all fours, a rabbit herself, and cooed over her shaken little family that was supposed to be mine.

CHAPTER TWO

"YOU KNOW WHAT we should do? We should drive to Vegas."
I'd been there once before with Eli for his twenty-first birthday. That wasn't *really* doing Vegas.

"Oh my god, *yes!*" Michelle said. "I need it after this shitstorm of a year."

"It'll be like *Swingers*, but like with women. And we won't be picking up any male strippers working the skank shift," I said. "Let's text Jared and see if he can hook us up." Jared was my fifth-grade boyfriend. We used to hide in my tree house and take quizzes about who in the class we would want to make out with, marry, live with, and so on. We always picked each other. This was, obviously, before he realized he was gay. Or came out. Whichever. Now he lived in Las Vegas, taught film courses at the local university, and had hookups for everything from hotels to shows. He got us a room at Hooters (the hotel).

My red Nissan Versa was a dynamo. The first stick shift I had ever owned and totally bare bones. One Christmas, Eli had given me his spare Jeep keys wrapped in a jewelry box. We were visiting his family in a no-name Oregon town. "You'll either learn to drive a stick and drive us home, or we're not leaving," he told me. I learned in ten minutes.

"We're gonna need to rally hard when we get there," Michelle said, curled into the passenger seat and taking tiny sips from the bottle of Jack, overly cautious that a police car would zip by. We were scheduled to drive into Las Vegas at dusk, and there was no way we were missing our first night out.

"I'm on it," I said. Coffee still worked wonders on us,

especially with a few heavy pours of whiskey to sweeten it. The drive took us from Portland down south, past the highway town where we grew up. We stopped for breakfast there and nothing more—a proper visit with our moms was scheduled for the drive back.

Right across the California border, we stopped for gas and Michelle took a photo of me at the pump. Oregonians notoriously either don't know how to pump gas or do it terribly. It was the second time in my life. "You look so proud of yourself!" she said. I was. We were on the stupid side of thirty, just a few hours from what was bound to be a shitshow in Vegas, and both with kind-of grownup jobs. She worked at a luxury purse and shoe store, inching towards management. I wrote grant proposals at a tiny nonprofit that targeted Portland's just-starting-to-get-noticed African American community. I got called thick there and didn't mind.

Creeping into Nevada, the telltale signs of where we were began to spread like disease. We were hungry to see one of the rural brothels, hoping it looked like Quentin Tarantino's The Titty Twister in *From Dusk 'Til Dawn*. It didn't, or at least not the one we saw. It just looked like a truck stop cum hotel. (The Latin cum for those who prefer to keep things clean). It had "heaven" or "angel" or something in the name that was instantly forgettable, and I felt a sharp pang of sadness for the men inside.

"What do you think they do?" I asked Michelle. "Just walk in, not embarrassed at all, and point to the girl they want?"

"I feel bad for the girls who don't get picked," she said. True. But then again, when a man's paying for it and you're lined up like cattle, what are the odds you'll get picked? You have to be the hottest one there, or at least the hottest within whatever niche might be up for grabs. Asian, big fake boobs, MILF status.

When you roll up to Las Vegas by car, you can see it coming for miles. It looks like an oasis at night, a dropping of fluorescence into an otherwise dark, dead desert. Driving by the sign is a must, and you have to do it slowly (evening traffic doesn't allow anything else). Jared met us in the hotel lobby and helped us carry our bags and bottles of liquor to the room. I don't know if I still see the same little boy in him or not. He got tall. He got experienced. Something in him died in the desert, too. "Dinner?" he asked. "Drinks?"

"Both."

Now, just because I had lost The Weight in college doesn't mean I got skinny. I was what average should have been, or maybe a bit heavier. I still had a double chin in some photos, and always regretted wearing shorts in them. My thighs weren't overly big, but my calves were notoriously too slender. It looked like I supported myself from the knees down on lollipop sticks no matter what my weight. I got down to normal by low-carbing it. That's it. No exercise (I heaved after twenty minutes on the elliptical machine), no calorie counting, and certainly no cutting out alcohol.

Dinner was a buffet, and I got dizzy with how many trips I took and cheap cocktails I drank. As long as it was low carb, it was legal. I was equipped with a stomach that knew no ends. In my whole life, I had never felt "full." I've never once thrown up from drinking, even after once consuming an entire fifth of tequila in just eight hours. I pretended to know what people mean when they said they could burst, or couldn't take another bite. Around people, if sober, I would steal their cues, copy how they acted when they were done eating. Put down my fork when they did. In private, I could take down an entire carton of eggs turned egg salad, no problem.

God. We drank a lot of liquor at dinner.

I brown out, I don't black out, and I'm not proud or happy about that. I don't do particularly stupid things when I'm drunk, but I'm obnoxious. I spill drinks. I wave my hands around too much. And I only remember sparks of the night before. I'd rather not remember anything at all. Here's what I do remember: Jared took us to a gay club, the only place where we (as women) had to pay twenty bucks to get in and he paid nothing. We decided to try and get married. Trekking from chapel to chapel, Jared yelled at every guy remotely in our age range, "Hey, you're hot! You wanna be my best man?" We clung to each other like the drunks we were. And we found out that, no matter what people say, it's not as easy to get drunk-married in Las Vegas as you think. In fact, nobody would marry us.

The next morning, Michelle and I woke up in bed with Jared slumped on the floor. She was slightly less drunk than the rest of us had been and had taken photos the whole night. Jared and me making out under a gazebo. Jared trying to eat my head. Me peeing in the bushes.

"Did we make out?" he asked, dragging himself out from under the fog of half-drunk, half-hungover.

"I think so," I said, staring at the proof on Michelle's phone.

"Gross," he said. "But I guess it was twenty years coming. Check that off the list."

Breakfast was another buffet. Cheesy omelets that could be weighed by the pound. Berries (surprisingly low carb). Bacon, ham, and sausage. I passed on the sliced tomatoes.

My Nissan got a flat tire along Route 66. It was a Sunday, not far from an infamous alien shop where believers and non-believers flock. The entire day was stolen from us. The tow truck arrived, Michelle and I squeezed thigh to thigh inside the sweaty old man's cab. "Where you headed?" he asked us as he unhitched my hatchback from his rig.

"San Diego. Then LA, San Francisco, and back to Portland. But Tijuana first," I told him.

"You're going to Tijuana by yourself," Michelle said. There had been reports stretching all the way to Oregon warning Americans to avoid Mexico, especially Tijuana, as the drug wars heated up. "And you are *not* taking the car there to get raped, killed, and have it stolen leaving me stranded in California," she said.

I didn't really care that it was my car. "Then I'll walk," I said.

And I did. She dropped me off at the border and I

strolled right across, very aware that I was not only the sole non-Mexican heading there, but the only bleached blonde, too. Immediately on the other side there was a towering pharmacy promising everything from Viagra to Ritalin. Children started hustling me at once, grabbing at my pants and holding their hands like cracked supplication cups. I had just a fleeting moment of feeling bad before physically pushing them off me like they were dogs humping my shins.

I spent the day there, wandering marketplaces and getting stared at. Everyone assumed I didn't speak Spanish, thank god, because it was rusty at best. "Hey, I know you," men would yell-whisper from doorways and alleys. "Come here, I have what you need." Their accents were that thick, syrupy cholo variety that I love, and maybe they did have what I needed. But I was too scared to find out. Or maybe self-preservation had just kicked in on auto pilot. Instead, I bought a scarf, a magnet, and followed the sign back to the American border when nightfall began to poke at the sky. Not even I'm stupid enough to drink in Tijuana alone.

This was, technically, my very first time out of the country. It was in the early aughts when Americans didn't need passports for Mexico. I walked through the small immigration station like I owned it, my privilege washing over me like cologne. *"Disculpe. Disculpe. Aye, Disculpe! Señorita!"* And an officer was on me. My brain had pushed his Spanish right back out my ears. *"¿Hablas **Español**?"*

I opened my eyes wide at him, the universal sign for "Oh shit/save me." *"¿**Inglés**?" he asked, and I nodded. "You need to fill out this form."*

Even with my fried white hair and skin fairer than my mom's, there was something about me. "You look something," people would say, and when they guessed it was always Latina. Mexican, to be exact, though I blame that on growing up along the I-5 corridor. There's something not quite right about me, something that doesn't fit into one of the holes we so desperately want to place one another in. It doesn't matter that my eyes are the color of cut grass or that my nose is nondescript. It's in my cheekbones. The way I look in a braid. There's just something Other about me.

Back in San Diego, we stayed in the Gaslamp District in a cheap hostel. I sat cross-legged on the floor, trying to curl my hair in front of the single mirror in the room. Michelle spent an hour walking up and down the street looking for decent coffee. When we checked out, I left a carpet burn in the floor I half-heartedly covered up with a towel. They never called us about it or the burning rubber smell.

The two-week trip turned increasingly less eventful. Los Angeles gave us another excuse to get drunk, this time in West Hollywood. We each bought the cheapest thing we could find on Rodeo Drive, at the Lucky store of course (the only place we could afford). I went off my low carb diet, kind of, for my one exception: Pinkberry, original flavor, no toppings. We moved up to San Francisco where it was cold like all summers in the bay area are. Hiking through Chinatown, I sought out souvenirs. A welcome cat was a given. I chose one with a turtle on its chest, Michelle took the one with a duck. Then something pulled me close, a clay bucket full of stones with Mandarin words on them. I picked up the one with "love" etched into it, and I have no idea why. Love was the last thing I wanted.

I hadn't thought of Eli at all on the entire trip, even though our divorce had just been finalized two days before we left. Even though it was the World's Easiest Divorce, it still takes time for the paperwork to process. I hadn't felt like I would have been cheating on him had I fooled around with anyone when we separated, filed papers, and I moved out. Still, I hadn't. The few months living with Michelle had been richly steeped in her own flings. We would go out, she would meet a guy at a bar. If she decided he was a go, we would sneak away to the bathroom together so she could pull off her Spanx and hide them in my purse. I have to say, for all the men she brought home, I never heard any squeaks or groans from her room. Or maybe I was just too browned out to have functional hearing.

Nothing picked up again until we nestled into Oregon's sleepy Central Point town and temporarily went our separate ways to spend the night with our moms. Michelle's mom, an obese woman who's the poster child for man hands, has always hated me. She tried to pit us against one another, obsessed with us competing, but we never did. We simply never wanted the same things.

My mom is an alcoholic, but the sip on vodka all day/slip it into her diet soda kind. Not a binger. Our relationship had been patch-worked back together, sort of, four years after I left at sixteen. Maybe it was my dad's death that did it. Or maybe one of us just got bored. When she found out about my leaving Eli, she gave one of those deep, shaky sighs that are so well practiced. "You're making the biggest mistake of your life," she said. "He's decent, college educated. What the hell else do you want?" She had spent about thirty minutes with Eli during our entire relationship.

That night, after the requisite visit in the musty living room where my mom and I smoked a bowl together and laughed at how my dad truly went out in a blaze of glory, she began snoring in front of the television she kept on around the clock at a deafening volume. I began craving a dive bar, and something more.

Whiskey Creek is the kind of hole in the wall you see in movies about small town life. Two pool tables, a massive square footage, and whiskey poured in quadruple for just four bucks. I put on skin-tight jeans, a skin-tight shirt, and too much makeup. I was by far the most fuckable thing in that place.

I picked him out easily, playing pool with his friends. They were all out of place, young college boys looking for something beyond the offerings of the college town nearby. I don't have a problem approaching men, but most of the time I still prefer to let them come to me. It's easy. All you have to do is walk by them, just a touch too close. Eye contact is optional, but moves things along faster. If you prefer a buffet, sit at the bar closest to where orders are taken. Every man in there has to come to you, and their wallets are out so it's easy for them to offer you a drink.

It took him about twenty minutes. "Can I buy you a drink?" It was cute, echoing the line he'd heard in movies.

"What took you so long?" I asked. I was ready to go.

"I ... I didn't think someone like you would be single," he said. It took him a little longer to shuffle through his limited experience at this and pick out that line.

He was six years younger than me. I forgot immediately what he said he studied, but I was right about the college. He had come here from an even tinier town in Iowa, *actually* from a farm if you can believe that. I imagined him sucking a dry sprig of straw in the autumn. He left his friends, and I drove us back to his place. Thank god it wasn't a dorm, but close. A shared townhouse just blocks from his campus.

And the sex? The sex was mediocre and forgettable, like first time sex usually is. He was fast, the movements, not the time, but not rough. And he just seemed so god-damned grateful. I never knew whether I was glad to have done it or not, but I'm not one to obsess over numbers. I'm safe, always, assuming that everyone has HIV unless I've seen day-of paperwork that says otherwise.

Still, it was my first one-night stand. I wanted to commemorate it, and grab a keepsake but he didn't have any welcome cats. Instead, in the morning, I got up before him to pee, grabbing his tee-shirt in the process. Mine had somehow disappeared. I got dressed in his dirty boy-bathroom, and when I walked out he was up, sleepy-eyed and not as much like a stranger as I thought he'd seem.

"I'm keeping this," I told him, pointing to the shirt covering my braless chest. "See you around." It was the kind of line I'd probably seen on some television show, but it felt incredibly empowering.

"Bye," was all he said. He didn't even have to ask if I wanted coffee.

iii.
Toast and Blowjobs

IT WAS OUR Christmas tradition. With my feet tucked under my rump, I sank into the fake leather couch, my embroidery all around me. Embroidery was easy, but took too long. Even with the outline of the roses clearly screen-printed onto the fabric, I didn't want to take the time to make all those moderately-sized stiches, so I cheated where I could. Long, loose, sloppy stitches in blood red to get the blossoms blooming faster. My mom didn't care. She sat in the matching, cracked loveseat opposite me, looking at the television and listening for the crunch of gravel outside.

"Can I have toast?" I asked, and she automatically got up to make it. I was seven, I could have easily shoved more of that cheap wheat Wonderbread into the toaster myself, but it tasted better when she did it. She didn't skimp on the margarine and grape jelly. It would be my fourth piece in the past hour.

It was just past midnight now. I had never stayed up all the way 'til dawn—we usually gave up by then. One week before Christmas, my dad was right on schedule. Every year, he would disappear. Well, not really disappear, because he always came back with hints of where he'd been. Still, Mom went through the motions. Starting at about nine o'clock, she began calling the hospitals. "Is there a Jamie Tyler there?" she'd ask. There never was.

She handed me the paper plate with the steaming hot toast that sucked up the bright yellow margarine like a starving sponge. At eleven o'clock, she called all the local police stations and jails. He wasn't there either. Actually, she hadn't gotten a "yes" from a jail since I was too young to remember this ritual.

Next it was all adult television until two in the morning, when we'd finally pile into the minivan and start driving bar to bar, looking for his truck, the one with the "Ford" letters rearranged into "Dorf" for some reason. Sometimes we'd find it, and she'd get gobbled up inside the thick black doors only to reappear minutes later, all traces of worry erased by pure pissed-off-ness. Usually we didn't and my dad would creep back home a week later, his jeans smelling of piss and his neck like a perfume-beer cocktail.

I looked down, and the toast had disappeared. It left black crumbs on the plate like a sad little offering. I was still hungry. On the television, a fat woman was mad at her boyfriend. She was yelling at the talk show host. "How could he?" she scream-sobbed. "That (bitch) bleep! That (fucking) (slut) bleep bleep! I caught them," she yelled.

"Now, you're saying," said the host calmly, his smooth voice filling the living room, "you actually caught your *best friend* performing oral sex on your boyfriend?" The audience oohed as their thirsty eyes lit up, wanting more.

"Yes!" she screamed even louder. I didn't get it.

Turning to my mom, whose eyes had drifted to the window that faced the driveway, I asked, "What's the big deal? I mean, they were just *talking* about sex." For the first time that day, my mom smiled. Actually, laughter struggled out of her mouth.

"Is that what you think oral sex is?" she asked. She had always been overly generous and matter-of-fact about sex. It was her way of compensating for being told nothing as a child of the Depression. When she was thirteen, she came home from school crying because a boy had accidentally brushed his crotch against her butt as he squeezed down the narrow school hallway. She thought she might be pregnant. I don't ever remember *not* knowing how sex worked. Penis in vagina, sperm comes out, and if you're lucky (and want it) you get a baby. If you're not, you get an STD and die.

That night was when I learned what a blow job is. And what eating pussy is. It didn't sound very appetizing, but at least I figured out why the fat woman on TV was so mad.

"Put on your shoes," Mom said. "We're going for a drive."

"Can I have some toast to go?" I asked, and she walked dutifully back to the kitchen.

CHAPTER THREE

WE'D ONLY BEEN BACK from Las Vegas for one week, but it was more than enough time to recover. Friday night, and the Portland bars were bellowing their siren's call that lured us with their false promises weekend after weekend. Michelle and I had our favorite, Cellar, a tiny martini lounge in the pretentious Pearl District where the bartenders knew us and didn't care if we occasionally got too drunk to remember to pay the tab. The doorman had a not-so-secret crush on me, and looked like a shorter, younger Woody Harrelson. He was safe, because he knew better than to blatantly hit on me, so I could hide in the entryway with him, suckling on cigarettes while Michelle circled the insides like an antsy shark. But this night was different.

"It's dead in there," she said, joining us out front. It was. Only a handful of barstools were claimed, and the dark corners weren't lit up by women settling into the light of their phones. "Let's go somewhere else."

"It'll pick up," Abe said, feeling slighted at the vicarious insult even though he'd only held the door open for two people the entire time I'd been standing with him.

"Nah, let's go to that new place, Cake," Michelle said. It was the only club supposedly for the twenty-five and up crowd. What that really meant was that any woman with a legal ID could get in, and the bouncers could operate on a whim when it came to letting men in.

"Okay," I said. It was walkable, and I'd soaked up all the validation from Abe I'd needed that night. Besides, Cake was just five minutes away. He shrugged and we tottered off in our too-high heels and too-short dresses, huddling elbow to elbow in the evening that cooled like forgotten comfort food.

Michelle and I didn't wait in line anywhere. Her looks and tits hanging out compensated for me, but bouncers adored us for more than that. We could hold our liquor, or at least we looked like we could. We weren't obnoxious too early, and besides it was just eleven. We talked to them and made it a point to be nice to those who held the keys to the kingdom. Cake swallowed us fast, and we were hugged tight by the pulsing, the sticky floors, and the cougars prowling the perimeters. This was more like it. I'd only had one drink at Cellar, and that wasn't anywhere near close enough to crack my buzz requirements, but it didn't matter.

"Oh my god, Josh is here," Michelle said, pulling me behind a pillar. Josh was one of her domino hookups, one of the many that had happened consecutively a few weeks ago. A ten-night stand instead of one. But he refused to let her touch him before or after sex (or even do it at his place). He also made fun of the baby booster in her backseat.

"Ignore him," I said. Every quiet girl's go-to strategy.

"Whatever. I need to pee," she said. Peeing at Cake was like walking the gauntlet then waiting to meet the queen. You were guaranteed to get groped at least once en route, and with just two women's toilets you'd be gone at least an hour. "You coming?" she asked.

"No, I'll wait," I said, and she rolled her eyes as she began the trek solo. I liked being alone in places like this; the anonymity was intoxicating (no fourteen-dollar cocktail required). Surveying the crowd, it was easy to see all the ploys, the games, the hopes for the night. We humans, we really go all out with these mating rituals. The hours getting ready, the requisite drink buying, dry humping to drums and electronics, the pretending we don't all want the same thing.

"You wear a wicked grin." And there he was. He'd slipped in front of me so fast and quiet I hadn't even noticed. We were the same height with my heels, which meant he was about five eleven. Raked, black hair coiled like snakes to his collar, framing his golden skin. Thick-framed black glasses, and lips so full they embarrassed over-ripened plums. And the accent, the accent was a heady molasses of somewhere I'd never tasted.

"I'm not smiling." I don't know why I said that. With attraction, I turn into a bitch.

"Are you one of those people who needs to be drunk to dance?" he asked.

"No," I said. Then I smiled.

He led me through the crowd like he controlled it, his broad shoulders clearing the way for me. His hand grasped mine, warm and dry. The hands were too big for the rest of him, like a puppy who hadn't grown into his paws yet. I could smell his cologne from an arm-span away, something deep and dusky like him.

On the dance floor he pulled me strong, close, and I let him. "Chirag," he said, and when I told him my name, he repeated it. Usually, people call me Jessica. I say Jennifer, but they hear what they want. He didn't. Beneath the throbbing light, blanketed in the heat from everyone around us, he dipped his chin down, daring me to kiss him. But I don't work that way.

I shoved him, lightly. "I'm not that easy," I said. I don't get close fast with people I like. My heart battered against my ribs like a bird stuck in a cage, a familiar feeling even though it had been years. I wanted to set the winged beast free and clip its wings at the same time.

"I didn't think you were."

Michelle had parked herself at the bar, vodka cranberry in hand as she giggled with the middle-aged woman next to her. Chirag and I scooted in, his arm around my shoulder like it belonged there.

"I made a friend," Michelle said, ignoring him. It was our modus operandi: Don't acknowledge one another's hopefuls or conquests until given permission to do so. Otherwise, you were bringing them into the fold prematurely.

"Hey, how's it going?" Chirag asked the older woman,

and she immediately pulled him close. Held on too long. It was a bleeding red flag waving wildly to get my attention, but I had already waded in too deep to mind it.

"You smell so good!" she told him before turning to me. "Doesn't he always smell *so good*?" That was it, she was staking her claim. "Always," like she'd threaded forever into him already, but was letting me borrow her toy for the night.

"This is Jennifer," he told her, and I was forced to take her hand. It was cold, wet, and limp from her gin and tonic.

"I have to go," she said, smiling sweetly at him and Michelle before letting the darkness bundle her up.

"You scared my new friend away," Michelle said, moving her pouty lips back to her straw.

I shrugged. "She needs to make the most of the time she has left," I whispered. It was cheap, and I only wanted her to hear, not Chirag. "Look what I found," I said, pointing to him with my eyes.

"This is Michelle," I told him as she looked him up and down.

"So you're why I got deserted at the bar," she said.

"Let me buy you a drink to make up for it," he said, already nodding to the bartender.

"I like him," she told me, loud enough for him to hear. She tugged on his blazer, making him lean down to her. "We're a package deal, just so you know," she said. "And I don't mean that in the dirty way."

"Good to know," he said.

The taxis were chewing up staggering passengers outside, eager for the drunken revelers who weren't good at math come two in the morning so they tipped much higher than they ought to. Chirag smoked a cigarette while Michelle and I flanked his sides. She was ready to go home, and I certainly wasn't leaving with him—but I didn't want to leave yet, either. He'd already put my number in his phone, not asking for my last name. That meant there weren't any other

Jennifers in his phone, which was highly improbable. He probably saved me as Jennifer Cake or Jennifer Cake 6.26.09. I was one of the most common things to come out of the eighties. Jennifers, scrunchies, and spandex.

"We should totally take a picture!" Michelle said. She was now four free cocktails deep, but still in wingman mode. "You two first." I knew what she was doing. It was for The Book. We'd started it just last week: a big, black photo album where we planned to put photos, details, and ratings of men we hooked up with to various degrees.

Chirag wrapped me to his chest, his other arm dangling the cigarette at the end while Michelle snapped the photo. "Now all of us," she said, crouching in the middle and stretching out her phone for a selfie. We got bonus points if there was a picture of all three of us: her, me, and the random of the night. "It's freezing-ass cold," she declared as she checked the photo for too chubby cheeks or blurry makeup, deleting and editing the ones she looked best in. "Let's go home."

She had driven, and I'd bought all the time I could. "Okay, bye," I told Chirag slowly. I should have let him kiss me on the dance floor. His lips were the plumpest I'd ever seen, the focal point of his whole face.

"See you tomorrow then," he said, flicking the cigarette to the gutter.

"Tomorrow?"

"It's Sunday," he said. "I figured you wouldn't have another date lined up on God's day."

"God and me don't party like we used to," I said. "What did you have in mind?"

"Dinner, drinks, maybe you could show me some of the restaurants around here. I only moved here two months ago, you know."

"Yeah, okay. There's this one place open late on Sunday. They have alligator bites and frog legs and stuff." Plus, they wrapped up the leftovers in these ornate tinfoil figurines. I'd always thought it would be so romantic to walk out of a restaurant holding a swan heavy with Creole drippings.

"I'm vegetarian," he said. Indian, of course.

"Oh, sorry!" I said. Vegetarian. Where the fuck do you eat vegetarian? "I'm sure there's something—"

"We'll figure it out," he said. His smile blasted the night's blackness, shamed the light pouring from the red Chinese lanterns overhead. "I'll text you."

Scuttling back to her car, Michelle and I rehashed the night. "He's so your type," she said. He was, and I hadn't even known it. It wasn't just the accent, it was the gravel beneath it. His voice was so low it sounded like the deep groans of the ocean. I couldn't fathom what he could have sounded like as a child. The blackness of his eyes matched the inkiness of his hair, so opaque you couldn't tell where the pupils ended and the irises began. But it was how he touched me, held me, that gut-punched me hard, a rabbit shot of want. There was no hesitation, no shaking, no fumblings to make me hedge. I knew I could give myself fully and not wonder or worry if he would take care of it all—of all of me.

"What happened with Josh?" I asked.

"Nothing," she said. "He was talking to some girl. She was Asian."

"Oh, so he's got like full yellow fever now," I said. She'd seen him with a scattering of girls before. They were always at least part Asian. "What are you?" he'd asked her when they met. She explained her Hawaiian half, her European mother, without a trace of offense.

"I guess," she said. "She was thin." Michelle and I had both packed on weight after the teenage metabolism slipped away. Hers had stuck while I sloughed mine off, and hers continued sticking like icing. She wore it well, all thick hips and mountainous chest, but you could tell the heaviness was starting to strain. She needed pushup bras, carefully cinched belts and those masterful, practiced creams and powders to keep pace with the beauty she'd taken for greedy granted all those earlier years.

"Anyway," she said, "who cares. Someone's getting *laaiiidd*." Her singsong voice echoed down the street.

"Oh, I'm sure. Hold my Spanx, please," I said, pretending to reach for her handbag. Diverting the sexual mentions back in her direction and domain kept things easier. She didn't understand. I don't fuck people I really like. It's not like I had a lot of experience with that. After all, I had been with Eli for my entire adult life. The asshole Scott before him. A little rendezvous with an older banker between Scott and Eli. And the Iowa boy just one week prior. I didn't exactly have an army of precedents to consider before Chirag. But I knew. I knew I couldn't be easy with him.

Like the cougar at the bar. Something told me they hadn't had sex. Fooled around, maybe. Made out, probably. But she was simultaneously too overprotective and too flippant to have been clawing up the bedsheets with him. But she'd wanted to. She'd offered herself in some way, or every way, and he hadn't taken the bait. Nothing's as sad as a rejected offering, left naked never to be blessed.

He texted as promised, and part of me was shocked. I didn't really know how to "date," kind of like every other twenty-something in the first decade of this scrambled new century. Did men ring your doorbell? Did that whole three-date rule still apply (did it ever?)? How could I dress to make him want to fuck me, while also making it clear I would simply love to, but clearly can't because I'm a lady? Would I have to do the whole fake reach for my purse thing, and exactly how semi-drunk could I be to seem outgoing but not an alcoholic? I only had a few hours to prepare, and I was charged with not only seeming just interested enough, but also dreaming up a destination that was vegetarian friendly and not too awkward for what was awkwardly a Sunday night date.

I chose Due, a half-martini, half-fondue restaurant on Northwest 23rd Avenue, a mile of a street that was overly packed on Saturdays and a ghost town on Sunday nights.

Cheese and bread was about the most vegetarian thing I could imagine.

At six, Chirag texted me again that he was outside, his humming gray Nissan Versa squeezed tight into the tiny cul-de-sac. A pang of disappointment tugged at my heart. There would be no doorbell ring, no do-woop moment of opening the front door. But maybe that's just how it is now—women are beckoned from their homes like dogs hearing a whistle. Eli and I didn't have to deal with cars and doorbells 'til we were established, in deep. We simply walked across campus from one Greek house to another.

Sliding into his car, so familiar to mine, Chirag leaned over and kissed me, firm and gentle, before saying a word. The stiffness of his jacket crackled in the quiet, and I couldn't see his eyes for the sunglasses. "We have the same car," I said.

"It's the company's."

At Due, only a handful of other tables were busy. Chirag scanned the menu like it mattered, flipping past pages and pages of overpriced, overcrafted martinis. We were both quiet. Fuck. The single whiskey I'd downed before he picked me up had done nothing.

"They're known for their fondue," I offered.

The great thing about fondue is that it's very low carb. At least if you get it with meats instead of bread (not an option tonight) or vegetables that doubled as cheese vehicles (the only option tonight). Forget the wine they add to it and the staggering calories. I explained to him as I avoided the bread cubes about my aversion to sugar. To carbs. To anything that might sneak more fat onto me. Instead of thinking me strange like so many men do (or wrongly obsessed, like so many women do), he seemed impressed. "That must take tremendous willpower," he said, and I felt free—allowed— to chew on low carb vegetables and wine-drunk cheese with abandon.

Halfway through a 007 gin martini (extra dry) and the sadly small pot of sizzling cheese flanked by baby carrots, sliced radishes and stubby celery, Chirag said simply, "It's not enough."

"What isn't?" *Me?*

"The food. I need something more," he said. It was the most he'd offered the entire night, and a strange way to cut it short. I wanted to go to the bathroom and text Michelle. "You know anywhere else?" he asked, and I realized he meant going somewhere else together.

At Del Toro, right up the street, the expansive restaurant was shaking with energy. I ordered stuffed jalapenos, Chirag a heavy vegetarian plate. The heat in my mouth lit my insides like kindling. He ate like I imagined he made love, greedily and with his entire body. Between hungry bites, I learned about him. It eked out between his perfectly crowded, crooked teeth.

"Jains don't eat meat," he said. "Actually, the really traditional ones don't eat meat, eggs, or anything that grows underground. Carrots, ginger, those kinds of things. It's dirty, and there might accidentally be insects on them. But most people in my family eat the underground foods."

"So, Jains are like—" I began, searching for the words.

"Kind of like Hindus," he said. "More conservative. I'm Gujarati, and Gujaratis are Jains. We believe everything with a heart has the same value. Insects, animals, everything. Extreme Jains don't even fly in airplanes. Planes kill bugs by design."

As a child, I had seen a cartoon of an old Indian man furiously sweeping as he walked. He didn't want to mistakenly step on any insects. I didn't know such a man actually existed.

Chirag continued to devour his food, big fingers working in tandem with his heart-shaped face. When the plate was wiped clean, and the peppers battered the good kind of rawness in my throat, he looked at me and smiled. "Where now?"

Nightlight was a seedy joint on the outskirts of the urban university campus. From the looks of it, it had been around well before the wide-eyed teens descended en masse on downtown with their bulky backpacks and rain-soaked jeans, and it would be there long after. It was a "black bar," an important distinction in a city where segregation and gentrification were meanly apparent. It also had the best and only chronic live jazz in Portland. The crowd was so mixed it was blended, but with a penchant for attracting those with gray hair, wrinkles etched into faces with a heavy hand, and old schoolers who were curious about us but ultimately just didn't give a shit. Of course, there was no cover.

Inside, the smoke was thick as a comforter and the jazz quartet wailed a blend of mid-century favorites with their own concoctions. The crowd swayed in unison, some pensioners trying out a few seconds of west coast swing between slugs of tequila. It was as if Sunday night wasn't pressing in all around us.

Here, I felt more at home. More alive. I had practiced dutifully all through college, grad school, and beyond to look like I belonged in pretentious places. I learned how to eat roe from my fist, order a drink, hold chopsticks and read a menu. I think I faked it pretty damn well. Still, for all my practice, I was the same inside. Here, I didn't need to pretend.

Chirag got us drinks from the busy bar that drew the crowds from all corners. They were cheap and strong. It was so loud, the mourning saxophone and drunken shouts, that he didn't ask me to dance. He just grabbed my hand and led me to the dance floor that grasped sticky lusting at my shoes.

It was the same as the night before, but a world away. When he tucked his chin again, I let him. I didn't back away from the dare. His mouth a sliver away from mine, he forced me to close the distance.

I've never liked beards or scruff, and he had none. Whiskers would whip me raw, leave rug-burn evidence on my face. His mouth enveloped mine, lips otherworldly soft. His tongue reached into my mouth, exploring and forging new paths that had never been unearthed before. Walking as one to the wall, it gave me the solidity to press back. The thin fabric of my tight shirt did nothing to mask the space beneath us. His hand snaked its way up to cup my jaw, move my mouth the directions he liked. For song after song after song we were emblazoned there, stuck hard against the wooden wall as couples and groups thronged and vibrated together, not looking or caring what we discovered and conquered in our secret little world.

Somehow, it became three in the morning, the deadest of night. Michelle had been doggedly shaking my phone with her texts. "Where are you?" "How's it going??" "Are you spending the night with him???" My phone stayed nuzzled deep in my purse while she drained its battery from miles away.

I had work the next morning, a day of aligning budgets and narratives for yet another local grant we'd likely get (the byproduct of being the only non-profit serving African Americans exclusively). Chirag had work the next day, filled with testing telecommunication technology for Intel. Every Indian in Portland worked at Intel or Nike. You had a fifty-fifty shot of guessing right.

He drove us through the early morning fog, needling into Michelle's short street littered with economical cars and crossovers with Baby on Board stickers. In her driveway, he kissed me more. "How does someone who doesn't eat sugar taste so sweet?" he asked, and I loosened at the guts it must take to whisper such a thing with sincerity. My lips were raw, but wanted more, like the abused get itchy for another blow. When it stops, you miss them. Along the horizon, the blackness began to hint at the pink light of dawn barreling like spring frenzy straight towards us.

"I'll call you," he said. But he never did.

An Inch to Pinch

"UGH, I am so fat," my mom said. We were in the front room. It was supposed to be a bedroom, but she used it as storage and a sewing area. It was always freezing, and it's where she kept her closet. I never understood why my dad got the one in the bedroom. "Just look at that," she said, standing in stretchy pants and an ugly bra, squeezing the doughy white roll of her middle. "God, how did I get like this? I used to be so thin—not that I realized or appreciated it then," she said. "You know?" I was eight. I didn't know.

"That's it," she said, taking off her bra and releasing the smell of drugstore Chantilly perfume into the air. "Liquid diet starts tomorrow." Her nipples were big and long, like an African woman's. I hoped mine didn't get like that.

"What's that?" I asked. A liquid diet. It sounded exotic.

"Just liquids until I lose this," she said. "I need to lose at least twenty pounds." I didn't know what twenty pounds really was. Was it a lot? Did it take a lot of work? I wasn't even really sure how much I weighed.

"I wanna do it, too," I said. It sounded challenging. It sounded fun. My mom just laughed. "You don't need to, not like I do. You are *just perfect*, my little Indian princess. But okay." Okay. "My dad, he used to always pinch my upper arm and say, 'Gettin' a little *fat*, aren'tcha? Gettin' a little *fat*?'" She always made this mean, high-pitched voice when she talked about her dad, my Papo. I didn't particularly like him, that tall German-looking man, but the loathing in her voice was a face slap. "But it's true," she said. "You can always tell when a girl's going to be fat by her upper arms, even when she's thin."

As she pulled on one of her gowns, I sized up my upper arm in the mirror. It was big, wasn't it? I'd never noticed before. Especially when I let it press against my side like that. I tried to picture the other girls at school and realized the slim ones, the pretty ones, they didn't have fat arms like that. Theirs were slender and elegant, so frail that you could easily see where their arms popped out at the shoulder and elbow because the bones couldn't help it.

"You know how you can *really* tell if you're getting fat?" my mom asked, seemingly to both of us. "You can pinch an inch. That's what they call it. Pinch an inch of fat in your fingers anywhere, and that's where you need to lose weight."

I didn't want her to catch me, but I covertly began pinching my body. My thighs, my arms, my hips and stomach. My stomach was the worst. There were definitely plenty of inches to pinch. I would do it, I would go on a Liquid Diet and get rid of this gross fat and get those slender ballerina arms like the popular girls at school.

I lasted less than a day. Such a pathetic failure. But I got *hungry*, I couldn't help it! I tried sticking my fingers down my throat, a toothbrush, but nothing. I knew you could make yourself throw up and lose weight, but my body wouldn't do it. I tried just chewing my food and spitting it out, but that was worse than not eating at all. My throat muscles grasped at the food, pushing it down. So I just watched my mom instead—the daily weigh-ins, the baking in the tanning bed (tan skin makes you look thinner), and she came to me so proud with some results. "I lost five pounds!" she exclaimed one week later, looking at me expectantly. I didn't know what to say.

"Is that a lot?" I asked. I really didn't know.

"You little shit."

CHAPTER FOUR

CHIRAG NEVER CALLED, he texted. And that was how I came to know him. It was a dangerous way, but the modern way. For all the decades women were so scared of answering the phone, the three-day rules, the screening and the smiling into the phone to sound happier, prettier and more feminine, we yearned hard for those days after they died. The buzz of a text can be addictive, but it's like taking a shot of beer. It was just enough to remind you of what you were missing, but not nearly enough to get you high.

The dates began to pile up quickly, but never a Friday or Saturday night. They were never offered, kept in the back like the good china. And I didn't push, instead distracting myself by making my own dates with Michelle. Part of me was thankful for it. I had come up with the arbitrary number of six dates for sex. If three was the standard of the 90s, doubling it had to work, right?

I was also terrified. I'd never had sex with someone I was overly attracted to. Someone I had no control over.

Women, we're trained not to initiate if we like someone. Initiations are earmarked for when we're on the prowl, know we won't see them again, and honestly (or at least largely) don't care. Otherwise, we still knew to be a little distant. To act a little prudish while still wearing shirts too low or pants too tight. Balancing—between good girl and whore, tease and flirtation—it's exhausting.

I emailed my best college roommate, Sam, all about him. She'd scampered off to the United Arab Emirates after dropping out of her Ph.D. program. Spending a year in South Korea just like me. She and her husband worked at the most twenty hours per week, were given a five-bedroom villa by the government, and were in Nepal one month, Turkey the next. For all those years I was with Eli, I listened with furtive envy to stories of her hellish dates with the men she left scattered and confused in her wake. It wasn't until her husband that a calm crept over her, steadied her feet and stopped the spins. Now it was my turn. But I couldn't explain quite rightly what was so perfect about him. And to her, his name was funny.

"How's Chichi?" she would ask, and I'd get irrationally mad.

On our fifth date, a sledgehammer came slamming down. It wasn't preceded by a brigade, or even a warning.

"I've never been in a relationship," Chirag volunteered, but with the lilt in his voice he had when he was leading me down a conversation pathway he knew I might not like. But this didn't seem like that big of a revelation. A twenty-seven-year-old Indian who hadn't had a girlfriend? A man who'd lived with his family as an undergrad because he went to university in Mumbai just a few miles from where he lived? I had seen enough movies to know that Indians don't "date," especially while living at home.

"Oh."

"I never will," he said. There it was. "Twenty-seven, it's the age you're supposed to get married in India," he said. "But I get an extension being on the other side of the world." Like he was getting out of something vile.

"So how much time do you think you've bought?" I could not act like I cared. I would not act like I cared. And why *did* I care anyway? I'd been away from Eli for less than six months total. I didn't want to get married again, at least not anytime soon. The pressure I'd felt of the *Oh my god, I'm twenty-seven, I need to get married **right now*** had dissipated after I'd done it. Like I could check that off my to-do list.

"Who knows?" he said. "I'll take what I can get. If I ever do get married, it'll be arranged. That's how my community's always done it." Gujaratis stick together, that I had learned. They live together, work together. Decide who's marrying whom together, apparently. And suddenly, the idea of marrying him, which I hadn't even rolled around on my tongue yet, was all I could taste. All I wanted. Because he'd so prematurely taken it away.

Distractions are a deadly thing. We spent hours in his car, making out like teenagers until the latest of hours. "Get a room!" strangers would shout as they walked by, weaving between cars. He would tug gently at my hair until I whispered, "You can pull it harder," and his fist was instantly buried in the nest, yanking my head back to expose the throat. We splattered hickeys on each other, mine covered the next day with summer scarves, his with rolls from a hoodie.

At five in the morning, parked in Michelle's driveway, I straddled him in my jeans so worn down thin they threatened to burst open any moment. The seat was laid back, his hands roaming my thighs and hips. Whenever they started to seek my breasts, I'd move them away. This is what it means to have power as a woman.

After two weeks of it, my chin and lips were rubbed raw, but they'd gotten used to the abuse. After each time in his car, I left more pieces of me behind. "The car is covered in blonde hairs," he'd text me the next morning. And I felt victorious, like a dog that had peed generously all over a favorite mailbox. Just let another bitch try to slink in, my evidence was everywhere. In his car, on his neck, in his phone.

I could feel his hardness between my legs and the stick shift digging into the side of my knee. The Black Eyed Peas played on the radio, the official summer anthem of the year. The frequency of his reaches for my chest increased as my rhythm riding his jeans-laden groin did. I came fast and hard, soaking all the way through the denim. I faded as the song did and the streetlights turned off. "I have to go," I said, and he let me, without a word, following me only as far as the hood of the car where he perched and lit a cigarette.

Michelle was already up, her two-year-old screaming for something to bandage the loneliness. "Oh my god, what happened to you?" she asked and I caught a flash of myself in the mirror. My mouth was angry red and swollen, my hair sticking up like a lunatic's.

"Chirag," I said, settling onto the floor of her bedroom while she swayed back and forth with her little boy.

"You're crazy," she whispered. "So, I heard from the bank."

"Yeah?"

"They're kicking me out in thirty days." She hadn't been paying the mortgage in over a year, not since Chris had checked himself into rehab—but not before breaking into their home, stealing all the cash, and then emptying out the bank accounts. He'd spent it all on meth, cocaine, and a dash of heroin three days later.

"It was a good run," I said. "Where are you going?"

"I'm moving in with my mom," she said. "God, I really don't want to. But I don't have anywhere else to go."

I knew I'd be leaving, too. It had been a good few months, the kind we'd always talked about as teenagers. She and I, together, pouring heavy-handed drinks to fill the moats and voids in our own little castle.

I could glean a few hours of sleep before work, and Michelle didn't go into work until noon. Nesting in her bed, the baby fell asleep curled against her back. I stretched out, the smell of Chirag wafting off me. When the sun reached the window and woke me, a heavy weight had spread pins and needles down my arm. Michelle was spooned into me, her head on my bicep and iridescent saliva making its way across my skin and to the mattress. It was the end of what was meant to be, and the sadness spread over me heavy as fog. I would never see her like this again, cradled by the morning light and trusting me so completely. That evening, she nursed two bottles of wine while I made whiskey diet cokes that fueled my scrawling of Robert Frost on her stair-well wall. She scratched our initials into the underbelly of the kitchen cabinets. We thought we were so clever.

The week of packing, tossing, broken nails, and lost shoes whipped by with only texts for company. Michelle's transition into her mom's house was as easy as it could be, propped up with movers her mom hired and storage units her mom paid for. Me, I was surprisingly easy to please when it came to living arrangements. I'd lived in the equivalent of a closet with Eli in London where you could lay on the bed and touch the kitchenette, shower stall, and door to the basement hallway all at the same time. At Michelle's, I slept in her room with my suitcases vomiting clothes from the hallway. Children who grow up with no siblings on the same streets as orchards are supposed to need space, need room, just like we need sleep and food. I was an anomaly. I carried my home within me.

I took the first place I found in the newspaper, a basement studio rented out by a power lesbian couple. It was on the outskirts of one of Portland's in-the-process-of-gentrifying neighborhoods, Sellwood, and the home itself was breathtaking. Historic, perfectly restored, and on a hill of a corner lot. The basement had a separate, tiny kitchen, a separate, tiny bathroom, and a living room-bedroom paneled in 70s faux wood. There were two basement windows, eking in just enough light, and something incredibly comforting in living below the earth. It was like being held by the soil, guarded by the earthworms. It took just two hours to move in, hauling a bed and couch gifted from Michelle that didn't have a home at her mom's, my own meager belongings, a handful of New Things, and nothing else.

Chirag knew about the move, of course, and all was quiet most of the weekend. He was quiet most weekends. Sunday, moving day, my phone vibrated at noon. "All moved in?"

"Yes. Have new lamps, no scissors to cut tags with."

"Want me to come over?"

"K."

For each of the five times I'd seen him, I was at least one glass of something deep when he arrived. It smoothed out my jittery edges. Made me talk a little more.

Two hours later, the Lilliputian studio was mostly pieced together. I used salad plates instead of regular ones, an attempt at portion control. They stacked in the cupboards with mismatched glasses and mugs teetering beside them.

"Where's the door?" he texted. The house was an unusual setup, with the private basement door opening in back. Any of my visitors had to walk the long pathway where they were silently vetted by the landlords whose dogs lit up the quiet like a firing squad. Through the lattice garden door, past the compost bin, and hovering below the kitchen window, I had my own bell. Giving someone directions to this hideaway took long texts and awkward explanations.

When the doorbell rang, the whiskey had melted my insides just enough. Chirag took up the entire doorway, with flowers, and scissors still in the pack, in his hands. "Still need scissors?" he asked.

"I like it," he approved, surveying the cave that glowed with candles and twinkle lights strung across the living room-bedroom ceiling. And he meant it. This place was me, through and through. So unassuming you'd almost miss it, mostly hidden but soothing and steady on the inside. Sitting on the suede couch, he pulled me on top of him, kissing me deep while I held onto the purple, furry blanket slung over the back to feel something soft against the roughness. His hands pressed hard into my waist, making their way to my ribcage. Like always, I pushed them away. "What's the big deal?" he asked, a peppering of frustration breaking through that rock hard façade for the first time.

"You'll see," I said. Not now. Not like this.

I technically worked in a hospital near the Lloyd District. The office was an in-kind donation to the non-profit, an attempt to soothe race-based guilt and maybe drum up some positive PR. That meant the parking sucked but many of the hospital perks trickled down to us, including an on-site gym. It was minimal, but did the job. The day after my move, I began going there in earnest. Twenty minutes on the elliptical turned into thirty, then forty-five, until finally an hour or two was nothing. I watched the calories light up the screen like firecrackers, forcing myself to get to an even number. I couldn't have 578 calories burned when 600 was so damn close. 750 was even better. 1,000 ideal.

Here's what they don't tell you about losing weight: You'll never look like you did before. At least I wouldn't. In college, the weight piled on fast and I took it off even faster, but my skin just wasn't elastic enough to snap back in place. Plus, my stomach was never exactly flat to begin with, not even when I was a teenager at a moderate weight. After the college shedding, I had loose skin. Folds of skin. I looked like I'd given birth and my nipples pointed straight down. My breasts looked okay in a push up bra, and I knew how to dress for my body. I had grown bingo wings, flabby skin with a little fat hanging down heavy from my upper arms like a bat. I never wore tank tops or short sleeves, and knew three-quarter sleeve shirts were my best mask. But naked? If it was a huge disappointment to me every morning, I could only imagine the look of disappointment when someone else saw it. Like opening a Christmas present so sure it was jewelry only to find a pair of socks.

I needed to lose enough weight to be desirable, but I didn't know what "enough" was or even how much I currently weighed. At mirrors, I would hold my stomach taut, first one hand at my sternum and the other at my pubis, and then one on either side of my waist. There. Smooth, tight and taut. I had tried it all. Dry skin brushing, wet skin brushing, hundreds of sit-ups a day for weeks, wearing a corset most hours of a day and piles of cocoa butter. Nothing.

I was also still depending solely on low-carbing it for weight management, and I was starting to play loose with the guesses. Dinners with Chirag were always rich—tender steak cuts dripping with butter (did it really make a difference that I swapped the potatoes for asparagus)? Salads from the Cheesecake Factory with their low-carb cheesecake as dessert (did having Caesar dressing on the side, notoriously the lowest carb option from restaurants, make up for everything else?). The constant cardio made me feel better, more determined, when I was riding that machine to nowhere, but my clothes seemed to fit the same. I still had that same, flat Cherokee butt, the bane of all Indians who salivated over lower body curves. My breasts still sagged. It still looked like I'd spent years with a belt cinched too tight at my belly button, with a pudge both above and below. The hourglass figure was there, forced into being by a big rip cage and hip bones, but it was my only saving grace. I began adding yoga to my regimen, scouring online for all the free classes available. I'd tried it once in college, but it was some weird hybrid where the teacher drilled us incessantly about Sanskrit phrases and we didn't actually do any poses.

I wandered into a real yoga studio and barely made it through the first class. "Downward facing dog is a resting pose," the lithe instructor said. *Was she fucking insane?*

"You worked out three hours today? Straight?" Michelle asked when I called.

"Well, not straight. Morning, lunch and after work," I said.

"Man. I wish I had that kind of willpower."

"How's it at your mom's?"

"It blows," she said. "The kids are sharing a room and she's all up in my business. She signed me up for Christian Mingle! Made the profile and everything. I made her take it down."

"Not quite there yet?"

"Kill me if I get that desperate. Besides, I'm horny, not looking for a husband. I don't think Christian Mingle is the place for that."

"You never know," I said. "Those bible thumpers might be the kinkiest of us all."

Hump Day

MY CYCLE STARTED like a plague the summer before sixth grade. The sweltering months meant weeks on the reservation with ancient relatives who I never remembered, listening to them chattering in Cherokee while my name was dropped like garnish in the middle. *Cherokee, Cherokee, Jennifer, Cherokee,* as rheumy butter from corn dribbled down their chins. My dad has lost all the language; it had been beaten out in the Indian boarding school. Granddaddy long-legs the size of Frisbees hung from the door frames, and the tap water in every reservation home tasted the same: rusty, earthy, and a bit like blood.

This time, we drove from Oregon to Oklahoma, renting a Mercury instead of trusting the minivan which I thought looked like a retarded whale. The Cougar was sleek, new, and smelled of Other.

My period began in a gas station bathroom with fluorescent red blood licking down my chubby white thighs. Shit.

I knew exactly what it was, my mother having over-prepared me. And I didn't want a big deal made of it. Instead, I wadded up tissue in my rust-stained underwear even as the pangs like a chainsaw cut through my insides. Because I wasn't going to ruin this trip. This time, it wasn't just the reservation. This time, we were spending a weekend with my rich, much older cousin in Kansas City.

Katarina, or Kat, was in her thirties with two kids a little younger than I. She produced movies in LA, slipping back and forth between her sprawling Midwestern craftsman and a studio condo in Hollywood. She was beautiful, looked

Indian, and I was nothing like her even with all of my praying for it.

I was embarrassed immediately when we arrived on her street. The slick Mercury looked decrepit in her pristine driveway, cozied up next to her idyllic landscaping (I'd never seen edging) and out of place beneath her perfect home. Luckily, no one paid me much mind. Besides commenting on my hair, which my mother had freakishly permed only on the front half and left the back straight—poodle in front, flat and split-ended in the back—few people noticed me at all.

One of Kat's kids was at day camp all day long. The other was too young to be interesting. The adults talked, and Kat cooked dishes for breakfast I'd never seen before. Eggs benedict (I preferred scrambled with each forkful dipped in jam), which were runny and got cold too fast. Quiche, which was like a thick egg pizza but not nearly as good. She drank coffee, which permeated every inch of the morning. My mom drank orange juice in the morning. My dad, Coke.

After pulling the constantly bloodied napkins out of my underwear and into the bathroom trash and asking incessantly for Tylenol for "a headache," I found refuge in the backyard. It was blowed, mowed, sodded, and shyly offering up new blossoms. Kat also had dogs, one boy and one girl. The boy dog was particularly boisterous.

He followed so close to my heels to trip me, jumping up and lunging at me, his big maw smiling. Behind the custom dog house, made to look like a miniature of Kat's, he knocked me down good and began a slow grinding into my thigh, his back arched like he was constipated. Between his legs, a shiny, pointy, wet dog penis bloomed out of its hairy shaft. He rubbed it brusquely against my thigh, my shorts having ridden up to my hips. And then I understood.

After a few seconds, he stopped. Nothing happened, no sperm shooting out like I always thought it would. But he turned aloof, indifferent, and ran off to sniff at one of his old crap piles (or his sister's). And I was alone again.

It disgusted me, that dog penis, but it was the first time I'd been aware and engaged (willingly or not) in any kind of sexual act. I found one of his toys and tempted him close with it. Interest piqued just enough for him to come for a closer inspection. Drawing him back behind the dog house, away from any prying eyes from the picture kitchen window, I leaned down and held out a piece of bark dust between his legs. I didn't actually want to touch the dog penis, it was revolting. I didn't know what I wanted.

I didn't see it again, not the entire weekend. As my blood dried up and the pain waves subsided, so did the dog's interest in me. But it stuck with me. Not the initial violation itself, but my own perversion. It was that second time behind the ridiculous dog house that branded me for good.

CHAPTER FIVE

I WAS GOING to do it. Friday morning and I'd been settled in the new place for a full work week. "Gorgeous morning, gorgeous," was the text I got as I booted up my computer at work. It had been a month since we'd met, and I still hadn't texted first. These workday morning greetings kick-started what would be hours and hours of back and forth. As a test engineer, Chirag had a lot of downtime. And me? I had my own office and a boss who considered it a great achievement if she made it into work at all.

"What are you doing tonight?" I replied. This was it, address the monster full on. Silence, blank screen. Sometimes he had sudden distractions at work, but this was a different kind of silence.

"Have plans," he said. Plans. I was baby-fresh to all of this, but I knew what it meant. Still, pushing it a bit wasn't guaranteed to break my fantasy. Maybe it really would just stretch it a bit.

"Doing what?" I asked. I'd never questioned him before, not like this.

"You really wanna know?" he asked. No.

"Yeah."

"Got a date tonight," he said. Seeing it spelled out, those four words, smacked like a hit to the temple.

"You upset?" he asked. Yes.

"No."

"Good. How's work?"

"Busy, gotta go." I hadn't done that before, but there wasn't much of a precedent set. I mean, he'd flat-out told me he'd never had a relationship, never wants one, and if it's forced upon him it certainly won't be with someone like me, some milky American who only looks white. His texts the remainder of the workday were answered sporadically after meanly-plotted windows of waiting.

"Don't be mad," was the last one he sent before I left the office, phone at the ready to text Michelle who had to keep her phone in the break room until she left at five.

"We're going out tonight," I texted her.

"What? Why? I have the kids." Chris took them seemingly at random, usually "forgetting" them on Friday and Saturday nights in an effort to keep Michelle out of the bars (and the beds of others).

"C." She knew. It was all I had to say.

"He's an asshole," she said.

It was fine. I would go myself, sidle up to an empty barstool and wait for a distraction. I emailed Sam, trying my best to seem happy. She'd up and left me here, in this godawful country, while she sent me postcards from France. Photos from Amsterdam. And she deserved it, didn't she? She was the only person who'd never been cruel to me and she was so incredibly beautiful. What must it be like to have everything so easy like that?

I got to Cellar early to stake out a good spot. My bartender was manning the long bar, poured my glass full and charged me for a bottom-shelf drink. "How you doing, baby?" she asked, and I forced a smile to complement my plus-sized tip.

Here's the thing about living in the city where you went to college: ghosts are everywhere. They try to hide behind a new layer of fat or a mask of crow's feet, but you see them if you look hard. We all haunt the same spaces. Krystal was my second roommate in college, right after Sam. We met in the sorority, same as Sam, but Krystal was a different breed. She was dumb, truly dumb, in that sad kind of way that makes you wonder how she could function a full day without getting hit by a bus. Our freshman year, she became much more interested in cheap blow than school, going to class less and less until she let a strip club that pretended to be a burlesque show swallow her up. Blonde sorority girl turns coke-snorting stripper is the kind of cliché that only comes true in porn and Portland. Krystal was a true living legend. Although our final days together were brutal, with my finding straight razors, mirrors, snowdust, and naked men strewn about the living room and her throwing a shoe at my head, it's as if she'd forgotten when she spotted me. Maybe she had.

"*Jennnnn*," she screeched in that Minnesota-thick way she had. She was on something, clearly, but nowhere near gone. "You look so good! You look so good! What are you drinking?"

You could have a "conversation" with Krystal without ever opening your mouth. You could disappear for the night, steal her designer handbag, call her a slut, and she'd never even notice.

But here, here's something worth noticing: Krystal wasn't alone.

"This is Chantel," she said, gesturing to a show-stopping woman behind her. She had that kind of toasted skin I love, brown springy curls, and a body like I'd never seen in person. Her entirety looked airbrushed, down to her aura. "We work together," Krystal whispered loudly, leaning in and giving me that look. Of course.

"Hey," I said.

"You're so pretty!" Chantel said, as if she were at work right then. She couldn't turn it off. I know what I am. I know how I look. She was a world away from me.

There was no being alone once Krystal found you. No matter how high she got, she had a penchant for tracking familiarity like a hound. I could either leave, or I could let her entertain me for a while. Because of Chantel, I stayed.

We moved to the long table in the center, where men did lazy circles to sniff out the drunkest and we could keep an eye on every nook and cranny. "What's your ethnic background?" Chantel asked me. Hmm. She didn't talk like a stripper.

"What?"

"Your ethnic background. You're not all white," she said, like she was revealing something I didn't know.

"Oh. Half white, half Cherokee," I said.

"Isn't she pretty?" Krystal said again, her eyes roaming the room and her fish lips nibbling around for the straw. Nobody was listening to her.

"Me, too," said Chantel. "Well, half black, half Cherokee. Obviously," she said, her perfectly straight teeth shining like jewels. Was it incestuous to fuck someone from your tribe? There are so few of us left.

From behind Chantel's shoulder, I caught a movement. A way of walking, uber pronated, that I couldn't miss. Chirag had walked into the bar, a towering, chunky and mousy brown woman behind him. He passed me, inches away, looked dead into my eyes and widened his own. He didn't say a word, and the woman followed like a loyal puppy. Together, they took up a corner booth. I watched him lean in and whisper to her, his plump lips working their magic. She smiled, pulled at her skirt and sat up straighter. He made a move for the bar, ordering drinks and taking dinner menus. They weren't going anywhere and the Cellar was pressing in.

No. No, it wouldn't be incestuous to fuck another Cherokee.

Chantel lived stumbling distance from Cellar, and I felt Chirag's eyes boring into my retreating back. Chantel and I, we lost Krystal at the bar, a flash of understanding between us before simultaneous excuses of going home. It was never difficult to leave Krystal at any place brimming with booze or something to sniffle up her nose.

Thank god, by sheer happenstance, my nails were cut short that night. Chantel was easy, in all the right ways. Soft and responsive like only women used to loving women are. Her studio apartment midway up a highrise smelled like her, a combination of sweet sweat and floral dryer sheets. Being with women, just in those moments, can be so much simpler because we both know each other's cards.

In Chantel's too-soft bed, I undressed her with voracity. Again, women can be so much simpler. Slip hands over her just waxed thighs, across her curving hips and pull down the thong over flexed calves while we explored each other's mouth, tongue, teeth. Pull the slip of a dress over her head, let it get caught in her natural curls, a makeshift blindfold so I could look freely at her baby face without her seeing and knowing all. Watch her breathe in more air, faster, guessing where I'd touch her next. Her breasts were half silicone but perfect, not needing the casing of a bra, and the implants slid underneath muscle to make them still feel natural and barely a whisper of a scar.

Her dark nipples were already hard, small and taut in the way only women who haven't breastfed have, dotted with miniature bumps and begging to be licked. Suckled. Send a pleasure wave down her stomach to between her legs. Only with women do I like this overt kind of control. To take charge. To make them sit back, arch their back for more, and always (always) make them cum first.

She tried, weakly, to reciprocate in tandem, reaching for the hem of my dress. It wasn't what either of us wanted, but I pulled it off myself and dropped it on top of hers on the floor. With her petite curves between my legs, she snapped off my bra easily, traced the teardrop weight in her fingers and flicked her tongue across my nipples while holding herself up with one arm. I was already wet with my want for her. Her concave stomach with the bellybutton that barely hung out. Her spreading hips with the faded stretch marks like a faint spider web. Her Indian cheekbones flanked by the most delicate of ears.

I pushed her back down, firmly, and she accepted her position as I worked my way down her body, kissing the bottom rungs of her rib, the swell of her hipbone. Her wetness and sweat tasted familiar, something comforting. My tongue tip moving across her clitoris drew her hands into my hair, showing me the rhythm, the pressure she liked best. I learned her, her body, in seconds. She liked very light flicks, breathing room between each one, followed by sucking on her clit in patterns she couldn't fully predict.

When she started grinding into my face and her juices began spilling down her inner thighs, working into her violet bed sheet, I worked one finger, then two and three, into her to give her something to really ride, my mouth never leaving her. Even through her heavy breathing, the rustling in my head as she gripped my hair tighter, the quiet squeak of moans escaping her, I could listen to her body getting closer. She bore down hard on my hand, my mouth, while I stroked her g-spot. I pulled at her nipples gently with the other hand, then harder as she arched in response. When she was on the brink, I slipped my hand from her nipples, through the valley of her own juices, and circled the rim of her anus while she shuddered through the waves and soaked my hands and chin with her cum.

She looked happy. Safe, held. "Taste yourself," I told her, and she took my dripping fingers between her swollen lips, licking and sucking them clean before pulling me down to her to enjoy the rest of her juices swimming in my mouth.

"Let me return the favor," she said, propping herself up and grazing my thigh with her hand. "What's the most you've ever cum in one night?"

I woke up snared in Chantel's sheets and legs with four texts from Chirag on my dying phone. "You up?" at nearly two in the morning. "Still upset?" right after the bars closed. "You there?" a few minutes later, followed by "Ok, goodnight." Apparently his date hadn't ended the way he'd wanted, maybe guilt mixed with fear was setting in—or maybe he thought all of this was perfectly fine for real.

As much as I wanted to sneak out, barefoot and quiet, Chantel was semi-stirring. Besides, Portland was small.

Small enough I may see her again.

"Hey, I'm taking off," I whispered after pulling my dress back on. The bra and underwear were nowhere to be seen, a casualty of the night.

"Hmm, okay," she said, barely opening her eyes. "You know where I live if you're bored some night."

"Yeah. I do."

I trekked home with the smell of her consuming me, sticky and sugary with just a touch of salt, like the ocean. I still hadn't responded to Chirag, and it being a Saturday he'd be sleeping 'til after noon anyway. Instead, I called Michelle.

"Did you go out?" she asked.

"Yeah, for a while."

"Find any good?"

"No. But I saw Chirag. On a date."

"Mother fucker. What did you do?"

"Nothing, I left. What's up with you?"

"Well," she began, breathing one of those deep sighs that indicated she was about to make a "revelation." "I have a date. Christian Mingle. He's a former model and musician."

"Of course he is."

"He's Hawaiian," she said.

"Well, that's an interesting twist." People. We come from all over, islands of paradise and bustling third world metros, just to fall into the depths of someone just like us.

I didn't hear from Chirag all of Saturday, and well into Sunday. It made sense—he wanted to keep his weekend nights free. I felt certain I could go back to Cellar if I wanted, whenever I wanted. It was my place, and letting him stay there Friday night was a gift. I'd staked my territory, and I was here first. He wouldn't be back. Still, I was full for the weekend and didn't need any more ego stroking (or any other kind). Come his Sunday afternoon text, I'd made up my mind.

"Okay, here's the deal," I texted when his requisite "Gorgeous morning, gorgeous" rolled in.

"What's that?"

"This is going to be a don't ask/don't tell arrangement. You do what you want. I just don't want to know."

"You want me to lie?" he asked.

"Kind of. I just won't ask."

"Okay." And the inky blood between us crafted a promise just like that.

vi.
The Die in Diet

PAPO ALWAYS SMELLED the same, like old man and dust. Mamo, I don't remember her. She died when I was too young. But my mom says she loved me and that she was the most wonderful woman ever. "And she was so thin," my mom bemoaned. "A tiny little thing. Why couldn't I get her genes? She didn't even weigh one hundred pounds, but Dad would still tell her she was getting fat. Said if she didn't lose some weight, he was going to trade her in," she said, shaking her head in disgust.

Every other Saturday, we went to Papo's place in Jacksonville, an old gold-mining town turned tourist trap. There were laws that you couldn't change any of the signs without the city's permission. It was a National Historic Treasure. I liked the Children's Museum and the Britt Festival in the spring. I liked the deer that snuck around Papo's yard, eating the roses my mom planted when she was a teenager. I liked his big backyard, the little bridge my dad had built for him, and pretending to get lost in the hilly woods beyond. I liked that I could fit underneath all the beds in the house (you couldn't do that at home) and I loved the apple butter Papo made me from his trees in back. But I didn't like him.

He looked at me with his hard blue eyes, the same ones my mom got that had gone milky in her. He had a full head of hair, but it was white and always gelled. He didn't move much, just watched me and wrestling on television from his lounge chair.

I sat kitty-corner to him while my mom vacuumed the spare bedrooms and dusted the ancient furniture. I always wished someone would turn on the fireplace—I'd never seen one burning before. But it was never on.

"Come here," Papo said suddenly, gesturing to me. He only touched me when he felt like he had to. I wasn't prepared for this. I moved to him slowly, like an animal angling for the bait even though I knew it was stupid. "Do you want a peanut?" he asked, showing me the bag of fluffy, orange circus peanuts. I liked them well enough and associated them with one of the Good Things at Papo's place. It was the only place where I had them.

I reached for the bag without a word. "That's probably not such a good idea after all," he said, pulling the bag back. His thick thumb and forefinger grasped my arm. "You're going to be a husky girl!" he said. "Yes, you are. Better be careful."

"Dad!" my mom said, appearing in the doorway with a wheezing vacuum in hand. "Jennifer, go outside." I went to the front patio where I could hear everything through the picture window. "How dare you?" my mom hissed. "You did that to me, I'm not going to let you do that to her. If you say or touch her *ever again*, we're never coming back. You understand me?"

"Okay, okay," Papo said. "Jeez, I was just joking."

When Papo died, just a few months later, I wasn't sad. It was kind of fun hanging out in the hospital for so long, waiting for him to die and mom to cry. The couches were a soft material, not fake leather like ours. And I don't care what people say about hospital food, I thought it was pretty good.

"Mrs. Taylor," a towering doctor said to my mother as we huddled in the waiting room. "Can I speak to you a moment?" I watched their whispered exchange, the doctor's practiced speech and my mom's slumped shoulders. As she began to cry, I peeled another lid off a chocolate pudding and licked it clean.

CHAPTER SIX

WE WERE ALMOST six weeks in and almost no days went by without a text from Chirag. Definitely no weekdays. On a random Tuesday, thirteen days before I turned twenty-eight, we went for dinner and a movie. In the dark, my breath caught in my chest when his hand swallowed mine. I tried not to breathe, willed my hand not to sweat, like he was a wary wild thing I'd scare away. At dinner, he picked apart the vegetarian options while encouraging me to order the most expensive of things. Lobster tails and truffle butter. I didn't even particularly like lobster—it felt like it was the money, the decadence, I was consuming.

"I can't stay long," he said. "Work in the morning." We both had work in the morning. Trampling down the basement stairs, a flood of heat greeted us through the front door. I'd left the oven on by mistake, the door open. The oven was empty, thank god, but filled the room with a dry heat. He smiled, "It feels like Bombay," he said.

We rarely talked here; instead he pushed me against the refrigerator before I could take my contacts out. We kicked off our shoes while he cradled the back of my head to keep it from cracking against the hardness. I wanted to keep him, to keep this, and so when one of my nipples peeked out from my dress and he dove for it like he was starved, I knew.

In the cramped space, the bed was just a few steps away. For all our kissing and everything buts, I didn't really know what to expect. I knew the softness of his skin, like lukewarm butter, from my hands sneaking under his shirt. I knew the insanity of his broad shoulders, the big arms, and the softness of his stomach. Still, with him on top of me and un-buttoning his shirt like lightning with one hand, I didn't expect this. He was a man, built like one and handled me like one. I was so used to Eli, who I was petrified of crushing, especially at my biggest. Even when I'd lost the weight, my thighs were still double his size. With the college boy, I didn't even bother to look. For once, I felt protected. Feminine. Like my body wasn't something to apologize for.

With the top of my dress already pushed down, it gathered like a petticoat at my waist. Chirag's weight on top of me, at least seventy pounds heavier, felt like nothing. As he unbuckled his belt, I slid his jeans to the floor with my feet. At the same time, he moved down between my legs, sucking hard on the soft spots of my inner thighs, already bursting the blood vessels closest to the surface. His tongue in the crevice of my thighs, working towards my clit, it was warmer than I expected, like being washed in an ocean of him.

His tongue, his thick fingers, they brought me close but I wanted him inside me. Now. There was an aching empti-ness in me I hadn't known existed. I pulled on his shoulders to bring him up, tasted myself on his mouth while he dug a condom from the discarded jeans before ripping it open with his teeth. Rolling onto his back, then rolling it on, he pulled me on top of him while pulling my dress over my head.

We fit together, easily, like we were supposed to. His cock was sized for me, wide but not overbearing, just enough that I could close my fingers around it. As I lowered myself onto him, he threw his head back, an "Oh, fuck," es-caping, made richer with the accent. The ride was slow, de-termined, his muscles tensing against my clit with every slow thrust. "Get on top," I said, relinquishing control, and he flipped me like it was nothing.

Burying his face in my neck, he fucked me faster, choos-ing his own favorite rhythm, and when he came the deep boom from his gasping vibrated through my body. I could feel the rush of him, even with the condom, the pulsing of him pushing against my g-spot and kick-starting my own pleasure pangs from my center to all of my extremities.

When he'd emptied himself, he rolled onto his back and pulled me with him. I curled into the crook of his arm, face resting on his smooth chest and a sliver from his warm, brown nipples. He kissed my head with a tenderness I hadn't known before, and I didn't bother to wake him. Or to clean myself, get up, or move for fear of scaring him away. It was the first time he stayed the night, and we woke twice throughout the darkness to explore each other again. By morning and oh-fuck-morning-commutes, we hadn't mastered each other's bodies, but we got close. We got close.

"It's my birthday next Monday," I told him, finishing my second whiskey, straight and on the rocks, of the night. Ninety-five calories.

"Then you'll be the old one," he said. For a span of just a few weeks, June 16 through August 17, we were the same age.

"Yeah," I said, rolling my eyes. "But I'm doing the celebration on Saturday. It's just at Cake, the bouncer reserved a booth for me. Just Michelle and a couple of other friends. You should come."

"I don't know," he said. "I won't know anyone."

"You know me," I said, pointedly. "And Michelle. Besides, how else do you think you meet people?"

"Not my thing, really," he said. "And I might have plans, I don't know." I didn't understand. Just a couple of weeks ago, he'd mentioned he was going to a friend's birthday party at Holden's Bar blocks from Cake. On a Friday. An "older" friend. A female friend. She was turning forty-five and he asked me for suggestions for a gift for her. It took all my strength not to spew something hateful, like Depends or mom jeans.

"Well, whatever," I said. "You know where I'll be." If a birthday wasn't a big enough lure to force a weekend night out of him, I didn't know what was.

"We should celebrate on your real birthday," he said. "Monday. Dinner, movie, whatever you want." It was not whatever I wanted.

That Saturday, I squeezed into a gold sequined dress with slim straps and a black velvet bow at the sternum. Shit. It had fit okay when I bought it in London, but that was almost four years ago. Now it was tight, the zipper complaining. Apparently all the low-carb dieting in the world wouldn't make up for monstrous calories, nor would hours of plugging away at the same cardio machine. But it didn't matter right now. I had talked a comped hotel room for the night out of my boss, a leftover in-kind donation from a recent philanthropy event. Bottle service was on the house, compliments of Cake's bouncer, Evan, who hollered after me one night, "I have a crush on you!" and I just smiled at him, that "smile like sunshine" he chased even as he was surrounded by easier catches.

By ten, it was still early. Empty. Evan had brought me the biggest, most jaw-dropping bouquet of flowers I'd ever seen, and a pang of guilt flooded me. I wasn't a tease—I didn't even have it in me to know how to do that. I never said or acted any way that should make him think otherwise. "I just wanted to," he said with a shrug when I tried to protest.

"Happy early birthday!" Sam's email lit up my screen. "What are you doing? Let me tell you, 30 is pretty great so far! You better listen to your older, wiser friend. I will have a glass of wine for you tonight and on Monday. Miss you tons, I hope you're happy." Her warmth touched me, the heat of the desert in her words. I wished she were here, like the old days. Like college when we spent four nights a week in the gay bar where almost nobody called me fat even as they fell to their knees and worshipped her.

Within the hour, I was circled by my small clutch of friends who'd stuck nearby, too scared to venture far. Michelle, couples who had paired off when we were in college together, remnants of sorority sisters. As the hour eased towards midnight, I couldn't help it. My eyes kept drifting to the door, to the coat check, to the long and sweating bar. It was a packed house (it always was) and the birthday drinks were coming at godspeed, but I felt entirely, selfishly alone.

At midnight, when carriages give way to pumpkins and drunk girls lose their slippers, an arm squeezed around my waist and pulled my head to the familiar chest. "You came," I said, trying to look and sound like I didn't care. Chirag shrugged. "What else did I have to do?"

I could see Evan watching from his post at the door. He didn't like Chirag. Had told me as much earlier that night. "What are you doing?" he'd asked me, and I couldn't answer. How could you explain it to someone? How could Evan explain why he was stuck on me when I was perhaps even more of a dead end than Chirag? "I just want you to be careful," Evan had said. "You deserve more. And know that when he shows up and you're not here, I don't let him in. He can stand in line all night for all I care. I don't give a shit."

I'm sorry, Evan. You deserve more, too.

But I can't stop, control, or reel in what's charging through me. "I have a hotel room tonight," I shout-whispered to Chirag, the music pouring deafness into our ears.

"I know," he said. "You told me." Even in my semi-drunken haze, the shame of a brown spot outing you is palpable.

"Hey," I leaned to the table. My table. "Hey! Guys, I'm gonna go," I said. The pain in my feet suddenly became noticeable. I was hungry. There was nothing here for me anymore, nothing more to wait for.

"It's just midnight!" Michelle said. "We've only been here two hours. It's your birthday!"

"I know, I'm sorry. I'm just tired," I said. She gave me a look. That look. But I just didn't care.

The flowers were heavier than they should have been, especially when I had to squeeze past Evan to leave with nothing but a side hug as a thank you. "You want to go anywhere else?" Chirag asked.

"I don't care."

"You hungry?" he asked.

"I could eat."

"I was thinking, since it's your birthday weekend and all, maybe tonight would be the night I'd try fish." What? What about the little soul, the thousands of years of religion, the face-slapping to all the Indian gods?

"But why?"

"Why not? It's good for protein. Besides, I started eating eggs when I was in Boston at grad school, you know." No, I didn't know. "Just don't eat them much now because of the cholesterol."

"If you want to, but I don't want to be the one getting blamed for it."

"Who will ever find out?" he asked with that grin I couldn't look at directly for long, like it would somehow burn me from the inside out.

Portland's food cart pods are open late. Well, some of them. Some don't open 'til midnight and serve drunkards while chasing off homeless kids until dawn. We parked at the Fourth and Alder pods, cozying up to a Vietnamese food truck. "Grilled halibut with extra sauce, steamed veggies," Chirag told the ancient, wrinkled man, like he'd ordered it a thousand times. I got the same.

At the decrepit picnic tables folded into the parking lot, with Christmas lights strung truck to truck and a melting pot of aromas filling the air, we unwrapped the tin foiled paper boats. What would it be like to eat meat for the first time when you're almost thirty? I imagined it would taste and feel disgusting, like you're fully aware you're an animal consuming another animal. That's how I feel when I try to eat meat stoned. I'm just hyper aware of the flesh, the tendons, the cartilage that can sneak in. I'm strictly vegan when I'm high—for four full hours if the weed is good.

Chirag dug into the meat with the flimsy plastic fork,

the butter saturating completely through the poor thing.

The white, melting blob raced into his mouth like it was nothing. Natural. Not an affront to the gods, his family, or one of the oldest traditions on earth.

"What do you think?" I asked.

"It's okay," he said, and then ate the entire thing. As did I.

The hotel was just blocks away, perched like royalty above all the other high rises in downtown. Carrying Evan's flowers (Chirag brought me none—he brought me nothing) was strange in the boutique lobby. In the suffocating elevator. They overtook the room, which felt cheap since it was free and begged for.

"I want you to know," Chirag said. "I wanted to come. It's just, it's kind of awkward, you know?"

"Why? Because people will assume things?"

"I don't care what people think," he said. "I've never really liked the whole big group, big party thing."

"You're with big groups, at big parties, every weekend night," I said, the liquid bravery coursing through me.

"That's different," he said. "I'm not really there. But, you know, I like you. Nothing has changed, though. I'm still who I am. Things will still play out the same way. But just because I 'have plans,' it doesn't mean anything."

"So what the hell is that supposed to mean?" I asked. This night had taken a sharp, veering turn into territory I didn't know.

"If you want, we can be monogamous. Just not exclusive."

"I have no idea what you're talking about."

"I don't want to sleep with anyone else. The dating, the flirting, that's fine. That's fun. I don't get jealous, and you shouldn't either. But I've never liked sleeping around. I've never had a one-night stand, and I don't intend to." Well. This was interesting. And I'd take what I could get. Besides, what harm was dating anyway? The details, the rules—

kissing, groping, I didn't want to get into it. I didn't want to feed my imagination.

"Okay," I said. "I'm in."

It was the first night either of us had sex in a hotel room. In the morning, I left Evan's flowers to die under the fluorescence of the bathroom light.

vii.
A Game We Play

I FOUND OUT two weeks before sixth grade started that I was going to a new school. But we weren't moving any-where. "Mrs. Dodge is *definitely* the best teacher in town," my mom said. "I always wanted you to be in her sixth-grade class, but now she's moved to Central Point Elementary, and so are you." And that was it. No discussion, no goodbyes to friends, no final year in elementary school at Jewitt. I had always been an honor roll, straight-A, flawless student because there was no other choice. My mom refused to be-lieve that anything besides perfection could come from her. When I was four, she tried to teach me to read, the proper names for shapes, and all these other tasks early. I remem-ber being overwhelmed and overworked getting flashcard after flashcard shoved in my face. "It's an octagon!" My mom yelled when I couldn't remember. "How fucking hard is that to remember?"

By this time next year, I'd be in junior high where there were no recesses—but I heard we got a mid-morning break where we could buy snacks from the cafeteria or vending machine. They had milkshakes, nachos, and soft pretzels. The idea of a real "break" where we'd use money to buy something beyond pre-determined portions on plastic trays was exhilarating.

I wasn't that heartbroken about the school switch. My best friend had been held back in second grade, so I never saw her at school. The next closest friends were boys who lived on the same street as I did, and we hung out because it was convenient and they wanted the toys and open kitchen policy at my house. No big loss.

The first couple of months in Mrs. Dodge's were brutal, memorizing the longest word in the English language (pneumonoultramicroscopicsilicovolcanoconiosis), the presidents in order and year, all the major bones in the body, and every morning started with copying a book for ten minutes in perfect cursive. The over-achiever in me thrived, shriveling up only for the math segment and (increasingly) science. Mrs. Dodge had a soft spot for creativity, whether it was writing, painting, sketching, or performing. I excelled at them all. After being forced onto the stage my entire life, from jazz dancing to folk storytelling, I adored being center stage on my own terms. I was quiet, not shy, and stages gave me permission to showboat. I scooped up the lead in the sixth-grade play and all the art and writing contests with ease.

I'd also found a new best friend, Vanessa. She lived on the other side of town with parents who didn't hover as we tucked into games or television. At recess, we played Pog and marbles, talked about boys, and practiced making teacups woven in our hands with stretchy strings.

"You know who likes you?" she asked. "Matt!"

"Eww!" I squealed. Matt floated between our class and a special needs class. He was big but not fat, like a bulldog. Really, he was sweet, but an easy target. He'd been kind to me, showing me his cat-eye marble one afternoon on a break from play practice.

"Thanks," I'd said, putting it in my bag.

"Oh, I—sure," he'd said. Then, I realized he was just showing me, not giving it to me. But I was too embarrassed to give it back.

On a rain-soaked January, my mom picked me up like always, but with that familiar harshness in her voice. "What the hell is wrong with you?" she said, before I could even close the door, her mean face coiled into itself. She reached over and slapped the back of my head, snagging a finger in the tight part of my ponytail. My body tightened as the guessing game began. Sometimes she flipped out for absolutely no reason, trying to trick me into admitting to something she hadn't a clue about. Just in case.

"What?"

"I got a call from the school today. There was a *petition* being passed around? Saying *I* did all your homework for you? What the fuck, Jennifer? Apparently almost your entire class signed it!" I didn't know what she was talking about. Shouldn't I know what she's talking about?

My mom had been extremely dedicated as a Classroom Helper, dutifully coming to school with me every Tuesday and Thursday morning. She helped the stupid kids with reading and complained at night that she was there to help me, not "all these retarded brats." I didn't want her there at all. It was shameful, having her buzzing around me, like I needed a babysitter even at school.

"I don't know what you're talking about!" I said.

"Right. Well, apparently it was your little *friend* who started it. Vanessa." Vanessa? That wasn't right. We'd just had lunch together, chicken nuggets and crinkle fries. We figured out how to make woven bras instead of teacups afterward.

"If it wasn't for some kid. Matt? It would have had every fucking signature of your class in it. He turned it in to your teacher," she said.

I never told him thank you. And I went to Vanessa's slumber party the following weekend like I didn't know a thing. I even kissed her during spin the bottle, and didn't mind when the wet flicks from her lips slithered between mine and got swallowed up to become a part of me for good.

CHAPTER SEVEN

"YOU'VE NEVER HAD a Christmas tree?" I asked. It was a stupid question.

"No," Chirag said. "I just don't get it. What's the point?"

"Well, it started as a pagan ritual. I mean, Christmas is aligned with winter solstice because it made it easier to convert pagans. Jesus was really born in the spring. But Santa is actually the Holly King flying through the night sky, the decorated tree just kind of got mixed in." I could tell I was losing him, and what did he care about the origins of Christmas, anyway? "It's just fun," I said.

"I'll go to the farm with you," he said. Even as a non-Christian, it was still a big deal for me. This time of year was always marinated in screaming fits when my dad finally dragged himself home from the week-long bender. I associated Christmas with closets that smelled like piss because he kept getting drunk and mistaking closets for bathroom. We had a fake tree my mom "named" Jolly in an attempt to make it seem real, but it wasn't. It was dusty and plastic.

It had been over three months since the birthday incident and the agreement to be monogamous but not exclusive. I still didn't know what that meant, but I didn't particularly want to sleep with anyone else anyway. Still, I knew it was dangerous. Humans, we have casual sex to keep ourselves from getting too attached to any one thing. Any one person. I'd already come up with a brilliant idea in September to chain myself to Chirag even tighter.

It was a quintessential Pacific autumn day—crunching leaves, pumpkins on porches, the whole deal. He'd just pulled himself out of me, and we were both drowsy with post-orgasm agreement.

"Since we're not having sex with anyone else," I began, "why don't we just get tested and not use condoms? I have an IUD anyway." That, of course, launched into a giant explanation of what an IUD is. Yes, it's the safest form of birth control. Yes, safer than condoms. No, it's not new, I've had it for years. In fact, I got it before South Korea because I didn't want to bother with getting birth control pills there.

Chirag was still wary. "Okay," he said, and actually made an appointment for an STD panel.

It's not like anyone likes condoms, and I was craving something even closer. I didn't think he had an STD with how obsessive he was with condoms and avoiding pregnancies. I knew I didn't with regular screenings every few months. It was about being extra sure, and getting that piece of paper from him—the closest I would get to anything of merit.

For two months, we'd been having unsafe sex. It was his first time, and when I eased myself onto him with nothing between us, his eyes widened like it was his first time, period. Afterward, when I told him, he said, "It *was* like the first time." That was something nobody could take from me, from us.

We drove for miles through the Oregon back roads, searching for that idyllic Christmas tree farm I'd found online. It was just how I imagined: a big, red barn on a hill that housed local honey sticks, handmade garlands, and ornaments. The fields stretched for acres, and you could choose to cut the tree yourself, or tie a flag on it and wave down a worker to cut, shake, and bundle it for you. We chose the latter, me afraid of spiders and sap and Chirag never opting into manual labor at all if he could help it.

He picked the tree, a blue spruce with hearty branches and no bald spots. It was short and a little fat, made to fit into my basement apartment. The whole thing was supposed to be romantic, and at times it was, but there was heartbreak in the act. This living thing, a newborn in tree years, was picked by us for slaughter. The chainsaw was deafening, and it only took a few seconds to slice through the trunk. Chirag smoked a cigarette while the poor thing was toppled, picked up, and violently shaken to make sure it looked its best. As it was dying in the pasture, happy couples and families sauntered by, dragging their own kills gleefully behind them. It would live on, a half-life, for just a few weeks before being left at the curb to be chopped into tidy pieces.

But Chirag loved helping to decorate it. We each picked out an ornament in the barn—he a sparkly candy cane and me a rustic-looking pair of ice skates. I'd never ice skated in my life. We pulled out my other ornaments from the closet, keepsakes I had collected from around the world. A black cab from London, crystal ball from Prague, mini-bull from Spain. Ribbon was wrapped around the tree, lights untangled and strung, and the discount velvet tree skirt tucked dutifully below.

He kissed me in the glow of the lights, tangled between the displaced tree and couch. "Why don't we just try to be together?" I asked. "For real?"

"You know I can't do that," he said, either exasperated or sad. I hoped for sad.

"Why not? Just to see."

I'd like to think he wanted to, not that he was simply beaten into submission. We were in deep now. It had been six months of this. Talking most days, all day, and carefully avoiding topics of what we did on the weekend. He was too ensnared to let me go completely, and I knew I had him cornered.

"Okay," he said. "Okay, we'll try."

"Omg, Sam!" I wrote to her. "We're 'official' now. God, he was a tough one to crack." I didn't like showing my real emotions in emails, and barely over the phone. I was the type who needed a proper sit down so I could read a person's eyes, their expression and the shift of their bodies. "How are things in the middle east?" She wrote back that she was happy for me, that she wanted me to find happiness.

It lasted two weeks. I was elated the first time he called himself my boyfriend. My computer was acting up, he fixed it, and when I said thank you, he replied, "That's the benefit of having an engineer boyfriend." He gave me weekend nights, and for once—for once—let me go to his place.

That was another of his anomalies. He was constantly at my place, or we were out. His flimsy excuse of "living in Hillsboro where nothing happens" wasn't holding anymore. What was he hiding? A wife? A live-in girlfriend?

I pushed him hard, flexing my new rights, until finally he conceded. "Just be forewarned, I don't have much furniture."

The one-bedroom apartment smelled like him and oily, spicy Indian food. He wasn't being modest. There was a cracked desk, a single desk chair, and a twin mattress on the floor with no sheets. The kitchen counters were covered in bottles and spices in a language I couldn't read. It was a boy's apartment, but also an apartment that wasn't a home. It screamed transitional. Temporary.

"Let me cook for you," he said. He'd never offered before, but had often mentioned what he made for himself. Palak paneer. Moong dahl. Chai.

In the kitchen, I watched him prep the black dahl, spilling the hard lentils into the pressure cooker that squealed every few minutes like a needy toddler. In a sauce pan, he soaked green peppers into a variety of spices. Cumin, mustard seeds, and asafoetida. Ready-made rotis and parathas sizzled over the open gas flame, flipped every thirty seconds with salad prongs.

"Try it," he said, gesturing to the bubbling pot when the thickened lentils and oils were combined. It tasted like health, like the earth, and like something wildly foreign. It exuded heat, it was comfort. "Here," he said, removing papers from an oversized moving box in the living room. We ate on the floor, leaning over the box. Every few bites, he would feed me by hand, dipping a torn-off piece of roti into the dahl. I didn't know then that it was an Indian's sign of love, of caring. It's what parents still do for their grown children when they rarely see them anymore.

That night, he taught me how to make chai. Boil black, Taj tea in an open-topped kettle. Add in grated ginger and two scoops of homemade chai spices. He had bottles his mother ground by hand in Mumbai. A little cinnamon, cloves and cardamom (green, cracked open with my teeth). Add equal parts milk once the boil begins, and sweeten as you like. For me, it was Splenda to keep the carbs at bay.

"Will you oil my hair?" he asked. I didn't know how. "I'll tell you how." He heated the blue Vatika bottle of coconut oil in the microwave for forty seconds, handing it to me with a small tea cup. "Be careful," he said. "It's hot and messy." Pulling off his shirt, he tapped the top of his head. "Just about three tablespoons," he said. "Now rub it in." After a few minutes, he reached up and shook his own head, gesturing for me to do the same. He tapped his shoulders, wanting a shoulder massage. "Gracias, babydoll," he said. "You want me to do you?" It was all nurture, a heady warmth spreading with the oil. "Women in India, they oil their hair every day," he said. "The smell makes me think of home."

His twin mattress had no fitted sheet and only a pilled, thin blanket for warmth. He kept the heat in the apartment in the 80s to feel like home. I didn't mind any of it. We spooned into each other, streamed the Food Network on his laptop, and experienced one another in this new environment. Sex on a twin mattress takes finesse, balance and creativity. I drilled every sight and smell into my memory. The way the ceiling vaulted towards the door. His open closet with Nike shorts spilling out. The suitcases in the corner with the BOM tags still attached. And I didn't mind any of it. I loved it, and soaked it in.

The next morning, I woke up at six to drive the thirty

miles home, then the fifteen miles to work. He slept through it all, the alarm and my peeing in the bathroom with no insulation between the rooms. "I'm going," I told him, and in sleep, he pouted his lips and tilted his head for a kiss. Yes. I could live like this.

Now, easing into December and the holidays, I felt nervous. I had it all, exactly what I wanted. Him committed to me, albeit begrudgingly. When I met Michelle for cheap drinks, I was spilling over with nervous excitement.

"You sure about all this?" she asked, looking doubtful. Buzzkill.

"Oh my god, just be happy for me," I told her.

"Okay," she said. "Oh, and I meant to ask. Can you stay the night at Chirag's next weekend? I want to use your place for the Hawaiian guy."

"I thought you weren't talking to him since he fell asleep in the middle of going down on you."

"He was drunk," she said, as if that was normal. "Besides, he's only in town for two days." As much as I hated sharing sheets with her men, I felt obligated. After all, I'd stayed with her without paying rent for three months.

She had my spare keys, and I had a guaranteed entire Saturday day and night at Chirag's. We had settled, over the months, into something that resembled ease and comfort. We were almost like a normal couple. But I was still curious. I still wanted reassurance. I searched for his name and his favorite handles online. He still had dating profiles on nearly every site, the common ones as well as one looking for BBWs. Was I a BBW? Did I care? (Yes, I cared a tremendous lot).

I knew I had a ten-minute window when he went for a shower, stupidly trusting me with his laptop that streamed a Bizarre Foods episode on Cherokees in North Carolina. He never logged out of his email. Most of the inboxed items were boring—work emails, credit card statements, promises of the cheapest airfare. I went into his chat history, but there were so many with Indian names and Hinglish that it was impossible to unravel. Then I searched for "gorgeous."

"Gorgeous morning, gorgeous," he had messaged a woman I'd never heard of. That morning. Was I already here when it happened? Was I on my way? I couldn't remember when I'd arrived.

The chat didn't last long, but it pulled up photos she had sent of herself. I know I'm not pretty, but she *really* wasn't pretty. At least forty years old with that crunchy, mousse-drowned hair we all tried in 1993. She had deep crow's feet and wrinkles by her mouth like she didn't just chain smoke, but performed expert fellatio on cigarettes. White trash, through and through—we recognize our own.

As for Chirag, he'd sent her some old photos of himself. "As promised," one said, and it was a photo of him with a shaved head from grad school, single stud in one ear and a practiced smirk. I'd never seen it. Didn't even know he'd ever shaved his head or had an earring.

Waiting to hear the water shut off was maddening, and as my blood pounded in my ears I felt lucky that at least he'd be the vulnerable one, wet and naked with just a towel.

"Do you want to tell me something?" I asked as soon as he came through the door, and I heard my mom in my voice. Charging him with something elusive to see if he'll admit to more.

"No," he said. "What's wrong?"

"I know," I said.

"Know what?"

"About the woman you were emailing this morning!"

"So?" he asked. He seemed genuinely confused.

"So! So what the fuck?"

"It was just flirting, babydoll," he said, running a towel through his hair. "That's all."

"No. You can't do that," I said.

"We never talked about what we could and couldn't do."

"It's implied," I said. "Otherwise, what's the fucking difference between what we're doing now and what we were doing before?"

"I don't know," he said, and I realized he really didn't.

The aching sobs were starting to flutter in my belly and work their way up my throat. The stinging at the eyes had started, and I knew there was no stopping it.

"Don't cry," he said, squatting beside me. "I didn't know."

"You'll never know."

"You're right," he said. "I don't think this is going to work." The last of the walls I had built up came sputtering down.

"Please," I said. That was it. Pathetic. I was begging, actually begging, and I didn't have a damn thing to follow it up with.

He leaned against the wall, the wet towel soaking into the carpet, and shook his head slowly. The determination steely in his eyes. "I'm sorry," he said.

For twenty minutes, we went back and forth. Me offering apologies that weren't due and somehow forgetting all about the woman in the emails. I had everything this morning, and now it was all taken from me.

It was getting to the point where the pain was so tight in my throat, I couldn't speak. The tears were drying up, and the dry heaving was setting in. "One more kiss," he asked-told me as I picked up my things, and I obliged. I fucking obliged, because I would take whatever I could get.

"I do love you, you know." It was the first time I had said it.

"Me, too." And the pounding afternoon rain washed me clean as I trekked to my car.

I called in sick to work on Monday. And Tuesday. Hell, better make it Wednesday, too. The day I left his place, Chirag's taste still on my mouth, I didn't want to crash Michelle's night even though all I wanted was my own bed and company. Instead, I picked up three bags of sugar-free chocolates and checked into a cheap hotel in the town between his place and mine. The bags of Reese's, Hershey milk chocolate and Hershey dark chocolate rushed through me, the laxative effect from sugar alcohols keeping me on the toilet for hours with my stomach twisting up. I wanted to feel empty, and I wanted something to taste good on my tongue.

Finally, when Michelle texted me the next day thanking me for the "sex room" and how hot The Hawaiian was, I couldn't hold it in. She acted kind and sorry and called Chirag all the names she was supposed to, but I could hear the "I told you so" pulsing through the words, and it's not what I wanted.

"How's the honeymoon going?" Sam emailed me, teasingly. I didn't reply. I couldn't. What could she possibly say?

One week later, Saturday rolled by again, so steady even when my world had crashed into dust. "You want to see me?" Chirag's text blinked on my phone. I couldn't help it.

"Yes."

"I was in Seattle. I have something for you." I hadn't known about Seattle. I didn't know if it had been planned and kept from me, or an escape because maybe he was hurt, too.

I spent two hours getting ready, curling my hair and applying flawless makeup. I chose the outfit carefully, to be tight at the waist and chest, but cover my arms. When he arrived at the basement door, he seemed a stranger. It had only been a week, but I was cruelly reminded that I didn't recognize him at all.

"Here," he said. It was sugar-free saltwater taffy and a ceramic, dragon-covered teacup from Seattle's Chinatown. "It made me think of you."

"I don't know what that means."

"I do," he said as he slinked back into my apartment.

"I tried," he said. "But this, just, I don't know. I'm going to India at the end of February for six months. Work."

"When did you find out?"

"Officially last week. But I kind of knew since August."

Figures.

"So what does that mean?"

"It means we have about two months, and we can make the most of it if you want."

He pulled me close to him, and I breathed in his smell. It, unlike the rest of him, was familiar. And my addiction to him was so strong, happy tears snuck down my face. I buried my cheeks in his shoulder so he wouldn't know.

Two months. Yes. Yes, I would take what I could get.

viii.
Alligators and Candy

"TELL ME YOUR first memory." The therapist looked at me with friendly, curious eyes. This wasn't my choice. My mom had sent me here after I started "acting out" (Michelle had given me a makeover three months after we sold cookies together, curling my hair loosely and straightening my bangs into one big swoop) and "not being herself" (I quit piano, quit Girl Scouts, and wanted to play basketball. My mom said sports were for stupid kids who couldn't handle academics. She didn't realize I was secretly one of those stupid kids).

My first memory. I couldn't tell where the stories I'd been told ended and my real memories began. "Well, my mom said—"

"I'm asking what *you* think. What *you* remember," the therapist said. What I think. I had no clue what I thought. But a memory popped into my head like it had been bursting to get out and leapt at the chance.

"Taking a bath," I said. This room was too small. It smelled strange. A smoking stick burned in one corner and the therapist wasn't wearing socks with her shoes.

"Good. How old were you?"

"About four, I think."

"What do you remember about it?" She just seemed to actually *care* so much, I wanted to feed her and make her full.

"I had this alligator squirt gun that I loved. My favorite bath toy. My mom would put blue food coloring in the bath-water because I didn't like the rust color. We have a well, so, you know." She nodded like she did.

"Anything else?"

"My dad came in. I mean, that was normal. We didn't lock the bathroom door."

"What did he do?"

"Nothing. I think he was going to shave, or get his razor or something."

"He didn't say anything to you? Or you to him?"

"No, I don't think so. I don't remember."

"Why do you think this is your first memory?"

"Like, there was nothing weird about it. But the bubble bath—my mom used dish soap—it had mostly disappeared. Those bubbles don't stay long. And then my dad *looked* at me, like really *looked* at me, and I just felt really embarrassed. Like I just then realized I was naked. I don't know."

"So what did you do?"

"I shot him in the face with my alligator."

"Uh huh," she said, making a note. "So you're telling me it's not a good memory of your father."

"No ...."

"Is that common? To have bad memories of him? Are there positive memories you associate with your dad?"

I didn't want my dad to be the bad guy in my memory, or anywhere. He wasn't a bad guy, I didn't think. He was just never around; and when he was, if something off happened, then that's what was going to get wadded up in my brain. "Yeah, sure," I said. "I remember good things."

"Would you like to share one of those?" Not really.

"Well, I mean, it's not like one *specific* memory. More like something that always happens."

"Go on."

"Usually when he comes home from work, he brings me candy. Sometimes he'll call and ask my mom what kind. But it's usually Reese's."

"You mean like one of those mini ones? By cash registers?"

"No, like the regular pack. Well, a king size. Or a king-sized Hershey bar."

"A whole candy bar?" she asked, looking up from her notepad. Her pencil stopped moving. "Every day?" she seemed surprised, and I felt like I'd let out a secret I was charged with keeping.

"Well ... yeah." Was that weird? Suddenly it seemed weird.

CHAPTER EIGHT

YOU CAN STRETCH out two months spent forgiving if you really want to, and it can slap you in the face like a rubber band. Make every day count, every moment. I stopped searching for Chirag's name online. Sometimes he gave me a Friday or Saturday night. Sometimes he didn't. When the timing was too late, and I knew I wouldn't see him, I'd drag Michelle out to the bars with me when I could. If I was alone, I'd message Sam while at the bar, but only if there were no prospects. Sometimes I'd even email my mom back. She never got Chirag's name right, always said "Cheersomething," but I minimized screen time on my solo nights anyway—nobody approaches you if you're loving on your phone.

But Michelle and I, we both started drinking coffees to stay awake, whiskey-free. We'd both done too many stupid things in the grip of a brownout. The occasional cocktail snuck in, but let's face it. They were getting expensive, and I had an entry-level non-profit salary.

"You want to go somewhere for the long weekend?" Chirag asked me. Martin Luther King Jr. Day, the random three-day weekend in the grips of a sleepy, cold, and wet Oregon January. The thought of being with him for three straight days equally thrilled and petrified me.

"Where?" I asked.

"You choose. Somewhere we can drive." It didn't take long to research the perfect place: an exotic animal sanctuary along the coast, a five-hour drive through the thickest of Pacific forests. I'd heard of it before. You could pet, play, and feed baby tigers. Black bears. Mewling little lions. For fifty more cents, you entered with a sugar cone full of seeds and the animals that roamed wild descended on you en masse. Goat kids butted at your shins while the deer came close with their soft, velvet lips, and the peacocks stayed in the back, confident of dropped pieces that would soon be theirs. They were too proud to huddle like groupies.

Chirag booked a hotel and I got the oil changed in my car. Three days before we left, a head cold gripped him fast. Part of me thought he was faking. Was he really so frantic to back out?

"What do you want to do?" he asked me, pinching the fold between his eyes like all men do when they're stressed. "You still want to go."

Yes. "That's something you need to decide," I said, working my mouth around the "right thing" to say.

"No, you decide," he said. How was I to decide what he wanted? Guess until I got it right? I knew what he wanted to hear. "No, you'd better stay home and rest. It's okay. Another time." Maybe that was what I was supposed to say—but I knew there would be no other time.

"You can either be sick here, or you can be sick there."

He laughed. "Then I'll be sick there."

We left early Saturday morning when the fog still hugged the roads like a lover begging not to go. The Nissan maneuvered down Interstate 5, past the bad-smelling mill in Albany and the hippies in Eugene. When I turned off onto the back roads, the weaving between the pines turned sloping, dangerous, and sexual. In sixth gear, Chirag's hand found its way to mine, worn and familiar. Now, he asked, "Do you mind if I read?" and I didn't. I'd never seen Oregon presenting herself like this, spread eagle and so wanting like she was in heat.

Arriving at the coast hotel, it was already dark. He'd chosen the nicest one, but that didn't mean much in this tiny town. The gift shop was open late, filled with too-expensive things nobody needed. "You want this?" he asked, holding up a stuffed sea lion with sad glass eyes. I wanted it more than anything.

Fueled with painkillers and caffeine, he forced a dinner out of himself. We were the only ones in the restaurant that was supposed to be fancy, and ordered seafood because that's what you're supposed to do at the ocean's side. Cocktails were ordered because that was what you did, too. Drink Sea Breezes by the sea. Sex on the Beach before sex at the beach. It was practiced and easy between the sheets that smelled unfamiliar, and we left a piece of ourselves far away from everything else.

The illness lost its grip through the night, and by Sunday morning Chirag had only a catch in his voice as a reminder. For once, it wasn't raining, but the storm clouds were on edge. Anxious. A bitter January sun struggled over the horizon, lighting up the huge billboards counting down the few miles to the animals. "Three more miles!" "Get wild, two more miles!" "Almost there!" And as we pulled into the dirt parking lot of a decrepit manufactured home, another: "Keep going! 80 Miles to the Drive-through Safari! You are captive, they roam free."

"Not very impressive," he said, sizing up the paint-peeling house. Was this all a sham? Only a handful of cars were in the lot, all parked far away, the tell-tale sign of employee parking.

Opening the doors, you could smell them. The Wild. It was all around us. And a big cat, it roared some shattering secret from behind the old cedar fencing as the first fat droplets of a storm rolled in.

"We don't get many winter visitors," said the should-be-retired woman at the counter. "But I must say," she said, leaning in like a conspirator, "it's the best time to come. Nobody's here, and the animals love the rain."

For less than the cost of a movie out with popcorn and soda, we went through the back door to the sanctuary, full ice cream cones in hand.

Wallabies loped around their bark-dusted, penned-in area, nuzzling at our hands for treats to be dropped in their mouth. A gorilla glared at us while we snapped photos of him chewing on breakfast, eventually making a big show out of getting up and turning his back on us. Deer, donkeys, birds, goats, and lambs strolled around as they wished, bored with us after they'd bombarded us for food.

The sanctuary itself was small, no more than one acre. Some of the animals were being rehabilitated, destined for release. Most were protected or in breeding programs to re-populate their dying species. What pressure that must be, and what loneliness to watch everything that's like you dying.

"I wonder if they know," I said.

"Know what?"

"That they're the last." A white Siberian tiger lounged pressed up against the chain link fence. An identical fence was just two feet from it, separating us by a scratch more than an arm's reach. In key areas, there were holds cut in both fences, allowing for clear camera shots. The tiger, he was used to humans and mildly curious. They really don't get many visitors this time of year.

Crouching down to his level, I tilted my head to the side and the tiger did the same. As I moved, left to right, so did he. The sign said he was old, eighteen (a grandfather of a tiger), but play was still etched into his bones. Chirag began filming as the tiger mirrored me. "Would you like to meet his cub?" An employee had braved the pouring rain, bundled into his worn rain boots and a puffy jacket.

"His cub?"

"Saigon here has sired dozens of cubs in his life. The youngest is four months old now, young enough that you can feed and pet him if you want." This. This is what we came here for.

The tiger is India's national animal. The Royal Bengal tiger is found in almost every region of the country, rightly dubbed Lord of the Jungle. Chirag had little tiger motifs peppered throughout his apartment. A striped lighter here. A random bobble-headed tiger there.

"It's not right, you know," Chirag whispered to me as the keeper disappeared. "Keeping wild things in cages."

"They'd be killed otherwise," I said.

"At least that's a life."

The keeper emerged from a backdoor of a small covered area. It was dry, the only place in the sanctuary that was, with hay scattered around a walled-in area the size of a bedroom with just a tree stump in the middle. "This is Kama," he said. "He's got a lot of energy this time of day." Kama was the size of a Sheltie, with thick paws too big for his frame and wondering blue eyes that scouted ours with curiosity.

"I'll keep hold of the leash, just in case," said the keeper. "But don't worry, he won't go far. Here, these are some of his favorite toys."

Kama's toys were made for big, rough dogs. A thick knotted rope and industrial-grade rubber rattles. We were in the earth immediately, hay poking through our rain-soaked jeans. "It's rough," Chirag said, running his hands along Kama's back. I held the rope knot behind my back, making Kama circle in the hunt. Like a house cat, he crouched and shook his rump before attacking. The strength that ran through his body, which he wasn't even close to realizing, I felt in my bones when he pounced.

"Would you like to feed him?" the keeper asked after ten minutes of us bathing in Kama's scent, his fur stuck to our jackets and woven in our hair. "He still likes to take a bottle, even if he's a bit too old for it. Soon enough, he'll be eating hearts like all the others."

"Hearts?"

"There's a horse farm up the street where they're cared for 'til they die. Old race horses. They donate the bodies to us. Lions, they love hearts the best."

We sat on the bench while the keeper showed us how to cradle him. Between us, the cub's heat radiated into our own. I held the bottle upward and at an angle while Kama latched on tight. As he suckled, his back pressed into Chirag's ribs, he lightly grasped my forearms to keep the warm milk close. His eyes grew drowsy as he began to softly knead my exposed skin, tracing light etches into me, and I loved it. This scarring, this proof that it had all happened.

"I'll take a photo," the keeper offered, already reaching for Chirag's camera. It was beautiful. Us, rain-drowned and dirty, with our little tiger baby in the middle.

"Just so you know. Just so you know," Chirag began, his eyes big and voice mock-serious, "I can't top the tiger for Valentine's Day." This, this he would give me. It fell on a Sunday this year, making Saturday night the Ultimate High Pressure Date Night. "So, you tell me. What do you want to do? Or are you not into it?"

"I'm *so* into Valentine's Day," I said.

"So, what we doing?" he asked, dropping the articles and verbs, settling into his cozy speech. The, are, is—they're all useless words to him. Extra work.

"Let's go all out cheesy. Romantic restaurant with oysters. That *Valentine's Day* movie is opening. Dessert and champagne."

"Let's do it," he said, in that stupid-lilt voice I imagined he would use when playing with a child. He was leaving on the twentieth.

Saturday night he picked me up, complete with red roses and sugar-free chocolates. I wore a ruched black dress that somehow knew exactly how to hide my bra straps; he wore expensive jeans, black blazer, and sleek shoes. We ordered everything at the little boutique, French diner downtown. Duck breast with exotic spices. A dozen oysters on the half-shell with loads of horseradish. Wine and three desserts.

The theater was, of course, packed-in tight. "You wanna just skip it?" he asked.

"No. Let's try it." We squeezed into the front row, the only place with chairs left together and watched all the beautiful celebrities try to find love. Taylor Swift and her huge teddy bear. Jennifer Garner and married McDreamy. They weren't all happy endings, and we were overdressed.

"Where to now?" he asked, and a tiredness washed over me. This was our last weekend before India swallowed him up again.

"Let's just go to a dive bar by my place," I said.

"You sure? You don't wanna go for more dessert?"

"They'll have dessert," I said.

They didn't. They had watered down cocktails and a sad, sparse crowd. Empowered by the gold liquid, I got needy. "Will you email me?" I asked.

"When I can. I don't know what to expect there. It's Bangalore, not Bombay, and I'll be in the field a lot. I don't know how the Wi-Fi will be."

"When will you be back?" I asked.

"You know. Middle of August."

"You sure?"

He didn't want to answer. "No," he said. "Not really. That's what they say now, but contracting doesn't have any security."

"Oh."

"Hey," he said. "Bibijaan. It will be okay, so no being sad. You'll see."

"Okay."

"Okay," he said mimicking me. "I love you."

"Love you more."

In my balmy basement, he spooned me, wrapping his arm around my chest and breathed heat into my hair. "Don't be sad," he whispered. "It'll go by fast."

"I'm not."

We didn't have sex that night—the first night we just slept, and held, and breathed everything in. It was as it should be.

The following six days were filled with shopping. Laptops and iPods for his cousins, good knee braces for his grandfather, watches for his parents, aunts, and uncles who lived in the family home. Polo shirts for his brother, and scotch for his friends. We raced from store to store, grabbing chocolate wafers you can only get in America and swooping into restaurants with starved abandon. Spice-infused kisses in his car, good slow sex, easy fast sessions, and me memorizing the curves of his face. The mole that looked inky blue, like a tattoo that almost got started, between his nose and lips.

"You don't have to take me to the airport," he said. "My flight's at six, I have to leave by three in the morning."

"I'm taking you to the airport," I said. There would be no argument.

That last night, he stayed with me, suitcases lined up against the wall like a firing squad. Music streamed from my laptop as he worked his way between my legs, my body already knowing what to expect. "You're so fucking wet," he said, sliding one finger into me to see how ready I was. Slowly, lightly, he captured my clit between his lips and began a light flickering with his tongue. His finger was still inside me, solid and thick. I pushed against it, wanting more, wanting to be filled up with any part of him I could get. He ducked lower, tracing my wetness with his tongue from my opening back up to my clit, running the juices across it. My fingers wove into his long curls, pulling him closer and starting to fuck his face, steady and hard.

"Get on your back," I told him. Straddling his face, I lowered myself onto him while he gripped my hips to control my ride. Unbuckling his jeans, I pushed them down and freed his cock, the pre-cum already spreading wetness across the denim as if I needed anything more to get him inside me. Pushing the foreskin down, gently, his own captured wetness spilled down his shaft as I took his tip into my mouth. He dug his hands deep into my thighs, lapping me up harder as my wetness spread. I could feel it, warm and sticky, coating my legs and dripping across his cheeks.

Taking him all the way in, I was thirsty for the taste of him. Of the pre-cum, of his skin like silk. And then I remembered the mints in the bedside table.

"No, don't stop," he said as I raised myself. Upright, him still working my clit and circling my g-spot with two fingers, I grabbed the Altoids and rode him to my edge. Cupped my breasts and pulled at the hard nipples while I cracked the mint between my teeth. His cock stayed stiff, my saliva still coating it. When I got too close, I moved back to all fours to slow down, took his shaft and began lightly stroking him while taking the tip into my mouth.

He didn't realize it at first. Letting the menthol wash across him, releasing him from the warmth of my mouth and a blow, the hardness skyrocketed in my hand.

"Oh. Fuck," he said. "What are you doing?" But he was fucking me with his hand faster and began working my clit when he could, between deep breaths and groans.

I took him all in, letting the mint do its job as I did mine. As he started fucking my mouth, I pulled gently at his balls and took him to the back of my throat. "Come here. Come here," he said suddenly, flipping me over and sliding into me. The mint spread from him to my insides, to my clit, as our rhythm began. We were already both so close, when he came it lit me up from deep within and made me cum with him. Demanded it. His cock emptied into me, pulsing with his heartbeat, as I gripped him tight and came against his hardness.

We had to leave for the airport in three hours.

Part 2

ix.

Planes, Trains and Elevators

IT WAS MY VERY first time on a plane, at least that I could remember. I was told that when I was two, we flew from Medford to Miami to visit Disneyworld. We stayed at my Aunt Carol's house (Kat's mom). There are pictures to prove it: me on my dad's shoulders. My mom looking young and tan in the pool. But I don't remember. Were we ever really like that?

This time was different. I was fourteen and a freshman in high school (always and forever the youngest in the class). As part of the advanced English/History class, the annual trip to Washington DC was a huge deal. Our chaperones were just our two teachers, Mr. Bukavitsky and Mrs. Deene. No parents, no teacher's aids, no nothing.

I didn't like Mr. Bukavitsky. By seventh grade, I had grown to my full height, my full curves, and (especially from the back) looked totally grown. Men started catcalling on the street, approaching me in malls and offering rides. Asking for numbers. I imagined Mr. Bukavitsky would do the same if he stumbled upon me in a strange town where his job and jail time weren't so solidly on the line.

During our one-day sex ed class before the trip, he showed us graphic videos of STDs in a pitch black room. I had no idea what this had to do with English or History. Herpes in full flare mode and caressing groins and hips. Penises that looked like they'd been mutilated. It was like a porno, but a sickening one. Throughout the fifteen-minute video that felt like eternity, he came and sat beside me, leaned close and started talking about nothing. "How is your homework going? Are you enjoying the books?" as vaginas and scrotums rolled on the screen.

But Michelle was in the class, too, and we were sharing a hotel room together. The students got to pick their room-mates, and I felt badly for those without friends in the class. On the massive 747, the seats got moved around and the class separated. I was by myself in one of those long, stretchy middle rows that seated ten. Mr. Bukavitsky and Mrs. Deene were a world away, past a curtain and bathroom. A hoard of military men and contractors were on board, draped in fatigues and tired eyes. One sat beside me, and somehow there was nobody on either side of us for this red eye flight.

Jamal said he was twenty-seven and in contract security for the marines. This somehow meant he could have dread-locks instead of those close buzz cuts, but he still wore the heavy boots and tan camouflage. He was glorious.

"Quiet, huh?" he asked after two hours in the air. "Silent but deadly, I like that." And then we were kissing, just like that. I'd never kissed anyone before. But the entire plane was asleep, the lights dimmed and no eyes were prying. Ja-mal drifted his hand across the top of my chest, just below my collar bones. My shirt was low-cut, as it always was as I tried on my new body and pretended to be older than I was.

I told him I was fifteen, like a year would make any dif-ference, and he told me I was beautiful.

I pushed his hand away, but not because I wanted to. Because I thought it would make him want me more. He laughed.

When the plane landed, we headed to the terminal down different aisles and I told Michelle I slept the whole time.

The monuments, the museums, the politics of DC were pointless to a fourteen-year-old girl. Instead, I loved the free day we had. I took the train to the mall and bought ridiculously high, platform shoes. Michelle went elsewhere in an effort to seem cultured, but I knew what mattered to me.

On our final night, the class was going to the theater. Everybody dressed up, and I wore a black dress that licked at my thighs and my new black heels. Giggling, arm in arm, Michelle and I stumbled together down the hallway, going room to room to try to scare the boys while they were in their boxers or size up the girls to see who looked fat. Who looked hot. Who looked different. The class was spread out onto multiple floors, and once we'd exhausted our own level, we scrambled to the elevator to finish our mission. Mr. Bukavitsy was inside, alone.

"Wow," he said, looking us both up and down. My legs like a shaking colt. Michelle's thick thighs and swollen calves. "If only you girls were eighteen," he said, shaking his head sadly.

When I got home from the trip, I was changed. Jamal changed me, in a good way. Mr. Bukavitsky in another. I told my mom what happened in the elevator, carefully leaving out my own dalliance on the plane. "Okay, Jennifer," was all she said, keeping her eyes steady on the television.

CHAPTER NINE

TWO YEARS SINCE Chirag came back from India, as promised, with suitcases full of kurtas for me (and other women's kurtas not in my size, which he pushed aside), sugar-free dry-fruit sweets, darker skin and photos of the Taj Mahal and petting Asian elephants. He had written, sure. Almost daily. "It's incredible here," he wrote when he got back to the hotel from the Taj Mahal. "I wish you could see it." His hair was shorter when he returned. It took a few days for his normal scent to settle.

I couldn't help it. One month after he left, even with the near-daily emails, I searched for his handle online and immediately found it on an Indian dating site. Community: Jain. Complexion: Wheatish. Family financial status: Moderately wealthy. Looking for: Just friends, short-term dating, long-term dating. He hadn't checked marriage, but long-term dating? A little icon flashed that he was online when I found him. It was three in the morning in India.

Of course I'd looked up tickets to India, but then what? Get a visa, spend thousands of dollars, and show up for what? It was a romantic notion that had no roots in this world. So I just let it go. I let it go, and when I picked him up from the airport after his six-month absence, there was no romantic scene in the terminal or epiphanies. I wore lingerie under a long coat, even though I was dying in the heat. "You're crazy!" Sam messaged me when I told her my plan. "I've always wanted to do that," Michelle said. But as soon as he embraced me, he said, "I need to go to the DMV right now." I went to the DMV with my winter coat buttoned to my neck as I sweated through a cheap corset. My period was almost starting, and he was so exhausted he fell asleep while I gave him a blow job. But then, we simply settled back into what we had been before.

Two years. That's two years of fights when we ran across one another on dates with other people. Like that two-month fling I had with the man 25 years older than me. He looked like a slimmer George Clooney and was Italian, but with a drowsy Manchester accent. It was a lovely distraction until he got mistaken for my father. Two years of Chirag gesturing at me to be quiet when he called India on Sunday mornings. Two years of flexing my willpower to not search his email when he left the room—why was I looking for something I didn't want to find? Once, a chat with an aunt. In reaching English, she asked him when he would choose one of the girls from the bio-data they were sending him. "I will, Auntie," he said.

"R going to wedding 2 Feb. good venue. Maybe 4 ur engagement too?" she asked.

"If you say so, Auntie."

"Good boy."

I never did see any of the girls' photos or bio-data that were apparently flooding his phone. Part of me wanted to. Maybe I could help. Pick out a nice, plump, non-threatening thing with hair thinner than mine and bad skin. Maybe then we could still go on, giving her space to cook and play housewife, but otherwise we'd be uninterrupted. God, I'm ridiculous.

I told my mom about my delusional goals because she was getting too old to judge what was ridiculous and what wasn't. And she was drunk all the time. "Maybe he *should* just get married," I told her once over the phone. "I could be a mistress. It wouldn't be that bad, don't you think?"

"If you say so, Jennifer," was all she said. Sam kept asking about "Tinny" in every email, and I only answered when I could get by with minimal lies. Once, Michelle was out with her cousin and began shaking my phone to life at one in the morning.

"Omg, fucker C is here," she texted. "We're at Cake. He's talking to some OLD woman. Serious cougar."

"Don't do anything," I texted back.

"Too late."

"What'd you do? What'd you do?" Nothing. "Eff, Michelle! What did you do??"

"Nothing big!! Just walked by him and said he could do better. Kind of loud."

"What did he say?"

"Nothing!! Don't think he even saw it was me."

"Are you at Cake?" Chirag's text flew across my screen.

"No."

"You sure?"

"Pretty sure."

"Ok."

I texted Michelle, making sure not to message him by mistake. "He just texted me!!"

"Lol!"

St. Patrick's Day fell on a Friday. I tugged on a green bob wig and found myself at Midnight Hour, a French bistro with a long bar and white linen table cloths. Compliments flooded toward me, from men and women alike. Two men, one a lanky Asian and the other from Lebanon, sidled up beside me. "I love your hair," the Asian said. I think he thought it was real.

"Thank you."

"We're both from Seattle, visiting for the weekend," he explained. "My friend here, he's planning to open a restaurant in Portland next year."

"I already have the one in Seattle," his friend said. "But Portland, I hear it's the up and coming foodie city."

"That it is."

"Are you meeting anyone tonight? Are you alone?" The Asian asked.

"No. And yes." I had texted Michelle earlier to say, "Bartender at Midnight is giving me free drinks! Come here."

"No," she'd replied. "I'll only come if YOU buy me drinks."

"I'm broke. What difference does it make?"

"I only hang out with GENEROUS people. Sorry." Bitch. Sometimes she was like that. So tonight I was alone with my green wig.

"So, what do you say?" asked the Asian. "Want to be our tour guide?"

I took them to Cake. Of course. The three of us grasped each other on the dance floor, the alcohol flowing through us. Chirag loped through around midnight, but in all the green he didn't recognize me. Another boring brunette followed on his heels. This one was short. He swayed her like he did me, all those years ago. When he dipped his chin down to her, she laughed a drunken wail and threw her head back. Back to the Asian and Lebanese guy. What were they doing? Oh, fuck, they were kissing. I was trapped. I had to get past Chirag and the girl to leave. I could make it. With my disguise, I could make it.

I didn't make it. His eyes were drawn to me as I stumbled past.

I couldn't text Michelle. Sam wouldn't answer in time. Shoving the keys into my car, I fell into its safety and called my mom. I didn't care that it was the witching hour, I knew she'd be up. The alcoholism fed her agoraphobia which fed her insomnia. She was always up.

"Jennifer?" she asked. "Jennifer, what's going on? What's wrong?"

I was blubbering so hard I could barely speak. "Chirag," I said. "Chirag ...."

"What happened?" she asked.

"He was there. With some girl ...."

"Oh, baby," she said. "I'm so sorry. I wish I could take the pain away." I did, too. It was hateful, but I'd dump it on her, on anyone, by the ladleful. I just couldn't take it anymore.

At two, he texted me. I was still slumped in the parking

lot. And I went, of course I did, with my tear-streaked face and hoarse voice. But I was so heartbroken I forgot my keys in the car. Left it running, but locked. In the morning, someone had busted out the window but got too scared to go all the way. My car was on empty and my winter coat was stolen out of the backseat.

This year I'm turning thirty. I'm not sad or scared or scrounging my hair for grays. It's more like, "It's about time." For Michelle's thirtieth birthday, we went to Seattle, had too many Spanish coffees on a boat tour, and decided to photograph thirty different men giving her thirty spanks to celebrate. It was the easiest project ever. She ended up bringing one of them back to the hotel—Tyler, seven years younger than us and a Costco worker. But he swore his family was secretly super wealthy, even though he didn't have a car. He and Michelle kept in touch, and six months after her big 3-0, he got drunk and dove headfirst into a ten-inch deep "pool" on a mini golf course. He was paralyzed from the neck down. How fast everything can change.

But not me. I'm in purgatory, in limbo, totally unable to let go. Michelle's tired of hearing about it all while I grow tired of being privy to her patterns: girl finds boy, girl fucks boy hours later, girl can't understand where he goes. I guess it's a better story than mine: girl finds boy, girl ties her center to him, girl gets dragged in the dirt until her body shuts down.

I'm not saying there weren't good times, magical times, times that reminded me that this, this is truth. It's not wishing, not hoping, not some idealized notion of what True Love is. I loved Chirag simply as fact, like saying Burnside is vomiting up prostitutes at an alarming rate or that the best secrets are the ones shared, or the best food made by someone who loves you. I couldn't stop.

There were some interesting characters sprinkled in with him to offer a little extra kick. They gave me something to do on his disappearing nights. There was the towering

Chinese attorney who took me with him to get a tattoo on the first date. He was a re-born, fired up Christian who ultimately said he wanted to give it another shot with his ex. She was a stripper with three kids from three different men, but he assured me she was a good Christian deep down. I, of course, was not. There was the clichéd lesbian who volunteered at a cat rescue center, but all those yellow eyes staring at us from the foot of the bed freaked me out (and she kind of looked like my little sister in the sorority anyway). The Gold Star who gave me shit about being with men, but she reminded me of a young Winona Ryder with tattoos so that made up for it until I saw how thick and burly her black hair was, shaved haphazardly on her mound in mean-spirited morning light. Oh, the Jamaican who lucked into the country on a lottery visa. He was a chef at a snooty patisserie and took me hiking on Mt. Tabor on our first date with a bottle of rum in his pocket. His accent was so burly I spent most of my time asking, "What?" He had "about three kids" back in Jamaica and dreadlocks to his hips. There was the American-born Confused Desi (ABCD) I met in Cellar at closing time, one of the top-ranked doctors in the country. Akash and I became confidantes, me bemoaning my love for Chirag and he tucked behind high walls and once—just once—breaking down crying that he would always be alone. He was forty-two, a highly functional alcoholic, and would tell me, "You're so young. You're so young. You don't know what you think you do." I told him once, as we danced on his penthouse balcony in the Pearl District to "our saddest songs" (his was REM, mine was Peter Gabriel's "The Book of Love"), I told him, "Kiss me like a teenager." And for once he did.

None of them mattered. They stroked my ego, filled in the dead space, and gave me something to keep my mind busy on the nights Chirag fell quiet. In one month, I would be thirty. Wasn't something phenomenal supposed to happen? It would happen to Sam first, of course, on the other side of the country. Maybe she would tell me, or maybe she would keep it a surprise.

The last weekend of July, a far-flung acquaintance, Octavia, threw a Thanksgiving in July party. She was a classic American-born Chinese girl who refused to be wrong about anything. Did I invite Chirag? Of course not—by now I knew better. Besides, her party was on a Friday night and the sheer Americana of the whole thing wouldn't register well with him. Better I go on my own, forcing myself into strange territory. At least it would down one more Friday night.

I arrived early, armed with an apple pie and pumpkin-flavored vodka. Octavia was hunched over the stove, mashing potatoes in between yelling at her dog to be quiet. There was just one other person there, a reincarnation from my history books.

In college, I had a crush on my resident advisor, Josh. He was five-foot-ten with close-clipped black hair and mournful, drooping eyes. Josh had the kind of bulked up chest and arms that were a pinch of genetics and mostly gym dedication. I never spoke a word to him.

"This is Fernando," Octavia said, gesturing with a garlic-splattered spoon to her only other guest. "Jennifer," she said, nodding to me.

Fernando was perched on a barstool, a beagle/basset hound mix wriggling in his lap. "And this is Bagel," he said as the squirmer licked at his face. His face. It was exquisite. Cloudy whiskers and perfect teeth, save for a slight gap in the middle. His forearms and biceps tightened in the skin-hugging tee as he struggled to keep the dog at bay.

"How do you know each other?" I asked.

"College," Octavia said. "He's the *nicest guy*." There was something about him. A gentleness, a kindness, which was evident in his eyes. In how he moved. When he climbed down the townhouse steps to let Bagel out, I whispered to Octavia, "Is he gay?"

"Fernando? No!" she said. "Why?"

"I dunno. He just seems ... nice."

"He is ...." she said, like she was just slapped with some

terrible realization about me.

As more people poured in, arms full of green bean casseroles, homemade cranberry sauce, and seasonal wines, I watched Fernando. He didn't know anyone else, and seemed as out of place as me. Instead of joining the riot around the table, he looked gently at Bagel and helped Octavio clear the dishes as they mounted.

"You know what's stupid?" one of her friends asked, a mountain of a guy with an impressive beer gut. "Running. Running is fucking stupid. Fucks up your knees, fucks up your feet, and have you seen the average runner's body? Nothing to brag about!"

"Jennifer just started running," Octavia said, her eyes starting to sizzle as she sat back to see how her strategy would play out.

"Yeah, well," I said.

Beer-gut guy was already bored. "You'll fuck up your knees," he said again as he took another slug from his bottle.

"I like to run," Fernando said. "I don't do it much, but I'd like to."

"I want to do a half marathon," I said. "I keep a bucket list—a real one. Written down and everything. I thought about a marathon, but that just seems like too much."

"Did you know less than five percent of the world's population has run a marathon? I don't know about halves, though," Fernando said.

"I'm turning thirty soon, so I figured better now than later."

"Thirty?" he asked. "I thought you were younger."

"Why? How old are you?"

"Twenty-five." Oh. That's right. I'm older than Octavia.

"Well, if you ever want to run together, let me know. O has my number," he said.

I didn't hear from Chirag that night. Or on Saturday. Something was off. As the sun slid under the covers of the Portland skyline for the evening, I texted Octavia. "Hey, can you give me Fernando's number?" She did, without a single question. He replied immediately, no games and no wondering. I didn't know if it was a date or what, but we planned to meet at six in the morning at the Portland waterfront for a run.

I had only been "running" for about a month. I woke up feeling fat and thought, "Fuck it. I'm going to run 5k right now." Of course I had to look up what that was: 3.1 miles. I mapped it out online. It was forty blocks down and back. Not bad. Who cares that I hadn't run since Junior High when the "weekly mile" was all that constituted the day's PE class?

And I did it. I ran a 5k without stopping. I didn't time myself, but my legs are long and I'm stubborn. I couldn't walk the next day, but that was normal, right? Shit. I had no idea how this morning thing was going to go with Fernando. And then Chirag texted at midnight. "You up?" Yes. Of course I was.

Chirag was in one of his moods, the kind you can't get him out of. If he's made up his mind to be moody or pissy, he doesn't want you to charm him to another personality— you just have to ride it out. I think it's the Gemini in him. Tonight was one of those moods when he just wants silent company while he watches Jersey Shore reruns and pretends I don't exist.

We didn't have sex that night, and I swear I would have left if he didn't live so goddamn close to the waterfront. As soon as I gauged his mood and saw that I was just filler, I told him, "I'm going to bed."

"Okay."

"I'm meeting a friend for a run at six tomorrow, so I'll be gone when you wake up."

"Okay."

The alarm started vibrating too soon, and I was nervous as I pulled on men's running shorts (I hate how my thighs jiggle in the women's), a short-sleeved tee and Nike running shoes I got for a discount at the employee store. I wear foundation, always, partly for the sunscreen and partly because when you're this fair, every acne reminder sticks around for years. Eyebrows filled in, ponytail up high to distract from the roundness of my face, and a smear of sunscreen on my arms and legs.

I was nervous. Oh, god, I was nervous. Parking the Nissan along the vacant streets, I wove my way through the homeless camps to the west side of the Morrison Bridge. He wasn't there. My phone was in my car. I would wait. I would wait, but how long? The clock on my iPod showed 6:05. 6:10.

"Hey!" Fernando said, appearing from behind me. "There you are. I texted you. I parked on the other side of the bridge, and it was raised for the ships to pass through." The ships, I hadn't even seen them. They coasted along the Willamette River which shone with all the rays of the morning, reflecting the Oregon green. "Have you been waiting long?"

"No, I just got here."

He was faster than me. Smoother than me. In so much better shape than me. I'd never talked to anyone as I ran before. Actually, I'd never run with anyone before. It was odd, not having Tupac and Ani DiFranco in my ears. I forced yoga breathing into my voice, steady and liquid, as Fernando pointed out what he thought was beautiful. The Canadian geese stalking the discarded bread. The older runner couples with their matching jackets. How the Newport Bay restaurant seemed to be its own little island on the water. Running, it gave me something to do with my hands, with my feet. I didn't have to look at him, and that loosened up the chains in my mouth.

"I need to talk to someone about financial planning," Fernando explained. Oh, that's right. We were talking about Life Stuff. "I've been working in a lab since getting my chemistry degree a couple years ago, but now I really need to start working on my MD."

"MD?"

"Yeah, I want to be a surgeon. Always have. I've taken the MCAT and applied to a couple of schools, but didn't get in. But I can't just keep floating forever. I actually quit the lab just to give myself a kick in the butt."

"My adoptive parents are financial planners," I said. They were Scott's parents, though technically they became my legal guardians for insurance reasons when I was a teen. It was easy, all they needed was written consent from my parents that I was officially abandoned. Both my parents signed it within the day.

"You're adopted? Me, too!" he said.

Oh. "Well, really they were my legal guardians. I didn't meet them 'til I was sixteen. Long story."

"That's nice, though," he said. "My mom adopted all of us, my two brothers and me. We were all born in Costa Rica with different bio moms. She was a nurse doing Peace Corps there. She lived there twenty years! But she's from Oregon and we moved back when I was thirteen."

"Do you miss it?"

"Nah," he said. "But I'm thinking of going there for my doctorate. I have dual citizenship. It's a lot cheaper there, and pretty easy to transition a Costa Rican MD to the US."

He was leaving? Then what the hell was I doing out here?

We'd looped back around to the bridge, and by now the streets were waking up. Saturday market vendors were dragging their organic parfaits, hemp-made bags, and artisanal cheeses into the booths. More runners were spreading across the paths like hot foie gras, and the fat tourists began to waddle from their cars. "That was fun," Fernando said.

"Yeah. Thanks for meeting me."

"Do you want to get together again? Maybe go for lunch or drinks or something?"

"Sure," I said. "Just let me know."

"I promised my mom I'd help her with a huge yard project. But what about next Friday?"

A Friday? He was offering me a Friday when I looked like this, all red face and greasy hair? "Sounds good," I said.

As soon as I got to the car, I called Octavia. "Why didn't you tell me the hot Latino was going to be a doctor?"

"Would it have mattered?" she asked with a laugh.

Well, this was a first. Not a chirp from Chirag all day Sunday. Usually these days were filled with going to the movies or helping him shop for a designer shirt he'd never wear. Whatever. Then Monday came. Nothing. And Tuesday, nothing. It'd been three years since we met, and I still didn't contact him first. Wednesday. Thursday. Well, fuck him then.

"I met someone new," I emailed Sam, filling her in. Maybe if I put it in words, it would make it more real.

"Good! I want you to be happy," she wrote back.

Fernando picked me up in his aged sedan with a gym bag in the backseat and dog hair coating the insides. "Where do you want to go?" he asked. "Not because I'm too lazy to choose, but because you know downtown better than I do. Otherwise, we'll end up at a restaurant known for pies with lard and where I know the owners."

"Pie with lard sound good," I said. It was one of those family restaurants off a busy highway with too many temporary drawings and promos on the windows. "Early bird special!" "Best pie in town!" "Hungry???"

I ordered cottage cheese and eggs from their breakfast-all-day menu. "So, I, I don't eat carbs," I said. "Pie always sounds good, but I can't do it."

"Why not?"

"Oh, you know. The whole Indian predisposed to diabetes thing. Plus I'd rather skip carbs than cut down on eating."

"Indian? I figured you were something."

"Why? Because one whitewashed person recognizes another?" He looked something, sure. But the fairness of his complexion didn't give away the Tico heritage. His name, of course, did.

"No. It's the cheekbones," he said. Once he'd downed two slices of pie and I'd picked at the curds on my plate, the bill came. "Let's split it," I said, administering the test. He just shook his head and left too much cash.

"You up for anything else?" he asked. "Your call. I picked the pie."

"What about karaoke?" I asked. My first sober karaoke was a few years ago after spending countless hours singing to Ludacris and Nicki Minaj. It put me on stage, where I felt wrapped in warmth and could move people with my voice.

"I won't sing, but I'll watch," he said.

The Furnace took up space in China Town like it owned it, the only karaoke bar left in the downtown area. The waits were two hours, the seating was fiercely wanting, but the crowds were so tremendously happy. It's where you could sway in unison, rope your arms around strangers without getting a hand slipped up your skirt, and where everybody peed together in one of the two, tiny individual bathrooms.

It didn't disappoint, and for twenty bucks you could move to the top of the list. I chose something safe, a Kanye song I'd done a dozen times before. "That was so good!" Fernando said, adding a layer to the buzz from the stage high.

Just two drinks sneaked down my throat, but they didn't have the potency they normally did. My vision stayed sharp, and we shouted at one another over horrific Journey songs and an amazing "99 Luftballons" sung entirely in German by an old man with gray hair so thick and coifed it had to be a wig. A good one.

"I need to go outside," I said.

"What?"

"I need to go outside!"

The trampled-on street with the low brick buildings was panting with energy. Toppling drunk girls in Kelly Bundy dresses grabbed at each other, men they just met, and complimented the drag queens on the corner. "Oh, my god, you're so pretty!" they screamed. "I wish I had legs like that!"

"I've never been here, it's awesome," Fernando said. I checked my phone. No texts.

"So are you going to kiss me or not?" I asked. It was after midnight and I was getting restless.

"What? I don't know, I don't usually move that fast."

"Look. I have enough friends," I said.

It was a challenge, a cheap one, but I didn't care. He moved in fast, a shift in his eyes, and pushed me against the brick. It wasn't bad, but it was rough, the thickness of his emerging beard raking across my face.

x.
Sluts, Spics and Other Four-Letter Words

I MET ROSA at the end of freshman year of high school, mysteriously flanked in a Latina name even though her red hair and freckles gave her away. We recognized the outsider in each other. My mom didn't like Rosa *or* her mom, a quiet and seemingly scared animal who couldn't have possibly produced a child as beautifully wild as this. Rosa's oversized heart was hidden inside a body everybody identified as Whore. I didn't care, and became a whore by association. Sure, we talked about sex. We were fourteen-year-old girls. Rosa never spoke in concrete terms, and I wasn't sure if she'd really "done it" or not. I didn't care. But she dressed the part—mini-skirts, platform Mary Janes and a vinyl baby backpack. It was 1995, the year *Clueless* came out and before dress codes were enforced in small towns.

Together, we also brought Kerri into the mix. She was too big and too quiet, so I settled comfortably in the middle somewhere between Rosa's cartoon-sized personality and the lump that was Kerri watching from the sidelines. I hoped to soak up some of Rosa's charisma like good leftovers forgotten on her plate. I also hoped to look like More with Kerri at my side for comparison. I was using them, yes, and they me. But the thing is I actually, truly, wholly liked them both.

The trio of us trekked to the mall every Saturday. Every Sunday. It was the only place to go, a hanger-on teenage remnant from the *Fast Times at Ridgemont High* era. Here, we flirted with boys (or hoped they flirted with us). Wait, that's not right. The boys were usually men. Or almost men. And that made it even better.

"We should hang out sometime," Carlos said outside Orange Julius, his voice dripping in a rhythmic Mexican accent. He was eighteen and handsome, with bright white teeth that cut through my awkwardness. He means Rosa. Or me. Or both. On either side of him, his little cousins size us up. They were too young to be interested in girls, but not too young to follow Carlos around aimlessly.

"I have a free house on Friday," I said. I don't know why. The house was free, true. It was my dad's birthday and for once my parents were going out. It was a first. My mom had begrudgingly said Rosa could stay over. The pieces fell together like colorful candy.

"Cool, cool," Carlos said. "Give me your number. I'll bring my boys and we'll chill." Besides the marine, I had never kissed anyone. I'd certainly never had a real party. I'd never smoked or drank. And I had no idea what Carlos expected of me.

Friday night crept up fast, my mom asking me numerous times if "we're sure we're okay." What she was really asking was, "Are you sure that little bitch isn't going to make you do something stupid?" She hated Rosa's knee-high white socks and her too-tight babydoll tees even though I'd taken to wearing the same things.

Carlos came as promised, complete with the two little cousins and two friends. I'd dragged out a warm case of beer my dad had forgotten about in the barn out back. Rosa and I pulled the cover off the billiards table on the big covered patio. The "bar," an illegal living space my parents had converted out of a detached garage, was unlocked with a secondhand couch and TV. Time lost all meaning. I didn't drink—partly out of fear of what would happen, and partly because I didn't want it to run out. Rosa had disappeared somewhere with Carlos, and I ended up on the couch with his friend Javi.

Silence. We didn't talk. But the television was on, he was an entire cushion away, and I was happy in the quiet with no pressure and *Ren and Stimpy* dumbly rolling on. And then the crashes began.

"The fuck, man?" Carlos yelled, stumbling out of the house and into the patio-garage area. My dad followed him, blood pouring from his head. The cue stick in Carlos's hand was splintered and bleeding, too. "We're leaving, okay? You don't fucking touch my cousin though, I'll fucking fuck you up, man."

"Get the fuck out now, you fucking spic," my dad said, that angry prison growl rising in him.

"Jennifer! *Jennifer!*" my mom was screaming inside, looking for me. God, I hate her shrill, cracking voice. I hate how she says my name. I hate how she ruins *everything*. Javi was off the couch and at Carlos's side in seconds, grabbing the rest of the boys as they backed into the gravel driveway.

"I knew it, I knew it," my dad said, and I saw the drunk glaze in his face. "I knew some shit would happen, and I knew when I saw that fucking wetback car in the driveway."

I don't know where Rosa went. Maybe she went with them, maybe she was hiding in a urine-smelling closet. In the living room, my dad faced off with me while my mom railed about how stupid I was from the hallway phone as she called the police who kept asking so loudly I could hear, "Is anyone hurt? Is anybody there hurt?"

"What, are you some slut? Just giving it away to any nigger spic you see?"

We don't all have fight or flight. I get paralysis, but my emotionless face makes it look like I'm determined. My dad had one of his ashtrays in hand, the too-heavy glass kind he loved, light blue with ripples.

He was only four feet from me, but when he raised it behind his shoulder I didn't move. I knew it weighed at least five pounds. I knew it smelled of his Winstons. I knew it could tear apart my face, crack in my skull and flatten my nose. Would I still get Carloses and Jamals with such a face? Would my brain give in? Maybe I was calling his bluff. Maybe I didn't give a shit. I didn't even know myself.

I heard the ashtray fly by my head, so close the gust of it

rustled my hair before it broke like confetti into the mirror behind me.

"*Jamie!*" my mom bellowed, tears raking mascara down her face. He simply walked to the bedroom, like it was nap time, door slamming.

Did he miss because he was drunk? Or because he wanted to?

CHAPTER TEN

"WHAT YOU DOING?" It had been ten days since my pocket had shaken with his words.

Silence.

"You mad?" Chirag asked.

"Where've you been?"

"Busy."

"Whatever."

"Don't be mad. You wanna come over?"

"No."

"Whatever."

I began to scatter. I needed something to glue all those wriggly parts back together and Fernando, sweet and stable, remained constant. He called, he didn't text. It was strange and old-fashioned, like a circus act from a bygone era.

"Hey, good lookin'," he said with his usual morning call. He pulled it off, without a trace of irony. "What's going on?"

"Not much," I said. "I booked skydiving tickets for my birthday this morning. And got a run in."

"It's crazy nobody will do that with you," he said. "By the way, I reserved my own tickets for the same day and time. I hope you don't mind."

It was a bucket list item I'd been circling for a few months. When I'd brought it up to Chirag, the answer was an immediate and unsurprising no.

"Seriously?" I asked.

"Yeah, it's always sounded fun," Fernando said. "What better time to do it? If you're free, we can go for a hike or something afterward since it's kind of in a rural area."

"I'm having my party later that night," I said, "but we

should have time." Michelle's mom was out of town, visiting family in southern Oregon, and had let her commandeer the house for an aging college-themed party. Flip cup, keg, and all to wave farewell to my twenties. I hadn't even mentioned it to Chirag before he began to fade. I knew dragging him would be a battle I was getting too weary to keep fighting.

One week 'til my birthday. Chirag had remained frozen on the other side of the Willamette River, save for the occasional cryptic messages. "Were you at Furnace last weekend?" he asked. I was of course, with Fernando pressed up against me. Chirag wouldn't be in a place like that, but his friends would. Maybe his dates would. Maybe my actions were being reported back to him, as if he hadn't left the cage door wide open for me.

I didn't reply. Surely he'd come through for my thirtieth, right? It was on a Wednesday with celebrations the weekend before. That meant I was clear and guilt-free for Fernando, skydives and parties with a middle of the week mountain to stare down.

"You have stuff here," Chirag texted me on Thursday. Six days to go.

"So?"

"So what you want me to do with it?" The passivity stung like a splinter.

"Throw it away, I don't care."

"No. What you want me to do with it?"

"I. Don't. Fucking. Care."

"Whatever."

Friday. The day I usually snuck out of the office early, letting the Portland Indian summer lull me into patio bars and complaints. Instead, my boss came in. Stayed in. She's never appeared on a Friday before, as if it were some holy day only she observed.

"Can you come in here a minute?" she asked.

Her office took up an entire corner of the donated

space, with papers buzzing everywhere, balanced precariously on dying plants and broken printers. "Look. You checked out a long time ago," she said. Shit. Was this about the missing comma in the last grant spreadsheet? It had to be that goddamned comma.

"I'm sorry," I said.

"No, you're not," she said, leaning back so her chair squeaked. "And I don't blame you. It's damn boring work. But here's the deal. Our funding is ending this quarter. You know that. We're shutting down all the programs but one, and we just can't keep staff on anymore."

"Okay," I said. The air in the room got soupy thick.

"I need you here through next week, though," she said. "At least to get this last philanthropy walk out of the way."

"Okay." Strategies and campaigns for making money began to struggle through my head already. I wasn't a crier, a beggar, or a sit-back-and-worrier. I was a plotter, no matter the stink of the shit heap.

"I can give you this," she said. "It's a layoff. You can collect unemployment. I'll report it next week."

"Thank you," I said.

"I like you, you know," she said. "And I don't like most people." I did know. And see how much that mattered?

"Eff that job," Michelle said when I got to her place that night. Her mom was already gone, the kids with Chris, and her wine collection was beginning to take over the pantry. "I *wish* I could have unemployment and quit mine. It's making me hate people. Do you know how much you'll get?"

"Yeah," I said. It was the first thing I had looked up. "Enough to live, and I can defer my student loans. I just need to prove I applied for, like, five jobs a week."

"Enjoy the ride," she said. "So is Chirag coming tomorrow? Fernando? Both? That would be good."

"Oh, god. Fernando, yes. Chirag, I think it's done and I don't even care."

"I've heard that before," she said, popping another wine

cork into her big collection jug. "Fernando's nice. I like him. But he's not your one."

"We'll see." I hate being told what I already know.

On Saturday morning, Fernando picked me up at dawn, two minutes after I found my first gray hair. It sprung like a snake right from the front of my forehead. How had I never noticed before? Or had it arrived overnight to announce the new decade?

"You hungry?" Fernando asked. I was, for something that would make me feel better and not fat. Burger King breakfast sandwiches with the croissants removed and extra-large diet Cokes, my version of bottle feeding. My dad always told me the first thing I crawled for as a baby was his glass of Coke on the ground. When I got older, I would pour Coke in a bowl and drink it with a spoon, like it was stew. It made it last longer, and I liked the metallic aftertaste in my mouth.

"I'm excited!" Fernando said. If I died, it would be with him. Was that right? Should I die with someone who was so blind he couldn't see me clearly?

Skydiving isn't what you think. You don't show up, get strapped up, and then thirty minutes later you're barreling through the air. It's hours of training, of lessons, of practicing landing in a gymnasium so that you don't skin your butt on the fields outside. Finally, finally, you're chewed up by a tiny plane that looks like it should have been put to the grave long ago. By now you're tired and on autopilot, no idea how one foot is going in front of another. And it's cold. It's so terribly cold all the way up there.

"You ready?" the guide shouted to me over the shrieking, thin air blasting us from the open belly of the plane. Who's ever ready for this? "Just lean here with me," he said. I could feel him pressed tight to me, our bodies bound together. Did he ever get hard when he was doing this?

I was wrong. I wouldn't die with Fernando. I would die with this young kid with blond dreadlocks whose name I didn't remember. "Let's go," he said, and I let him push me into the sky.

"What's your name?" I asked, but he couldn't hear me.

It was incredibly loud and colder than this kind of blue should be. My eyes stuck to his special watch that spun like a dervish telling him rates and numbers I couldn't understand. It's such a long time to fall through the open like that, what must it feel like to jump from a building? From a bridge? Is it different if you're leaping for suicide or because death by jumping is better than consumption by fire? There's too much time to think. All your regrets and stupid moments reel through your mind's eye one last time, and if you forgot to tell someone you loved them or that you were sorry, well that's just too bad now, isn't it?

"That's it," the guide said, and yanked the parachute cords hard. This floating was different, like how Alice must have felt when she went down the rabbit hole with her skirt popped out. Where was my blue dress and fat calves? This was soft, quiet, and the beauty of the Oregon horizon spread at our feet like carpet. "It's beautiful, isn't it?" he asked.

"It is."

"Thanks for not throwing up on me. You can never tell who will."

The landing was soft, natural. One second you're descending through goose flight patterns, the next your weight is squarely on the earth. How ridiculous we are to desperately climb those heaven stairwells just to tumble right down again.

"That was awesome!" Fernando said, landing a few minutes after me. "How'd you like it?"

"I don't know. I'm not sure why I wanted to jump so badly."

"Maybe you just needed to."

From the farm spreads of Molalla, we took the winding route to the Silver Falls trails outside of Salem. It was barely the afternoon and hours before the party. I led because, like a horse, I get stressed when someone's in front of me.

It's not about winning—it's about not being left behind. Dragonflies mated along the water, and the streams were bubbling with the excitement of yesterday's rainfall.

"I've lived in Oregon for twelve years, and there're so many places I haven't seen," he said.

"I've lived here basically off and on for thirty years, and it's still a wild thing," I said.

He kissed me in the archway to a cave along an empty trail. It should have been romantic, with a song swelling in the background, but it wasn't.

"Hey!" Michelle said when we arrived with a pregnant keg in Fernando's back seat. "I cleaned and decorated," she said, presenting a ping pong table turned flip cup station in the garage with linen-scented candles lining the shelves.

"Fancy," I said.

"How was skydiving?"

"It was diving. Out of the sky. It was good."

For some strange reason, a handful of old friends from college came. They all looked so *old*. Maybe they were feeling nostalgic. A guy I used to fool around with, but never fuck, also showed up with eight of his friends, including a girl who tucked unopened bottles of tequila into her purse before stumbling back out to her car. Tito was an asshole. We'd met in a hotel bar when he gallantly intervened as a very large, very drunk man tried to bully me into a corner for I don't know what. Tito and I had one official date at Huey's, one of the city's oldest restaurants that turned Spanish coffees into a performance and served duck on Thanksgiving. But when I wouldn't do more than kiss him, he shook his head. "You know I only asked you out because I thought girls in hotel bars were sluts."

"Why would you think that?"

"Why else would you be in a hotel?"

"Why were you?"

He shrugged. "I was looking for something easy. You're really a disappointment." He caught me during one of my downturns with Chirag, so I accepted it. We kept talking online, sometimes for hours while I was at work. He'd tell me about his dates, I'd drone on about Chirag. He told me he'd never date anyone who didn't have a doctorate like him—anything else was laughable. My degree was laughable. I was laughable. He said running, as I got a little better at it, was only for sad people who needed validation. "I'd much rather chase a ball around a field," he said. "What you're doing is pointless."

Once, in a drunken night out when he tried to put his hand on my thigh and I pushed him away, I told him, "If we're both still single at forty, we can do one of those pacts, you know. Get married and all." I was joking, being stupid, but his face changed and he got serious.

"If I'm not settling now, I'm certainly not going to settle then." But I just didn't learn. Another time, I got sad-drunk and told him I didn't know what to do. "I have all this loose skin from losing weight," (*compliment me, tell me how thin I am now*) "and there's nothing I can do! You're not supposed to get a tummy tuck until you've had all the children you want."

"That's quite the catch-22," Tito had said. "You can't get a decent body until after you have kids. But you can't find anyone who'd want to fuck you, let alone have kids with you, until you get a decent body."

Stooped on the front steps with him at my party, sharing a weak joint, he sucked in deep and said, "Boyfriend, huh?"

"Something like that."

"It won't last," he said. "I mean, *I'll* never fuck you. I have standards. But I'd let you blow me. You seem like you might be good at that. So when this whole thing with the Latin boy is over, just let me know." Tito's current girlfriend was steps away, playing flip cup with her horse face and al-most-Chiropractor degree. I went back inside for a drink, but his friend had already stolen most of the bottles and laid them to bed in her trunk.

Fernando was an easy drunk, high and happy off a few

beers. "Hey!" he said. His eyes drooped at the corners, constantly sad even as the light shone from deep within. He looked like a young Marlon Brando, a young Mark Ruffalo. Why couldn't I be happy with this? What was wrong with me?

"Hey," I said, letting him hug me close. He always smelled clean, like bleach and dryer sheets.

We escaped to Michelle's room, Tito's words still swimming in my mind. "I want to tell you something," Fernando said. "Just to, you know, be totally open."

"Okay."

"When I was thirteen, in Costa Rica, a bunch of guy friends and I were hanging out. And we all decided to have sex. I didn't like it, but just thought you should know." Well. This was interesting. Any slivers of hope I had of forcing happiness with him folded up and died.

"Oh. Okay. Like giving … receiving …."

"Both," he said.

"With just one, or …."

"Everyone. We all took turns both ways."

"Oh."

"Just, you know, I didn't want to hide anything," he said. He wasn't ashamed, embarrassed, or anything. Shouldn't he be? Was this the beer? "Hey," he said. "I love you."

"Oh. Love you, too."

Wednesday stalked me quietly, slowly, like a good prowler. I applied for unemployment and did the requisite on-site testing. Tuesday, nothing. Wednesday. The day. I had made up some lie to Fernando about how I might have to work really late because of the philanthropy walk planning. Really, I was buying my time and my space. What if Chirag surprised me, came to my door with flowers and some excuse that would erase my memory?

"Happy birthday!" Sam messaged me. "How's it feel to be old like me? I hope you do something incredible. I miss you so much."

By eight o'clock that night, I gave up. I removed his

number from my phone, but it was just for show. It was branded into my brain. I cried hard, but in ten minutes everything was dried up. I just didn't have it in me anymore. Instead, I called Fernando. "Hey, we just got done with everything. You still want to hang out?"

"Sure," he said, "Let's go wherever you like."

Over dinner of carb-free steak and asparagus, I realized: This was it. I was unemployed. Fernando had no job, either. He was living with his best friend from college and his friend's pregnant wife. Neither of us was moving anywhere, and he was so blindly trusting in me.

"I've been thinking," I said. "Why don't you just go to Costa Rica now and do the MD? I mean, what's stopping you?"

"Not much," he said. "I'd like to save more money, but I guess that's like having a baby. There's never a good time. I don't like having debt or student loans and I've saved about $30,000. I guess that would be a good start."

"Are the semesters there like they are here?"

"No," he said. "Actually the 'first term' is in January to go with the first of the year."

"So, when is the deadline for applications then?"

"I'm not sure. Why? You trying to get rid of me?" he said with a smile.

"No. I'm trying to go with you."

xi.
A Box for Re-Gifting

"HEY! Nasty ass slut! Yeah, I'm talking to you with your nappy hair." This was the gauntlet of high school hallways. Sophomore year. When I signed up for cheerleading tryouts, it was montages of 80s movies that fueled me. I overheard two girls in the office, whispering about the signup list, and was shocked when they glanced over my name. Did they really think I belonged?

"Oh my god. Diana Denton? She's trying out? She's so *fat*," one said. I didn't think Diana was fat. I didn't know her personally, but I'd *know* if she was fat. If she was, what did that make me? Size eight, 36C bra, and always the most generous loop in a belt. I was far from thin.

I thought cheerleading equated to popularity, but that must have been from an era long gone. It didn't do anything for me at all except make boys leave notes in my locker of how they wanted to "dip into me all night long" and how they "loved seeing those black panties under the cheerleading skirt." I don't know if the other girls got them. Did they? Was it part of the swag, like pom-poms and car decals?

"Fucking slut," the girl said to me, about me, whatever to me again as I walked passed. I had no idea who she was, and only a hint of what "nappy" might mean.

Everybody could drive except me, including Michelle. But she'd just met Chris and lost her whole self in one weekend. He made her cold sores flare up, with a side order of beard burn and chest hickeys. "You know cold sores are a kind of herpes," I told her in geometry class, loudly so others could hear. I wanted to shock her into acting normal again, to say a single word that wasn't about Chris. But she looked at me like I was a stranger who sickened her and moved seats. It'd been three months since we spoke. I saw her new-old Toyota parked in the student lot, a Chinese deep red, but had never been inside. I didn't even know if she'd slept with Chris yet.

Me, I hadn't slept with anyone. Hadn't kissed anyone, hadn't been asked to "go out with" anyone, nothing. I was a slut because of my short skirts. Because of Rosa. How big my tits were compared to my waist. Because I didn't smile. Didn't raise my hand in class. When a teacher asked me why during a conference, I told the truth. "Why do I need to prove what I already know I know?" I asked. The teacher just shook her head in wonder. "But, Jennifer. You're so smart." Boys, they froze me. At least the ones I liked. Until Nate.

I met him at the mall as I wandered alone while my mom picked out ugly bras without underwires at Montgomery Ward. "Yo, you have a light?" he asked, as if he could smoke inside. I just shook my head. "Nice tattoo," he said, pointing to my ankle. I'd drawn a rose in black sharpie, filled it in candy red.

"It's not real," I said, as if I'd been caught.

"Doesn't matter," he said. He was eighteen (of course), with these cold blue eyes and night-black hair. And he smelled of nothing I'd ever known. "You don't look full white," he said. Not an accusation, just an observation.

"Neither do you."

"Half white. Half Portuguese," he said. Portuguese. Something besides Mexican, the sole Other in this small town. It sounded exotic, and I had no idea where Portugal was.

Yo. You have a light? That question is what scooped me up and gave me a place to give away my virginity, like it was something I'd been keeping in a closet to re-gift.

I never wanted to lose my virginity to somebody I cared about. It would mean too much, give them too much power, because I knew they wouldn't stay. So when Nate and I were officially "going out" for a couple of weeks, I really didn't care when he picked me up with hickeys flanking his neck. "Saw my ex. We didn't have sex, though," he said. That was fine. We still dry humped to Ginuwine's "Pony" in the far reaches of the airport parking lot that night.

Nate lived in a trailer with his twin brother and mom, neither of whom I ever met. I guilted him into taking me to winter formal, where he lasted twenty minutes before dragging me outside to finger me as he pressed me against the gym wall. It didn't hurt.

But the sex, that hurt. It hurt more than I'd prepared myself for. "My mom's working the night shift," he told me, and I knew. He jimmied open the front door that never fully locked and pulled me into her room with the king-sized bed and the white comforter that glowed in the dark. He never turned the lights on, I couldn't see his face, and he didn't know. He didn't know. He probably thought I was a slut just like everyone else. Maybe I was, maybe the title was just premature.

"Do you have something?" I asked as he squashed me hard into the comforter that smelled of smoke, kissing me deep. I can't believe I forced that question out. But I couldn't bring myself to say "condom."

Nate sighed, "Yeah. Whatever," and disappeared in the bathroom. This was it. It would be done, and I wouldn't have this burden to protect anymore.

The searing that tore through me when he jammed it in spread to every part of my limbs, through my brain, and sprang out my eyes. Every single thrust was like getting a seppuku through my organs, but I didn't shout. I sucked back the tears. I didn't even have to take off my skirt, shirt or bra. And it was over fast. Nate rolled off me without a word and pulled the condom off as he walked, pant-less but shirt covering his groin, back to the bathroom. I never even saw it.

My underwear became a makeshift towel, and I buried it in my purse when it was drip-heavy with blood. And my eyes? They'd adjusted somewhat to the dark, or maybe the gutting had sharpened my senses. Either way, I saw the slaughter. It looked like a murder happened on that bed. The room was an abattoir. Nearly half of the pristine white comforter was covered in my redness. It must have gushed out by the bucketful, and more had started to creep down my leg.

"Let's go," I said as soon as Nate reappeared in the doorway, clinching my legs tight to hold it in.

He didn't see my mess then, and I didn't say anything. I never said anything. I didn't return his calls, and he gave up after just three days.

I bled so heavily for a week that even the super thick pads had to be changed every hour.

So, yeah. That was sex.

CHAPTER ELEVEN

"TWO WEEKS UNTIL the deadline at UCR," Fernando said. "Are you sure about this?"

"Yeah," I said. "Yes. Let's do it." What else was I going to do?

The unemployment checks had started rolling in, and both Fernando and I were hustling on the side, picking up side gigs where we could. In late August, we worked a booth at the end of the Hood 2 Coast relay race, giving away free juices and offering carnival games to the teams that spent the past full day trading sweaty slap bracelets as they worked their way from Mount Hood to the Oregon coastline. We were "brand ambassadors" for a muddy warrior race, handing out granola and getting a free entry to the obstacle course. There, I overheard a girl ask for his number while he worked the cash register and I the granola machine. "I ... I can't," he told her. He sounded devastated. But later, together, we rolled over logs in the river, slid down manmade muddy terrain mixed with earth and other people's vomit. We were "corporate modes" handing out free shots and t-shirts at a local country bar. I picked up an interim director position at a local hospital, too—I just couldn't escape a full-time job surrounded by the sick and dying.

The interim job stopped the unemployment, or really delayed it. The pay was double what I was making before, and I got an official-looking badge with "Director" proudly printed in bold. It came with free rides on the Portland Streetcar, and I pretended to lose my first badge so I wouldn't have to turn it in when the job ended. You never know when you might need a free ride. My job was to oversee the shutdown of one of the philanthropy programs, to govern a killing. I trudged to a decrepit office from the 1960s in quivering heels while Fernando raced to put together transcripts, recommendations, and essays translated into Tico Spanish and apostilled by the state department. My boss was a typical Portland lesbian who glanced with wariness at my shoes. She was at first indifferent towards me, and then very unsure. But I let the department check off that desirable "Native American" box for their proof of diversity.

The emails I got from around the departments were so creamy with female apologies and emojis that I could feel my intelligence sinking. *Hi there!! I'm SO glad you're on the team! It's so nice having a new face around the office. J You're a great writer and I'm so impressed by the work you've done so far. J Really great stuff!! Just one little thing and it's NO big deal (seriously!). Can you pretty please cc Karen on the DAS project from now on, too? She really likes to be in on the loop, too, and has some really great insight on it since she's been here for OODLES of time!! That would really help us out a bunch! But really great work! Thank you SO SO MUCH!!*

Oh, fuck. My replies were consistent. *Hello, Yes, I will cc Karen going forward. Thank you.* Or *Thank you for reaching out, I will take care of your request this afternoon.* It wasn't enough.

My new boss called me into her office after just three weeks. This isn't the "usual" calling into an office. This took some serious legwork. Getting to her office required taking a special lift system to the waterfront, then a trolley or bus, before finally walking the last few blocks to her office that was nowhere near the hospital.

"Jennifer, I'm going to be frank with you," she said. "There are, as you know, a lot of women in the department. Mostly women. And, well, if you want to get ahead here, you have to play the game. Do you understand what I'm saying?'

"Not really." Games, games I'm not good at. Unless you count refusing to call someone first.

"Use some more flowering language in your emails, you know?" she said, choosing her words carefully. "Maybe some smiley faces. That goes a long way here."

"Do you think my emails have been rude?"

"Well, no. Not overtly. Not exactly. No."

"But you want me to be more 'flowery.'"

"Yes, exactly."

"Would you say the same thing if I were a man?"

She didn't have a reply, and for a moment the corporate walls shook between us. She didn't want to stick a damn winking face on her emails any more than I did. "I don't think this is going to work out," she finally said.

"Neither do I." Back to unemployment it was.

"Are you seriously going to Costa Rica?" Michelle asked. We were at one of our rare Sunday morning yoga classes together. She preferred the instructors who told us we were perfect and beautiful just as we are, and warned us not to push ourselves too hard. I preferred the classes full of pain, punishment and not a word of English.

"Yeah, why not?"

"I don't know. I don't think you'll be there long."

"I've lived in London and Korea," I said as we rolled out our mats, mine as close to two mirrors as possible to watch my form and see how thin my stomach would look *this* time in downward facing dog.

"That was always temporary though," she said. "What's this?"

"Fernando's program is four years, then he'll come back here for his internship and residency," I said.

"And what are you gonna do? Just follow him around?"

"I don't know yet, but I have nothing else going on. And cost of living is cheap there, plus unemployment will still be deposited as long as I'm looking for a job."

She pinched up her face. "It's like you don't even want to be here."

"Not really," I said. "What's keeping me here? What's

here for me?"

She had no answer for that.

"I got in!" Fernando said, showing me an email in Spanish with only a few words I could pick out. My limited high school Mexican Spanish was sad at best. Central American Spanish was an entirely different monster.

"That's great!" I said. "Congrats!"

"So, two months," he said. "I really want to spend this last Christmas here with my family, and my uncle can get us standby tickets the day after for cheap. Are you in?"

"Completely." I had already partly packed my apartment and shipped some boxes down to my mom's where they would likely be ripped apart by rats or stolen by the meth dealers down the street. But what did I need with yearbooks and photo albums? I would take nothing with me but my computer, bathing suits, shorts, and essentials. I couldn't get out of here fast enough. Even though I avoided the haunts where Chirag might be, you never know where ghosts might appear—deserted parking lots. Grocery stores. Movie theaters. Anything was fair game and Portland was getting small. If I put an ocean between us, would that be enough? I knew he'd play stowaway in my heart, in my mind, but there was nothing I could do about that. The only thing I could do was pursue physical distance and try to force happiness down my throat with facades.

Is this what most people think happiness is? Fernando took me to his mom's favorite Chinese restaurant in old town Tigard along with his two brothers and his best friend from high school, a girl named Anna who was clearly in love with him. She teemed with so much jealousy and hatred in my presence she refused to speak at all, happy to simply gaze at him in adoration.

"You know Anna's in love with you, right?" I asked him afterward, hot little leftovers between us in the car.

"Yeah, well, I've kind of always known that. She's not my type ... physically," he said. She was dull, certainly. Average body, pale freckled face, reddish hair, and mousy all over.

"Then why do you still hang out with her? Don't you find it cruel?" I asked him.

"No. She knows we'll never happen. I basically told her that once," he said.

"That doesn't make it okay," I said.

At dinner, with that big lazy Susan in the center of us all, his brother with fetal alcohol syndrome tried out my limited sign language skills. His other brother, Ramon, watched me closely with searching eyes. "Ramon, he's always hit on every girl I've brought around," Fernando had told me. "Not that there were many, but you know ... most of them went for him." Ramon was short with greasy hair and swagger he hadn't earned. A high school dropout who leeched off their mom even as he was squarely in his thirties. He couldn't drive thanks to too many DUIs, but worked at jewelry stores sporadically. My introduction to him had already happened, at his insistence and online. When he connected with me on Facebook, I thought nothing of it. Fernando's mom and friends had, too. But it was that early message that snared me and gave me a peek into what this family really entailed. With all the kids being adopted, it had led to a risky competition without the blood ties that ensured fair game.

"Hey," Ramon had written. "How's it goin, haha?"

"Good. How are you?"

"Doin ok. How's it going with my brother? He's such a fucking loser dont ya think, haha."

"No. That's not a very kind way to speak about your family."

"Haha, I was just joking but srsly, whats up wit that? Why r u into him?"

"I'm sorry, but I haven't even met you and that's not really any of your business."

"Haha. Must be cuz ur an ugly, fat bitch just like him haha." I deleted and blocked him at that point. In person, he was much quieter—but because I knew, I could see that restless hate stirring in his eyes.

"Ah, Jennifer," Fernando's mom said. "You're going to ruin my plan! I've been trying to get Fernie and Anna married for ten years now!"

"Mom," Fernando said.

"Oh, she doesn't care," she said. "Did you know they got 'married' in senior year of high school? For Senior Day, there was a wedding booth set up where the kids could dress up and take photos. I have it still hanging on my wall." And she did, Anna looking ecstatic and Fernando embarrassed. It was a huge blowup that overpowered the hallway, like it was a real wedding.

"Well, they had ten years to figure it out," I said, not able to look Anna in the eye (if she were even looking at me), but hoping my words stung deep. If Fernando were a fire hydrant, I would have pissed all over him right then, right there, right in front of them all.

The holidays rushed in and melted together as they always do. I did our makeup, Fernando and I, like zombies and we dressed up in black tie and went to Cellar for Halloween. It was nearly empty, and not a trace of Chirag. Did I want him to see me like this, all huge hair and tight dress with a beautiful Latin man at my side? I don't know, but I liked to tease fate and sometimes slap it in the face to wake it up.

Thanksgiving was spent at Fernando's mom's where he helped her cook, raked her leaves, and made me a special no-sugar-added pumpkin pie filling. My Costa Rica visa came through, with the caveat that I'd have to do a visa run every three months and be out of the country for seventy-two hours each time before being readmitted. Those would be my escapes, alone. I pictured how Medellin, Colombia would look with the remnants of Escobar still lurking through the city. The contemporary high rises in Panama. The quaintness of Nicaragua by bus. I only knew of these places from books and movies, but was so sure of their magic.

"I got the tickets," Fernando said, "for three days after Christmas, it turns out. But I was thinking, you said your friend Sam would be in Mississippi for the holidays visiting family? My classes don't start until the second week of January and our layover is in Atlanta. It's just a short drive to Oxford. Do you want to go see her?"

Of course I did. The threads between Sam and me were double-knotted in college and thus break-proof. It didn't matter that she went to study abroad in Australia our junior year and missed our birthdays, only fifteen days apart. She sent me a postcard about how she spent the day vomiting blue curacao into the toilet on her twenty-first and wishing I were there. I was who she called when her great love left her and she got so drunk that she woke up with her own shit all over the floors and walls. I went to her when she began her Ph.D. in Georgia, where we got high and ate sugar-free cupcakes. She followed me to Korea, albeit a year too late. I wanted to follow her when she moved to Abu Dhabi after grad school, but my body was too sick of teaching to continue.

"That's the beauty of standby," Fernando said, smiling. "You can pretty much show up when you want and hope for the best."

On Christmas morning at his mom's, gifts were exchanged but nothing large was given to us. A calendar of Portland to remember it by when nothing but palm trees and whistling buses surrounded us. A sock monkey ornament for Fernando to keep at his mom's. Luggage tags. It didn't seem real, that in four days all this cold and rain would be behind me. It was like walking to the plane that would dump me out all over again, and my feet just kept going through the motions even as my insides slowed down.

Christmas night was the first time we had sex at his mom's house, quietly like little mice in the office-guest room on a twin bed. It was perfunctory and Just Fine. At first, Fernando had told me, "I don't go down on women, I just don't like it." I was shocked, stunned.

"Have you—done it before?"

"Yeah, with my high school girlfriend. It just wasn't good."

Talks about Costa Rica had already begun, and I'd written off our first few trysts as lacking because of unfamiliarity and haste. "Uhm, either you go down there, or I'm not going *down there*," I said. I had already had who I really wanted ripped away from me, with Chirag's hungry tongue put on the shelf with a lock. I'd be damned if I was going to be stuck with subpar sex, too.

I had to teach Fernando, which I'd never done before, but it wasn't difficult and it paid off in my favor. What is good sex, anyway? Everyone likes to think they know what it is, but they don't. One person isn't necessarily "good" or "bad" at it. It's whether you complement each other, get off the same way, and how much you're pulled to that person no matter the consequences.

So, no. The sex wasn't bad. It was better than nothing and sometimes, sometimes, in just the right moments, I could pretend it was who I wanted.

I'd been running religiously every other morning, letting the sun wake me up and roll me into the dead of Portland winter. The distances were short and made my face sting, but I was doing it. Two days before leaving, my nightstand shook, and I just knew. Instantly. Like I'd been expecting it.

"Why didn't you just slap me?" Chirag's words flashed across my phone.

"Why didn't you hit me? Tell me how stupid I was?" Did he know I was leaving? No, he couldn't know. I'd blocked all means of him finding my plans, my plots and my pleas of escaping. It had been almost six months—almost six heavy months. Shouldn't I be healed by now, or on my way there?

I couldn't help myself, my fingers raced across the keyboard of their own volition. "I just couldn't do it anymore."

"Let's do this. I want to be with you. For real." All the tugging of the past few years flooded my system. Backed into a corner, we always attack.

"Will you marry me? Right now?" I asked, even as my suitcases were packed in the corner. Even as my passport was getting ready to open wide for a Costa Rican customs stamp.

"I can't. I can't do that right now. But let's see ...." the ellipses told me he was still typing. Fuck this.

"No. Now or never. You choose."

"It's not that simple, babydoll. You know about my family."

"I don't know anything about you. But I will tell you this. I'm moving to Costa Rica in two days. This is all up to you now."

"You're moving? For good? With that guy?" He was never good at lying, not outright. I knew he really didn't know at all.

"Yes."

"Can I see you?"

"That's not a good idea."

"That's not an answer."

It was a terrible idea, one doomed to fail and poison the world of palm trees ahead. The world of marrying a gorgeous, Latin surgeon who had a heart too big for his chest cavity. That's what all women are supposed to want, right? A soap opera doctor who would never stray, just like a good puppy tied to a tree.

"I'll be there in 30," I said.

My arms directed my car, already slated to be sold by Fernando's roommate when we left, to Chirag's with no effort. The body remembers the curves and lanes it loves. For the first time, I didn't bother dressing up. He didn't get my made-up face and sprayed perfect hair. He was getting dirty jeans, a ponytail, and a swipe of chap stick.

In the looming tower of his condo, I didn't recognize the new doormen. These ones hadn't seen me tear-streaked in the elevator in a green party wig. They hadn't seen us making out in the underground garage. The anonymity was comforting. And his door. It was the same, with the post-modern "art" on the placard that looked like graffiti from a distance. With a knock, I heard that familiar shuffle from the other side.

xii.
Yes, No, Goodbye

NOBODY BUT Rosa and Kerri knew about Nate, and that's how I kept it. I was still one of the whores at school, just no longer a virgin one. I'd settled into a pattern with these out-liers. At a school with an off-campus lunch policy, it was too delicious to pass up. We began slinking the two blocks to Kerri's house at noon every day. Most days we never went back. Instead, we pooled resources and bought a Ouija board from the toy store at the mall where I had a crush on a lanky boy with dark hair whom I couldn't bear to speak to.

When I was eight, my mom forced me to watch *The Ex-orcist* as a warning. She believed in God "just to play it safe" and had me baptized for the same reason in front of a church full of cheering white people. She altered the words to the "Now I Lay Me Down to Sleep" prayer to exclude "If I die before I wake" because she thought it would give me nightmares. But it was the stories she told me about her own Ouija play in her twenties that made me pay attention. She asked it if she would ever have children, and the board told her no. When she asked why, it said, "Stop bc pills." Obviously, she thought. Birth control pills weren't very con-ducive to getting pregnant. But she stopped anyway—she wasn't having sex. Three months later, those pills were pulled from the market for allegedly causing fertility prob-lems. If it wasn't for this board, I might not exist.

What could it tell me? The three of us hovered over it like vultures over the dead. But it couldn't speak with cer-tainty. Phone numbers of celebrities or anything that wasn't already buried deep in our hearts. When it became too frustrating, we tried playing Light as a Feather, Stiff as a Board and mimicking scenes from *The Craft*, but nothing worked. Only the Ouija worked. Sometimes.

"When are we going to die?" Kerri asked it one day.

"Don't ask it that!" I said.

"Why not?"

"I don't want to know." She rolled her eyes and said, "I do."

"R," the board began. "2 ... 0 ... 2 ... 3 ... 2 ...."

"God, you're going to live forever," I told Rosa.

"That's the plan, beautiful," she said with a giggle.

"What about Jennifer?" Kerri asked.

"Stop it!" I told her, but the planchette jerked hard. "J ...." it began, and then it grew dizzy. "J ... J ... J ...." It circled aimlessly, like a dog with worms.

"This is stupid," Kerri said. "What about me?"

"1," it said. "8." It stopped hard.

"Well, shit, I don't have much time," Kerri said, lighting a cigarette. "Hold this for me?" she asked, handing me the smoking cigarette so she could put away the board. Her mom knew about the Ouija, but didn't like seeing it out. The cigarette was wild and foreign. I tried to hold it like an old movie star, like Bette Davis might.

As the days shuffled on and we dug deeper into Ouija, I began to notice something. Something disgusting about myself. The words in my heads, the thoughts, they moved the planchette. I could think anything, and it would spell it out. I swear, I swear to god I wasn't actually pushing it. It was my brain, my mind, something far down deep inside me with wet, blinking eyes. Was I the only one feeling this?

"Do you like me?" Kerri asked, teasing the board. *Bitch*, I thought. Not because I thought she was, but just to see.

"B, I, T, C, H," it said.

"Well, screw you, too," Kerri said.

"I have to tell you something," I whispered to Kerri the next day. "I think I can, like, move the board. With my mind."

"*You're* moving it?"

"No, not like that. I—I can't explain it."

Chapter Twelve

HE ANSWERED the door in worn-out basketball shorts and a Nike tee-shirt that was cracking along the graphics. Were we here, now, where we didn't have to pretend anymore? I thought maybe that buzz between us would be gone, faded, after so many days of make believe. But Chirag pulled me close, without a word, and I remembered what Home felt like. Like this, his chest too big and arms too thick. The smell of the oil in his hair and the type of Tide to wash his clothes. "I'm sorry," he said. And I said nothing.

The condo was the same, with strewn-about clothes and takeout containers fighting for counter space. I scanned the cherry wood floors and dark corners for something strange, unfamiliar. A bra I didn't recognize, or makeup that wasn't mine. But it was as if nobody had been here since me. And he'd kept all my things.

"Why now?" I asked.

"I dunno," he said. "I kept thinking that maybe with some more time, it would be done. But it wouldn't stop. I've only cried for a person twice in my life—once when my grandmother died and I was in Boston, unable to go back home. Then you, for the past six months."

"Did you know? That I was leaving?" Sometimes the answers we already know are the most important.

"No," he said. "I tried to find you online at first, but you'd blocked everything. Are you happy?"

"I don't know. Happy enough."

"That's the other thing. I knew you were dating somebody, but I didn't know it was all this. I didn't want to get in your way."

"You've been in my way for years."

"You haven't left yet," he said. "Stay. Let's try this for real."

"You've said that before." There was a resolve in me. Not to move on, no. But I needed Costa Rica, the physical distance and the foreignness to baptize me. To hell with the casualties I dragged behind me in the sand. "I'm going. I'm going."

He didn't say anything, just shook his head like the words would tumble out right. "I was stupid," he finally said. "You know I'm dumb."

"It's too late now."

"You once said you'd wait for me," he said. It was true. I'd once bet my life I would give him all the time he wanted, all my time he could manage.

"And I'm still waiting," I said. "I'm just not doing it here anymore. And I'm not doing it with you."

"It'll be different," he said. "I promise you."

"So you'll tell your parents, then? Right now. Call them and tell them about me—not that you want to marry me, just about me."

The internal fight was palpable on his face. "I can't do that," he said finally.

Stupidly, I went to the bathroom. Flushed the toilet and ran the tap as a waterfall of "Fuck, fuck, fuck" dribbled out my lips. The tears tiding on my lashes faded away without escaping, but I blotted my eyes just in case. And there it was. A used condom at the top of the bathroom trash bin as I threw the tissue away. His housekeeper came every Friday. This was very, very fresh, and the years of anger flooded my system like it was new.

The coldness that creeps in when this happens makes me walk with a purpose. Glazes armor over my eyes. "You think that," I told him. "You think you can just get what you want. Well, let me tell you something. One day you're going to tell your parents about me. About this white-looking girl and I don't know what's going to happen then. I don't know if I'll even be on this side of the world. But believe me, you will tell them."

"Maybe you're right," he said.

"And what's so wrong with me, anyway?" I asked. "You're almost thirty years old! So what if I'm American, if I'm not a doctor or an engineer? What, because I'm Native I'm the wrong kind of Indian? Maybe you're the wrong one. You ever think of that? Maybe we both are."

"It doesn't work like that, they don't think like that," he said. "But, no. No, you're not the wrong kind."

I stayed all day, into the night. Fernando was easy to lie to, like a still trusting animal with brand marks and cigarette burns all over his body. I wish I could say the physicality between Chirag and I had waned—like it was supposed to, like ending honeymoon periods promised us. But Chirag's skin on mine was still flint on steel. He was familiar and then a stranger, all at once. And I didn't mention the condom lurking steps away.

Naked and covered in a film made of both of us, he asked, "Did you ever try to think of me when you were with him?" I suppose it wasn't a time to pull punches.

"Sometimes," I said.

"Did it work?"

"No. You don't feel like anyone else."

"Yeah," he said, running through the women in his head. "I know. I tried, you know. To have a one-night stand. Find a girl in a bar that reminded me of you and just take her home. I couldn't do it. I always went home alone."

"Not always."

"No," he said. "Not always. But never right away."

The day before leaving, I was getting too close. Pushing my luck too far. Fernando was amenable, believing that I was saying goodbye to mysterious friends he'd never met.

"Can I write to you?" Chirag asked.

"I guess. I can't stop you."

"How long will you be gone?"

"I don't know. I've sold everything I have."

"Let me prove it to you. Prove it to you in my words."

"You can try. I'm not promising anything, least of all returns."

"I want you to take something of mine."

"What?"

"Whatever you want." I hadn't been thinking of such a thing, but it was one of his watches. His collections turned in fancy watch collection boxes, being constantly showboated and wound. They were way too big for me, even if all the possible links were taken out. "That one," I said, pointing to a silver and deep blue one.

"I'm glad you chose a watch," he said, placing it in a velvet pouch.

"I will wait for you," he said. "Wait for you like you waited for me all those years."

The goodbye didn't leave me room to cry. Instead, I just breathed in his scent, tried to memorize the feel of his skin and flesh in my fingers.

Our flight left at night and Fernando and I got a grand farewell. His family, Michelle, and a sprinkling of his friends gathered for cocktails and dinner at a beach-themed restaurant just twenty feet from the security checkpoint. "I can't believe my son is finally going to be a doctor!" his mom said over and over, shaking her head in wonder.

"Hey," Michelle whispered. "Who's the tall guy?" pointing with her eyes at one of Fernando's friends.

"You won't wanna come back, bro," Ramon said. "It's fuckin' paradise there, man."

"I remember what it is," Fernando said.

There were hugs and cheek kisses and a smattering of Tico Spanish amongst all the goodbyes. Central America was still days away—we were scheduled to land in Liberia on New Year's Eve. What would Chirag do this New Year's Eve? I hadn't asked.

But first, first was Sam in Mississippi. Our emails were sporadic, but without any hint of passivity. Sometimes she was busy, sometimes I was, but we always came back 'round together. She was beautiful like Julia Roberts, petite with freckles and chocolatey eyes. But it was her smile, plus-sized and brilliant, that made her special. When we'd met, her hair hung in ropey tangles to her waist, but now it was short. Bleached blonde to make the thin, fine mess of it look thicker.

I'd watched Sam fall hard in Australia, felt the surging in her letters. She'd fallen fast and deep for a boy named Tim from California, also in her exchange program. When they came back to the States, she flew nearly every weekend to see him and spent any spare second locked up in her room on the phone. I met him once, on a rare occasion that he came to her. I was unimpressed and he didn't say much. But she was happy in a way I'd never seen so I tried to will it into being for her.

After months of flying to California, the two of them had arranged a dual summer internship in northern California watching birds and collecting data for the Forest Service. It was two months of being tucked into a cabin with no human interaction besides each other. Tim picked her up in San Francisco, and as she rolled her luggage to his car, he said simply, "I can't do this anymore." He left her, but didn't leave her, in a busy airport with two months of analysis in front of them. "So ... what do you want to do?" he asked.

"I want to stay," she'd said. "I want to stay and I want these two months with you. Will you give me these two months?" And he did. In my head, it was begrudgingly. But he gave her those birds, the wild ones who could fly where they wanted and hadn't a clue they were being watched.

I imagine the worst of her heartbreak was processed in those woods. When she came back, she was different, quieter, and I didn't know what to say. But months later she went to grad school in Georgia, perhaps as far away from California as she could manage. There. I visited her there.

During her PhD, she regaled me with stories of her dating mishaps. I was with Eli, and she was responsible for my vicarious love life. She told me about the Indian guy who took her grocery shopping on a first date so they could choose items for a picnic together. About "Cheese" who demanded she stare him in the eye the whole time he went down on her, then asked her "What are *those*?" as he fingered the stretch marks on her thighs. And then there was Sean. "You'd like him," she said. "He's your type of guy." Sean was from Mississippi and followed his fiancé to Georgia, where she left him for someone else. He stayed and went to grad school, too, because he had nothing better to do.

Sam was above Sean, and he knew it. He worshiped her, even though she drank too much on their first date. She told me she still stalked Tim online, and thought he was dating someone. Sean, he was her Eli.

That was so many years ago. Sam married Sean three weeks before I married Eli. I don't think she told him much about Tim, or about the time her and I tried kissing in college and she laughed in my mouth. "Just do it," I had told her. It was her first like that. But her beauty, even when she half-heartedly offered it to me, was beyond my grasp and that's where we drew the line in permanent ink. They both dropped out of their programs. Their marriage was sustaining. Did Sean still think he was the lucky one, or had it all evened out?

When Fernando and I landed in Atlanta, the line at the rental car center snaked forever. Finally, at the front of the line, I began digging in my purse for my phone. "Next!" called a man's voice. I looked up, and every booth was empty. A young black man manned each one, all five looking at me expectantly. I went to one at random. "*I* didn't call you," he said, gesturing to the man next to him. "Fuckin' think we all look the same," he said under his breath, about the woman he assumed was white.

The drive to Oxford was uneventful, the landscape flat compared to Oregon. Sam was hidden away in Sean's parents' house, in the same town where they'd been married. She hugged me tight, and I had to bend down to her as always. His mom had fallen for me at their wedding, probably because I was too self-conscious to have breakfast in my pajamas like Sam did. His mom had wanted a proper southern girl for her son, and the roots from my parents must have been showing. My Oklahoma dad, my Arkansas mom.

That night, with Fernando in the back room talking with Sean's father (the local town doctor), Sam whispered to me, "He reminds me of Eli."

"He's *a lot* better looking than Eli."

"I didn't mean looks," she said. "You're going to walk all over him." We watched Pedro Almodovar's *The Skin I Lived In* and talked about how beautiful he-she was and how implausible the plot. Sam loved Almodovar, watched *Bad Education* and *Matador* over and over. I think she lusted after the loveliness of his freakishness, so unlike her slow and steady kind.

After our bags were re-packed and hugs passed back around, I asked her, "You'll come see me in Costa Rica, won't you?"

"I don't know," she said. "I looked at tickets from the UAE and they're not easy. I'll try."

Leaving the freezing cold of the south wasn't hard. We would spend two weeks on the western coast of Guanacaste where monkeys perched in trees on the street and coconut water was sold on the corners. It's where Fernando's family lived, on his dad's side, complete with a massive old home that everybody shared when they wanted to escape to the beach. San Jose, the capitol where the university lurked, was smack in the middle of the country, hours away from Liberia. You had to crawl over rainforests to get there.

It's just a few hours from Atlanta to Liberia, and the plane jetted in at noon. Descending, I took in my new home. It didn't look as I had imagined. There were palm trees, sure, but also a lot of brown. It was flat in this part of the country. It wouldn't count, wouldn't be real, until the plane's wheels touched the ground. I scrolled through my iPod and put OneRepublic's "Good Life" on repeat, setting my own soundtrack to this new beginning. I could will *this*, right? Can't we will a good life to blossom?

xiii.
A De-flowering

"ISN'T THIS PLACE a little too adult for you, young lady?" He looked like Blane from *Pretty in Pink*, squinty green eyes and perfectly styled hair—and a smile that held nothing back.

"I'm fifteen," I said. "My mom teaches line dancing here before the live music starts." He couldn't have been that much older than I was, but had that broad-shouldered V-shape that so many boys my age were left wanting.

"Ah, that explains it," he said. "Actually, that's how I'm in here, too. I'm eighteen, but my dad's performing tonight." Every week at the Rodeo Railroad, my mom brought me to her dance lesson where she (for once) shouted at other people. It was embarrassing, but I liked being in that big bar, pretending to be older and sitting by myself on those high, hard stools. I asked for diet soda in cocktail glasses and pretended I was a lady sipping something that turned her loose and beautiful.

"I'm Scott," he said.

"Jennifer."

"So where's your mom at?"

"Oh, I don't know, she usually hangs out afterwards with her friends."

"Isn't she afraid some rapist is going to snatch you up?"

"She can only hope."

Scott was *barely* eighteen and had dropped out of high school last year to follow his dad around Oregon towns playing whatever gigs he could muster up. He had no plans for a GED, and his career goals were solely getting hired on *Saturday Night Live*. I wasn't attracted to him. I recognized that he was an attractive guy, and would make others jealous, so by default I accepted his advances. He wore Abercrombie clothing, and scoffed when I'd never heard of it (there was no Abercrombie down here).

"We're in town for, like, three nights I think. Then my dad is going to go stay with his parents in their RV park for a while on the coast," Scott said, after he tried his best at two-stepping and swing dancing with me. "You should give me your number," he said. "Maybe we can hang out before I go."

Richard Chase, serial killer, chose his victims by going door to door and trying the locks. If they were engaged, he moved on. If not, he saw it as an invitation to come in. The invitations we hand out, how many do we know about? How many demons do we welcome into our foyer to serve them tea?

Scott didn't leave three days later. Instead, he stole me around the city, sliding his hand under mine while we jolted around in his 1985 BMW. "This is nice!" he said when he saw "the bar" at home. "It's so unfortunate it's not being used. I could totally stay in here and your parents would be cool with it because it's not like *we're* staying together or anything. Then I wouldn't have to leave."

For some god knows why reason, my mom said okay. I had known Scott for three days. He called her ma'am, promised to get a job right away, and that he would never, ever be in the house after ten o'clock. My dad had nailed the windows in my room shut when I was nine after he found my fake journal entries about sneaking out of the house, so my mom felt pretty confident Scott wouldn't be sneaking in. I'd left my kid journal open and propped up on the dining room table, begging to be read. My dad found it when he sat down to his usual dinner: "salad" of lettuce and cheese wrapped in saran wrap, and whatever my mom had cooked on Sunday for the whole week. Roast beef and baked potatoes. Ham and black-eyed peas.

When my mom confronted me about the journal, I cried

and ran into the field. Later, I wrote a note that said, "I'm sorry," and taped a quarter to it. That should buy her forgetting.

"Now you need to get a job," my mom told Scott firmly. My dad just glared at him.

"Yeah, yeah, I will," he said. He did, three months later, pumping gas. After fucking me gently on the floor of the bar. In the pool. In my bed and the living room couch. I got on birth control and he got off condoms.

He sighed, "I just wish you were a virgin," he said. "It's really too bad, because *I* waited until I really loved someone. I kind of think I deserve the same. But oh, well, I guess that's not in the cards for me. I'm just not that lucky." I should have waited? I felt like I *should* feel guilty, but I didn't.

Scott took me to school, picked me up for lunch, and waited in the parking lot an hour before the last bell rang. I stopped going to Kerri's house. Most days, he would bring flowers right to my final class. "I took them from a graveyard!" he said with a laugh.

"Who's *that*?" girls would ask me. "He's so hot!" They didn't need to know the flowers were stolen from the dead, whose stinking bodies were nourishing the grass between our toes.

"Some more flowers for my sweet," Scott said, handing me a bouquet whose petals were already wilting. "This flower looks a little roughed up—kind of like yours!" he said. "Just kidding."

"I lied, okay!" I said as I got into his car. "I didn't have sex with that guy before. I mean, we made out and stuff, but that was it."

"I knew it! I knew you were lying!" he said. "You obviously didn't know what you were doing. But *why* did you lie? How am I supposed to believe anything you say now?"

"I don't know, okay? I just wanted you to think I was more experienced than I was."

"Okay," he said, a smile scrawling back across his face. "Okay. So I was your first?"

"Yes." Forget the bloodied bed in the trailer. The quakes in my organs.

"You absolutely swear? You're not lying again?"

"Yes, I swear."

"All right. Good. Well, it'll take me a while to trust you again, but I think I can. After some time. After you prove yourself to me. I'll do my best, but it's really up to you."

"Thank you."

CHAPTER THIRTEEN

"WOW, you've got a lot of luggage!" the Americans behind me in customs said. "How long are you staying?"

"I live here." I live here. I was testing it out, seeing where it hit my palate. It didn't taste so bad.

"Really? I'm so jealous," said one of the women. Fernando was in another line, the Tico national's line.

The Liberia airport was small, like Medford's, and we had to de-board directly onto the tarmac. January is "winter" in Costa Rica, making it a constant 80 degrees. It wasn't humid, was barely balmy, and reminded me of my wedding on Maui where I sealed in ink what I knew was wrong.

Fernando's cousin, Maria, picked us up. She weighed all of ninety pounds and was working on her law degree. "Hola!" she said. "Soy Maria." That's all I understood before she launched into a tirade of Spanish.

"Que?" she asked Fernando when he said something to her quietly. And then, "No Spanish?" in flawless English, not a whip of an accent. "You'd better learn," she said. "I'm only going to speak Spanish to you from now on so you learn." I was tired and she was too thin to argue with.

His grandfather's home was a stately thing with three stories and dark, heavy wooden doors smack in the middle of little downtown Liberia. It looked too big and out of place like it didn't belong. I met too many aunts, uncles, cousins, and far-flung relatives to keep them all straight. All their names ended in an "o" or "a." The house filled with Spanish, and after the obligatory cheek kisses and introductions I was ignored. Ticos are small. I was very aware of how white and spreading my thighs were in my khaki shorts.

"Do you want to walk around town?" Fernando asked me. More than anything.

He bought Diet Coke for us in plastic bags from the *soda,* local slang for a corner store. That's how it's done. Glass bottles are popped and the clerks pour the brown fizz into cheap plastic baggies so they can retain the glass for themselves. Nobody paid me much attention. The Guanacaste region is rich with foreigners and squat tourists, McDonalds and Subways and Burger Kings. The town square was looked over by the imposing white Catholic Church and teenagers snuck breast squeezes and fast kisses on benches beneath the Guanacaste trees.

"Are you hungry?" he asked and I said yes, just to stay away longer and avoid eating at his grandfather's. A half-bar, half-restaurant sizzled with red neon lights and called to me with its open patio. "Cervezas," it promised. "Imperial Beer."

"Here," I told him. He ordered for us, of course. Spicy tortas de carne that were like nothing I'd had before. I don't know what they did to the meat, but it was glorious.

"Not too hot? Not too hot?" the waiter kept asking, looking concerned as I scooped the red chili-infused meat into my mouth.

"Fine, fine," I said. The chortling busses kept stopping right in front of the restaurant, scooping up tired passengers as the sun set. Someone had scratched out the lower leg of "Ruta" on the stop, making it read "Puta 23."

"We'd better get back," Fernando said. "The family is going to start celebrating soon." That's right, it was New Year's Eve. It didn't feel like it. Last New Year's, I'd asked Chirag what he was doing.

"Going out with a friend," he said. Well then, hell. So was I.

Like most holidays Chirag stole from me, I somehow ended up with Akash. We found each other at Cellar, him stroking Krystal's hair in a corner booth. No. I didn't want Akash, but I'd be damned if I'd share him with Krystal. I drew him away down the two blocks to his penthouse that looked like an eighteen-year-old had won the lottery and thought, "A penthouse! That'll do." There were alcohol bottles, dirty clothes, and papers strewn so heavily through each room that you couldn't see the floor. He was already way too drunk. That was the night he started crying.

"Why?" he asked me. "Why am I going to be alone? What's wrong with me?" Fuck. This wasn't any better than staying home alone. I didn't want to, but I stayed with him. He passed out in bed, his pager dying on the nightstand while I watched *Saturday Night Live* because I couldn't find the remote to change it.

In the morning, as he stirred, I rolled in his direction and he shoved me away. That was it. He wasn't worth anything anymore. Creeping to the door barefoot just in case he wasn't faking sleep, I shame walked to the street in my cheap-looking black dress doused with champagne.

At Fernando's, everyone was just starting to eat. I thought Tico food would be easy for me, like Mexican. A lot of meat and vegetables, but this was different. Everything was wrapped in carbs or too awkward to eat without them. Everyone would look at my weird habits. Plus, we'd just eaten but I couldn't be rude.

One of his aunts watched me closely as I carefully picked out just the meat and vegetables from the pots. She muttered something in Spanish and though I didn't know what it was, I could tell she was saying I was taking only the best, most expensive pieces. Fernando answered her, and I could understand "diabetes" and "low carb." She didn't believe it.

When one of his cousins asked if I wanted a drink, it took all my strength to say, "Sure," instead of "Oh, god, yes." But it was beer. Fat-making, sluggish, kind-of-warm beer. Beer never got me drunk. I got full and slow-feeling way before it could. I nipped at it slowly, knowing it and the carbs weren't worth it while his cousins began dancing salsa on the patio. I was good at salsa—I'd danced competitively in South Korea. And I loved being the center of attention. But something here was off, and I pretended I couldn't dance when Maria asked me to join. Rightly, she rolled her eyes and gave a mean laugh.

"I need to check my email," I told Fernando and stole away to the attic, our designated room. The house wasn't air conditioned, which was fine—it you weren't in the attic. Here, it was a steam room, the first step into hell.

There was a message from Chirag. "Happy New Year, babydoll," he wrote. "You're two hours ahead of me, and I know you might not get this. But it's almost 2012 now, and I wish I were with you. I'm staying in tonight, email me if you get a chance. Love you." In that roasting attic, I wanted to write back with everything in me. But when my message was clacked in, and the "Love you more" was signed, the internet disappeared and my laptop began to fall into sleep from a tired battery.

I'd bought as much time as I could. I had to go back downstairs. It was almost midnight, and Fernando's family was gathered around the small pool. There had to have been at least twenty of them. The boys lit firecrackers on the concrete, the girls moved in lazy circles in the pool. "*Feliz año nuevo!*" they howled as the countdown began. Fernando kissed me at midnight, a sparkler in his hand and me so very, very aware of all the eyes darting towards us.

San Jose looked like it didn't belong, a bustling mini metro surrounded by volcanoes that still rumbled. I'd found work in the thumping heart of downtown right before arriving, teaching English at a culinary school. It came complete with a semi-permanent visa promise once I'd completed the Teaching English as a Foreign Language (TEFL) certification. For four hours each day, I ducked into a classroom and trudged through curriculum. Then it was another six hours of teaching students who had no interest in learning. Two hours per day on the bus. At least. We were living in Maria's father's closet now, a twin bed folded into what was supposed to be a pantry.

After two days, Maria threw a sizzling pan against the wall and screamed at Fernando for using some drops of milk for his coffee. "I'll buy you some more milk, calm down," he told her.

"Fuck the milk!" she said. "It's not about the milk!" And she looked at me. English. I was supposed to hear this.

"I can't take it anymore," he told me. "We're moving right now, I don't care about the cost." When we shoved our dirty clothes back into the bags, she smiled, kissed our cheeks, and I could hear the deadbolt click behind us.

I hated teaching. I despised it in Korea, in my graduate program, and while in London. But I was an American with an advanced English degree in Costa Rica. What else was I supposed to do?

"I'm sorry," the director of the school said when I handed over my TEFL certificate. "We just can't support any more visas. But you're welcome to keep teaching. Part-time. Quietly."

"I just spent two thousand dollars on this certificate because you promised me a work visa," I said.

"Well ..." he said slowly, "who do you think immigration will believe? Me or you?" I realized the Skype interview, the contract, it didn't mean anything. But I stayed. I was still getting unemployment coupled with a now very under-the-table job.

And I wrote to Chirag from the two-bedroom home in Moravia Fernando had overpaid a deposit on. There are no addresses in Costa Rica. Addresses are directional and depend on landmarks. We lived in "the green house 150 km from Pollo Loco no. 13." Nobody would ever find me if I disappeared.

There was a mangosteen tree in the backyard, which was adorable for a day until I had to spend every weekend picking up rotting fruit. Every house, including ours, had tall steel gates backing up against the sidewalk. Beggars would come daily, hourly, door to door hollering "Upe!" I hid when I saw them, crouched down on the couch. Men with machetes followed next, clanging along the metal bars and offering lawn cutting services. Tarantulas nestled into the backyard beneath their trap doors. Sometimes I could see them scurrying across the yard.

"What if they get inside?" I asked Fernando. "Will you kill them?"

"You can't kill them!" he said. "That's like trying to squish a bird with a broom!" And the national bird, a thrush, screeched from dusk 'til dawn. I called it the Doodoo bird, its incessant, "Doo-doo-do, doo-doo-do, doo-doo, doo-doo, dwip! Dwip!" drilling a madness into my skull. Sometimes it stopped unexpectedly. Sometimes it tried out an addition to its insane song. When it went quiet, I went still and hoped it was dead. *Was* it dead? It was so silent outside. But, no. It always started again.

I became Craigslist desperate, scouring the pit for something—*anything*—I could do for money that wouldn't make me leave the house. Keep me from going *out there*. From getting a quick film of grime and dirt rained down on me from the city garbage.

"We need furniture," I told Fernando. We'd been sleeping on a comforter on the tile floor for weeks while cockroaches scurried over us. I would have slept in the hammock outside if the dengue-full mosquitoes wouldn't have descended on me like a plague. My one bright spot of the day was the neighbor's dogs, Stella and Mischa. One white, one black. They didn't care about my bad Spanish or stare untrustingly at me from their post. They raced to me every time I was outside, licked at my palms between the gates. Fernando talked to the neighbors, who wanted to get rid of Mischa. He was too old, that black lab. They'd bought Stella to make Mischa feel and act younger again, but it didn't work.

"They said you can walk Mischa," Fernando told me. "Whenever you want. Here's the code to their gate. They want him gone." I walked Mischa every single day. Together, we poked around the neighborhood, and I bought him cuts of expensive meat from the carniceria. He loved me, and I him. Just as we were.

Wal-Mart is a fancy place in Costa Rico. Much more than Mundo Pequeño. It took an hour to get there by bus. We found a bed frame, mattress, couch, and table. "Cuanto es?" I asked a clerk. There was no price.

"Ah. ¿Inglés?" he asked. Thank god.

"Yes."

"No se, I ... I don't know. There's no price."

"I know. That's why I asked you." Fernando looked on in awe.

"Well. You know as much as me then," said the clerk.

"Can you, like, look it up or something?"

"Eh, tranquilo, tranquilo," he said. "Pura vida." I fucking hate that saying. It's everywhere here. Pure life, my ass. That's all *anyone* said here. "It's no big deal," he said, and walked away. Next to the table was a much cheaper one with an easy to unstick tag. I grabbed the sticker, stuck it on the table we wanted, and told Fernando, "Take it. Let's just buy it like this." The cashier didn't look at the freakishly low price twice.

Fernando asked the cashier something in Spanish. Whatever the answer, it wasn't good.

"What'd you say? What'd you ask?"

"I asked how long delivery would take."

"And?"

"Up to ninety days."

"But we live ten miles away!"

"I know."

We left with nothing but what we could carry and cradle on the bus. A hair dryer, dish soap, food and shampoo. In the parking lot, I just couldn't take it anymore. The bag broke open, spilling our meager belongings all over the concrete, and I broke down crying. Fernando looked like he wanted to join me, but instead he just held me and said,

"I know. I know."

"This is a miserable country," I wrote to Chirag.

"So come home. Come to me."

"I can't."

"Well, we're getting settled!" I wrote to Sam. "It's very different from anywhere else I've been. How are you?"

"I'm pregnant," she wrote. "I'm freaking the fuck out."

"Jennifer? Where are you?" Michelle wrote. "You haven't been online! I need to tell you about my latest boy drama." Her, I didn't write back. Not right away.

I could feel the tension in the culinary school getting stickier. More dangerous. New twists were being added. They didn't like me, and I didn't belong there. I walked Mischa in the evenings and told him all about it. He panted in empathy as our hips ground up the hills.

By midnight, I was refreshing Craigslist every night, filtering by "telecommuting" when I found a spiteful posting in the writing gigs section. *I need a fantastic, flawless writer who will <u>actually</u> meet deadlines and has a professional attitude. No hacks, no students, no losers. I'm a professional and I expect you to be the same. Don't waste my time. Send resume and writing samples. If you can't follow these (very simple) directions, don't bother. Put 'pro' and your last name in the subject line so I can tell that you can, at the very least, follow basic directions.*

So it wasn't just here. Assholes were everywhere. I had nothing better to do but reply. I was professional, I always was. "I'm curious what kind of response you expect with a condescending post like that?" I wrote. "Even if a quality writer did read it, they wouldn't apply."

Within the hour, I had a response. "I Googled you," said "Ken." "Master's and director experience, huh? I'm assuming you wrote grants. Send me a sample?" It was a challenge, a demand to showcase my skills. Of course I could write. He may as well have called me chicken. "Good stuff," he said. "You want a job?"

Yes. More than anything. Give me something to hold onto.

"I ran a big newspaper for twenty years, now I have my own writing services business," he explained. "One of my clients needs a writer to create 300-word descriptions for 500 children's trading cards, all based on Portland-area destinations. I'll pay you $100 each, including for the test sample. I'm hiring three writers, but the client is ultimately choosing two. You interested?"

Three hundred words for one hundred bucks a pop? It would take me fifteen minutes to write those, tops. Five days and one sample later, I got my response. "Well," wrote Ken, "turns out the client only wants you. How many can you deliver per week? I'll pay with PayPal."

As many as you want, Ken. The first hundred dollars was already in my account.

"I quit that effing school job," I wrote to Chirag.

"Good. You seemed miserable. You coming home?"

"I am home." This was not home.

It was February, and Fernando had been in school for one month. "These professors are idiots," he said every night as he rounded his now sagging back over his books. "They're making me take an English proficiency test now— and making me pay for it of course."

"Don't they know you're a native English speaker? That you went to an English high school and undergraduate program in the US?"

"They don't care," he said. "I speak better English than the people administering it." He got 90 percent on that test. Some of the questions had wrong multiple-choice answers. I saw it myself.

Ken's work began to grow. He referred me to others. On a whim, I emailed a local tourist company operated by a Canadian and asked if they were hiring writers. "Your portfolio's great," the owner said. "We have no money to pay, but would you be interested in writing for comped trips? I can get you hotels, transportation, entry fees to attractions, etc." Definitely. Of course. Get paid to see the good parts of this place? I mean, it had to get better, right?

It did. For Valentine's Day, I was sent to a butterfly farm followed by a coffee farm tour. At the butterfly farm, blue morphs scattered around me while translucent beauties dried their wings. Butterflies slowed down at feeding stations, suckling on opened fruits and juices. "They're drunk," said a worker. "We put alcohol in the fruit. They like it." I'm right there with you, guys.

Inside, employees were bent over lit-up stations, carefully putting golden and iridescent cocoons in packaging. "We ship these all over the world," a host explained. "To places where they're in need of these species. Costa Rica is home to more species of butterflies than anywhere else in the world."

And the butterfly release. God, it was incredible. When new butterflies with barely dried wings were ready, they would be brought into the meshed-in sanctuary—a space big enough for me to spend hours walking through—all bundled up together in what looked like a laundry bag. "Watch out!" said the host, flipping the bag open. The butterflies flapped with madness, surprised at their new way of traveling. But they were fresh and got tired fast. Most flew right at me, smacked against my face and clothes, and clung with gratitude to every inch of me. For a few minutes, I was their savior and they made me magnificent.

"I've been writing," I told Chirag in one message.

"I know."

"No, I've been writing. Poetry. Like I haven't in years."

"That's good, babydoll. What you gonna do with it?"

"I don't know yet. I'm thinking about trying to publish it. At least send it around and see." I was having my work published already, of course. My write-ups of butterfly farms, coffee tours, and local restaurants were coupled with a photo and byline. But that wasn't what I wanted to write about. I wanted to write about Chirag, about how the distance wasn't keeping us apart. About how this strange country reminded me of him, oddly enough. His brown hands as I counted colones into bus drivers' palms. His lips, which I'd found in a young boy's pouty face. His black hair, everywhere. Everywhere.

My first poem was picked up by a fairly reputable American journal. I ordered a copy for Chirag, had it sent to the condo whose address I knew by heart. "How to Oil an Indian Man's Hair." It was our memories, his directions, my remembering us back into life.

xiv.
Identity Crises

AS I GOT INTO Scott's car for him to take me to school, he pulled a small box out of his pocket. "I got something for you," he said. It wasn't wrapped.

"Contacts?" I asked. "But I have contacts."

"These are brown contacts," he said.

"Okay ...."

"Brown eyes are so much prettier than green. Like Natalie Portman. Damn, she's so beautiful. Don't you think? Green eyes are kind of, like, reptile-like. They're weird."

"But you have green eyes, too."

"Not like you, though. Mine are normal green. Yours are like, *really* green. You should put them in now," he said, dumping the box in my lap. I did. They weren't prescription and I couldn't see very far. The person staring back from the pull-down mirror looked almost like me, but not quite.

"That's so much better," he said.

Leaving me at the front gate with only two minutes to spare, lest I have time to stray and talk to a boy, I walk-ran towards the blurry building. An arm slid over my shoulder at the halfway point. "I miss my friend," Michelle said. It had been months. I'd been watching her, sure. I thought I'd lost her.

"Me, too."

"Who's that who dropped you off?"

"My boyfriend. Scott."

"He's cute!" she said.

Kerri didn't think so. Well, she probably thought he was cute enough, but something about Scott made her antsy. They'd met a couple of times, and Scott told me afterward that she was weird. "She's just quiet," I said, taking offense for her. Like me. "No, she's weird," he said.

Somehow, I had wrangled both of them into going to a basketball game on a Friday evening. I don't know why—I hated watching sports. But it seemed like a very high school thing to do. "Okay, but I promised my mom I wouldn't leave school grounds," Kerri said. "She's been all on my ass lately. So you have to promise you can't blame me if he wants to leave and I have to stay!"

"Okay, okay I promise," I said. I didn't know what she was flipping out over.

Scott lasted one quarter before he was ready to leave. "This is boring," he said. "And I love basketball! So that tells you how boring it is. Let's go to a restaurant or something. Drive around."

"I don't know...," I said, searching for words. Kerri was screaming at me with her eyes.

"Come on, this is lame."

"We can't, Kerri's not allowed," I said, laughing and shoving her lightly. Immediately she got up and, without a word, stalked out of the gym.

I should have gone after her. I should have apologized to the stars for her, but I'd never said I was sorry to anyone and meant it. How hard is it when you mean it? Those words turn into boulders. Instead, I just let her go.

"I told you she was weird," Scott said.

CHAPTER FOURTEEN

I COULDN'T RUN in Costa Rica. I tried. Treadmills were the only option—it was deadly to be on the streets at full speed, winding around potholes while the constant horns blared in fear and anger. But the treadmill I just couldn't do. Boredom spilled out my pores and something in the air made it so I couldn't breathe in fully. "Did you ever run, Mischa?" I asked him on our walk. He didn't answer. He probably never had.

"Do you want me to teach you how to lift?" Fernando asked when I complained that I felt fat. Every day, we walked to the hot, dirty little gym on the corner. He showed me proper form and laughed when I shook my head "no" without my realizing it whenever I'd had enough of chest presses, flies, kickbacks, and rows. "Hey, look," he said. "They have yoga classes here." Yoga. Like math, where everyone knows the same language and nobody would realize I didn't belong.

I still plugged away at the elliptical, but followed Fernando around his weight training. Yoga became a daily ritual, where I could fill in the spaces I didn't know, get relief from Spanish, immerse myself in the Sanskrit. My body was wrung out like a wet cloth; I could feel my muscles lengthening. Actually *feel* it. Maybe it was the heat, maybe it was the humidity. But I slid into wheel, crow, and headstands with an ease that had always stayed far, far out of my reach before.

And the work, it kept pouring in, and the words back out of me, an ouroboros of a cycle. Every poem I wrote was for Chirag. I couldn't help it. Even when the setting was the overgrown rosemary bush out back or the rainforest where the travel company sent me ziplining, it all came back to him. I picked up a contract writing web content for an insurance company at $75 per 200-word description. They wanted every state, then every major city in every state. I was drowning in the work, in the words, and used my contracts as a way to keep space between Fernando and me. He suffocated himself in books while I pulled the wordy soil over me all day. All night.

During my first visa run, to Medellin, I didn't realize Americans need yellow fever shots to get *out* of Colombia, but not in. The city was modern and clean, but I had a fall-apart hostel with an iron bed and a shower with just a garden hose pulled through the window and a sink that had recently crashed to the floor, spilling porcelain everywhere. "Better than our shocker shower!" Fernando wrote when I emailed him about it. The infamous Tico shocker showers looked like an American contraption at first blush—until you realized there was electrical wiring alongside the shower head. Each cleansing came with a fifty-fifty shot of a small electrical zap. But not enough to kill you. It couldn't be that easy.

In Medellin, I didn't have to pretend. I could write to Chirag with abandon, tell him about the obese Botero sculptures all around the city. The jolly street vendor yelling, "¡Fresas *fresca*! ¡Fresas *grande*!" as he peddled his strawberries up and down the street. He made it all sound so sexual. I sent Chirag sexually charged stories about us, too. About him. About how I wanted to feel his thumb on my clit and his hardness inside me. But the real things, the things that mattered, I could only get out in poetry.

Back at the airport, the desk agent started chattering in a different kind of Spanish to his friend. "You, eh, you stamp? Where?" he asked.

"It's in there," I said, thinking he meant the immigration stamp.

"No, no. Es ... yellow fever? Where?" Fuck. I just knew.

Right then, I just knew.

"I don't ... I don't have it?" It was a Saturday. There's no way clinics would be open until Monday.

"You need," he said. "You need." Then he handed my passport to his co-worker and they both started laughing. I knew why. The photo was taken when I was at my heaviest, about 250 pounds of disgustingness. "He say. We think," said the agent, "you look *so much better* now. This. You stay like this," he said, a command.

"Steroids from cancer make you fat," I said. I'd never had cancer. "Is there anything I can do about this stamp right now? I need to leave." I need to get out of this country.

"Let me see my boss," he said, muttering Spanish into a walkie-talkie. "He coming."

His boss had a moustache fuzzy as a caterpillar, and walked faster when he saw I looked white. "I'm sorry," he said. "There's nothing we can do. Well, there is, but—"

"What is it?"

"Well, you could buy another ticket through Panama to Costa Rica. You don't need shots to go from here to Panama, or Panama to Costa Rica. But it's expensive."

"How much?"

It was an extra $600 on top of the ticket I already had. "Just give it to me," I said. Fuck it. I was making a lot of money. And I couldn't bear it anymore, the freezing garden shower and the sexy strawberries in the street.

Fernando picked me up at the airport in the thousand-dollar white station wagon he'd bought when taking the bus, which required hours to go a few miles, began to gnaw at his sanity. His school would have been walkable in America. A long walk, but still. Here, with all the ditches and pollution weighing you down, and all his books, it just wasn't.

"I've been thinking," I began. "All these local clients asking me to write about Costa Rica? There's a huge medical tourism industry here. I mean *huge*."

"I know," he said.

"You can get plastic surgery for, like, a quarter of what it costs in the US."

"I know."

"What if I got a tummy tuck and breast lift? It's probably the only time I could ever afford it."

"If that's what you want."

"It is."

Chirag still asked me daily, between his promises and declarations of love, if I was coming back. When. He asked what color couch I'd like because he was buying a new one. "It's your couch," I'd written back. "It will be ours," was the reply.

If I were going back, I needed to be better. Thinner. No amount of working out was going to get rid of this baggy skin that hung at my waist like a skirt. Those sad, sagging breasts. What if I went back with a flat stomach and perky tits? Would he really, truly want me then, enough to tell his family? I had no solid plans, not yet, but I knew surgery like this would take some serious recovery time. The scars on my wrists from the teenage years looked like thin spider veins now. I didn't even mind them.

"Will you help me set up an appointment?" I asked Fernando.

"Sure."

I went to the first doctor whose name sounded non-Latin and whose website was in English. A lot of Western doctors relocate to Costa Rica where they can manipulate the tax system, the medical rules, and bask in the glory of charging what they like in a country where cost of living is ridiculously low. "Now," the doctor said, a gangly white man with glasses, "I think you're a very good candidate for a tummy tuck. Very good. But your breasts, I'd recommend implants as well as a lift."

"How big will they be without it?"

"I can't really say for sure, not until we get in there. But I'm guessing maybe a small B or a full A." I wore a DD, had for years.

"Uh, no. No, I don't want implants." For some reason, *that* was crossing the line.

"Okay, your call," he said. "But ... I also recommend spot liposuction. Just to get rid of some pockets of fat left over from before you lost the weight."

"Where?"

He began circling everything that was wrong with me with a Sharpie. The insides of my knees (really? My *knees* were fat?). My saddlebags (I hadn't even noticed). The insides of my thighs (okay, he got me there). "You know what, actually, if you're up for it, I really think you should get a thigh lift, too. It would really help with the sagging that liposuction just can't fix," he said.

"Then what about my arms?" I asked. I was impulse shopping. I hated my arms, but they hadn't even been on the list when I'd arrived.

"Oh, yes," he said. "The arms definitely."

"But I don't want the big scarring," I said. "I don't know what's worse—fat or a huge scar to my elbow."

"Oh, no, no," he said. "You're a good candidate for a mini upper arm lift. The scar would be thin and just go about five inches from your armpit to your bicep. About here," he said, creating stitches with his Sharpie. "You could still wear short-sleeved shirts," he said.

"Okay," I said. "Okay. Add it on."

"Is next week okay for you?" he asked. "The receptionist can schedule your appointment."

"Sure."

I only wrote Chirag about it when the non-refundable deposit was paid and I was already going off most of my supplements in preparation for the nine-hour surgery. I'd never had a serious, cut you open surgery in my life. I'd never been put under.

"You don't need it," Chirag wrote me. "But you'll do what you want to do. Call me before you go in?"

Call him. I hadn't heard his voice since I left at Christmas. "Okay," I replied.

The morning of surgery, Fernando had school so I took the bus. I feigned being too nervous the night before for sex—and knew that after surgery, if I made it, I had endless excuses ahead of me. "Wish me luck," I told Mischa as I scurried out the gate. He was confused. Why was I leaving so early? Without him?

I almost missed my bus stop, it looked so unfamiliar from these high windows. Descending, I was in front of a movie theater. *The Skin I Live In* was playing. It was the only film showing. Really? Did this mean something? Fifteen minutes until my appointment. The glass double doors of the clinic glistened across the street.

My phone was a pay as you go burner, one that Fernando couldn't and wouldn't trace. That was sheer luck and cheapness—not planning. Chirag was waiting.

"Bibijaan," he said. "Where are you?"

"Outside, across from the clinic." His voice sounded just as deep and gravel-strewn as I remembered, the familiarity of it stinging my eyes.

He sighed. "It'll be okay," he said. "Don't worry."

"I read about this stuff. A little," I said. "It's not the surgery that can kill you. It's the anesthesia."

"It'll be okay," he repeated.

"I should ... I should go in," I said. I didn't want to be sad before getting cut open and Frankensteined back together.

"I love you," he said. "Call me when you wake up."

In the clinic, everyone was rushing around like I wasn't about to risk my life for a flat stomach. Like I hadn't just paid $12,000 cash to be put on the butcher's block. They made me remove all my jewelry, all my makeup, even my nail polish, and left me cold and shaking in an icy changing room with just a thin robe for comfort. The prep nurse didn't speak any English.

"Hello, there!" the doctor said as he strode in, cheery and alert. He began circling all my problems again, took photos (no face showing), penned codes into my skin with his faithful Sharpie. "Now, we're going to try and do everything at once, but I can't absolutely promise that. You may need to come back after you heal for the rest of the surgeries."

"I can't come back. I need this all done now."

He looked me curiously in the eye. "We'll do our best," he said.

I walked into the operating room, though he offered to wheel me in. No. I wasn't broken yet.

"Alejandro here is your anesthesiologist," the doctor said.

"Hola," the man with the mask whispered. He wore glasses. I couldn't see his face.

"I'm going to go scrub in," said the doctor. "I'll see you on the other side."

"Tranquilo," said Alejandro as he adjusted the gas over my face. *I can't see your face!* A nurse grabbed my arms and pinned them down to crucify me on the table. And it was so cold. It was so ungodly cold. I once volunteered at a veterinary clinic for a few days, where they strapped female cats down just like this to spay them. When the cats were under, their heads lolled sideways and their tongues hung out while the vet scooped our intestine, made some nips and then shoved them back in. They looked so funny, it had made me laugh. Would I look like that?

"Count down from ten, porfa," said Alejandro. *Show me your face.* "Breathe deep." Ten. Nine. Nothing was happening. Oh fuck, oh fuck, oh fuck. Was this a huge mistake? Would this masked man be the last thing I ever saw? Eight. Seven. It wasn't working. *Your gas isn't working!* Six. That's all I remember.

"You need to breathe!" a woman screamed. God, she was annoying. Leave me alone. "I need you to breathe!" she repeated. *Shut up!* What was her problem? I *am* breathing. "Breathe!" Fuck, it was cold. My arms hurt. "There you go. There you go. She's breathing!" she said.

I woke up in a hospital room that looked like the ones back home. My body hurt all over, but in a dull way, not those really painful sharp ways. *Just stop it. You did this to yourself. There's no point complaining now.* Okay. Besides, the pain wasn't really all that bad. It was the cold that was unbearable. It was so, so cold. Some kind of weird rubber snowsuit-like things were wrapped around my legs, slowly squeezing and releasing them. They were heated. I was rolled into mounds of blankets, but the cold was coming from deep inside.

"You awake?" asked a nurse who appeared at the doorway.

"Are they all done?" I asked.

"¿Que?"

"The surgeries. Did they do all of them?"

"Si, yes," she said. "All done."

"I need ... I need to go to the bathroom."

"Number one or two?"

"I need to pee," I said.

"So pee." I need you to help me, bitch! I can't move. "Go ahead," she said. "It's okay."

"No, I need—"

"You have catheter." A what? Nobody told me about that. She reached down and held up a bag, already full of yellow. "You believe me now? You already use it." I tried, waiting for the sensation of wet warmth between my thighs that never came. I felt a little better, but still like I needed to pee. Just not quite as badly as before.

"Where's my phone?" I asked.

"All your things here," she said, pointing to a bucket an arm's reach away. "You hungry? We have chicken noodle soup." *Don't eat!* my mind screeched. *You just had all that fat sucked out of you. You'd better keep it off.*

"No," I said, "I'm not hungry."

"Okay. You buzz if you need me."

I called Chirag immediately. "How long has it been?" I asked.

"About ten hours. How do you feel? Are you okay?"

"I don't know. I'm fine I guess. I'm so cold."

"It'll be okay."

It took hours to feel warm again. In the hardest of times, I wanted to die—truly die—because I couldn't handle the iciness anymore. But it thawed, slowly, and I found the one channel in English. It was a marathon of *The Middle*, a show I'd never watched before, but the unimportant crises of the characters circled me in warmth. Somehow, I dozed off again and when I woke it was morning.

"I need to work," I told the nurse, and she begrudgingly brought me my laptop from the chair across the room. All the tubes tied me the bed.

"You should rest," she said. "You hungry? Grilled cheese for breakfast." God, I was hungry.

"No, not hungry," I said as I opened my laptop. The weight it put on my stomach was comforting even in the dull ache. A body armor.

"You have to eat. This morning, you have to," she said.

"Okay." She brought the triangle pieces that smelled like heaven. I let them cool so I could peel away just the cheese. No carbs, no carbs. I squished the bread and shoved it deep in my bag.

"Your boyfriend, he call and say he come soon," the nurse said when she picked up the empty tray.

I refused to be rolled anywhere. When Fernando came, I was already three assignments deep and counting the money in my head.

"Hey!" he said. "You look better than I thought you would."

"I think I look better than I feel." It was a little hard to walk when they de-tubed me, but not much. I was just slower than normal, and with bandages on most of my body I felt awkward. Like everyone was watching.

"This bodysuit, you need to wear it at least four weeks," the doctor said when he checked me out, Fernando by my side. "And the compression bra. These are what will reshape your body. Right now, your skin is trying to 'stick' back to the muscle. We cut through a lot for this surgery. It's more invasive than a caesarean. It'll take time to heal. Only remove the bodysuit to shower. There's a flap here at the bottom, see? So you can just unlatch it to use the bathroom."

"Okay," I said. I hadn't known I'd be strapped up like some acrobatic freak. I did almost no research. I was too scared of what I might find.

"And this," he said, "this is what's going to drain the excess fluids for you. I'll probably be able to remove it in a week or so." I hadn't even noticed. A tube ran from somewhere in my midsection, under the bodysuit, into this little disc the size of a smoke alarm that was already dribbly with blood, puss and yellowy things. "You'll probably need to drain it from time to time. It's easy, see?" he said, tapping the little plug. "Are you okay doing that?"

"I'll do it," Fernando said. "It's pretty cool." He was deep into med school now, so I was the ideal roommate/lab rat.

"Great," the doctor said. "That's about it! You'll have liposuction massages every few days. The receptionist will give you your schedule. Any questions?"

"What about painkillers?" I asked. I didn't need them, but I liked to hoard them. Just in case. Sometimes I would take two Vicodin just to check out for a while.

The doctor smiled. "It doesn't work like that here," he said. "Take some Tylenol if you really need to."

The liposuction hurt the most, a kind of bruising that felt like it went all the way through my bones to the other side. The cuts, though, barely even registered. Still, I refused to look down when I showered. I only felt the poky little stitches with my fingertips. But those liposuction massages, they hurt like a motherfucker. And the damn nurse kept trying to clean my bellybutton during massage appointments.

I crab-crawled backward and away from her every time. "We need to do this," she said. "The doctor, he make a new bellybutton for you. Need to make sure it's clean." It didn't hurt, necessarily, but the thought of anything coming near my bellybutton, let alone a Q-tip that would dive deep, made me nauseated.

"No, no, no, no, no!" I beg-yelled until two other nurses had to hold me down for the violation. "You such a good girl otherwise," the nurse said sadly. "No complaints like the other Americans. They so weak, but you, you strong. Just this. This, why you have to be so panicked over?"

I got used to peeing with the bodysuit. Kind of. I still wore underwear over it as if I needed to, and twice I pulled down only my panties and pissed all over the bodysuit, forgetting about the flap. I couldn't sleep in the bed with Fernando anymore. Part of it was the mattress being too soft, and part of it was being too close to him. I took to sleeping on the hard couch, and he moved onto the floor beside me. Once, three days after surgery, I woke up covered in blood. I didn't want to wake or alarm him. "Hey," I whispered. "Hey."

"What's up?" he murmured in his sleep.

"Don't freak out, but I think ... I think something's wrong."

With the light on, I could tell it wasn't fresh blood. The drainer had come open in the night and I was blanketed in my own, sick insides. But I kept working. I interviewed Costa Rica's most prominent living poet with the drainer tucked as discreetly as it could be into the back of my pants. The poet offered me a joint while he showed me his backyard and library. I couldn't believe I was getting high with this pseudo-famous writer while my sickness leaked down my pants.

It was May. I ached to work out again, could feel the fat from lack of movement start to slither back on. "You want to see?" the nurses asked at every appointment while they checked my scars and I avoided the mirrors. I was still too scared. "It look good! You look so much better. It healing so good," they said, trying to cajole me into it. I wasn't having it.

Two weeks later, I almost fell over at the Wal-Mart deli counter because I tried to lean my hip against the now-familiar railing. But the doctor had taken my hip. Cut it clean off. The rail was farther away than it used to be.

"I want to see Irazú," I told Fernando the next morning. "I need to see the crater."

"You sure you're up for it?"

"I'm bored. I'm going crazy."

"Okay," he said, and drove me to the volcano's rim. The blue below was so brilliant, it looked like a cartoon. It was hard to walk to the rim, but I made it.

"What's that?" Fernando asked me, and I looked down. Shit. One of my scars had started bleeding. The effort of hiking had stretched the stiches clean apart.

"It's nothing, I'm fine. It's kind of pretty, right?" I asked as the redness burst like spring.

xv.

Gambling

"YOU EVER NOTICE how your dad always turns off the computer when someone comes in the room?" Scott asked.

No. But I didn't pay much attention to my dad anyway. The computer was kept right in the living room, one of those big, lumbering models that relied on dial-up and AOL discs. "He does," Scott said. "I think he's having an online affair."

"That's stupid," I said, but that weekend when my mom went to Reno for a line dance convention—the first time she'd taken a non-family vacation that I'd ever known—my dad acted quick.

"I'm going to Eugene for a big auction," he said as soon as he dropped my mom off at the airport. "You'll be okay here, right?" This was weird. He'd never leave Scott and me alone, and he'd never been to an out of town auction. Ever.

"Uh, sure," I said. A weekend alone together? Done deal.

"Let's look at your dad's email," Scott said as soon as the gravel stopped wailing under my dad's tires. Okay, fine, if it would shut him up.

His email was so stuffed with porn I couldn't believe it was all being contained. "Who's Sharon?" Scott asked, as if I knew.

Their emails went back for months. Sharon was also married, for about twenty years, and hated her husband. She lived in some tiny town called Silverton, closer to Portland than Medford. "Be there soon," my dad had written to her just that morning.

"Love you, can't wait to see you," she'd replied. We found photos. She was petite with black hair curled like a 50s

179

housewife with fair skin and red lips. She looked like an aging Snow White.

"Got him!" Scott said with glee in his eyes. Crap.

"So what the hell are we supposed to do now?" I asked.

"You should tell your mom," Scott said seriously. "She deserves—she deserves to know."

"She hasn't even landed in Reno yet!"

"You're right. We should wait 'til Sunday. Let her have some fun, let your dad have some fun!" he said with a laugh. "Let *us* have some fun first." Okay. Okay.

I wasn't mad about the affair. It's not like Sharon was the first. I always knew my dad fucked around, and who knows? Maybe he'd had this real kind of affair before. Once, as he was barbequing steak out back and I hung around watching the blood sizzle out, he turned to me suddenly and said, "You be careful. You have that wander in you, just like me. Can't be still. You be careful." I hadn't known what he'd meant.

Scott and I splayed across the living room floor, watching MTV and having the kind of sex that left me with good, roughed-up hair. On Sunday, I called my mom's hotel room. "Jennifer? What's wrong? Is it Boots?" Boots, her stupid deaf, fat dog. He was all she cared about.

"It's my dad," I said.

"What? Who—what happened? Where is he?"

"He's not here."

"What do you mean he's not there? Where the fuck is he?"

"He has a girlfriend. Up north. He's there. We found the emails." That shut her up. But the static, it was so loud.

"I'm coming home. *Now,*" she said, and hung up.

"Your dad's in *trouble* now," said Scott, eager to sit back and watch the explosions. Shit. What did I just do?

CHAPTER FIFTEEN

"SEE?" the doctor asked, patting the wounds after pulling out the last of the stitches. "Perfect! It's healing so nicely." Finally, weeks later, I looked. It wasn't me. The flat stomach, the belly button a different shape. I could feel my legs, I could feel my chest, but in my middle nothing. Tracing my fingers over the flatness, it felt like a foot that had fallen asleep.

"I can't feel anything," I said. The doctor shrugged.

"It's nerve damage. It happens. We cut through a lot, remember. It can take years for sensations to return. Or they might not ever."

"My arms look lumpy," I said. They were half their size, sure. But unnatural.

"That will settle," the doctor said.

"So ... how long 'til I can work out again?" I asked.

"Whenever your body tells you that you can," he said. "You'll probably find that you tire easily, and there's a *tiny* bit of your arm that's still healing. Right here, see? But otherwise, you're okay. The body, it heals so quickly. It's an amazing instrument, isn't it?"

I turned sideways to look in the mirror. No dips, no swells in my stomach. "Yes. Yes, it is."

The tourist company was sending me to La Fortuna waterfall, then the Venado caves, and finally to Manuel Antonio. At La Fortuna, I'd stay in a five-star resort and take a horseback ride to the waterfall. In Manuel Antonio, a catamaran boat around the coastline. And for once, for once, Fernando could go with me.

"This is incredible," he said, maneuvering the complaining station wagon around the jungle roads. "I can't believe you get paid for this."

"I don't get paid," I reminded him. "It's just free."

"Same thing," he said. "Hey, you want some queso? Trust me. It's not like in town."

Along the sickening sharp rainforest roads, little huts popped up at random with square, rusty signs. "Queso Fresca!" one said, and there was a smidgen of a dirty pathway to pull over. "It's palmito," Fernando said, dropping a white ball into my lap. "Try it."

"I've had it," I said. He brings it home from the cheese shop.

"Not like this."

He was right. It was a wonder ball, perfectly straddled between salty and sweet. Rich. Creamy. My tongue had never known anything like it.

"Amazing, right?" he asked. "There are some good things in this country. Not much, but some."

At La Fortuna, the resort was expansive with hot springs of various sizes and degrees that were spread throughout the greenery. Towels shaped into swans floated on the beds. Dinner was a buffet with so many meats, cheeses and vegetables I didn't bother keeping track. I downed a saketini, a glass of sheer vodka and sake with nothing else, but struggled. Maybe it was my new stomach, but I just didn't need it anymore.

The Venado Caves were a short drive away, with the tour starting as the first rays of sun snuck over the volcanic horizons the next morning. "These caves were under the sea for millions of years," explained the guide as he fitted us with rain boots and headlamps. "Only recently has it risen to the surface. You're one of the first few humans to ever experience it."

"Why do we need these boots?" I asked. They were already rubbing at my heels.

"Sometimes the water gets neck deep. It's not too bad

this time of year, though," he said. "But, just so you know ... people get claustrophobic down there. *Really* claustrophobic. I know I already told you, but if you get stressed in the dark or have claustrophobia, you really shouldn't do this. I won't be able to take you out the other way."

"I'm fine. We're fine," I said.

"Also, there are a lot of bats. They won't bite if you don't bother them, but they can fly quite close to you. They don't have the best sense of direction. Oh, and it's strange down there. Prehistoric. There might be things, odd things, that you've never seen before. If you feel something touch or crawl on you in the dark, don't panic. Just ... don't panic." What the hell?

He led us down a rolling path, alongside pastures that looked like they were out of children's books. "Here we go," said the guide, "watch your head. And just—don't think about what's in the water." Darkness. In seconds.

"Here, you'll see fossilized remains of sea life preserved in the walls," the guide said, using his headlamp to highlight the ancient whale bits. "See its teeth? Look up. All those little moving bodies? Those are the bats. They don't like the light." *Then maybe you shouldn't shine it on them.* "Okay, all lights off. *Off!*" he said. In the blackness, the bats rustled. The water dripped loudly. There were somehow echoes, a cough in the corner. "How do you feel?" asked the guide. "So quiet, you could go mad. Okay, lights on, follow me," he said. "This one's a tight squeeze." It was a true underworld, and we weren't supposed to be here. Tarantulas lined some of the walls—I held my breath, willing them not to see me. As we crawled, thigh deep in water, through the next opening, something scurried over my hand. Oh, god, what was it? *What was it?* I don't want to know.

"Oh my!" the guide exclaimed. "Come here, come quick." He dangled a wiggling, deadly looking monster from his fingertips. "This here, their name in English ... what you say? Tail whip scorpion." It was mostly spider, a little scorpion and lashed with long, slender limbs at the guide's face.

He laughed. "Don't worry," he said. "They look dangerous, but they're not." Letting it go, it raced into the crags, back to the darkness.

For thirty more minutes, we followed his voice, his light deeper inside the earth. What if I died right here, buried with all these beasts? Could I find peace here? "You notice how you can see more?" asked the guide. Yes. I thought my eyes, my body, were getting used to this hell. It was hot, not cool like caves were supposed to be. "That's because the end is near," he said.

Then I understood. Slowly, coquettishly, the sun peeked out from between rocks ahead of us. "Don't go fast," said the guide. "Wait by those rocks up there, the ones that look like a ship. Let your eyes readjust to the sun." Fernando and I leaned against the rock ships, the ones which had been sunken deep in the ocean for all those years. "I don't think we were supposed to be down there," I said.

"Yeah," he agreed. "Maybe not."

We got a flat tire on the way to Manuel Antonio. "Tranquilo," Fernando said, trying to make me smile. "We'll take a taxi the rest of the way and have this thing towed." He couldn't afford it, but wouldn't let me pay.

Manuel Antonio isn't as convenient as most of the other tourist towns, but some Americans swore it was the only place to go. There was a rainforest there which had more overall species in its small designated space than any other place on earth. Monkeys, sloths, strange tree raccoons, and insects somehow lived together so close, so harmoniously. The gentle hike was easy enough for my new body. My freshly birthed thighs and emerging arms. We ate seafood, of course, and I ordered a whiskey. It didn't taste good, but it seemed the thing to do.

But by evening, on the catamaran, words were building up in my throat. I couldn't do this anymore. I always got seasick. Why didn't I remember this? We were all sick, everyone on the boat throwing their heads over the railing. Fernando's face was pale as we sat starboard, surrounded by happy, honeymooning couples. "I can't," I told him. "I can't do this anymore. I'm going home."

"I know," he said, that safe smile on his face.

"You knew?"

"Not that you were going. But that you wanted to. And I understand. I don't blame you. This country is a hell hole, and nobody sees it."

"I'm sorry," I said, and an Indian couple next to us asked him to take their picture. They'd been married six days. Those were the last words I said before both of us ran to the rail and vomited all those expensive oysters right back into the ocean.

"When are you leaving?" he asked on the drive back with a brand new tire and a car that smelled, now, of cigarettes. It was early June.

"I actually found a yoga teacher training program in Puerto Viejo. It starts June twentieth through August first. I thought I'd apply. Do that first. If that's okay."

"Anything you want is okay," he said. "You want to stop here?" It looked like a little farmer's market. Did I want something to remember this by? But I could give him this. I should give him this.

One of the young hustlers started following us around, pointing out jewelry, artwork, anything he thought I might want. "Where are you from?" he asked.

"She's American," Fernando said. "I'm from here."

"Right," the boy said with a laugh. "Fucking poser Americans. You all want to be us."

Fernando said something in Spanish, then, "Believe me. I wish I wasn't from here."

A few stalls down, a piece of the country snared me. It was a bowl, a gorgeous bowl, with rich swirls and dark smears. "Heartwood," said the elderly woman. "My son, he make them all. Come from heart of local tree." This. I would carry this hard, beautiful heart home with me.

I waited until Chirag's birthday to tell him, though it took all my strength to not spill it all over the messages. Instead, I told him about my work. About the unearthly caves and the blandness of Manuel Antonio. About the latest places my poetry was published. Finally, it was June 16. I waited until Fernando left for school and called from under the patio while Mischa bathed my hand between the gate slats with his warm, rough tongue.

"Happy birthday," I said as he answered, groggy with sleep. "You're old like me now."

"Yeah, yeah," he said. "What you doing?"

"I thought you might want a birthday present."

"What's that?" he asked.

"I'm coming. August second. I'm coming back."

No reply. His breath caught in the lines, and then a shaking. "Thank you," he said. I pretended not to hear the tears in his voice. "Thank you. Thank you. I fucked up bad before, I know. But I promise, I promise. I'll spend the rest of my life making it up to you."

"Let's not talk about that right now."

"But why so late? Why not now?"

"I got accepted into a yoga teacher training program on the Caribbean coast. It's intensive, six weeks, up in the jungle. It's something I need to do."

"I get it," he said. "I'm waiting."

"Are you sure you don't want me to drive you?" Fernando asked. "I will."

"No, I'll take the bus. I want to."

"And I won't see you when you get back for your flight?"

"I think that's for the best. Don't you?"

"Probably," he said. "I'm sorry. Sorry I brought you here."

"It's not your fault," I said. "I'm the one who pushed for it."

"If it weren't for you, I wouldn't ever be a doctor probably."

"You would have," I said, although I didn't know. Maybe he was right.

"No," he said. "I wouldn't have. I would have kept making excuses. I would have given up as soon as I got here when it was really hard. Call me if you need to, want to, in Puerto Viejo. I'll be here."

"Okay," I said. "Watch Mischa for me. He won't understand."

"No," Fernando said. "But he's an old dog. He might surprise you. He's seen a lot I'm sure. But he'll miss you. We both will."

The bus to Limon took hours, my arm pressed against the buttery, sweaty arm of a woman who breastfed two children at once. The cityscapes gave way to signs of the ocean, but unlike the western coast there were no hints of America. No chain restaurants. No white people. It was glorious. Was this the Costa Rica I was meant to see?

Outside the city limits, I saw a woman get off at a deserted stop with a yoga bag strapped to her back. I hadn't notice her before. Was this it? I wanted off the trembling bus so badly, I didn't even care. I followed her.

"Are you here for the Samasati training?" I asked.

"Yes!" she said, her big brown eyes gulping it all in. "I read you're supposed to get off here and walk up the hill. It's supposed to be easier."

"What about the 4x4 special taxis?" I asked. That's what I'd read.

She shrugged. "I heard they were impossible to get. I'm Taryn, by the way."

"Jennifer." Together, we lunged up the hillside. Howler monkeys peered down from trees and blue morphs swayed across the path, more than I'd seen since the butterfly farm.

"Why did you come?" she asked.

"I was living here, anyway, in San Jose. It seemed like good timing."

"Whoa, you were living here? That's so cool. I wish I did!"

"Yeah, well, be careful about those wishes," I said. The

walk up the steep incline took two hours, and not a single vehicle passed us. The higher we got, the stranger the animals. The insects. It was getting dark, and pink streaky fingers reached across the sky.

"What *is* that?" Taryn asked as something like a lightning bug darted in front of us, a bright green light on its rear.

"I have no idea." Did it sting? Was it poisonous? Where the hell was this place?

Eventually, a log cabin came into view with *Samasati* scrawled across the top along with a painting of a gecko.

"Here for yoga?" asked the cacao-skinned girl with protruding teeth and a Caribbean lilt.

xvi.
Hide and Seek

MY DAD MOVED out the day after he got back from Sharon's, my mom with his clothes already crammed into old suitcases. He didn't deny it, didn't try to win her back. It's like he was happy he got caught. There were no rituals, no big hoopla made. One day his clothes were there, the next they were gone. His presence was already so sparse, it wasn't missed.

Kerri still wasn't talking to me. A coldness had settled on her and I was too stubborn and scared to try and slough it off. Michelle was completely in Chris's clutches. She may as well be gone, too. Rosa had dropped out. There was nothing left here for me. I started going to class even less.

I skipped school and made Scott drive me to my dad's company where he was a foreman. I'd never been. They had to call him over a loudspeaker, and he emerged minutes later between big logs being hauled to the chipper for slaughter. There was sawdust on his jeans. For once, Scott stayed in the car. Was this it? *This* was too much for him?

"Where are you living?" I asked my dad.

"An apartment across town. But not for long. I'm moving. I'm going to North Carolina, Cherokee country."

"Is she going with you?"

"Yeah."

"Take me with you."

"No," he said. "I can't."

"Yes, you can." He just chuckled.

"I guess I got out before you did. I have to go." Got out before I did? Was that a hint? A suggestion for a plan?

My mom was going crazy. Full, flat-out, totally insane.

Now *she* left porn on the computer and an adult, spiked, dog collar in the desk drawer beside the stapler. She got her nipples pierced (she told me). Once, I peeked in from the diamond window by the front door before jiggling it open. Thank god I looked, and I don't know why I did. She was naked, on all fours, while a big motorcycle-looking man whipped her with a leather strap while she whimpered with a ball gag in her mouth.

That night, Scott said, "Let's play hide and seek!" I hadn't told him about what I'd seen. In the dark, the old play equipment out back looked sinister. "Home-base" was the bar where he slept. I was the prey first.

It had been years, but I used to squeeze into the tall, tall bushes that lined one side of the property. They were dense and at least fifty feet long. I knew exactly where the biggest space was. I squatted for what felt like hours, listening to Scott prowl the property for me while my quads got stronger. Were there spiders in here? Yes, there had to be. There were spiders in here.

He sensed me like a good hunter. But he couldn't see me. Inches away, he picked up a small rock and threw it into the bushes, hitting me squarely in the forehead. It stung, but I didn't flinch. Didn't breathe. Didn't move. He was sure, but moved on, confused by my quiet. Then I made a run for it.

I could hear him on my heels, and he was faster. So much faster. But my heart pumped adrenaline through me like I really was about to get mauled. About to die. Closing in on the bar doors, I slammed into it to push it open wider, make for a victorious arrival—but my hand kept going. Through the glass door windows. Across the shards. The blood made it easier to slide through.

"Oh, my god! Oh, my god!" Scott cried. What?

There was blood everywhere. And my arm, my arm. I swear to god I could see the bone, and it was white. Clean, bright, shiny white. Shouldn't there be blood there?

"Fuck, Jennifer!" my mom said, running out the back

door. She dragged me inside and stuck my gushing arm under the faucet.

"Don't do that!" Scott said. "You need to compress it."

"I need to see!" she screamed. "I need to see! Don't tell me what the fuck to do." Eventually, though, she did wrap my arm in a towel. Just like Scott said.

My dad's older truck, the one he didn't use—didn't take—was blocking her in. "Go move the truck, I'll take you to the ER," she told me. I was dizzy. I couldn't remember how to drive it. And I parked it wrong, hanging too far out in the street. "Goddamnit, Jennifer," my mom said as she pulled out, me in the passenger seat, Scott in the back, "Go out there and re-park it right now." It's hard, with your right arm gone invisible, to move a vintage truck from drive to reverse to park.

I didn't let her go into the exam room with me. I was old enough to have a say. I knew she'd be pissed, but I didn't care. The doctors pumped me full of painkillers and said, "This is deep. We're going to have to staple this." The first staple shot like a bullet through my arm. "Still hurt?" they asked and injected more clear fluid into me. The second staple was a stab wound. "We can't give you any more painkillers," they said. "Your adrenaline's overriding it." I got thirteen staples in all and felt every single one.

My mom wouldn't let me win. When we got home, she threw a rag at me and said, "Go clean up that mess you made." You can't suck blood back up out of porous concrete, especially not just with your left arm, but you can try. And you can pick up the glass pieces. On one, a big chunk of my pale flesh jiggled like a crown. It was at least the size of a bottle cap. When I picked it off the glass, it was cold to the touch. Cold. That wasn't right.

I couldn't bring myself to throw it away with the glass. Instead, I tossed it into the bushes. Maybe it would make the plants grow big. Maybe an animal would eat it. Either way, I'd become something else, a wilder part of the earth.

CHAPTER SIXTEEN

THOR, the yoga certification program owner, spent his twenties as an engineer before realizing all the happiness had been siphoned out of him. Now he owned a yoga studio in Colorado and came to Costa Rica twice a year to save others from the corporate nightmare he'd narrowly escaped. He had a sunburned face and bright blue eyes, and his sandy blonde hair was just barely starting to silver at forty years old. We began practice every morning at 5:30, and when some women groaned (it was all women, all twelve of us), he said, "The monkeys won't let you sleep anyway. They love the sound of the tin roofs. You'll be up by five." He was right.

"Loosen all your joints, including the ones in your pockets," he said at that first sunrise class. First it was yoga. Then a vegetarian breakfast followed by anatomy class. A vegetarian lunch. Yogic history, lessons on how to compose a yoga class, and an evening yoga practice followed by meditation and a vegetarian dinner. This was every day six days per week, with Sundays a half-day.

We came from all over: America, Canada, and Australia. Somehow, I was put into Monkey Lodge, which was down the trails a bit from the main cabins. Most of the other women shared bigger log homes just steps from the dining hall. I was tucked into a small room with Laura, a Mormon escapee originally from Utah who'd spent the last ten years teaching at special education schools in Manhattan. She chewed her nails voraciously and was overly open. Next to us was Donna, a Canadian who'd just spent a year teaching English in South Korea. She seemed too soft and too blonde to manage much on her own.

Laura and I slept with the mosquito nets carefully wrapped around the twin beds. I kept a jar of peanut butter and low-carb cookies in my bag, even though Thor told us not to. But what if I couldn't eat the food they served? What if it was carby or I couldn't be sure if it was? "The monkeys will get it," Thor warned.

And they did. It was stolen two days later. While we learned how to give assists, we were taught how to survive in the jungle. "One of you will be bitten by a bullet ant," Thor said. "It's going to hurt like a pain you've never felt," he said. The ants, from the Amazon, had pinchers you could clearly see and they were big. They went where they pleased. "Shake your shoes out before you put them on," said Thor. "The scorpions here are transparent." He gave a demonstration in the circular room surrounded by meshed-in windows where we practiced. A little stinging thing came tumbling out and he swept it onto a newspaper to release it back outside.

I loved being here. I didn't want to be here. I had special arrangements to work in the evenings because I couldn't give up the money. I couldn't give up my clients. I'd ordered a special device to get a struggling hot spot even all the way out here, in the jungle. When the others found out, it bought me a kind of false popularity I'd always yearned for in childhood. But I didn't want to share, and they could tell. Only Laura and Donna used my computer regularly. I left it on our little patio table.

Monkey Lodge had three rooms in a row, but we only occupied two of them. At the end of the long cabin was a shared bathroom, like how I imagined some campgrounds would be. If we had to pee, we had to shove on our shoes and walk down there, through the dark, even if it was the middle of the night. Sometimes I woke up hours before the monkeys rained down and found my mosquito netting covered in spiders. In insects I couldn't name. They crawled around me curious, wanting inside. But thank god, thank god *these* spiders were little. Not like the ones outside.

In the jungle, the spiders were odd colors. Bright colors. They stretched as big as Frisbees, bigger, like those granddaddy longlegs in Oklahoma. One had made a web by our patio hammock, just one foot away. We didn't go near it, and it seemed to never move. It had just six legs. "It deserves this," I told Laura and Donna one night. "It lost two legs and still survived. It can be where it wants." I wrote to Chirag, to Sam, and Michelle. Even to my mom.

"There are things here I've never seen before," I told Chirag. "We have to call for special taxis that can handle the mountain terrain if we want to go to or from the town. Sometimes they come, sometimes they don't. There's a plant along the main trail here, I forget its name. But it's an hallucinogenic. One time last year, a girl tried to walk to the beach and back. She made it down, but on the way up she got so high from breathing in the air near it they found her crawling on the ground hours later, on the precipice of a cliff. She thought she was in heaven."

To Sam, I asked, "How's the pregnancy? Any weird cravings?" I didn't want to ask about gender or names in case she didn't want to tell. I didn't want to force her to tell me, "Sorry, this is a secret you can't know."

"I feel like a whale," she told me.

Michelle didn't tell me "I told you so" when I told her I was coming back. But she didn't hold back any punches when I told her Chirag was picking me up and I was moving straight in. "That's a stupid thing to do, but If that's what you think is best," she said. "So this guy I'm seeing, we've gone on a few dates but he just told me he's going to be a dad. I guess he got drunk and hooked up with a female friend who's been in love with him forever. He's not into her, but she's pregnant. Do you think I should still keep seeing him? He's hot. Men with babies are hot."

I could practically hear my mom drunk sobbing on her end, through her words. "Thank god," she wrote. "I didn't like you being there." Nobody but Chirag knew about the surgeries. About how an inch of my armpit had split open in bridge pose at the top of a jungle mountain. About how I couldn't do tree pose any more how I liked, with my foot tucked in tight to my inner thigh. About how my arms got tired fast in warrior two even though they were half their original size and should have felt lighter. How I couldn't even attempt crow pose right now. We had to memorize the Sanskrit names and use only them, but I couldn't keep the animal names and war-riddled references out of my head. Just off of my tongue.

"Nobody listens," said Thor. "Active listening, real active listening, it takes practice," he explained. "Even when we love the person we're talking to, even when we're really interested in what they're saying, we're still preparing our responses in our head. We're waiting our turn to talk. I want you to try something," he said. "Partner up with someone you haven't done a group project with before. Lie down side by side. Both of you keep your eyes closed. One person will talk, about anything that comes to mind, for three minutes. I'll keep time. It's going to feel a lot longer than that. The other person just listens. That's it. Then we'll switch."

I partnered with Gemma, the thinnest girl in the group. She would have been beautiful if she hadn't had gums that showed so much. She talked first. It started out simply, about how she felt being in the jungle (excited and kind of scared). About her job back in Florida at a yoga sportswear company. By minute two, she had started talking about what mattered. "And I don't know," she said, her voice starting to shake. "I think he loves me. I know he loves me. So I don't know what's wrong." She began to cry. Love. It's always about love. My instinct was to say something kind to her, to commiserate. But I couldn't. "Almost time," Thor whispered. "Thank you for listening to me," said Gemma, and I could hear the lightness, the smile in her voice.

I forgot most of my three minutes as soon as they were up. I'd been talking to Laura and Donna about Chirag nonstop for days now. But this was different. Gemma wasn't waiting to compare notes—she couldn't be. I told her about our history, my fears, and the "what if it all goes wrong?" About the man I was leaving here, my much better-looking, more prestigious safety net than Eli had ever been. I'd already thrown one back before. Were Eli and Fernando really so similar? "Thank you," I told her when my time was up

"Now, be forewarned," said Thor. "Things seem to come up in the jungle. Emotions, fears, all of it. I choose these places for a reason." Gemma and I didn't talk one-on-one again, but I felt the thread between us cement for life. We knew a part of one another, we who were strangers, that nobody else would ever know.

On the morning that Chirag's morning email said, "Twenty more days, babydoll," I was up at five with a pillow covered in blood. What the hell? There was no pain. It was gushing out of my nose. Great. There was no way I could spend hours in inversion like this. I sat up to let the red drain into an entire box of tissues, but it wouldn't stop. I trudged to class to tell and show Thor, who told me to wait until eight and take a taxi down to the local clinic. It was just a few miles from the base of the hill.

I'd never been to a local clinic. I'd always been to private clinics in Costa Rica, didn't even know the difference. By the time I arrived, it felt like half my blood was gone. The clinic was in an abandoned elementary school with a line of Ticos wrapped around it entirely. Most were barefoot, all were staring. I was alone, and as I walked from the taxi on the sidewalk to the entrance, my face buried in a bloody cloth, trucks of locals whipped by and whistled at me. I didn't care about the line, I walked right through the doors and to the reception desk, praying my white skin would do its job.

"Disculpe," I said. ""¿Inglés?"" she just stared at me. "Uh, doctor ...." I was starting to feel too dizzy.

"You have appointment?" she asked.

"No, isn't this urgent care?"

"You need appointment," she said.

"How do I make an appointment?"

"You talk to her," she said, pointing to the woman right beside her, just two feet away. There was nobody in line there, either. Moving to the other woman, who had obviously just heard the exchange, I said, "I need to make an appointment."

"You need to register first to make appointment," she said.

"Okay, how do I do that?"

"You talk to her," she said, pointing back to the other woman. What the fuck. I went back to the original woman. The blood was beginning to seep through my bundle of tissues. I felt a drop hit my toe.

"Look, I really need an appointment," I told the original woman.

"You need appointment, you talk to her," she said, pointing back to the second woman. They were both trying not to laugh out loud, hiding their smiles behind their small, tan hands. Fuck this.

I went back outside not giving a damn if I bled all over their floors. Here, I got reception. Barely. I called Fernando. "I hate this fucking country," I said between tears, telling him what was wrong.

"Do you want me to come there?" he asked. "I can come."

Yes. "No," I said. "No. I'll figure it out."

"Jenn ...."

"What?"

"Ugh, this isn't a good time is it?"

"I might be bleeding to death, what do you think?"

"I don't know! I don't know if I'll ever talk to you again and I don't want to make things worse and—"

"What? What is it?"

"They put Mischa down."

By some miracle, I got a 4x4 taxi that took me back to Samasati. "How are you?" asked all the girls who were now at breakfast. My yellow backpack was filled with bloody tissues and I'd taken off my cardigan to soak up more on the drive back.

"Not good," I said. "Not good." I couldn't hold it in anymore. I broke down crying, in front of everyone.

"You need to see a real doctor," one of the women said, the loud Australian. "Come on, I'll take you."

"No," I said, crying hard. "You'll miss the class, I don't want you to miss class." We could only miss so much and still get certification.

"I don't care," she said.

Brandy rode with me to the center of Puerto Viejo where the sole private doctor had a practice. He was used to dealing with Westerners who went off-track to this side of the country in search of the real paradise they'd heard so much about. The big sign outside his office said "Worm Removal Specialist."

"You have a very, very severe sinus infection," he said. The diagnosis took less than thirty seconds. "I'll write you a prescription, there's a pharmacy just two shops down. It's really raw in there." Brandy was in the stiff exam room chair across from me.

"What caused it?" she asked.

"Probably an incredible amount of stress," said the doctor.

After we picked up the prescription, Brandy looked up and down the street. On one side, you could see the surf. On our side, shop after shop offering handmade jewelry and seafood. "Are you hungry?" she asked. "We've already missed most of the morning and they'll be having lunch soon. We might as well make the most of escaping yoga prison."

We chose a restaurant that had a second-floor balcony and ordered tuna steaks and ceviche, all low carb and allowed. Brandy got wine. "God, I miss this," she said in her sing-song accent. "Aussies, we drink a lot, you know? It's good for you! That 'no drinking crap' up there is going to do me in. I'm sick of only having water to drink." It sounded like magic, how she said words.

"Say it again," I said.

"What?"

"Water."

"Ah, you Americans. You always like that. 'Water!' Please, waiter, more water! I'm parched and need water!" Her glass was full, but the waiter came at a half-jog.

I hadn't liked her when she had arrived. She was late and came booming into the first night meeting with all eyes on her. I thought it was an act, a plea for attention, but now I saw that it wasn't. She was just that full of life: she couldn't help but lap it all up.

With only ten days left, we were set to complete 108 sun salutations as the sun rose, which meant getting up even earlier than usual. All of us hated the howler monkeys by now, their incessant pounding and screaming on our rooftops. We didn't care about the monstrous spiders anymore; we swayed along in the hammock right beside the big blue beast. But this morning, I woke up minutes before the alarm and had to pee with a fervor. I didn't want to wake Laura with the light, but didn't want to risk putting my toe into a scorpion-filled shoe either. I'd just brave it down the outside patio barefoot, even in the pitch black.

I knew it when I felt it. This was a kind of obtuse pain that shot from my middle toe all the way up my spine and into my brain. A bullet ant. Bent over in agony, I could even see it scuttling away. I leaned against the doorframe to the bathroom and let the pain sweep over me. Breathe in, breathe the pain out. In a few minutes everybody would be up and I had 108 sun salutations ahead of me. I would not be the weak, crying, bleeding one again. I would not. "I got bit by a bullet ant," I whispered to Laura as we walked up to the expansive outdoor patio where we'd be practicing. Every step hurt. The patio looked over the lush greenery of the rainforest like something out of a movie, the Caribbean ocean in the distance. "Oh my god, are you okay?"

"I don't know." But I did it. She's the only one I told

until that evening. I stretched through the pain, put my mind somewhere else, maybe somewhere where Gemma would listen and Mischa licked my face. Upward dog, downward dog, jump forward. Halfway lift, forward fold, swan dive up. Hands throughout heart center, mountain pose. Hands back up, dive back down, jump back. Chaturanga, upward dog, do it all over again. I was the first to finish.

Most of the women immediately fled to the beaches for Sunday half-days, but I only went once. The ocean was buzzing with energy, and they staked out boys to flirt with. I got bored and walked back to the center of town instead of waiting for them. I wished that I could have joined in their giggling, enjoyed these moments. But I was too close to being with Chirag. That's all I could see.

As I walked back along the narrow road, men hollered from their cars and my shoes wore a blister into my heel. It was almost dusk when I spotted the town, and right then the van the group had hired slowed beside me. "What are you doing?" Taryn yelled.

"I just wanted to walk."

They took this night to prepare for graduation just a few days away. We all shoved into a liquor store to load up. "Jack," I told the cashier.

"You want mixer with that?" he asked.

"No."

"Oh, wow. You're hardcore," said one of the girls. "I figured you for a wine type. Or a teetotaler."

"Ha," said Laura. "They don't know you like I do!" She was right. Something in the jungle, in that small room, had opened us up to each other. She cried to me most nights, I less often. It was a war zone up there, and she my closest comrade.

In broken-up groups, we wandered along the beach town as the vendors set up shops for the night. Every evening was like a farmers market, food truck event, and salsa party that spilled onto the street rolled into one. I found a stunning beaded and leather bracelet with a single bead just a little misshapen. "¿Cuanto es?" I asked the boy.

He looked me up and down, trying to figure out how stupid I was. "Eight dollars," he said. It seemed like a penny, but I knew he was overcharging me by at least twice as much. I didn't care.

"Hey, hey!" said two of the girls to me, friends who had come together and stuck mostly with each other. "We're going to try and find some weed. You wanna go in with us?"

"Sure."

"Really?" they asked, surprised. "We were just asking, didn't think you would."

"I'm from Oregon," I said.

The weed shouldn't even have been called that. It was weak and dry. I'd have to smoke two bowls to feel anything, and it just wasn't worth the effort. "This is bad," I told them, leaving them to strain their cheeks for a high.

Graduation day, we all had to teach an hour-long class while Thor observed. I removed the clock from the wall and created a soundtrack of my own. "The Warrior" by Patty Smyth for the warrior series, and "Kissing You" from the *Romeo and Juliet* soundtrack for the savasana.

"I want you to picture someone you love. Someone who's waiting for you at home," I told them, walking them through a guided meditation. "Think about their eyes, their mouth, any anomalies on their face where you see only perfection." Chirag's melted cocoa eyes. His sprouting lips, his tattoo-like mole. As I walked, talking them through the memory of their loved one, pulling at their feet and massaging their temples, one tall, gangly girl I'd never spoken to very much began to cry into my hands.

Afterward, she apologized. "Don't be sorry," I said.

"It's just ... I left someone. Back home."

"We all did," I told her.

After dinner, with celebratory cake I couldn't eat and rich appetizers I wouldn't touch, the party house was designated and the joints and liquor began to get pulled out. Thor joined us, smoking like a pro and quickly settling into a deep philosophical talk.

"Oh, my god! Oh, my god! Roberto's here. Shh, shh, don't look!" Most of the women huddled together, darting furtive glances at the door. I'd heard about Roberto, the object of a mass crush. He was a surf instructor at one of the resorts and, apparently, the most godlike man in the country. He was good looking, sure. Maybe even beautiful. Seared skin, all abs from hours in the water, and sun-bleached dreadlocks. He was flanked by his friends, shorter Ticos who were hoping to soak up some of his loveliness and use it for their own gain.

On the patio, none of the women dared look at him. Wouldn't talk to him. One of them was already too drunk, but she was engaged. When she finally tried to flirt with him, the others pulled her inside and suddenly it was just me and him. I saw feet in the window. They were showing off their headstands, fueled by cheap wine. I moved to the now empty hammock, while Roberto perched on the railing like a kingfisher.

"You not drinking?" Roberto asked, searching for the right English words.

"Not like them," I said, holding up my little plastic bottle of whiskey.

"Ah," he said. "I no ... I don't ... I don't like alcohol much," he said. "Or people, too. Too many people," he said.

"You like the quiet," I asked him. Told him.

"The quiet," he said. "Yes." His smile was perfectly crooked. "That is why, too, I like the ocean. Surfing. Quiet." He pulled a joint out of his shirt pocket, raised his eyebrows at me, and I nodded. As he lit it, I watched the feet and heads pop up on the other side of the window. They'd forgotten all about him.

Passing the smoking, rolled paper back and forth, Roberto grasped the end of the hammock and began to rock me. "You lonely?" he asked. "For home?"

"I am."

"You, you are lucky," he said. "I never leave here. Never

even farther than Limon. I am never lonely for home."

"You're young," I told him. "You still can."

"No," he said. "No. I not so young anymore. Twenty-seven!" he said, as if I should be impressed.

"I remember when I was twenty-seven," I said.

"My papa, he own a banana, how you say ... plantation," he said.

"That's nice."

"He say I should not be in the water so much. He say it is, what ... time waste. My papa, he want me to own the plantation one day. But I ... it is not for me. Every morning, I care for the bananas before going to ocean, though. Papa, his rule."

"He probably just wants you to be stable," I said, though my heart was breaking for him. This weed was swimming in my head, and he looked so proud and strong up on that perch. But I could see the slight slouching in his shoulders already. The plantation weighing him down. I could see that he, too, even him, he would be old one day.

"My papa," he said, "he say the ocean will ... how ... swallow. Swallow me one day."

Everyone was hungover the next day except me. I took a separate bus to San Jose than them, claimed I got the time wrong when we'd all trekked to the station days before to get our tickets. "I think we all got so thin!" Brandy said. "Don't you ladies think?" Everyone nodded because they hoped. "But Jennifer," she said, "*she* got thinnest!"

"I did?" I guess it made sense. I hadn't been eating. I knew exactly how much I weighed when I came here thanks to a final check-in with the surgeon. 151 pounds.

"We only took two pounds total," the doctor said. "We have to measure." I wondered how much I weighed now.

I was done here. Laura and Donna and I had exchanged information, but that was it. Laura, with her offer of a place to stay in Manhattan and Donna with her optimism in excess. I wanted to go to the airport alone, to take the bus alone. As I waited to board at the international airport, full of happy arrivals on honeymoons and vacations, I counted my every step to the plane, every minute until take off. I would never touch this country again.

My layover was in Atlanta. I was reversing my movements. It must have been the joy that exuded from me, but everyone was picking up on it, soaking it in. "Hello, ma'am!" said a baggage attendant as he rushed by. At customs, an elderly black man motioned me forward. "Eight months in Central America!" he whistled. "Whoo-ee! I wish I'd done that when I was young. Are you happy to be back?"

"You have no idea," I told him, and he heard it, the sheer elation in my voice.

"You know what, honey?" he said. "I'm not supposda do this, but you wanna stamp this entry yourself?" I did, and I slammed it with a bang.

My flight to Portland arrived at seven in the evening. With an hour to landing, I squeezed into the airplane bathroom for a baby-wipe bath and fresh makeup. I knew I wouldn't want to waste any time in the bathroom when I got there. As we began to descend and the pilot told us the weather, I put "A Thousand Years" by Christina Perri on repeat. I didn't care if it was cheesy.

Every step through the terminal sped my heart. I counted the little runway prints in the PDX carport. Twenty-five. Twenty-six. And there he was, just like the first time, just like always. With a bouquet of roses and an air of nervousness cloying all around him.

Part 3

xvii.
Suicide Watch

THE CAST WAS TAKEN off one week before my driving test. "Have you studied? Did you study?" my mom asked daily.

"Yes," I said. I hadn't, of course. I'd let go of that straight-A need two years ago but was given pass after pass because I wrote good essays. Could bullshit enough in presentations. Lucked into the "business tract" now that I was going to be a junior and could escape those horrific math classes.

Scott came with us to the DMV, and I buckled into that barely alive whale of a van, embarrassed before the gray-haired administrator. He held a cracked wooden clipboard and seemed to want to be anywhere else.

"Pull out here," he said, pointing with his pen to an exit. Every move, every turn, he jotted down notes. I sat straighter, wished my skirt was longer. We were at the old Goodwill next to the train tracks that were so old there were no safety bars, no stop sign—the tracks had been out of commission ever since I could remember. Train tracks. Shit. There was something about them, wasn't there? I slowed, but didn't stop. A California stop, my mom would call it. The proctor made a note.

"I'm sorry," the woman at the desk said after we'd returned. "You passed the written, but it's an automatic fail if you don't stop at train tracks."

"But they're broken," I said.

"Doesn't matter." My mom had been hovering so close, I could smell her.

"Shit," she said, grabbing the keys from me and barreling through the crowds of Mexicans to the car. Scott and I sat in back of the van like she was an angry cab driver. Not that I had ever been in a cab.

"Fucking hell, Jennifer," she said. "Even *morons* pass driving tests. They give licenses to *retards*. You can't do shit right." Scott was giving me "I'm sorry" eyes from the opposite seat, which helped. It helped. But her crackling voice cut deep as always.

It's a good thing I no longer had anyone at school—nobody could ask how it went. Kerri had been swallowed up by the smokers. Rosa had, I heard, moved in with a black boyfriend ten years older than her. Michelle was trying to needle her way into the popular crowd while clinging to Chris whenever she could.

"Jennifer," said an older woman as she popped her head into English class the next day. "Come with me, please." Was I in trouble? What did I do?

I followed her clacking heels to a part of the main office I'd never been to before. "This is Mrs. Whitehead," she said, introducing a forgettable-looking woman in a dowdy dress. "She's the school psychologist."

"Okay."

"She'd like to talk with you."

"Sit, Justine, please," said the counselor. I didn't correct her.

"How are things?"

"Fine."

"I'd like to talk to you about your arm."

"My arm?"

"Would you like to tell me about it?"

"Not really."

"Justi … Jennifer," she said, looking at her notes. "When things like this happen, we need to take action."

"Things like what?"

"Suicide attempts. Cries for help."

"You think *I* did this?" The cuts from the bar door sliced up my forearm, with just the tiniest triangle rising over a major artery. Most were along the bone, on the outer part of my arm. If this was a suicide attempt, I was shit at it.

"Didn't you?"

"Can I go now?"

"Do you want to talk to someone else?" she asked, coming at me fast around the table. I couldn't help it, she raised her hand quickly and I ducked. It was an automatic reaction, not wanting to get the back of my head slapped. It never hurt, but it was annoying.

"Oh, you poor thing," she said. "You're not used to being touched kindly, are you?" I don't know what was wrong with me, but I cried. I cried in front of this woman who didn't know me at all.

CHAPTER SEVENTEEN

WE WERE HOME, the same condo I'd left eight months ago. Before the door even clicked shut, Chirag's hands were on my waist, sinking into the pools below my ribs. He was unlike anyone else, what I had fought dog-tired to imagine with all the other men. His mouth found mine with ease, pulling the worn tee-shirt over my head. "I have scars," I told him, and he looked. At the now fading slit from hip bone to hip bone, like I'd been gutted yet somehow survived. At the anchor scar peeking out from below the bra. At my for-once flat stomach.

"You are the same," he said, and walked me backwards to the Japanese-style bed that hovered inches above the floor.

He pulled off my jeans while unbuckling his belt and was inside me before either of our shirts could be taken off. The top hem of his chains chafed against my thighs, my new thighs. The first time they'd opened for anyone. After the days in the jungle, my limbs covered in bites and my whole self changed from the months in some place so alien, I was home. He explored me deep, like the first time, and I remembered it all. That last fight against the suede couch over there. The strange lipstick I'd once found under this same bed. The time I'd accidentally burned his desk chair while I straightened his hair with a flat iron. As he came, pushing me over the edge with him, he gripped my newly shaved-down hips and for once it didn't hurt. All the bruises had disappeared.

Back in America, it was easier to sniff out clients. A better internet connection and not feeling the tug of writing to Chirag freed me up. I collected them like some do beer bottles or expensive makeup. The day I arrived, August 2nd, was also Sam's birthday. "Happy birthday!" I wrote to her. "Just three more months to baby. How's it having a dry birthday?"

"I'm used to it now," she wrote. "I've decided to do an all-natural birth, no drugs. I wanted to do a water birth, but Sean says we're not buying a tub just for that. I think he thinks it's weird."

My birthday followed quickly, Chirag picking up a special, pink, glittery cake from a diabetic bakery. A small clutch of friends gathered at what was now *our* condo—Michelle and a couple of old sorority sisters. Leading up to the day, Chirag and I ate out almost every night, or at least ordered delivery from the Thai restaurant downstairs. The day I turned thirty-one, I could no longer fit into any of my jeans.

That was it, the day after my birthday marked a new kind of dieting. For the first time, I would count calories. I ordered a scale, but wouldn't open it until four weeks had passed. Maybe by then the number wouldn't be so terrifying.

My god, the calories in everything. *Everything.* I had heard that 1,200 was the number women needed to lose weight, but what about the calories in my vitamins? Especially the oils? I needed to count those, too, right? And so I adjusted the daily intake to 1,150.

I tried keeping track on special websites and apps, but found my own favorite low calorie foods so quickly that it became too much of a bother. I made an Excel spreadsheet and tracked it myself. Only 24 items fit in my limited allowance. And running, yes. I would start running again. I would run a half, I swear. New running shoes were picked up from the Nike discount store and I made a hybrid Hal Higdon plan of my own. Routes were plotted and four days per week I slogged towards my goal, slowly adding miles. I hated it. Men yelled, "Show me your tits" as I ran, though they began to disappear. I was hit twice by city buses that tried to turn on a red light as I loped across the crosswalk.

You learn the foods that make you feel fullest at godspeed. Tofu noodles, big bags of steamable broccoli. An entire carton of egg whites with sugar-free jam. And sex? How many calories did that burn? Did I get to count it? After one month, it was weigh-in. I tried not to drink much water the night before, pushed out as much pee as I could in the morning, and didn't even brush my teeth. I was 165 pounds. *Fuck*. How much had I weighed on my birthday?

"I think my pants are a little looser," I told Chirag as he got ready to leave to work and I settled into the couch to write.

"Good job, babydoll," he said, leaning down to kiss me before he left.

The numbers were all I saw. Fridays were weigh-in days, and the impending Thanksgiving was stressing me out. I didn't like to drink anymore, and would rather spend my calories on something else. Plus, I got stupid when I drank. I would eat and hate myself in the morning. Anyway, it slows down your metabolism. Morning rituals became very important. A glass of warm lemon water first thing. It kickstarts your metabolism and helps with oral hygiene. Nothing can go into your mouth for at least an hour. Then it's vitamins and green tea, another fat burner. I started intermittent fasting and lowered my calorie intake to 1,000. With the fasting, I gave myself four hours of a "feeding window" every day, just like bodybuilders do. That hour turned into just one eating session, period. I ate once, within thirty minutes, every twenty-four hours. And the weight began to drop.

Two or three pounds per week was normal, no matter how hungry I was or how much I worked out. The running continued, but I complemented it with spin classes and sometimes two hours each day on the elliptical. "You look amazing," everyone said when they saw me—which wasn't very often. But Thanksgiving. What would I do on Thanksgiving?

"Let's make it Diwaligiving," Chirag said, blending

Diwali with the American holiday since this year they were so close together. We invited all our friends for butter turkey, curried green beans, chaat-style tater tots and spicy home-made cranberry sauce. I couldn't control the calories, I couldn't tell how much was in anything.

Luckily, it was easy to hide my lack of eating in an environment where everyone was flying around. "I don't know how you do it," said one of our friends. "You're looking so good!" I smiled and left my already meagerly covered plate on the kitchen counter like I'd forgotten it. But still, I'd had some. I had to. I'd had some.

As soon as our friends left, I told Chirag, "I'm going to the gym."

"I thought you ran this morning?"

"I did. I'm feeling fat." I got in two hours on the elliptical, 850 calories, before the empty gym shut down early for the holidays. Fuck. I needed that 1,000 calorie mark. Needed it. The mystery calories began to spread into my fat cells and were making me chunky again.

But I'd found a new love: my old sugar-free laxatives. I had started to plateau around 130 pounds. It was the lowest I'd been in my adult life, but I knew it was nowhere near thin. Not *thin* thin. It wasn't just the calories, I realized. It was the weight of the food. Not all calories are equal! The lighter the physical food was, the more I lost. Every other day, I would eat nothing but two bags of sugar-free chocolates or four Atkins bars. The laxative effect was almost immediate. I tried purging, I swear I did, but I just couldn't. That was one thing where my body just said, "Nope! Not gonna do that." This was the next best thing. If I ate them and ten minutes later they were exploding back out of me, how could they possibly stick inside?

I was down to a size four.

Hiding my eating from Chirag was easy. He was on the way to work, at work, at the gym, or on the way home most waking hours of the day. I was never really big on dinner anyway, always hungry as soon as I woke. And he got the whole intermittent fasting thing, believing that I was eating when he was gone. In the condo, the garbage chute and recycling bins were just one door over. Him not seeing telltale signs of food consumption was normal. I obsessed over recycling and empty trash bins well before I had every calorie and carb count in the grocery store minimized.

"We never go out to eat anymore," he said, pulling me against him on the couch. That's because most restaurants don't list calories on their menu. Only fast food menus do—except some places. Some, you can find the calorie counts online. Denny's, iHop, Black Bear Diner. I searched them out like they were god, never telling Chirag about my strange new taste in these chains. But then, what if these counts were wrong? How could all these workers in all these restaurants put the *exact* same amount of oil on everything? Oh, my god, what if these calories listed didn't even count the oil? No. No, it was safer to eat at home. Safer in my bags of chocolate-flavored laxatives.

The day the scale hovered at 120 before dropping to 119, I felt lightness in my bones.

Kate Moss weighs 107 pounds and I'm the same height. *Fucking fat whore*, I told myself. There, that was good. Stop bolstering myself up, I could do with some humility. I wasn't thin, not even close. I was normal at best, and who wants to be that? I knew my BMI range—116 was the lowest, 145 the highest. What was I doing almost five pounds above the lowest? I couldn't even get that right.

"You lose any more weight, you'll disappear," called the doorman after me when I came back from a run and I grinned like a lunatic. How much more weight did he mean? How many 'til beautiful?

But the weight loss, it wasn't *working*. It had been six months, and Chirag hadn't told his parents. He hadn't talked about marriage or anything of permanence. What did I come back for? *Lose enough weight, and you'll be enough.* More, I needed more. But I was plateauing and I couldn't go without eating every 24 hours. It didn't matter if it was just a bag of laxatives, I needed something or I'd scream. I began weighing myself every hour.

If I dropped at least one ounce, I could have some water. If I dropped two, I could have a stick of sugar-free gum (five calories), but I had to do two minutes of jumping jacks to burn it off (it was usually worth it). If I lost three, I could have some mustard (zero calories, but that sodium). I began to eat so much mustard to make my stomach shut up, dipping my finger into the yellow sludge, that it bleached my pinky nail. I stopped wearing polish. It was probably adding part of a fake ounce to the scale anyway. If I didn't lose any ounces in the day, I had to drive back to the gym for the third time and spend twenty minutes in the sauna, sweating it out. I knew it was just water weight, but didn't care.

"I'm worried about you," Sam wrote. "You look so thin in the photos." Didn't she have a baby to worry about now? Theron was born November 2nd in a Middle Eastern hospital. Sam had begged for drugs, but by the time that sense kicked in, it was too late. "It's like being ripped in two," she told me.

By the time my birthday came around, I'd made it. I was 115.6 pounds and thirty-two years old. At thirty-two, I was beautiful. Right? I was under the minimum BMI. *Am I thin now?*

Barely, said the voice inside. *You're barely thin. Size zeroes today don't mean shit. Vanity sizing. This could be a fluke.* Right. I needed to lose five more pounds, give myself some buffer space. Just in case.

It was the end of September, the leaves shifting in the city below us, falling to the cement to die. "How much do you weigh now?" Chirag asked.

"One hundred and ten." I was so proud.

"Come walk on my back," he said. I was so light— it's what he asked his eight-year-old cousins to do in India. Was I really this light? Like a slight Ashiatsu-giving Asian woman? Were my bones hollow now, and could I take flight from the balcony?

I clung to the wall for balance as I stepped across his expansive back.

Halloween and no need for a costume. Half my hair had fallen out. At first, I thought I was just shedding, like your natural hair cycle does. But it was coming out in clumps in the shower. I saw myself in a CCTV monitor going into Fred Meyers and even from that grainy distance, it was clear: I looked like I had male pattern baldness. I began parting my hair in the middle and wearing a low ponytail. Then a braid—ponytails make hair fall out faster.

At the same time, a fine layer of peach fuzz had sprout up on my face. Lanugo. I had heard about this. When the body has so little fat it can't regulate its own temperature, it compensates. How fucked up is that? The hair on my head was falling out and being replaced by a werewolf-like coating. I was 108 pounds on my best days, but it still wasn't enough to be beautiful, was it? It didn't make Chirag love me enough to risk his world. Michelle begged hard to go out on Halloween, and even though I wasn't up for it I forced it. At least I got to wear a wig to hide my shame, and a skin-tight latex cat suit with a padded bra. I looked like a cartoon, unbelievably thin. Strangers asked to take pictures with me, the living comic book girl who you couldn't tell was balding underneath. That my cholesterol was soaring as my body began to eat my heart. "You're no fun anymore," Michelle said. "You don't *eat*." I just shrugged. She wanted someone to validate her own, consistent binging. She was fat.

I was too tired for sex. I didn't even want it—I wanted him, madly. Desperately. But I was just so tired. When you don't eat, you don't sleep, no matter how delicious it sounds. I started getting up at five. Then four. Now three was normal. My brain was always up, waiting for food even though the stupid thing should have known it wasn't coming. But I was thin enough to allow for cheat days now, right? I could have those?

I gave myself permission and went wild. One Saturday a month, I called it Faturday. Chirag and I would go food truck to food truck, getting a dish from each. He was just so happy I was eating, he didn't say a word. When I woke in the middle of the night those days, I would drive to the 24-hour doughnut shop. It started with just getting one. Soon I was up to six. I shoved food down my throat well past when I felt full or when it tasted good. My entire body ached, like every pore was bruised. I was so dehydrated on all other days that my skin was literally stretched painfully tight during these binges. A gas station bowl of Fruit Loops, large Coldstone ice creams, pizzas, and thousand-calorie cocktails. I had it all. When I weighed myself the next day, my bloated stomach felt punched. I would put on eight pounds, ten. Then it was starve, starve, starve until I got below 110 again. I got so good at this, I could binge every Saturday then laxative-starve my way back down just one week later.

"How can you eat so much?" friends would say when they'd see photos. "You're so little, I'm so jealous!" *You have everyone fooled.*

My low points were low. I shit myself more than once driving from the condo to the gym. Sometimes the laxatives kept on working for hours, but I was so grateful to get just a little more out, just a little lighter, I was thankful. My highs were high. That number hovering at 106. Not being able to find a single pair of pants in adult sizes, even in department stores—I had to shop in the kids' section and I pretended to complain about it to whomever I could. *Tell me I'm enough.*

It was December, and Chirag and I had been living together for nearly a year and a half. I didn't know how I was still running, but when I caught glimpses of myself in store windows as I glided by, I looked like a gazelle. I was so lithe, so lovely, like a ghost. I ran a 10k race in the freezing cold and somehow, somehow, I placed first for women. All I ate that day was a bag of sugar-free chocolates, stuffed down my throat minutes before the race began. When I finished, I didn't stop. I raced straight back to the bathroom (no lines, thank god) and had the most painful bowel movement of my life. That was winning. I ran off all those calories, then left any remainders in the toilet. All before I even collected my medal.

"So, I saw this ad on Craigslist," I told Chirag.

"Trolling for casual encounters?"

"Whatever. No, for like a publisher looking for poetry manuscripts. So I put together a bunch of my poems and sent it in."

"Oh. Well, that's good babydoll," he said, cutting the flaps off his New Seasons wok box to let it get room temperature and soggy how he liked it.

"No, you don't get it. They said yes," I told him.

"Yes to what?"

"Yes, they're publishing it."

"Seriously?"

"Yeah. I mean ... it's got a lot of stuff in there. *A lot.* About sex, drinking ... dieting. You think it's okay?"

"You do what you think is best," he said.

When I'd found out that morning, I felt high like the first time I'd smoked a joint and needed to move, move, move immediately. I started shoving up the steep hills towards the rose garden, along my favorite trail that wove towards the zoo. At the top, the winter garden above the Japanese ones, the scrambling began to settle in my brain. There was so much in there about starving. So, so much. Was that all I could write? Was that my muse? And what about the next book—would I have to go full inpatient, *Girl Interrupted* to make it worthwhile?

Fuck. I had just cornered myself into a starvation prison camp.

xviii.
These Boots are Made for My So-Called Life

"SHUT UP," Scott said. We were in his car arguing, like always. "Just shut up. You know what? You can just not speak the rest of the day. You don't have anything worthwhile to say anyway." Like a dog.

I was pissed because I'd caught him. We were at the mall, and a girl came up to him with that knowing look. Women know. There was something there. "Ariel is just a friend," he continued. "But you know what? I *should* take her out. Just to show you. If you can trust that I go on a date with her and nothing happens, then maybe you'll earn your right to speak again. You're so fucking stupid."

All I wanted to do was scream.

It was the beginning of my junior year, and I'd passed that driving test the second time around. I'd been saving for years to buy that 1985 red Mustang convertible with new, light gray leather seats. It had sat in the driveway for a year. I loved it. Even added on a sound system. It was years of working under the table jobs for family friends, every summer splattering cheese on nachos at the raceway for cash. But Scott had told my mom, as soon as my license was in hand, that a Mustang was too dangerous. She should trade it in for something safer. Now I had a Ford Probe with ugly maroon carpet, but Scott still wouldn't let me drive it.

When he dropped me off at school, my first class was AP English. It was one of the few classes I didn't regularly skip. The assignment was easy: Write a short story. But I didn't have any stories left in me. They had all quietly slipped away. I liked Mr. Robertson, a lost hippie man, but he just didn't understand.

That night, Scott worked. Thank god. Still, there just weren't any stories in me, and school was ridiculous anyway. Instead, I watched *My So-Called Life*. And saw myself. *This* was a story. I copied the dialogue and filled in the rest with descriptions of the surroundings. Expanded Angela's interior monologues. Made little twists that better reflected my life.

And I got caught. My mom was called in to Mr. Robertson's office. "At first," he said, "you know, I thought this seemed familiar? And then I recognized it. Plagiarism isn't allowed. It's not good," he said. The hippie in him couldn't bring himself to say "bad." "Do you have anything to say?" he asked me.

"No." My mom sat, freakishly silent for once, in the uncomfortable chairs.

"Nothing? Any regrets?" he asked.

"No. I got caught. So ...."

He looked at me in amazement, like I was a newly discovered insect that both shocked and appalled him. Leaning over to my mom, he whispered as if I couldn't hear him, "I've never seen anything like this before. Usually they cry. Or apologize or beg. This ... lack of emotion ... I don't know." My mom just shook her head in disgust. And I got off with a warning and a demand to re-do the assignment. I never did.

The ten-minute drive home was silence until we pulled into the driveway. "I think you're a sociopath," my mom said, and slammed the door behind her. Scott's car wasn't there.

"Oh, my god! Oh, my god!" her yells came from the back patio. I didn't want to go, didn't care, but something propelled me forward. "That fucker!" my mom screamed, bent over Boots, "That motherfucking psychotic freak! Look what he did! Look what he did to my baby!" Boots was breathing, but barely. It looked like stab wounds covering his torso.

"What ... what happened?" I asked.

"Your psychotic, retard *boyfriend* did this!" she screamed.

Did he? I doubted it. Animals were the only thing Scott loved unconditionally. "I knew it! He threw him over the fence and let the neighbor's dogs do this!" Okay, this I *highly* doubted, but I watched her reach to piece together a story that she liked in her head. One where she and Boots were victims against the world. As I turned to walk away, she bellowed, "Boots! Boots! Please don't die. You're the only thing I have left. The only thing I love."

Chapter Eighteen

"I'M GOING to India, first week in January," Chirag said.

"Oh." I was too tired to say much more, and thought maybe my legs were looking fatter than earlier in the day. Were they fatter? Was it just the angle? The pants?

"What day do you want to leave?" he asked.

"What?"

"Don't you want to come to India? Meet my parents?" It was November, but this was how Chirag announced things: all at once.

"Are you serious? Did you tell them?" *You're enough, you're enough. Look at that, you fat pig, you're finally enough.*

"No, I thought I'd tell them there."

"Don't you think you should *warn* them or something?"

"Nah, you're not that scary."

He wouldn't tell me what types of gifts to bring, kept saying that taking nothing was fine, but I knew his dad's birthday was while we'd be there. Chirag booked the tickets and I reserved a hotel on Juhu Beach. The Sea Siren opened onto the Arabian Sea, promised an internet connection and a gym. That's all I needed. I packed my most modest clothes—only pants and skirts that were floor-length and shirts with sleeves, ones I wouldn't have to use burn victim makeup with to cover my scars. Each piece of clothing was impregnated with a Ziploc bag of protein bars or sugar-free chocolates. Any day I could get by without eating, I'd take. I knew I'd get fat in India. Fat, fat, fat. Everyone said Americans came back from India "rail-thin," but those people hadn't had an empty stomach for so many months.

I packed Native jewelry for his mother, a bone pocket

comb for his father. Cologne for his brother, and baggies of bath products for his aunts and cousins. Boxes of eggless chocolates were hidden alongside my own, much lower calorie options, gifts for "just in case." For his grandfather, a Pendleton blanket.

"You go first," I told him. "Spend time with your family without having to worry about taking care of me." That was partly true. Partly I needed space to prepare in ways I couldn't tell him. But also, partly, I wanted a few extra days to make myself sick and work out even more. Indian women are thin, right? *Please, let them think I'm thin enough.*

I gave him a five-day lead and searched ravenously for a Hindi speaker on Craigslist. I found Rani, a woman in her 50s offering childcare service. "What would you charge for an hour of your time, just to translate phrases and record it for me?" She understood—she had left her family in India decades ago when she fell in love with a white man on a train. "His eyes, so blue," she said. "They brought me to America and I've never looked back." Her family didn't speak to her ever again, but here Rani and her husband were still together. Still married more than thirty years later.

Chirag and I had only been on a flight twice since I came back. Once to New Orleans where I nearly cried with every bite of po' boy I made myself take. There, we took an airboat tour of the swamps and bayous where alligators were pointed out to us by the driver. In a cooler, the host kept an alligator hatchling and passed him around. The little thing loved the warmth of our palms and barely moved, watching us with his slit of a foreign eye. "How stupid he is," I told Chirag as I held the rough scales in my hand, "he thinks we won't crush him for sport." It pissed on me.

The other flight was to San Diego where I secretly bought tickets to a backstage experience at the zoo to surprise him. We hand-fed rhinos, prehistoric-looking beasts. They were dinosaurs—all they eat is vegetables, and look how big they are. We took photos next to a cheetah and watched a wolf cub learn to howl. That trip, we drove back up north instead of flying and stopped in San Francisco. I tried to find the same shop with the Love rocks, but couldn't. Instead, we went to the original fortune cookie factory for souvenirs. I let myself have one (30 calories) and made Chirag walk up and down the hills for twenty extra minutes as punishment. I didn't tell him why. During the boat ride to Alcatraz, I almost got seasick and had to close my eyes the entire time. "Tell me when we're close," I said, and he shook me as The Rock came into view. "Look," I said, pointing to the rusting sign that said, "Indians Welcome."

"Which kind do they mean? Me or you?" he asked. I didn't answer, but bought a crumbled-off piece of the prison for too much money.

Those short flights didn't teach my new body what it needed to know: That there wasn't enough fat on my butt anymore to let me sit for so long. The first leg was to Seattle (fine). The second to Dubai (not fine). My bones ached as they pressed into the hard airplane seats. By the time we were over the Atlantic, I couldn't take it anymore. All the pillows and blankets propped under me weren't working. I had to sit with my hands under my ass just to bear the pain, all the while shaking my head *no* every time a snack or meal came by. My hands went numb after two hours, but I couldn't move them.

It's like they were fattening up farm animals on the plane. The food came constantly, keeping everyone in a daze. I could have brought my protein bars on board, but this was a challenge. I would not eat on a plane. I loaded up on water and diet soda, though. "I'm guessing no, again?" the attendant said as she wheeled by another mouthwatering trolley.

"No, I don't like to eat on planes," I said with a smile.

"I'm impressed," she said. "I wish I could do that." She was impressed. Everyone complained about the small airplane seats, but to me they were huge. I should get a discount, especially as the passengers on either side of me oozed over the armrests and into my space, into my ribs, with their flab.

I'd planned my flight to spend a week in Abu Dhabi after India, just me, Sam, Sean, and Theron. "What do you want to do?" Sam had asked, and we mapped it out. A camel race, trip to the falcon hospital, and (at her request) tons and tons of food. Michelin-starred restaurants, coffee at a palace with camel's milk and gold flakes on top. And endless, endless wine. Luckily, she also had to teach and attend class. I was sure at least some of the days I could get by without eating in front of her.

Flights into Mumbai are dreadful. Most arrive between midnight and three in the morning. Chirag was picking me up with one of his friends. When I landed, before the bags rolled in, I changed in the bathroom, piled dry shampoo in my hair, and applied flawless makeup. Yes, this is how I naturally look after twenty hours in transit.

The mosquitoes descended instantly, happy with the middle of the night humidity. Chirag looked the same here, where he was from—I don't know why I thought it would be otherwise. "This is Sandeep," he said. One of his best friends from childhood. He was a short, terse-looking man with thick glasses and bloodshot eyes.

"As you know," Sandeep said as he helped put my luggage in the trunk, "Chirag is really busy. I don't start my new position for a couple of weeks, so anything you need, just call me. My number's in this phone," he said, handing me a burner. "We can go out, drinks, whatever." Chirag had already told me I shouldn't leave the hotel alone after dark.

"Did you tell your parents?" I whispered to him in the backseat.

"Not yet."

The hotel was just a twenty-minute drive away, but by now I was on autopilot. I was hungry, hungry, hungry. Chirag helped me check in and walked me to my room. It was cold tile floors and a thin cover on a twin bed. "You're going to crash hard," he said. "Text me when you're up tomorrow." *Go away, go away so I can eat.*

I don't remember him leaving, but I tore into three bags of sugar-free chocolates. While I binged on my laxatives, I found my travel scale. It was a quarter the size of a regular scale and I had to stand on tiptoes to use it. I should have done this first. What was wrong with me? The dehydration from the plane made my waist look so tiny. Like an ant's. My thigh gap looked the biggest ever, at least one inch even when I pressed my feet as close together as I could. I wished I had brought my tape measure to see for sure how wide the space between my legs was.

I was fat already with the chocolates, but willing to risk it. And the grease in my hair and the dry shampoo, that was more weight. I only liked to weigh myself when I was freshly cleaned so no dirt could toy with the number.

Still, I stripped down and balanced on the scale, my teeth still coated with the fake chocolate. It blinked 105.4 at me. Amazing. But this was a different scale than what I was used to. And I had just eaten. And I was dirty. It should be less, maybe it was wrong. Or maybe I actually weighed more! I looked in the mirror again. Maybe my waist wasn't as little as I'd thought. The thigh gap not so wide. *You're useless, you fat slob.*

I slept through the entire next day. The sun was setting before I pulled myself out with a pounding headache. The gym. I needed to find the gym. It was sparse, but would do the trick. I spent an hour walking at the steepest incline before texting Chirag. "I'm up."

"Busy tonight, family stuff," he said. "You want to go out tomorrow?"

"Okay." Now I was wide awake and it was only six o'clock. What was I going to do?

"Want to get a drink?" I texted Sandeep.

"Sure. Pick you up in twenty."

He was trim, so I didn't think he'd eat much and I was right—he was a drinker. An alcoholic. We bonded over whiskey. To be polite, he offered me food, and I didn't want to seem weird so I had a few nuts. They're high in calories, but low in carbs. He told me about his romantic exploits, gems about Chirag's family that I didn't know. "His one cousin, Alia, she's even thinner than you—"

I stopped listening. Thinner than me? That means his family was used to thin girls. I knew it. They'd think I was fat for sure. It didn't matter that she was only sixteen.

The next day, Chirag picked me up at eleven. I hadn't eaten since the chocolates the morning I'd arrived and the handful of nuts with Sandeep. "You want to try Indian McDonald's?" he asked, and I did. My jeans were fitting loosely and I'd caught myself in the mirror by mistake. My arms and shoulders looked skeletal, just how I liked. Like a movie star. I could afford it.

My very first rickshaw ride was to McDonald's, how American tourist is that? The first few seconds in the black beetle-like three-wheeler, I was terrified. It whipped through the crammed streets inches away from cars and motorcycles. Nobody obeyed the traffic laws. The rickshaw got too close to the cows and street dogs roaming around and there were horns everywhere. Horns not like in Costa Rica. There, the horns covered up fear and anger. Here, it was a language. The rickshaws and cars were talking to each other. *I'm here. Move over. Go ahead.* "The Horn OK Please" stickers and paintings on nearly every truck summed it up. *You have a horn, use it, okay? Please? (Otherwise, you'll die. Sorry.).*

At McDonald's I got an Aloo Burger, a potato patty instead of beef. Chirag got paneer, that farmer's cottage cheese that he always cooked with spinach back home. The fries tasted the same, so I just had one. *You could have gone with none, you obese fuckup.* But screw it, I got soft-serve ice cream, too. It had been so long I forgot the calorie count—150 I think?

"Where you want to go for dinner?" he asked.

"We're eating right now!"

"We can still decide. Street food?" He knew I loved street

food, the cheaper and dirtier the better. But I could feel my stomach getting bigger already. Softer. *No, no, don't. You're so lovely when you're empty like a clean soup bowl.*

It *was* street food for dinner, even with my excuses, and it was incredible. The biggest, permanent carts on Juhu Beach opened at nightfall. Indian pizzas, pav bhaji, Chinese food, golas and more. Vada pavs and Thums Up soda and paan (chocolate and plain). Chirag's friends came, and I forgot their names instantly. Everyone was eating and the girls told me, "You're so thin! I thought all Americans were fat!" which gave me permission to eat, too. I loved it all except the paan, which had some kind of seasoning in it that made me want to wretch. But by far, the best was the pizza—the amul cheese that was salty and creamy, the crispy crust like nothing I'd had before. "Try this, try this," his friends would say, coming at me with forks and pinches of food. "It's not too hot?" they'd ask and Chirag would laugh, "She can eat spicier than any of us."

I wanted to show off, to prove that I fit in okay. "Try some gola," one of his friends said, a stick of ice dipped in flavored syrup.

"It's local water," I said.

"Go ahead," Chirag said, and I did. His friend lifted it for me and lowered it to my lips, a mockery of teabagging. It was just okay, not worth the bacteria risk. But what risk? The risk of Delhi Belly, of a stronger laxative than I'd known before? That was no risk. That would be a godsend. I had more.

The next day, I got away with not eating out and left enough room in my calorie allotment for drinks. Sandeep took us to his favorite bar where he knew the owner and there were menu items named after him. It was a warehouse-style karaoke and dance place with pictures of American rappers papering the walls and chicken wire separating the booths. "Kuchne," Sandeep said, pouring a local whiskey for me. "It means 'nothing.' So you can tell your parents you drank nothing, and it would be true." It tasted cheap, like I liked. "Teachers," he said, pouring the next. "This one is the staple bottom shelf whiskey here." It went down slippery and harsh. "You want to try Old Monk?" he asked.

"Nah, dude," Chirag said. I didn't know what it was, but I wanted it.

"Sure." They looked at each other and ordered three with coke. "You have to have it with Coke," Sandeep urged when it came.

"Diet," I said. "But I want to try it by itself first." They both watched me like I was about to swallow a sword, and I couldn't figure out what the big deal was. "It tastes like Jaeger," I said, which I liked, that cold black licorice, and they both laughed as they mixed their own concoctions.

"You going to sing? You going to sing?" the KJ was at my side, ignoring Chirag and Sandeep.

"Oh, uh, sure," I said, looking around. It was a big enough crowd. I hated singing to no one.

"Write it down here," the KJ said. "I can download anything." Nicki Minaj it was.

I love shocking people. To sing about fat asses when I had none, to use that low and dangerous voice when I looked so childlike I could float away. Let people underestimate you, that's the secret. Let them think they know who you are and then hit them across the face with a steel pipe.

"Did you tell your parents yet?" drunk Jennifer asked Chirag on the drive home. Drunk Jennifer is incredibly annoying.

"I will. I will, babydoll."

I only had one week left, then I was off to Abu Dhabi. His dad's birthday. "I told them," Chirag said on the phone the next morning. I had already been scouring the breakfast buffet, picking out grilled tomatoes and the onions from the omelet. I'd have to eat today, so the protein bars were out, too high in calories. But I needed something to trick my stomach to fullness.

"On his birthday? You told them on your dad's sixtieth

birthday?" I would, always and forever, be the thing that ruined this milestone. "How?"

"They started asking if I'd found someone, like they always do. If I wanted them to help. My mom had already told me last year that all the good ones were taken—that I was old stock now. They were just going through the motions, but I told them no. I'd already found someone."

"And?"

"I told them you were white. The next thing they asked was if you were vegetarian, and I said yes. I dunno. I told them you had a master's degree, showed them some pictures. And they asked when they could meet you."

"They weren't mad?"

"Not like I thought they might be."

"So, when?"

"I'll figure it out ... they know you're leaving on Sunday." I was grateful the countdown had already begun. How bad could it turn in seven days?

Bad. But not because of them knowing. It was my not knowing. Each day was like trying to sneak past a firing squad. The relief was brief because I knew it was temporary. But nothing. Day after day, we'd go to expensive restaurants. Out drinking with his friends. We went to the famous Halal Juice stand where I drank chikoo milkshakes and ate apple custard. To Leopold's, the restaurant near Churchgate that got famous from *Shantaram*. I'd read the book, but it was nothing like I pictured and the parathas were just okay. To the Gateway to India where we took photos by the docked boats and watched a skinny man save a drowning pigeon. I asked, begged, to ride an elephant, one with pink ears and freckles like the photos he'd shown me so many years ago when he was working in Bangalore. "No elephants around here," he said. "Maybe next time."

Chirag bought me too many kurtas from Fab India and cheap shoes that I loved from the streets. The vendors saw my pale skin and flocked to me in broken English. I hid behind Chirag, made him haggle on my behalf. "She's American, I'm not," he said so many times in Hindi I began to recognize it. Sandeep took us to his favorite falooda stand at midnight where we could stay in the car and the Iranian desserts came to us. I was wearing a long skirt and my ankles began to sting in the backseat. Flipping on the overhead light, I saw a storm of mosquitoes so dense battling for my ankle skin it looked like my feet had disappeared. There were hundreds and nothing I could do, so I just let them binge on my body while I collected more scars.

Thursday and still nothing, but my luck had run out. It was the pani puri from the day before, it had to be. I woke with a stomach that growled like a tiger and I half-crawled to the bathroom where my insides gave way. I texted Chirag for packs of baby wipes. It hurt to be alive. Every twenty minutes I made my way back to the toilet, kept forcing down bottled water and flushing it right back out of me. *How much weight was I losing? What's my number now?* I didn't want to look because I knew more was coming. I'd wait, wait 'til the number was the best it could be.

By Saturday it had stopped and I got on the glorious scale—103. So, so low. How incredible I must look, my ribs showing like a swollen cage and my collarbones erupted from my chest. I felt good enough for a light elliptical work-out where I could watch my almost-disappeared waist in the window reflection. I knew 103 didn't sound very low to some people, to *real* anorexics. But I was naturally big, big boned and took up so much space. My hips soared out like sails on a ship, my shoulders like wooden hangers. I looked how some looked at 90, 85 pounds.

Tomorrow I would leave for Abu Dhabi, and as my strength grew out of the sickness I began to get mad. Pissed. Roaringly angry. What the hell? I'd come halfway across the world, and his parents couldn't even meet me?

One hour into my Saturday workout and it was five o'-clock in the afternoon. The phone buzzed in the cup holder, "Meet the parents at 7," Chirag said. Now? They want to meet *now*?

"Wtf?" I replied, and he called.

"Sorry," he said. "They asked today again when they were going to meet you. I guess I was supposed to arrange it and I thought *they* were going to tell me when, so ...."

I had two hours and I was sweating. *Like the stuck pig you really are. You're going to get so fat in Abu Dhabi.* At least I was thin now. For the moment.

I can get ready fast. Shower in the hard water, blow out the hair. Foundation, eyebrow filler, cream blush and that's it. Jeans and a kurta. "Dress conservative," Chirag texted. I know, I know. "No matter what they say, if they're angry don't respond. Don't fight back."

"Do you know me at all?" I replied.

"Sorry."

It was 6:40. They'd be here in twenty minutes for tea in the downstairs restaurant. I played Rani's voice over and over on my US phone. Her words were burned into my brain. Please, god, let them roll out my tongue like butter. I knew his mother spoke not a whit of English, but his brother was fluent and his dad close enough. I needed a drink, to be loose when they got here.

As much as I loathed shooting whiskey—it should be savored, not downed like poison—I took a generous pull from the bottle. "Gonna be late, 7:30," Chirag texted almost immediately afterward. *Fuck.*

The whiskey punched me hard on an empty, dehydrated stomach, but the buzz faded fast, too. By 7:10, I was totally sober again. Twenty more minutes. I needed another shot. One more long, long drink followed by tooth brushing and gum. "Here, in the lobby," Chirag texted at 7:12. I was drunk, and the firing squad had arrived.

It was the longest walk of my life. Down the elevator, through the lobby. The restaurant was empty, and the four of them sat in silence. His mother was short, heavy, and smiled constantly, her hair thinning badly and dyed with henna. "Sundre," I said, pointing to the henna on her hand. *Beautiful.* "Mehendi," she said. She didn't care that I was white, I could see it in her eyes. His father was another story.

He was cold, slender, with a full head of thick hair. He stared at me hard, arms crossed over his chest. I bowed and Namasted like Chirag had told me to, but it did nothing to thaw the ice between his father and me. His brother had just the slightest whisper of resemblance to Chirag, but he was heavier. Going bald. Had bad skin. I was supposed to be modest here, even quieter than normal. But this was awkward. And I was drunk—I wanted to talk.

Was I supposed to be intimidated by his dad? I wasn't. And right now, I didn't care that he didn't like me—he didn't even know me. He knew my skin color, that was it. And he looked like Chirag when Chirag was unhappy. It made me want to laugh, that pouting. Next to me, Chirag was slamming his knee up and down like a scared rabbit. I longed to touch it to make him stop, but knew I couldn't. Then the quizzing began.

What did I do, what languages did I speak, was I vegetarian, what was my religion, what did my parents do. Chirag had prepared me for all of these, and he repeated the answers in Hindi to his mom, who continued to smile widely. In just thirty minutes the interview was over, but I didn't know if I got the job or not. The gifts. The words Rani gave me. It was easy to hand over material things, but the whiskey courage wasn't strong enough to force the words out. The fear had sobered me up and now I had to pee. Then we were in the lobby, Chirag's mom leaning on his arm. Then the front of the hotel. Then the parking lot, waiting for their driver to circle around. *Say it, say it, say it you fucking coward.*

"Uh, mujhe pata hai ki main Indian nahi hoon," I said to his mom. *I know I'm not Indian.* "Per mujhe Chirag, aur Indian culture hai, bahot prem hai." *But I like Chirag and Indian culture very much.* It was what Rani had told me was the best thing to say in this situation. His mother smiled bigger, grabbed my hand and pulled me close, a safer distance from the approaching cars. His father's hands dropped from his chest.

"You did good," Chirag said as he walked me back to the hotel.

"That was the most terrifying thing I've ever done."

xix.
Wolves and Sheep

"I WANT HIM OUT," my mom said on a Thursday morning. Scott was at work. "You choose, you think you're so grown up. He leaves alone, or you both go." Seriously? She was making me choose between him and her? What an idiot.

"Then I'll go," I said. "I don't care." She came at me to slap the back of my head, but I was a head taller than her and she was weak with arthritis. It was instinctual. I balled up my fists; she glanced at them, and backed away.

Honestly, I thought she was bluffing. But when I got home from school that day (driving myself now that Scott had picked up more hours at the gas station), the locks on the door had been changed. They actually worked for once, all shiny and new. A rag had been taped over the diamond window. And a couple of garbage bags with my clothes were on the front porch. Seriously? This was how she was going to play it? As I dragged them to the trunk of my car, she came outside. "Yeah, go!" she screamed. "Go live with your loser boyfriend!"

"You fucking bitch!" I yelled back from the driveway. It was the first time I'd actually sworn at her, and she slammed the door, scuffling back into her black hole. It was winter, and would be dark soon. Scott's work was only a couple of miles away.

"Get in," I told him.

"I'm working," he said. "What the hell happened?" he asked, looking at my mascara-dripping face.

"We need to go. Now."

"My car—"

"No, leave it." Amazingly, he did what I said. Something

new was in my voice, a resolve that scared him. As I filled him in, speeding to his apartment across town, I could see the plans rushing through his head.

"Fuck, fuck, fuck," he said. "You're a minor, I'm 19. Your mom's crazy, she's going to call the cops and say I kidnapped you!"

"Yeah. She might."

"What are we going to do?"

"I don't know. I don't know! Help me."

"Okay. Okay. Park a few blocks from my place. I'll go get the most expensive things, and some clothes." I'd never seen him move so fast, carry so much in one go. Stereo equipment, watches, a backpack of essentials. "How much gas do you have?"

"It's almost full."

"Do you ... do you think she's going to kill herself?"

"I don't know." It hadn't occurred to me, but she might. She might. Ever since my dad left, she kept thinking it out loud, but she was too scared of hell to go through with it.

"I'll call the cops from a payphone if you want. Have them check on her, it'll be anonymous. Then we're going south."

"South?"

"If she calls the cops, she'll assume we're going north, to Portland. To my family. They'll be looking for our cars on I-5 North. We need to stay off it, at least for a while."

After the call, I needled the car towards Weed, California and didn't need to stop for gas until after we crossed the border. Scott showed me how to pump gas, and we ate whatever we wanted from gas stations. He stole from the aisles as I distracted the cashier. Hyped up on adrenaline, we kept on going, circled around and took the less traveled highways back up to central Oregon aiming for Bend. "I have a friend there, we might be able to stay on his couch awhile. His dad's usually gone," Scott said.

When we grew tired, halfway there, I pulled into a shaded spot in a deserted grocery store parking lot. By six in the morning, a cop was tapping on the window. "You can't sleep here," he said. "Keep it moving." He didn't question my age, why I was here, nothing.

It was night by the time we rolled into the outskirts of Bend and snow began to fall in puffy white flakes. On the side of the highway, a wolf stood frozen, staring into the distance. I slowed the car, but the big white beast didn't move, just looked at us with boredom. *Don't you recognize me?* I begged him with my eyes. *I'm the same as you.*

CHAPTER NINETEEN

THE FLIGHT TO Abu Dhabi was just four hours, and Sam was waiting for me alone. She hugged me tight, and I felt the baby weight around her stomach. It had settled onto her thighs like a film. "Where's Theron?" I asked.

"Sean's watching him at home. He's not the most exciting thing at this age." Was this a country where pedestrians got the right of way? I tested it out at the road between the terminal and parking lot and was met with a flurry of honks. Apparently not.

Abu Dhabi looked like what it was: A contemporary city sprung, very recently, out of the sand. Everyone here had new money and not a clue what to do with it. So they bought Lamborghinis and kicked back in villas given to them by the oil-rich government. Sixty years ago the locals were living in tribes in the desert, then voila! Oil was found and now they were some of the richest people in the world. They ate gold and bought 24k bars around the clock from vending machines because they could.

Sam liked to shop in the "back rooms" of grocery stores where pork was kept like it was pornography. With eighty percent of the population in the UAE being westerners, the Muslims had no choice but to cater to the bacon-loving invaders. It tasted dirty, those ham slices and pork chops.

"I met the parents," I told Sam.

"And?"

"I don't know. After so many years and such a buildup, it was kind of anti-climactic."

"Do you think you're going to get married now?"

"I guess? I mean, Indians don't date. You only meet parents if you're basically engaged, but there was no talk about it. Chirag knows about engagement traditions in the US though. We didn't really get a chance to talk about it."

She nodded. "I want you to be happy."

Sam and Sean had jointly developed a serious drinking problem. Gin and tonics every night, at least a bottle of wine a day. She was a pro at the pump and dump. They'd get drunk, turn on the white noise machine to shush the baby, but it would put us all to sleep.

"So, I looked into the camel races," she said. "Apparently it's only done at dawn and it's a few miles away. Sean can watch the baby that early, so it'll just be us."

The next morning, she maneuvered the "black mambo," her nickname for the black SUV mom car they'd bought, like a fiend down the sandy-littered highway with no speed limits. Past an overturned school bus and two Ferraris that had collided in the blindness. People died every day here on the highways, holding their babies on their laps or out the window to make them laugh, keeping their own seatbelt clasps under their rears. "I think this is it," she said, pulling onto a long side road in the middle of nothing.

I was expecting a racetrack like horses or greyhounds back home. Big grandstands and cheering crowds. It wasn't like that. The men and boys, they raced to impress the sheikhs. If their camels were good enough, royalty took notice and they were rewarded. It was more about the prestige than any prize money. There were no crowds, there were no seats—and we were the only women for miles. Not to mention the only white women. The only women uncovered.

"What the hell?" she said. "Where do we go?"

The directions, if that's what they were, were all in Arabic. We rolled down our windows to see better, the settling dust storm from the night still making the air soupy thick. And then we saw the camels.

They barreled along beside us, out of the dark dawn air, so freakish and ugly in their canter. Foam flew out their mouths and men in red and white checkered dishdashas followed in Jeeps closely behind them. There was a rail that separated us from the camels, but nothing else. How fast was Sam going? Ten, twenty miles per hour? They seemed to appear from the mist, like dragons, and they were so unearthly tall and hideous.

I take that back. They weren't ugly. They were beautiful. Somehow, here, in this magic the ugly things turned into sheer beauty. I l liked that. But Sam and I, we didn't belong here.

She began keeping pace with one of the camels and the piles of men on the other side. These men were older with wrinkles deep as moon craters. They looked mean with their furrowed brows and frowns. *You're not supposed to be here*, the one who locked eyes with me seemed to say. *Go away, this is sacred. It's not for you.*

I don't know what was wrong with me, but I smiled at him. I waved, and he waved back, his face suddenly lit up bright as the sun.

At the end of the track, Sam slowed the black mambo as the camel came to a halt. Here, there were mounds of humps, some resting in the sand and others milling about. Men clumped into their own humpy groups, laughing and trading stories, some pulling out foil-wrapped naan from their white robes. They looked like priests, like religious beings from another time.

She parked and looked at me. *Should we get out?* asked her eyes. We'd been together so long words were only a formality. *We've done stupider*, my eyes answered back.

Wasn't that the truth. In grad school, the first time I visited her in her small Georgia town, we both shrieked, "Let's go to Atlanta!" It was the biggest city we'd ever be in together. I tracked down the biggest gay clubs while she found a hotel room. But first, we started at a country bar because, well, it was the south. That's what you do.

Some young white boy saddled up to us. "Your tits are amazing!" he said to me. He was wrong, my bra was amazing. "Are they real?"

I was semi-drunk already. "Yes! Do you want to touch them?" Only afterward did I realize we weren't in a gay club yet. "Let's go," I told Sam, and we hailed a cab outside. "Take us to the Jungle!" we told the driver.

"The Jungle? You girls sure?" asked the oil-black man. "That's a rough part of town."

"We'll be okay," I said.

It was early by gay standards, barely ten o'clock. The waitress was a towering queen with her blue leopard bra showing. "Leopards aren't blue!" I whisper-yelled to Sam after one strong cocktail and she snorted into her own drink.

"This one is!" she said. "Hey! Waitress? Ma'am? Can I ask you something?"

"What's that, honey?" she asked, strutting over with an empty tray.

"Do you have any E?"

"Sam!" I said. We'd talked about doing ecstasy on the drive over, but I didn't think she'd really ask. I'd only ever smoked weed before. Sam had done shrooms once, and said she freaked out in a barn thinking there were spiders everywhere.

"Are you cops?" asked the waitress.

"What? No!" said Sam.

"I need to hear you both say it."

"No," I echoed. Was that really a thing? I thought that was an urban legend, like men who lick your palms under the bed.

"Twenty each," she said, and pulled some blue pills out of her blue spotted bra. We shuffled to the one-gender bathroom together and leaned against the trough urinals.

"The blue leopard's hiding blue pills!" shrieked Sam. "I hope these aren't actually Viagra."

"Are you sure we should—" I began, but it was too late. She'd already popped hers into her mouth. Oh, what the hell. I followed suit.

"I don't feel anything," Sam said. People had poured in while we were hovered over the urinals and, as the only women in the place, a group of young black men immediately surrounded us.

"*Hey,* ladies," said one. We did a round of drinks with them before one asked, "You wanna go to a different club? I know somewhere better." That's the last Sam or I had remembered.

My heart was racing. I was having a heart attack. *I was having a heart attack.* Where was Sam? It felt like we were in a basement and there were bodies on the floor. Were they dead? I found her leaning against a doorframe. "I don't feel good," she said, swaying to music only she could hear.

"Come on, I need to get some air." The unfamiliar bar was dark and unmanned, some stools tipped over. Then we were climbing stairs. We *were* in a basement. Outside, it was morning, the sun just stretching over the Atlanta skyline. A bank across the street flashed the time: 6:30. We'd lost eight hours and I didn't know where we were.

By some miracle, a cab drove by. I had memorized the address of the hotel (when did that happen?), and Sam fell asleep in my lap. I felt like god. *Look at my superpowers! I will save us both.*

I pulled the blackout curtains shut in our room, but by then Sam was already passed out in one of the twin beds. I crashed, too, but not for long. What was that blinding white light? Was Sam up? Did she turn on the lights? No—above her bed was a crackling ball of fire. What the *fuck*? I stuck my head under the covers. What good was that going to do? But it was the only plan I had.

And what kind of person was I? I saw her limp body, vulnerable and blanket-less, and I said nothing. I just hid, hoping the poltergeist didn't see me. I left her. *I left her out there alone.* And then it was gone. I could see the blackness return through the comforter.

I didn't tell her, as I drove her car home, stopping every half hour so she could vomit out the window. Back in her little studio, we curled up in blankets, ordered take-out, and watched *The L Word* marathons. Weeks later, the demon was still driving me crazy. Or was it my dad? He'd only been dead a few years now. The questions were haunting me, forcing me to dig deeper. I found my answer online: It was ball lightning. I'd never heard of it before, but it could pass through windows. The pictures I found online were exactly what I'd seen in the hotel room, lighting up the polyester blankets like a firecracker.

Was stepping out of the black mambo stupider than Atlanta? There were stories all over Abu Dhabi, about women's bodies getting buried in the sand dunes and nobody caring. The men looked at us with mild curiosity, at our lack of abayas and our white skin, but then went back to their own conversations. We weren't so interesting after all. They had servants grooming their investments, coal-dark men from Nepal and Bangladesh. "You want to pet? You want photo?" one man asked. His few teeth were urine yellow.

"How much?" Sam asked.

"Free," he said, looking confused. "All free." He took a photo of us with a foam-mouthed camel and the sandy fog all around. For the first time, I looked thinner than Sam.

"I'm really worried about you," she said the next day as we waited to be let into the falcon hospital. "You're so thin. You're not eating."

"That's not true," I said. "We just had those Oman sandwiches last night, didn't we?" They were what the street workers ate. Rolls with sauce and potato chips. "And the camel milk lattes at the palace! We had those."

"But that's *all* you had," she said. "How much do you weigh?"

"I don't know." I knew exactly. Not enough. Too much. *Fat, no-good pig.*

Some falcons cost $100,000. Besides humans, they're the only species that get real passports for travel—stamps, photos, and everything. Because of how costly they are, and how much training it takes for falconry, it's the ultimate sport for wealthy Emiratis who have run out of things to spend their money on. The falconry hospital is open to visitors, and it's where all falcons go not just when they're ill, but for regular grooming. So they don't get scared, special goggles are put over their heads making them look like little, feathered, badass motorcycle gangsters.

The veterinarian removed one of the goggles so we could all put on thick gloves and let it perch on our forearms, posing for a picture. There were eight of us on the tour and I went last. The bird was heavier than I thought and looked at me with its black, black eyes. There was no emotion in there. Nothing in there at all. It snapped at my face.

"Hey!" the vet said. But before he could save me, the bird pecked again. Was this a threat? Play? He could have plucked out my eye in a second if he'd really wanted to.

Next, the vet put one of the birds under using the littlest gas mask I'd ever seen. "It's easier to trim their talons like this," he explained. "Come, look closer." The poor thing was so vulnerable. Even with death in its toes, it was useless like this. It was no match for the invisible gas.

On the drive back to her villa with all those rooms she didn't need, she said, "Tomorrow's your last day! Anything else you want to do?"

"I want to take some of this sand with me," I said, watching the dunes fly by. The sand here was brick red. Blood red. And illegal to take, like they'd run out.

"Really?" she asked. "I mean, there's a mason jar in the trunk if you want ...."

She pulled over to the side of the road. I stepped out of my flats and began hiking to the top of a dune. I don't know why. The sand was the same at the base, wasn't it? As I climbed, horns blared below, trying to reach the thin white girl who was, for some strange reason, hiking into oblivion. I dropped to my knees at the peak and dug the jar into the hot pebbles. Sand is just rock babies, mostly quartz, worn down, down, down over time 'til it was almost dust. One time, long ago, it was big and strong and beautiful. Quartz, one of the most expensive, desired stones in the world, and now look at it. This is what too much pressure, too much grinding, too much time could do to you. *Just let them try. Let them try to take this from me.* I wrapped the jar in kurtas with price tags still on them before tucking them in my suitcase.

Sam held me like I was disappearing when she dropped me at the airport, like she'd never see me again. Like a ghost with not much material matter left in this world. "I'll be in the US this summer," she said. "I'll try to plan it for our birthdays." Whenever I leave her, it doesn't feel like a hole appears in my chest. She's always there.

I arrived back in Portland on February 8, Chirag again with arms full of roses. "How was your visit?" he asked.

"Good. What I needed."

I was on a high, below 110 even after a month of some-times failing at dodging dinners and questioning eyes. I could almost see my chest bones beneath my breasts. If I'd let that plastic surgeon stick those implants in me, I'd have looked like a freak.

I needed something more, some proof of my thinness, and somewhere out there my silent plea was answered. An old co-worker posted on Facebook, "Hey! I have a designer friend who needs someone to walk for him in an upcoming show. The dress is for someone who's around 5'7, size 00 with about 34x24x34 measurements. No models in the show can fit this!! Message me if interested, no exp needed." That was my height. Those were my measurements. If Chirag was still on the precipice, would this force him over?

There were only four of us at the go-see and I was the thinnest of them all. "It fits," said the designer's assistant and a quickie contract was shoved in front of me. Those "models" with their big butts and thick thighs. How dare they feign to call themselves that? Only *I* could fit. Only me. The voice in my head had nothing to say.

I was out of place during the rehearsal. The women

were so tall! Like Amazons, broad shoulders and barely-there bodies. The tallest of all walked by me and said, "You have something there," pointing to my shirt. It was a small thread.

"Thanks," I said, picking it off.

"Oh, yeah, just leave it on the floor so it gets on someone else." Did she want me to walk that nearly non-existent thread to the trash? What was her problem? Later, she came by again as a photographer was doing lighting tests on me. "You're so cute!" she said. "You're so short! Isn't she so short?" she asked the photographer, who just grunted at her. I may not have been a tree like her, but I was far from the shortest one there. A lot of the designers had petite models and besides, she didn't know how to hurt me. She was stupid. What did I care if I wasn't six feet tall? She didn't call me fat. She couldn't. That's all I cared about.

I learned how to walk, how to roll my shoulders back, how to stride with one foot perfectly in front of the other in stilettos. How to pose, how to turn, how to give the pissed-off face to the crowd. After the show, Chirag took me to Dust, a club in Chinatown where there were free-for-all poles to climb on and VIP booths. *Did you see me? Was that enough? Am I thin enough now?*

I got my answer two days later. On February 12, as we were making gargantuan Valentine's Day plans, Chirag came home late. I was in my pink sweatpants with acne cream on my face and an oily ponytail. It had been a heavy laxative day, and all my energy had seeped out of my model-thin limbs.

"I got a package from India!" he said, holding it up. "I had my brother send it."

"Oh, yeah?" I said. "What is it? We were just there."

"Open it." Inside the beat-up box were all the makings for street pizza. Real amul cheese. A pack of the special, personal-sized crust.

"What's this?"

"Well ..." he began, "you know how in India, sometimes

you need to bribe people for what you want? You bribe the police if they bother you. The customs agent to not look in your bag. The waiters for the good tables. Well, this, this Indian pizza, is my bribe to you," he said, falling to one knee and pulling a gray ring box out of his pocket, "if you'll let me be your husband."

"Are you serious?" I asked. I couldn't help it, I was blind-sided. I was in pilled sweatpants.

"Yes ... is that a yes?" he asked.

"Oh. Yes!" The ring looked even bigger than it was on my long, skinny fingers.

I had everything I wanted, everything, and I was numb with the knowledge of it. My brain didn't know where to go, who to listen to. The ring was a halo band with a round center. Tiny diamonds were below the surface, propping it up big and proud. It decorated my hand like a chimney. Spider hands, Michelle called them. Michelle. I needed to text Michelle.

But it was almost Valentine's Day and she was in the throes of yet another messy, doomed, half-relationship. When I'd married Eli, she told me over and over, "I don't know what to say! I hate men, I hate love. So don't expect much celebration from me at the wedding." She and Chris had already started their rocky decline at that time, but it was still a few months away from methed-out crashed in the bushes bad.

But this. I wanted to share this with her, but didn't know how. I didn't want to throw it in her face, to force fake happiness out of her. Still. She was close and Sam was far.

"You free to meet up?" I texted her. Let's do this in person. Let's do this for real.

"No, Bo said he might come by later," she replied. Might. Maybe.

"C proposed," I said.

"Seriously???"

"Yes."

"You don't seem very happy about it." She tapped my

balloon just right with her pin, and let all my joy leak out.

"Don't let it upset you," Chirag said. "You know how she is. Come here, let me see it," he said, motioning to me from the couch. He held up my hand, so small in his, and watched the ring dance in the light. "You wanna stay in this Valentine's Day? Make pizza at home?"

Yes. Because that way I could forget to eat it. I could get thinner. If his family thought I was barely good enough this time around, I had to be better next time.

A Homecoming

SCOTT WAS ONLY half-right about his friend in Bend. Sometimes Josh could sneak us in, but most of the time his dad was around and wasn't having it. Now part of me was grateful that I had the big Probe and not the Mustang with the soft top. The seats reclined deep and we figured out which parking lots were safe. Josh gave us some blankets to keep warm and, slowly, Scott pawned off his items for cash. At Pilot gas stations, we could pay for showers if we started going too long between stays with Josh. We stole what we could, never once getting caught. Scott didn't want to tell his family right away, scared that my mom might still have the cops hunting us down. It wasn't unusual for them to not hear from him for stretches at a time. His mom had remarried in an obvious gold-digging move just a few years ago and Scott hated her husband. But his mom was flying high for the first time in her life. She'd had Scott when she was eighteen and in high school.

We lived in my car for six months. Almost all of what should have been my junior year. When summer began to appear, he finally thought it was safe. I'd only been to Portland once before—a sham of a time with Michelle when we were convinced we'd be picked for a national modeling scouting event. Only I was picked to send in more pictures, but the agent told me to get back in touch when I lost twenty pounds. I'd never been to the outskirts, to Aloha where Scott's mom lived.

He must have given her the lowdown when I wasn't around. Stacy was the kind of woman you could tell was pretty and popular in her youth, but now her butt had grown too big. They lived in a mint green, two-story house in an overly landscaped, planned neighborhood. I'd never been in such a nice house. Growing up, I'd always wanted a two-story home. They seemed fancy, kind of like having a doorbell did.

"I got ahold of your parents," Stacy told me, pouring us a kind of juice I'd never tasted. Pomegranate.

"Both of them?"

"Yep," she said, sliding the glass over. "I don't want any trouble here, but you—you need some kind of guardianship. For legal safety if nothing else. And insurance. I talked to our attorney. At your age, if your parents sign away their parental rights, we can become your legal guardians. But really it's just a formality to keep everything on the up and up."

"Do you think they will?" I asked.

She looked at me frankly. "They already have."

Of course, we couldn't stay in the same bedroom. I slept in Anjelica's room, Stacy's 13-year-old daughter from a brief marriage in her twenties. Anj's dad had custody, so she was rarely there. That didn't stop Scott and me from fooling around every chance we got.

"You need to finish school," Stacy told me. I did whatever she said. She was strong, powerful, and kind. I wanted to be just like her.

But there were roadblocks everywhere. I went to the high school in our district, the one Scott had dropped out of. Alone. I didn't tell anyone. In the admissions office, the counselor went over my situation. "At this stage," she said, "the district you were in—well, they're way ahead of us. You only need eight credits to graduate from here, and it's pointless to take just two classes. I recommend you go to Portland Community College and do their high school completion program. I think it's independent study."

I was crushed. I wanted a do-over. I wanted to go to high school where nobody knew me and I could have a real life. But I didn't. I drove to the community college and registered that day. One history class and one literature course. That's all I needed to graduate. I bought the books with money Stacey had given me and dedicated my life to it. In just three months, I was done. I "graduated" at sixteen, just weeks before my birthday. The community college had a huge graduation ceremony for all students, and I was able to attend. Walking that huge auditorium with thousands, it just wasn't the same. It felt fake.

And something else was wrong. I don't know how I knew, but I did. I still had my period, but I felt the foreignness inside me. "I think I'm pregnant," I told Scott, and he rushed to get tests. I was, test after test after test.

"What do you want to do?" Stacey asked. She'd been here before.

"I want an abortion," I said.

"Okay, okay. If you're sure."

At the special clinic downtown, she had to sign for me, but it was Scott who took me. There was an ultrasound. "Do you want to see?" asked the nurse.

"No."

"Okay. Hmm, that's strange ...."

"What?"

"I can't find a heartbeat," she said. "We'd need to do more comprehensive tests to see if it's actually a viable pregnancy or not, but it doesn't really matter if you want to move forward. Viable or not, you still need a D and C."

They had to dilate me first, then I'd come back two hours later for the abortion. The dilation stuck pain prongs through my insides. I couldn't get my pants back up after they stuck whatever it was inside me to start the dilation—I passed out and hit my head on the exam table going down. "That's the first time that's happened!" said the nurses. "Dilation ... isn't supposed to hurt."

"Help me," I said, pain tears springing out my eyes. The abortion itself didn't hurt. They loaded me with laughing gas and a nurse with gentle eyes held my hand and folded over me.

"You're doing good, almost over, honey. Almost there. Breathe deep, breathe deep." And I did. The purple elephants on her mask began to dance like Dumbo, and it took all my strength not to laugh as they pulled fetus parts out of me. If I laughed, they'd take away the happiness.

Afterward, in recovery, they brought me cookies and milk like I was a little girl. As soon as Scott picked me up, he demanded we go to Chuck E. Cheese for his friend's ironic birthday. I went, but spent the whole time in the bathroom. My insides spurted out, and it looked like raspberry jam. *Sorry, baby*, I thought, every time I flushed. *If you knew, you'd thank me.*

CHAPTER TWENTY

THE WEDDING preparations in India were moving fast without our input, and I was happy to have no part in it. Chirag's family added me to WhatsApp in one mad rush, sending me photos of fabrics and venues. I told him to tell his mom to make all the decisions. She didn't have a daughter, so I could give her this: all the picking, the choosing and decisions. All the fun parts of having a daughter. His grandfather passed along the message, "She needs to gain weight before the wedding!" and it made me giddy.

Laura had been messaging me from Manhattan, promising a free place to stay and an insider's guide to the city. I left in April, before the heat rained down on New York. Of course, she worked—public school teachers don't have the luxury of time off. Her apartment was just a few blocks from the subway, and when Chirag dropped me at the airport and kissed me goodbye, I already had visions of ironically romantic horse-drawn carriage rides through Central Park with Laura. I made room in my calorie prison for one New York street hot dog. One cupcake at Magnolia bakery. One slice of pizza from Lombardi's (I didn't know you had to buy the whole pie). I would do all the touristy things while Laura was in class, a hop-on, hop-off tour where I could see Rockefeller Center, the Statue of Liberty, and walk across the Brooklyn Bridge.

Months in foreign metros made it easy for me to maneuver Manhattan, and it was so much smaller than I thought. She lived in a quiet neighborhood in an old, one-bedroom walkup. Spare keys were with her super' and a note and blanket on the couch. "Welcome home!" she wrote.

"Be there at 6." I had dutifully packed my protein bars and travel scale. I couldn't risk the super laxatives here, not when I had to share a bathroom.

"Good lord, you're thin," she said when she saw me. That's *right*. The last time we met in person I was fat and in yoga teacher training. *Fat, fat, fat girl.* That first night, we just talked for hours as she dangled over the chair and I snuggled into her couch.

"I teach a full day tomorrow, but I'll text you when I'm almost done," she said. "We usually go for happy hour on Fridays if you want to join."

I woke up naturally at six and left before her alarm went off. The subway took just fifteen minutes to the Central Park stop and I began my exploration of the city that never sleeps. What the hell, it was *all* asleep. Every shop was closed. I had hours until my bus tour began and nothing to do. I walked that entire city until my hips ached. How many calories had I just burned? The only things awake besides me were diners (which had nothing for me) and newsstands. Arriving at the Brooklyn Bridge, I walked to the center and back. There. Check that off my list. By now, a few hot dog vendors were open so I shoved the voices aside and ordered one, plain with ketchup. It wasn't worth the calories, but I got a photo.

Near Times Square, I climbed onto the double decker bus to the top level. It was cold and my jacket was too light, but I had to do it right. For six hours, I was lurched around the city. The hosts swapped at one point, and the second one was livelier, pointing out places where movies and television shows were filmed. *Friends. Sex and the City.* We stopped near Magnolia's and I was thrilled to find a counter full of miniature samples, smaller than a bite. I took just one of each flavor and hoped that it didn't add up to one full cupcake. Calories saved!

By two, my arm was hurting. Did I strain it? I shrugged it off.

The Empire State Building looked run down. The Statue

of Liberty was closed, still being rehabilitated after Hurricane Sandy. I found out the big building with no windows was a data center. Data centers—that's what one of my new clients specialized in. God, my arm was *really* hurting. When the tour ended, I bought a Starbucks mug for Michelle in Times Square (she collected them) and a Christmas ornament for myself. For Chirag, a stupid tourist shirt and flip flops with apples on them.

I wanted to look fresh when I met Laura's friends, show them I could be a successful writer *and* thin. I could do it all! I had just started sending around my first full manuscript to publishing houses and had already racked up a few rejections, but those I was used to. In Laura's closet of a bathroom, I turned on the shower to the hottest level and peeled off my jacket. My arm was twice its normal size and had a deep purple snake looking thing wrapping around it that was rock hard. Not now. Not now. I didn't know what this thing was, but not *now*.

The closest hospital was two stops away, I had heard the announcement on my way home. "Hey," I texted her, "won't be able to make it to meet your friends, sorry."

Her reply didn't reach me while I was in the subway, clutching my arm and hoping it wasn't deadly. Did I have my insurance card? Yes, right here.

"Why???" her reply popped up as soon as I ascended the steps.

"Don't freak out, but there's something wrong with my arm. Going to ER at hosp near your place."

"I'm coming."

There were hordes of people, coughing people, bleeding people, people I'm sure were on the brink of death. But my arm, it was straight out of hell. The sheer monstrosity of it moved me to the front of the line. "What is it?" I kept asking, and got nothing but big eyes.

"I don't know, you'll have to wait to ask the doctor." That's all the nurses could say. During registration, they took my driver's license but still wrote down my name wrong. Jessica Charles. The Jessica I was used to, the Charles was my middle name and Papo's real name. My mom had hoped to buy his love by naming me after someone she hated, the hell with the fact that I was a girl.

Laura arrived at seven in the evening and talked her way into the back. There are two parts of an ER: front and back. The back is where you go if you look bad enough, but that doesn't mean you're much closer to treatment. It may as well be on the other side of the world. But Laura had a friend who was engaged to a doctor who worked this ER—just not tonight.

"Oh, my god!" she said, when she saw my arm. "I texted Raj," she said. "He's working in another clinic tonight, but he told me to get you out of here."

"Why?"

"This hospital," she whispered, leaning in, "it's ghetto. It's not good." I looked around. She was right. I was the only one who looked white. There were crazy people. Bullet-wounded patients. Some had police escorts.

"It's too late now," I said. "I'm registered, I've been here three hours already."

"I know," she said. "It's okay. He asked if you were white, and if you had insurance. I told him yes, and he said you'll be prioritized then." Her eyes moved down to my arm. "What the fuck is that?"

"I don't know, nobody knows." You could actually watch the snake moving, wrapping around my arm. It hurt the most in the crook of my elbow, but had stretched as low as my wrist and was encroaching on my shoulder.

"Did you call Chirag?"

"Not yet. I want to know what it is first." I wasn't scared, not yet. I don't know why. By midnight, nobody had come for me. Laura trekked across the street to an all-night diner and brought us back soup and cookies. I didn't even care, I ate it with gusto. Maybe it was going to be the last thing I ever ate. It was so crowded now, we were stuck in the middle of an aisle in what looked like lounge chairs. It was exhausting, but getting interesting. As we chewed the amazing cookies, tucked our feet beneath us, we eased back to watch the shitfest roll by like a parade.

"I ain't crazy, I ain't crazy!" a crazy woman screamed from a bed a few feet away.

"Ma'am, either you calm down right now or I'll have to sedate you," said a doctor. She tried to make a run for it, but police held her down while a nurse loaded her up. She flopped around like a beached whale for a second before going still.

"This is amazing!" Laura said as Orthodox Jew EMTs rolled in one of their own. In New York, that's a thing.

Laura fell asleep and at one a doctor came by. She looked younger than me.

"When did this start?" she asked, touching my arm.

"Ow, today I think. My arm started hurting this morning but I was out all day. I had a jacket on. I didn't see this until I got home at five."

"Do you know what it is?"

"No ... do *you*?"

"No, but it doesn't look good. We'll need to run some tests."

She stood from her crouch and began making notes at the nurse's desk just steps away. "Excuse me? Excuse me? Uh, could you tell me, like, the worst case scenario here?" I always wanted to know. Lets me prepare.

"Well, the *worst* case is we'll have to amputate your arm. But I'm going to try and avoid that." What? *What the fuck is this thing?* Grabbing my phone with my only good arm, my left one of course, I got as far into a corner as possible and called Chirag. It was awkward to rely wholly on my non-dominant hand, and I was already crying by the time he answered.

"I'm here, in a hospital and ... my arm ... I don't know. They said they might have to amputate it. I don't want them to cut my arm off!"

"What?" he'd been asleep. "What's going on?"

"I don't know!" Laura was suddenly at my side.

"Give me the phone," she said, and I handed it to her, unable to speak. I don't know what she told him, but she handed my phone back silently. The snake was almost across my shoulder, the doctor was gone.

"Excuse me," I said to one of the nurses, steadying my voice. "But this ... this thing is growing."

"Well, it's a good thing you're in the hospital then, huh?" she said.

By three in the morning, they'd found a gurney for me and I'd cried myself too tired to keep my eyes open. If I lost my right arm, how long until I learned to type with just my left? How much weight would I lose with it cut off? Could I count that lower weight? Was that legit? How would I leave Chirag? I couldn't give him a broken, disabled wife. I wouldn't. Breakup rehearsals began in my head.

The jostling woke me up, and two young, strong men were rolling me down a hallway. "How are you?" the black one asked.

"Tired," I said.

"Yeah," said the Latino one. "We all are." Well, fuck you then. You don't have a snake in your arm! I didn't know where they were taking me.

In the ambulance, the nice one stayed in back with me. He asked my name, my birth date, if I had insurance. "My card's in my purse," I said.

"It's okay, they'll take it later. What's your address?" I told him—the one I shared with Chirag.

"Uh ... do you ... do you know where you are?" he asked.

"New York."

"You're in Harlem. Girl, you're *far* from home."

"Yeah. I was ... I was on vacation."

They didn't cut off my arm. All the tests were negative for everything, at least everything to do with the snake. "You're underweight," said one nurse. "And your cholesterol's very high for your age and otherwise good health." She looked at me curiously. "Are you ... nevermind." In a last ditch effort, they put me on an antibiotic drip and the snake started to recede. In the new hospital, they brought me huge trays of food that I moved around so it looked like I ate. In the afternoon, a group of interns who looked like children wandered in. "I *have* to see this," one said. When doctors say that, you know you've got something good.

"It's fading now," I said. "You should have seen it yesterday. Actually, wait, I took pictures." They passed my phone around in awe.

I begged Laura to bring me my laptop and she did. I began practicing one-handed typing because I had no choice. There were too many needles in my right arm to do anything else. Chirag called every hour, asking if I was okay and if I wanted him to come. Yes, I was okay (no, I wasn't). Yes, I'd wanted him to come. I wanted him to come on the first day, without my asking. But I told him no.

"We don't know what that was," said the new, main doctor, a gruff old man who looked like he'd seen some shit. Just not shit like this. "But it's responding to antibiotics, so we're sticking with that. We're keeping you here three more days for the drip, then it's oral meds after that. But I have to put something on your chart, so I'm calling it cellulitis."

"It's cellulitis?" I asked, like I knew what that was.

"I don't know. If it is, I've never seen it present like *that,*" he said, making a note and walking away.

For three days everyone called me Jessica or Ms. Charles. I didn't correct them. Maybe they'd bill me wrong, too. I had self-employed insurance, and I was far out of network. With every drip in my tube, I could feel the debt piling up. I was released the day before my return flight.

"That was wild," said Laura. "Every time I see you, you go to the hospital!" I guess she was right. "Well, you've got about twenty-four hours. Are you up for anything?"

She had to do what I wanted, I was sick. We did the carriage ride, just like I had imagined. "I've lived here a decade and haven't done this," she said. "Can I pick the carriage?"

She picked the most fairytale-like one, full of purple flowers and a driver with a top hat. We careened around the park I'd seen all my life in movies, past the carousel and the boats on the lake. "It's so romantic!" cyclists cried out as we galloped past. I suppose it was. "We just got *marriiieed*!" she'd shout back to them and everybody whooped.

We got stuck in traffic on the way back for hours, her demanding I needed at least one gypsy cab trip before I returned. *Yellow cab, gypsy cab, dollar cab, holla back.* God, that was hard to say when you're five, wait, *six* baby bottles deep. Laura had hidden the little alcohol bottles in her purse, and we got stupid drunk in the backseat. "Excuse me? Sir? Sir?" I said repeatedly to the driver, a recent Dominican transplant who clearly didn't want to be escorting day drunk girls. "Do you have any Jay-Z? Can you put on Jay-Z? We want to hear Jay-Z if you could just—"

"You sit back and be quiet!" he finally barked at me.

"You got in *trouble!*" Laura said as the seat pulled her deeper into its crumb-filled pits. Fine. We didn't need him. He probably didn't have any Jay-Z anyway.

"Hey!" we started yelling to the stopped cars beside us. "Can you *slow down!* You're going *way too fast*, there are kids out here!" We said "Way too fast" in a German accent, just like in *Super Troopers*. The driver pretended he couldn't hear us.

For my last dinner, we went to Lombardi's. This was it—the oldest pizza in New York! We ordered a margherita and it came to the table sizzling. The crust was black in all the right spots, but all I could see were calories, calories, calories. How much was this costing me, really? I patted it down, trying to sop up the grease. The needless calories. "You take the rest home," I told Laura. "I just wanted one piece."

When I got back to Portland, Chirag checked my arm, ran his thick finger up its length, but by now it was deflated. The snake was gone.

"Where's the serpent?" he asked.

"Still inside me somewhere."

I went to yoga almost every day of the week, but only when I could get next to the mirror. I had to compare my thighs to others, make sure they were the leanest. Ensure that when my torso was twisted in warrior pose, my waist the slightest. There was nothing special about Thursday's yoga class. I'd had this teacher dozens of times before. She put us into savasana, my favorite part of her class. She'd always spray a new essential oil over us and tell us strange facts about our bodies. As she began her guided savasana this time though, she veered off. Not here. This was territory I didn't like. "I want you to think ..." she started in her slow, drunk-sounding voice, "about *five* things. *Five* things that you like about yourself. It can be physical, mental, emotional, spiritual, anything. Focus on those *five* qualities and be thankful for all they've given you."

Okay, five things. I could do this. One ... I don't know. Sometimes I was thin? Did that count? I mean, I was a good writer, but I don't know if I *loved* that about myself. It was just a fact, and it let me have a career that was easy. But love? "Now start slowly waking up your body ..." she said, "and wiggle your toes." It was over? It was over, and I couldn't think of a single thing?

I walked to my car, the '83 Trans Am Chirag had urged me to buy when he saw it online for just $15,000. It had been garaged for twenty years with only 18,000 miles on it. My childhood dream car with the big, golden phoenix emblazoned on the front and the yellow old-fashioned license plate: "JCT," my initials. It had been waiting for me, and it made me feel strong. I loved my *car*. But it had nothing to do with me.

That day, I made an appointment with the most renowned psychologist in the area who specialized in eating disorders.

The receptionist at Dr. Norwood's clinic was a stout, middle-aged woman who saw too-thin things all day, and she wanted to explain herself. "I used to be thin," she said as she checked me in. I hadn't asked. "I knew all the tricks. But things change," she said. She seemed sad about that.

Dr. Norwood was a blonde, slender woman with flawless makeup. She looked too young to have been doing this for twenty-three years. When she asked what brought me to the clinic, I was embarrassed to say it was a yoga class, but she didn't seem to think it strange. She asked all the questions I expected, but then took a sharp turn backwards.

"Tell me about your family." By now, I was used to this. I'd rehashed what was apparently my fucked up childhood over and over to get those scholarships in college. Committees love that messed-up stuff, the sicker the better. Dr. Norwood caught my mom in her teeth and wouldn't let go. She kept digging so hard I thought her nails would break right there, tear that perfect polish right off.

"Can we not talk so much about my mom?" I asked.

"Why not?"

"I've talked about her my entire life."

"Did you know that recent research points to some eating disorders having a genetic component? Did your mom every display any signs that you might associate with anorexia?"

No, my mom was fat. Wait a minute. Did she? Stories she'd told me that I'd long buried started cropping up. The meth she took to stay skinny, before anyone called it meth. How she only ate every three days. The liposuction, the constant dieting, the time I caught her running naked on the treadmill. "I'd like to recommend five sessions per week, Monday through Friday, to start," said Dr. Norwood. "We can modify as needed."

There were good sessions and terrible ones. She kept making me pull up the past over and over, look at it closely and then put it back to pick up another memory. "Tell me about your relationship with your father."

"I don't know, he wasn't around much."

"That's equally as important."

"There's really not much to tell."

"Think of one memory." Radio Shack. I'd forgotten about Radio Shack.

"Well, I was about twelve I think. Maybe thirteen, Junior High at least. My dad, he was Cherokee. Dark as a Mexican." Her eyes didn't flinch. Wasn't she going to tell me I didn't look Indian? "Anyway, my mom had put something on hold at Radio Shack for him to pick up. I went with him. My dad, he told the guy working there that his wife had put something on hold. The worker, he couldn't have been older than like twenty. But he looked at my dad, looked at me, and was like, 'Is *this* your wife?'"

"About you?" asked Dr. Norwood.

"Yeah. Like ... my parents had me late. My dad was I think 36 when I was born."

"How did that make you feel?"

"Embarrassed. I was twelve years old!"

"You developed early?"

"Well, yeah. I guess. But that—that wasn't the bad part." I was starting to tear up. *Stop it, stop it.*

"What was?"

"My dad—he never showed any emotion. Well, besides anger. But he was just so shocked. He looked so small. He just said, 'This is my daughter,' like he had to apologize for me. Or something." Only my breath was holding my tears in. "And I—I never went anywhere with him alone again. Never. Not 'til years later. And when he died, I felt so bad. Why did I care what some cashier thought?"

"You and your dad, you weren't the perversion there," she said. She was right, wasn't she? So why did I blame me and my dad?

She told me all the statistics. How anoretics (yes, I learned that was the correct word—not anorexics) had a forty percent higher chance of being alcoholics. A twenty percent higher chance of dying young. How more and more research was showing it wasn't just white, teenaged, privileged girls who suffered from it. Men did, too. Middle-aged women, too. Even thirty-something Native Americans. "A lot of doctors, general physicians, they aren't trained or educated on eating disorders. They miss clues which should be obvious or make recommendations that are harmful," she told me.

And then the biggest task of all: "You need to ask yourself, honestly, if you want to live."

"Yes. Yes, I want to live."

"Why?"

"I have an incredible life. I have everything I've ever wanted."

"Then why are you sabotaging yourself?" Was I? Is that what I was doing?

"I don't know, I don't know. It's like ... I set this precedent for myself. This really high bar. And while I was doing it, everything fell together. You know? And now—I can't go back. I can't get fat."

"Jennifer," she said, "none of that is tied to your weight. Do you really think your career will fail or Chirag will leave if you're a healthy weight?"

"No ... but what if his family says I got fat?"

"What if they do? Are you going to let people, no matter who they are, be solely in charge of your value? Your validation?" I guessed I was. "I think I know something that might help. Keep in mind, anorexia is for life. You can't recover from it. But you can be *in* recovery. There will be ups and downs. But this might help get you moving in the right direction. I want you to find a physical activity that you love. One that isn't dictated by calories burned or losing weight, but one that demands strength."

Running. It was running, I knew it was.

"Now, some ED doctors, they tell patients to not exercise at all. Especially someone like you, who has some exercise-bulimia issues to contend with." Bulimia, it's not just vomiting, although that's the most common. It's any activity that's designed to get rid of calories consumed in an excessive or dangerous way. I learned that from her, too. "But for you, I think it might help."

Anoretics are often perfectionists. Ambitious over-achievers. I might not be all white, or a teenager, and didn't grow up rich, but I fit the new mold of anorexia better than I thought. "Can you do that?" she asked.

"Yeah. Yeah, I can do that."

At home that night, when Chirag came through the door tired and heavy, asking how my session went, I told him. "I'm going to run a marathon."

"Did the doctor say that was okay?"

"She recommended it—well, something like it. She says to choose an activity that requires me to be strong. Where I have to take in nutrition."

"Are you sure about a full marathon? What about that half you wanted to do?"

"No. It's got to be a marathon." I ordered Brooks Ghost shoes that night, the waterproof kind built for the Northwest. They were dark gray with pink accents. I would only wear them for training, training races and the marathon. It was six months away, the Portland Marathon, and I scooped up one of the last entries. I would run over twenty-six miles, and I would do it three months before we got married.

xxi.
Some Fields Will Blossom

"JENN. Jenn, call me. Call me. It's ... it's about Kerri." Michelle's voice was cracking by the end of the message. Down There, it was senior year in Central Point. In another world, I would have been there but the valley walls had started moving too close. I hadn't spoken to Kerri since that night in the auditorium with Scott, but I knew. I knew she was partly behind all the girls I'd never noticed calling me a slut and bitch even more than normal in the halls. When did she get such powers? How had *Kerri* been the one to slip-slide up the ranks?

"Hey," I said when I finally got back through to Michelle. "What's going on?"

"Kerri, she ... oh, god, I don't know ...." Why was she crying? She hadn't even *liked* Kerri.

"You know, she wasn't in school. I guess she was with some girl riding ATVs in a field on Wednesday. It, she ... it was an accident."

An accident. An accident. "Is she okay?"

"No ..." Michelle's voice had gone up so high it disappeared, "she's dead. It's in all the papers here. The, uh, the funeral's in two days. If you can come."

What day was it? April 16. Eighteen. Kerri had turned eighteen last month. "Uhm, I don't know. Did she ... was it bad?"

"I'm not sure," Michelle said. "There are different stories. But the girl she was with, she said Kerri was alive when she left her. Stuck under the ATV, and it was too heavy to lift. The girl is freaking the fuck out, Jenn. She said Kerri was real calm. Really calm. Just told her to go get help.

266

Over and over."

"Oh, my god."

"And when she got back, with cops and everything ... Kerri was dead."

"Was it painful?" Why was I doing this?

"I don't know. For sure. But, uh, I heard that it took a long time. That she was out there alone for a long time."

"I'm not ... I don't know what to do."

"There's one other thing."

"What?" There's no other thing. There's no other thing.

"Rosa? She, uh, she asked me to get ahold of you." Rosa. I'd left her behind. In the mad escape with Scott, I'd pushed her deep into my recesses.

"Okay."

"She ... she just wanted me to tell you," her voice was cracking badly, almost splitting totally apart, "that Kerri forgave you. What for? What happened with you all?"

"It doesn't matter." God, it really didn't.

"So, are you coming? For the funeral?" Scott walked through the door, raising his furry eyebrows at my being on the phone.

"I don't ... no. I don't think I can."

"Jenn. What the hell."

"I can't, I'm sorry. If you ... if you see Rosa. Or her mom. Just. Just say I'm sorry."

"Jenn!" I hung up before she could layer on the guilt thick, like I deserved.

"Who was that?" asked Scott, dropping his gym bag on the couch.

"Michelle."

"And what did she want? Tell you about her latest drama?"

"Kerri died."

"Oh." That shut him up for a minute. "How?"

"ATV accident."

He clucked his tongue, opened the fridge for a string cheese. "I told you she was fucking weird," he said.

CHAPTER TWENTY-ONE

THIS TIME there were no excuses, no take-backs. I ran like my life depended on it. When the insomnia got shaken up, I used it, began running at four in the morning. I mapped out my plan, perfectly aligning a new Higdon program to culminate with a marathon on October 4. I wouldn't miss a day. "Ask or tell," Chirag would say to me in the evenings, our way of making new conversation.

"I ran six miles today."

"Way to go, bibijaan."

I'll admit it, I tried. I tried to run on 700 calories, but it didn't last long. I had a choice. I could either starve, or I could eat and run. I couldn't do both. Dr. Norwood didn't ask much about the running, she let me bring it up. For that I was grateful. When we first met, I told her, "Don't ask me about how many calories I eat or how much I weigh or I won't come back." "Okay," she'd said, and she'd kept her word. By week four, I gave up, moved up to 1,200 calories that was made up of spinach and tofu. Smoked salmon and whey protein powder. I watched my thighs start to thicken when I ran past shops and I tried not to care.

"Tell me something," Chirag said in May.

"Today I ran ten miles." Soon it was eleven. Then twelve, fourteen. I didn't know what runners were talking about as I tiptoed into their online world. Toenails falling off? Bleeding nipples? Shitting your pants" (that hadn't happened in a while)? On the 16-miler day, I got it. At mile 14, my chest began to chafe but I couldn't stop. The tips of my feet went numb. My nipples were rubbed raw when I got home, and it hurt too much to shower. The toenail on one foot was still there, but barely—and the whole toe was black. I researched, learned hacks and things to do that helped. But there was no stopping it altogether. These were battle wounds, pain I earned.

By June, I had it, a new kind of validation. "Ms. Taylor, we are extremely impressed by your poetry manuscript and would love to publish *Lions Love Hearts the Best* in our autumn lineup." I'd named the book after Kama, our tiger, who would grow up to feast on lion hearts. That night, when Chirag said, "Ask or tell," I told. What I didn't tell him is that it would be dedicated to him. *To Chirag. (Of course).*

"Let's celebrate," said Chirag. "This weekend, anywhere you wanna go."

"Cake," I said. "I want to go to Cake." We invited our friends, but nobody came. "Short notice" was most excuses along with a few "We're saving for a wedding, a baby, to buy a house." Michelle just didn't reply to the invitation at all.

"I've been thinking," I said as I scraped the whipped cream off the cocktail and brought it to my lips. How many calories? Stop it. "Maybe I should buy a place in Vancouver. Just for taxes. I could rent it out."

"Why don't we buy a place here?"

"Well, that would kind of defeat the purpose of buying. I'm just trying to get out of paying Oregon taxes."

"I know," Chirag said. "But if we don't buy now, we may never be able to afford to. Don't you want a piece of it? A piece of your home for keeps?"

"I thought we were moving to India in a couple of years." That was one of our deal-breakers, the product of a long conversation the night he proposed. He wanted to move back to India before he was forty, and I had nothing holding me here. I wanted a child, he demanded we adopt. Part of me was sad, that I wouldn't see his perfection reflected in someone else. Part of me was happy that I wouldn't see all my own faults passed down—including the anorexia. A sad part of me was happy that I wouldn't have to get pregnant-fat.

"We are," he said. "But we can enjoy it while we're here. Investment property. Rent it out or sell it for profit when we leave."

"Maybe," I said. He started looking that night.

For his birthday, I had booked six tickets a year in advance at Crater Lake Lodge. You had to: people come from all over the world to bask in its glory. I didn't know yet who we'd bring, but the two vans filled up fast. New friends, ones we'd met from old friends, and everyone all coupled up. Besides a Romanian couple, I was the only one of us who appeared white. "We best not scare the pale ones!" said the London-born Indian in the backseat with his Taiwanese wife. Both were doctors at a hospital, but never acted like it. We called her "Panda fucker" because it made sense one drunken night—she researched panda fertility. It wasn't until we were sober that we realized it seemed racist.

The mosquitoes were gluttonous at Crater Lake, and we got drunk early. I brought red Solo cups and we wandered around the rim trying to look sober. At dinner, we were the biggest, loudest table. I ordered bison and red potatoes, feeling only a little guilty. I'd done my best to shift my running schedule around the trip, but still needed to squeeze in a brief two-miler in the morning. Hungover and too full, I woke up at dawn and forced my way to a small stretch along the rim. The sun blasted pink back at me, and I was the only one awake.

Eventually the lodge woke with creaky knees and pounding heads. I was already two cups of tea deep by the time the first of the group made its way downstairs.

I hadn't seen Michelle in months, though I'd had a hand-carved box made with *Michelle, will you be my maid of honor?* carved into it. It had taken forever to find the right time to give it to her—she was always complaining about her latest romantic failure, and the timing was off. When I finally did, she cried like it was a real proposal. But then she disappeared. Went to a new friend's wedding in Jamaica where her ongoing fuck buddy also attended and moved his dick over to her friend she was sharing a hotel suite with. The wedding, from what I hear, was littered with cocaine snorting and Michelle making a big show about sharing cock.

I asked her to be my maid of honor because I missed her. It was my way of saying, "Come back."

But she didn't, even though she said yes. She was asked to be maid of honor for two people earlier that year, and posted incessantly online about how much planning she was doing. For one, she crafted a traditional bachelorette party complete with hotel suites downtown, dinner and penis party hats. For another, a guided wine tour and slumber party. I kept asking her when she was planning the engagement party for us. She kept saying she was too busy. It did happen, in July and it was lovely—though she roped in her friend Victor to help. He was nearly fifty, gay, and I'd met him once before. I'd given her our condo that day to decorate and cook, which meant we were kicked out from the early hours. Laura came, and we spent the day taking her around the city, to Voodoo Doughnuts and for hot chocolate flights at Cacao. When we were too tired to do anything more, we went back to Michelle's to nap. I was nervous for the party and had a glass of wine. Chirag fell asleep on her couch. The dishwasher was clean and full, so I rinsed the wine glass and left it in the sink.

The next morning, Michelle had left an angry text. "Wth happened at my house??? Dirty dishes in the sink and a pillow moved on my couch????" I didn't reply. She was almost gone.

Chirag and I couldn't find any houses we liked, except one. But it was a concept house, a "what could be," not a real one. A plot of land was for sale, the last piece of an old dairy farm. "You could build a house here!" said the realtor. "Any kind you want." Farmhouse sinks, quartz counters and subway tile bounced in my head, and we bought the land without knowing how much work it was.

It was my birthday, and I didn't want to celebrate. Michelle began texting me a week prior. "What are you doing for your bday?" she asked.

"Nothing this year."

"No! You have to! At least a movie?" Maybe she wanted to spend time with me after all.

"Ok ... new horror movie playing at LR theater. Friday at 7?"

"K."

On Wednesday, Chirag let slip that his friend's girlfriend wanted to have a surprise dinner for my birthday. He'd told her no because of the movie plans. A run team I'd found talked about a happy hour get together after our group long run on Friday, and I turned them down. Really, both sounded good. I wanted to celebrate. But for the past three years I'd held huge parties, paid for everyone's dinner (it's the Indian way) and entries to massive trampoline parks or roller rinks. It was becoming an epic free outing for everyone I knew, and I didn't want to pay for my friends anymore. But this? A surprise party, a well-intentioned beer after sixteen miles? Incredible—but I owed Michelle. We had history.

At four o'clock that Friday, she texted, "Sorry, can't make it" and I broke down. Called Dr. Norwood. "I don't know if I want to continue this. Maybe I should just formally end the friendship."

"That's something we can discuss next time you're here," she said.

Poor Chirag. He couldn't say, "I told you so" or "Why do you keep letting her do this to you?" He knew I wouldn't respond to that text and he did his best to make me forget. "How about we go out someplace special tonight?" he asked.

"No. I'm too fat, I shouldn't be eating." The words stabbed in a good way for a second, but it didn't last and he knew better than to say anything. And I cried—the entire weekend. "This is the shittiest birthday," I told him, knowing I was being a brat but I couldn't stop.

"Thanks a lot," he said, picking up the Jade yoga mat he'd bought me and the hand-knit yoga bag to store it in. I ran, though. I stuck to my schedule. Seven more weeks. I'd already put a half behind me on Fourth of July. It was a heatwave and on Sauvie Island where there was no shade. My time sucked, but I finished. I was used to picking up first now in all the smaller practice races. First for my gender and age, then just for my gender. I was besting those eighteen-year-old girls with their legs like horses'.

We had been inviting everyone we knew to the Indian wedding, knowing they wouldn't come. Except Sam, she would come. They'd moved back to the states for both their PhD completions. She'd left all but dissertation, ABD, in Georgia and Sean had never started after his master's. They knew they'd be broke and raising a young child, but it was now or never. It didn't matter to her that she couldn't afford the ticket. I'd booked a two-bed room for us at a different hotel on Juhu Beach. For three weeks leading up to the wedding, it would be like the old days. But with money. She and I, poolside and cocktails.

Michelle kept saying, "I'll go!" and then, "I want to go." "I'll try to come" and "I don't know if I can afford it" was next. My book was releasing days before the marathon. In the acknowledgements, I started with "To my forever friends, Michelle and Sam." I put Michelle first. I could say it was alphabetical, or because I'd known her longest, but the truth was I was begging her. Begging her to come back. Before I could even tell the publisher to send her a copy, before the marathon, I knew I'd lost her.

My longest pre-marathon run was twenty miles. That was almost a marathon, right? What's another 6.2 when you're already so close? I did it at four in the morning because I was too nervous to sleep. The low-hanging branches whipped at my face, and it was cold in September but by mile seven my braid was wet with sweat and flogging my back. Sometimes I came across old people walking their dogs and they couldn't hear me. Their dogs would turn around at my pounding feet, but they didn't give me away. I gave as wide a berth as possible when I passed them, but these were old neighborhoods with old, narrow walkways. "Jesus Christ!" they would yell as I passed. Their dogs would never save them.

I felt like a Terminator barreling through the night, the stop signs like bright candy pieces. I never ate before I ran—fasted, that's how I liked it. My stomach grew tauter and Dr. Norwood wouldn't like that, but I didn't care. I ate afterward. I finished when the sun was shyly beginning to rise, scheduled my stop to be four blocks from home to give myself a walking cool-down. Chirag wouldn't even be awake yet. As I came to a slow, my legs shaking and hair wild, a man about my age passed me in the other direction. "Hey, don't give up now!" he said. "You can keep going."

Fuck you. You try running twenty miles before dawn.

The morning of the marathon, I prayed for two things: no rain and a decent time. That was it. I knew exactly what my Boston qualifying time would be—3:48. I didn't know if I wanted it or not. It would come with bragging rights, but a responsibility. If I made it, I would have to do it. And I swore I'd never run again after this.

Chirag drove me to the starting point downtown. We had to arrive around five in the morning and it was freezing. He followed me as long as he could, taking videos and photos. Me in my cheap blue flannel zip-off that I could toss at mile three when I got hot and didn't care. My most comfortable running pants and sports bra. My shoes, now with over 300 miles on them. A braid woven tightly, and toss-away gloves.

How do you get ready to run a marathon? I jogged in place, trying to keep warm. The coldness never fully leaves an anoretic. It burrows into our bones and stays. There were thousands of people. When my wave started, I worked towards winding around them. Slow people, walkers, people who said their pace was faster than it was. I didn't lie about pace, even though I knew it leads to obstacles. The recovery stops were easy. At every water station (not juice station) I got to slow to slam it down. I got three gummy bears out of the cup they gave me, no more and no less (Dr. Norwood would hate that).

I didn't tell Chirag that I ate nothing that morning. I would do this. I would run a fucking marathon in a fasted state. The hardest part was all the people. They were so goddamned slow, and the streets so narrow. It wasn't until we'd gone both ways along the waterfront, around the northwest industrial district, up to Northwest 23rd and heading towards the St. John's Bridge that people got sparse. Now we were really running. With all the waves, I couldn't tell who had started before or after me, so the competition was just with myself.

The lead-up to the bridge was brutal and I wanted to walk more than anything. The incline slowed me, harshly, but I kept running. On the other side of the bridge was the good photographer. This is the shot you really wanted, with those green spires in the back. With every photographer, I slowed a little, tried to look peaceful yet determined for those good photos. I never looked at the camera.

On the descent from the bridge, we wove through neighborhoods in the University of Portland area, an unfamiliar landscape. Homeowners set out lawn chairs and grilled meat, cheering us on. Along the hillside, I passed a woman on a stretcher being hauled into an ambulance. It was mile twenty. God, she must be mad at herself. Around the Rose Quarter and then over another bridge back to downtown. This was it. We were almost there. Oh, thank Christ, a water station—but, no. It was beer. *Who the fuck wants beer at mile 22?*

All the marathon runners I'd talked to before, they were right. *Nobody* wants to hear "Almost there!" unless you're at mile twenty-fucking-six. But that's all anyone yelled. I preferred the quiet fans, the ones with signs that said, "All this for a free banana?" and "You think you're working hard? I got up at 5am to make this sign!"

The crowd thickened again at mile 25. At 26. I tried to look like it was easy in case there was a photographer I couldn't see or Chirag. I'd told him to meet me at the re-union area under "Z." Probably not many people would be there. Crossing the finish line, I couldn't slow down. I slammed my foot hard against that final tracker, knowing the device tied into my shoe was done. But it hurt to stop. To walk. "Where ... where's the reunion area?" I asked volunteers as they shoved chocolate milk into my hand. Chocolate milk? Who wants this after 26.2 miles?

"Oh, yeah, that didn't happen."

"Didn't happen?"

"No reunion area."

I didn't see Chirag, but asked a volunteer to use their phone. No answer. Shit. I couldn't sit, but I couldn't walk either. One block away was the results table, with times constantly being updated. There. I could make it there. A new list was being taped up as I hobbled my way there. "Jennifer Taylor: 3:56.25." Eight minutes. I missed Boston by eight minutes.

"Excuse me, can I borrow your phone?" The table of middle-aged women looking at me suspiciously. What did they think I was going to do? I certainly couldn't make a run for it with their phone at this point.

"Well, okay." This time he answered.

"Where are you?"

"The Starbucks. Where the results are."

"You already finish?"

"Just now. Yeah. I didn't qualify."

"I'm coming. I'm proud of you, babydoll."

"Bring the Vicodin. I can't walk."

"Anything else?"

"I'm hungry."

I wanted Red Robin, all of it. A guacamole chicken burger, salad with crunchy corn chips and bottomless fries. On the way there, four Vicodins deep, Michelle texted me. "I need to go shopping for Halloween costumes, you busy?"

"Just ran the marathon. Can't walk." She knew I'd been training. I didn't expect her to know what day it was, or to send me good luck texts like Laura had, though just last year Michelle had waited at the finish line for a co-worker, sign in hand, for "the other Michelle." She no longer talked to that girl. But I hadn't expected this either. Nothing. No response, not even a "good job." Was I so worthless to her if I wasn't readily available when she had no better options?

I could tell the lettuce in the burger was wilted, that the tomatoes in the salad were old, but I didn't care. I was ravenous. Fuck the gummy bears and their calories. And Michelle. I ate because I wanted to. Because my body needed it. And because I could.

At home, I pulled off the shoes and put them back into their original box, where I had been keeping training race medals and now the big, Portland rose-etched marathon one. On an index card, I wrote down how many miles were on the shoes, how many races, and my final time. It was a burial.

Symptoms of an End

STACEY SAID I was close enough to eighteen—we just had to find a landlord who didn't look too closely at my ID. I'd done the same to get a job. I applied in every women's clothing store in Washington Square, putting down that I was eighteen and Stacey as a "previous boss." She didn't mind. The Limited hired me to work the stock room and I finally felt like I belonged. Here I was, working in a mall and buying fancy clothes. Scott started working at Abercrombie, though our shifts were opposite and he was only on-call at ten hours per week. All the other time he spent playing basketball at the gym. There had been no word from my mom, and only occasional calls from my dad who had actually made it to North Carolina. He and Sharon were living in a cabin next to a goddamn mansion. He did expansions for the rich people who planned to use it as a vacation home and Sharon did the housekeeping. I wondered if she was happy now that she was in the thick of it, giving up her cushy real estate job and steady husband for my wild-haired father.

He called when he needed me, like the day I turned eighteen. Papo had left me $80,000, the miser had been comfortable the whole time and none of us knew. It was my college fund. My dad asked me to go to Merrill Lynch and sign some papers releasing the funds to him. He promised me $10,000 cash in exchange. That was a fortune to me. To Scott. I did it the same day and the funds were deposited immediately. I bleached my hair platinum blonde and bought Scott $2,000 worth of things he wanted. The money was gone in two months.

We had settled into a stewing hell of a relationship, pushed together into a one-bedroom apartment. Michelle and Chris meandered up north as soon as she graduated, and I could feel the jealousy seething from her. My very own apartment, and a nice one! New carpet and everything. She and Chris didn't have that yet. They were staying with his mom while Michelle let go of her dreams of college and Chris searched for a job in companies that would hire someone with a drug record and no high school diploma.

Two months into the year I turned legal, I was pregnant again. What the hell? I didn't realize my sensitivity to hormones, the sensitivity that made me throw up at least once a week, was making those pills null and void. For all my fails at making myself throw up, the pills did it for me—though not enough to make me thin.

"In that shirt, you're *almost* thin," Scott would say. He hung up pictures of Natalie Portman and Audrey Hepburn all over the apartment. When he found clothes that looked somewhat like their outfits captured on film, he'd bring them to me. Usually a size too small. "Better start working on that!" he'd say. My eyes were still brown. Watch how thin I'd be now, fucker.

I thought, You know, maybe I should just keep it. Hell, I've been religiously on birth control for *years* now and knocked up twice. Maybe that was a sign? Maybe the baby would look like him and nothing like me. At least I could give it that gift. None of my cat-like green eyes. My thin hair, my body that was turning to fat.

When I told Scott I was pregnant, all he said was, "How do I know it's even mine?" I made an appointment for another abortion the next day.

I wasn't the cheater. I watched him pet the hood of my car when he got home daily, to see if it was warm. See if I'd been out when I had no reason to be. I started going to beauty school and he hated it, but I had the upper hand. "You really think there are any straight men there?" He couldn't argue much with that. "What do you think I'm going to do?" He allowed me to leave the house for something besides work, but only for classes and back. Otherwise, he kept the keys.

But one day, one day I just didn't feel like going. I turned around and picked up our favorite Wendy's combo meals to surprise him instead. He didn't hear me pull into the garage. Couldn't hear my footsteps up the stairwell to our townhome. He was on the phone, his voice loud, confident he was alone. "Okay, I love you, baby," he said and hung up. I needed to get to the phone. *Needed the phone.*

When he saw me, he didn't say a word. We faced off, prepping for the showdown. I made a run for the phone, but he got back to it first, scratched at my arms when I wrestled it from him and searched for the "Redial" button. When I had it, he crawled off of me. Had he given up? "Hello?" said a girl's voice "Scott?" I hung up.

"It's not like that," he said. I could see him, actually *see* him, flipping through excuses in his head. "She's my manager, she has a crush on me."

"Get out," I said.

"Make me."

"Then I will." Instead of following me, he raced outside. What the hell was he doing? Who cares, this gave me time to grab a few things. Tires wailed out front and at the window I saw him whip his car in behind mind, holding my car captive. Oh, shit. His footsteps barreled back up the stairs and he blocked my way.

"You're not going anywhere."

"Move. And move your car now." He just laughed. I made a move to go past him, but he knocked me down. Jesus, he was stronger than I thought. The cold of the kitchen tile sucked at my back as his knee made its way against my throat.

The kitchen knife, the big one on the counter. With some superpower I shoved him off me and grabbed it, yielding it like serial killers do in movies, my knuckles on top of the handle. Like *I* knew what I was doing. "Whoa," he said, "whoa, whoa, whoa." I backed down the stairwell and he followed at a generous distance. Fuck, I forgot my bag. I can't go back now. In my car, the doors locked, I yelled at him to move his precious new Jetta. The one I paid the down payment on. "Just come out and we can talk. I didn't do anything, I swear!"

"Move your car. Right now. Or I'll move it for you." Stalemate. I turned the key, threw the car in reverse, and hit the gas as hard as I could. It couldn't go far—just two feet before it kissed his bumper.

"You fucking crazy bitch!" he screamed, "You're just like your mom!" he added, pulling the keys out of his pocket and moving the Jetta to the street. He didn't follow me, and I had nowhere to go. He told everyone I pulled a knife on him for no reason at all.

CHAPTER TWENTY-TWO

IT TOOK ONE FULL DAY of recovery to learn how to walk again after the marathon, and my legs shook like a colt's. Everybody was wrong. My body didn't crave running any-more—but it craved something. The next challenge. What now, Dr. Norwood? The following morning, hoisting myself up with my arms now that my legs had become useless logs, I pushed my way to the bathroom and pulled out the scale hidden below the towels. It had been nearly six months since I weighed in, but I knew I was bigger. Had felt my quads growing hard and bulky as I put on the miles. Shit, I should have done this yesterday. Right after the marathon.

I was at 121 pounds. That was it? Eleven pounds above the top weight I had arbitrarily assigned myself so many months ago. Then why did my clothes fit so differently? Why couldn't I pull up any of my skinny jeans, any of my kid jeans, above my thighs? I made an appointment to get my body fat tested. Measuring my waist, it wasn't much bigger than my lowest, hovering between 26 and 27 inches.

Thank god I could walk, albeit stiff-legged, two days later when it came time to clip me, dip me, and see just how much fat lingered against my muscles like frosting. "You're at 18 percent," said the administrator. "That's—that's good. Female Olympic athletes average about 19 percent. Professional cross-fit women are at 18 percent. You're per-fect, I can't recommend anything." Perfect. I was perfect. *Stop looking for validation from strangers.*

I didn't feel perfect, and I knew I didn't look perfect. Strangers stopped telling me how skinny I was. I couldn't remember the last time a woman gushed at my waist or men pretended like they weren't fascinated. Like they didn't love the fact that I had the body of a little girl. India was just two months away, and I wasn't stupid enough to think I could starve myself as easily this time. There would be family meals. Too many dinners out. Force-feeding by hand (to show their love). I needed another challenge, and I didn't need Dr. Norwood to tell me that. Something I could do in India, where the air was too rich with smoke, sand, and pollution to run, even if I wanted to. So, that was it. I would lift weights and I would spin. I would grow a butt that my Indian genes fought so hard against.

I'd been taking group lifting classes for so long, all in vain, and I knew what to do. It wasn't the sets that were hard—it was the protein pounding. Everyone said to shove protein down your throat as soon as you finished lifting, all while sipping on BCAA water throughout. How much protein was controversial, but I figured the more the better. Within sixty seconds of my new every-other-day-at-home regimen, I had protein in my hand and sliding down my throat. Whey powder, white fish, liver, and more. The muscle piled on everywhere I targeted like my body wanted it. Jeans got tighter. Bras began to hurt as my back expanded with new wings. Bigger ones. Stronger.

"You only have a few more weeks to back out!" Chirag would tease. This time we were flying in together, and I was armed with my latest obsession: books about eating disorders. Marya Hornbacher's *Wasted,* my most favorite, beloved one that I cried through, highlighting nearly every other sentence. Portia de Rossi's *Unbearable Lightness. Wintergirls.* I soaked them all in and found my sisters, the ones I'd looked for in college but had only uncovered Sam. I began talking about my eating disorder, my faithful ED (Mr. Ed), the one abusive boyfriend I'd never be able to quit entirely. I talked to anyone who would listen. I pounded statistics and weird discoveries and the latest research into Chirag's head like he was just as invested in anorexia facts as me. The genetic links, the men who suffered in silence. The idea that once we're below an ideal body weight, our ancestral instincts kick in. We were designed to not be able to see our reflections accurately at a low weight in case it was a bad harvest season. Otherwise, our ancestors might have given up hope, and that's not very conducive to a successful species. And I stopped drinking. Well, almost. Now, one glass was enough and it was usually wine—and usually because I needed to in order to be social. Not because I needed to forget.

"I need another tattoo," I told Chirag one morning. This is how they happen for me. I wake up knowing that a part of me is missing, but exactly where to find it. We drove across the bridge to Lady Luck. Like our house that we'd sprung out of the ground, I was also being built. Plans were being changed, blueprints altered. "Write 'C' down," I told Chirag as I checked in.

"This your first?" the artist asked. I was used to questions like this.

"No, I have a huge one on my back, a cover-up. And script on my ribcage."

"Really?" he asked, skeptical. "Let me see."

I lifted my shirt, with just the briefest of thoughts over whether he'd find my stomach flat enough. The feather on my back covered up stupid, temporary parts of my life. I knew when I got them I didn't want them. A sorority tattoo and a pentacle. The feather was huge and black, a Cherokee symbol. It had grown with me, shrunk with me. The Pablo Neruda quote I had penned into my own cage in Costa Rica. *A nadie te pareces desde que yo te amo.* You are like nobody because I love you. I did it for Chirag on the other side of the world, a testament to my permanence for him through an hour of searing pain.

"Okay," said the artist. "But this one. This one's gonna feel like I'm sawing your finger off. Ready?"

I chose a deep blue C to be emblazoned on my ring finger. Chirag's handwriting. Once the wedding bands piled on with the engagement ring, it would be mostly hidden. I would only see it in private, when I bared my hands and washed my face, the refection of his initial in the mirror. It would be my always something blue.

It didn't hurt like he said. My body remembered the unique sting of tattoos and made me start with my deep yogic breathing on autopilot. "Hope I spelled it right!" the artist said as he bandaged me up. I tipped him the same amount as the cost.

On the ride home, the familiar hum of my phone called from my purse. *We regret to inform you,* began the teaser on the phone's desktop. Another poetry rejection. I'd been sending out my second book manuscript for weeks. My skin had thickened against these form responses, but sometimes, sometimes they put in a little extra sting that was crafty. Swiping it open, the full letter from the Pulitzer Prize Committee spread its eager little legs. ... *although your book of poetry, which was nominated by an undisclosed nominee, was quite impressive, the committee has ultimately decided to award this year's Pulitzer Prize to another candidate.* What the hell? What nomination? To my left, Chirag maneuvered onto the highway and I struggled with my bloody, bandaged up finger to search my email. Sent, nothing. Trash, nothing. Spam. There it was, filtered six months ago. *Congratulations! Your book has been nominated for a Pulitzer Prize.* Well. At least I didn't spend all that time wondering if I was good enough.

"Did you get anything for my family?" Chirag asked. It was just a few more weeks to go, and this was a first. Him being worried that I would ever be empty-handed.

"Yes."

"What?"

"I'd rather not say." I loved surprises, keeping them even more than getting them.

"Please."

"Are you sure?"

For his mom, it was a photo of us in a crystal frame, the only one of just the two of us taken almost a year ago when we met. I looked lovely, didn't I? Like Angelina Jolie with the skeleton poking through. These days, I didn't take many pictures. For his mom as well, along with his cousins and aunts, I got us all matching Tiffany bracelets with the wedding date etched into them. For his grandfather, father, male cousin, and an uncle, Cartier money clips with the date. Just for his dad, a handmade hanger for his wedding kurta with "Father of the Groom" bent into the wire. A bottle of 18-year-old scotch for all his friends complemented with engraved flasks: "To nights we'll never remember with friends we'll never forget" followed by the wedding date. Their ritual of an all-night drinking fest on Sandeep's rooftop was coming, and I wanted my spirit there. I had "My ride or die" tee-shirts made, each pointing the opposite direction, and a Mr. and Mrs. Est. 20/1/16 matching set.

"Oh," Chirag said, thumbing the gifts.

"Are you upset you asked now?" By now, by now he should trust me. Giving gifts was something I was great at. Something I loved about myself.

"Yes."

He taught me how to say phrases I'd need to know and recorded them in my phone. There was no need for Rani this time. *Now we all have matching bracelets. These are eggless sweets from Portland. You look beautiful. She can't have spicy food* (Sam's stomach had turned on her in Abu Dhabi). He took me to get my nose pierced, a preparation for the hoop I'd wear on our wedding day. "Your eyes are going to water," said the piercer, but they didn't. I didn't feel the metal through my skin at all. That night, as Chirag stared at the new decoration, he said, "I don't see you as white anymore."

"I'm not."

"You know what I mean."

"How do you see me?"

"I don't know. You just are."

As the flight inched closer and the condo stayed barren of a Christmas tree to make room for the moving boxes that piled up, Michelle fell farther and farther away. I still tried, kind of half-heartedly. But every time I asked to see her she said no. Or "maybe" and then never followed through. Or yes and canceled even as I was on my way.

She snipped us apart entirely the only way we know how: on Facebook. It was a comment to a random, India-focused post. "Sounds amazing, wish I could go!" That was how she told me. There was no bridal shower, no bachelorette party. That same day, Victor messaged me. "Got my ticket to India!" he said. Really? He was coming? I hadn't spoken to him since the engagement party when he dutifully decorated and cooked under Michelle's instructions. It's like she was sending a stand-in, though he was coming of his own desire. I didn't reply to her.

One week before we left, she texted me. "We need to plan your bachelorette party." The words were soaked in guilt.

But I replied, and did my best to fake cheer. I sent her a list of names. She asked for email addresses. I didn't argue, didn't say, "Can't you message these people and get it yourself?" Instead, I did the work. Put it in a spreadsheet and sent it back, like she was my boss and I a lowly admin.

Two days before India. "Maybe we should do this when you get back," she texted. "Everyone's busy." Chirag and I had been engaged for a year now.

"I'd rather not," I replied. "Having a bachelorette party after I'm married is kinda weird."

"It's not weird!" she said. I couldn't hold it in. Here, here was the vomiting I'd always wanted.

"I didn't want to do this on text," I said. "But you cancel any plans or don't respond to my asking to see you. I don't think this relationship has been beneficial, for either of us, for some time now."

"Then why the hell did you let me throw you such a thoughtful, expensive engagement party???"

"All the gestures I've made, asking you to be my MOH, acknowledging you in my book, those were pleas. Last ditch efforts. I asked you to be part of my wedding because I thought. Hoped. You'd WANT to."

"I'd think you would cut me some slack. I've had a hard year." *You've been having a hard year for years.*

"Like I said, I didn't want to do this on text."

"Then when?" *You tell me. You tell me. You ask to see me, just once.* "Why did you let me throw you such an expensive party???" she asked again. Money. It was always about money.

"I never wanted this to be a burden. If the money is important, tell me the cost and I'll pay you."

"It's not about the money. It's about the time and effort." *Your time and effort can be easily bought. You mean Victor's time and effort?*

"Look, I really don't want to do this on text. I thought you might get defensive, counterattack, and not actually listen to me, and that's how it seems to be playing out now. But I've been talking to my Dr. for a year re. whether or not I should formally end our relationship."

"Seems like you've already made up your mind. Just wish you would have let me say my side of the story."

Michelle. You didn't even let me say mine. I said a tiny sliver of all the hurt and anger that had been fueling me up from the insides. She never messaged again, not even the day I left. At twenty-three years old, our friendship crawled into a dark space and whimpered as the heart beat slowed.

Sam's plane was scheduled to arrive in Mumbai just three days after us. Victor one week later. "Can I borrow something of yours for the wedding?" I asked her over the phone. Just one more day.

"Let me think about what to bring," she said.

Our flight left at five in the morning, which means a taxi right when the bars let out. We'd each slept just two hours, and I had a bottle of sleeping pills in a vitamin bottle. "He's not going to come," said Chirag, glancing up and down the road for the taxi. He was right.

Frantic calls were made to beg for a cab driver to risk picking up a rural fare in the middle of the night. We were living in a cell of a condo in Hillsboro deep, blocks from the property that we'd raised like a child. The final touches would be completed while we were gone. The apple tree groomed, the hardware and finishes installed. Six months ago, we'd buried a silver coin below where the foundation would be poured, a ritual from his Indian side. As he dug, I wandered the property counterclockwise with a smoking white sage in hand, whispering prayers to cleanse and bless the land. A ritual from *my* Indian side. The craftsman home had sprung up like a blossom, opening carefully into the world with an unsure skeleton and wondering eyes.

"He's here," said Chirag, picking up the heaviest bags.

xxiii.
Rites and Rituals

FOR TWO WEEKS, I lived in a cheap hotel where there was paid-for sex all around me. Scott couldn't find me here, and I knew he might be stalking Michelle. I burrowed into the stinking room because I deserved it. Didn't I? To wallow in my filth after all I'd allowed? I called my mom for the first time in four years, and she pretended like there hadn't been a fallout. We were unsure about each other, sniffing like dogs, but it was something. It was something.

One week in, and I was used to the bed whose springs scratched curios at my back. The sounds of faked orgasms and low grunting. Only my mom knew how to find me now.

"Jennifer?" she asked when she called, as if it could be anyone else. "You remember Rosa? I, well, I think she's dead."

Rosa. Michelle had told me she looked chunky at Kerri's funeral, but that the childlike giddiness in her had stayed. She poked fun at herself, at her weight, prematurely so nobody else could.

"Rosa?" I asked. No, not Rosa. Rosa couldn't be dead, she had too much life. "What happened?"

"I saw it in the paper. What was her last name?"

"Dietzle."

"It's her."

"Mom. What happened to her?"

"She killed herself." No. "Hung herself, it seems. It says her brother did the same two months ago." No, that wasn't right. Rosa was Catholic. Catholics don't kill themselves. They can't.

"When ... when's the funeral?"

"Let's see ... it says there's a service at a church on Saturday." Saturday. Two days. I'm coming, Rosa. This time I'm coming.

It seemed wrong, stepping into my mom's house with my black dress on a hanger. It was smaller and smelled dirtier. The carpet felt gummy beneath my toes. And my mom looked elderly, frail. More like eighty than in her fifties. "You don't want me to go with you, do you?" she asked.

"No, I'm going alone." I hadn't told Michelle, didn't want to scratch open that scab. She'd never liked Rosa or Kerri anyway, but funerals were new to us. Everyone wanted to dress up like they saw in movies and blot their eyes with a handkerchief. But this wasn't for play, this was real. Rosa and Kerri, they'd both been real. They were my only real friends during the blackest parts of high school.

Thank god, I didn't recognize anyone. I'd never been in a Catholic church before, and the body was kept solidly beneath the oak casket door. Was that a good thing? Shouldn't hangings offer a clean, beautiful death? That's what Rosa deserved, but I didn't know if I wanted to see her anyway. Touch her cold skin.

The priest was an asshole. "We can only pray for her soul," he said. "How she departed, at her own hands ...." Oh, fuck you. You don't know, you don't know her. If there was a hell, Rosa wasn't there. She'd put out the flames with the blue-hot brightness of her own soul.

On the drive back, my death-scented dress hanging in the backseat, I got pulled over for speeding. I always got pulled over for speeding. "What's the hurry?" asked the policeman.

"Funeral," I said. I didn't mention I was coming, not going. His eyes latched onto the black dress in the back. Something about me made him believe me.

"Oh. Okay. Well, uh, just try to keep the speed down, okay?"

"Okay."

"And, uhm. Well. I'm sorry."

"Me, too."

CHAPTER TWENTY-THREE

IT WAS A RARITY, lucking into a flight that landed at eight in the evening. Chirag's family came in hoards to the airport with his friends seasoning the mass. His mom, brother, aunts, and cousins I'd never met before. The energy of an impending wedding was contagious, amped everybody up and ensured rich foods and sweets were constant. It took four cars to get everyone there and back, and that was just the welcome committee.

Chirag's family was renting a four-bedroom apartment while they re-built the joint family home two streets over. The floors were all marble, the bathrooms each with a hose and no toilet paper. The travel packs of baby wipes I'd brought were pressed in my bra, against my heart. I hoped with everything in me that they'd flush during that first trial and thank god they did. And the gifts. Oh, my god, the gifts.

It was shopping, shopping, shopping and eating, eating, eating non-stop. At Dr. Norwood's suggestion, I'd left the scale at home and brought only stretchy pants. Hell, I threw the scale away. The baggy, harem-style pants and elastic-waisted maxi dresses hugged new muscles. New curves. "They're saying you're thin," whispered Chirag as his aunts chattered in Gujarati.

The day before Sam arrived, Chirag's mother brought out my wedding attire. It was traditional, one red sari and one white. I was to wear both. A hand-knit green silk blouse heavy with beading and which fit like a bra, letting Neruda's words peek out. "Your hair long now," she said.

"Ma's been practicing English," his skinny cousin Alia

said. Her arms were bony and slight, her stomach little but soft. She was blessed with genetics and her thinness reinforced by Bollywood standards. But she had no muscle. She was weak. "Do you want to see my sari for the wedding?"

She took me to a back room and pulled it out, a bright pink and green swirl. "I designed it myself," she said. "You know, I don't know why everyone's saying you're thin. From photos, I think you got quite fat. Especially in your arms and face." And I was thirteen years old again, the skinny popular girls' judgment raining down on me. *It's okay. It's okay.*

Do you really want to let other people assign your value? Dr. Norwood asked in my head.

Refuge was in my hotel. It was in mornings of lifting weights, walking on the beach and customizing my omelets to have only spinach and mushrooms. It was in waiting for Sam. The events at the family home blurred together, all bowing and "Jai jihendras" and trying to memorize faces to go with names. "You look pretty in traditional clothes," distant relatives would tell me. The little kids swarmed me like hungry mosquitoes, the first seemingly white person they'd ever met. "Auntie, you're *very* tall," they would say.

The day before Sam's arrival, we went to the shoe designer's home. "What style you like?" she asked me, and in unison "Traditional" rang through the apartment. My shoes were red platform wedges with hand-woven gold threads and beads through them. A single toe loop kept them on. "You want more jazzy?" she asked. "A gold anklet chain to the toe?" Yes, I wanted it all. I wanted to drip in it. For Sam, I chose gold platform shoes that would go with whatever color sari she chose.

"Size nine," I told her when picking Sam's shoe.

"Nine?" she asked. "So big!" Sam had hands and feet like Chirag, too big for the rest of her.

She arrived in the middle of the night, looking both rested and on the brink of passing out. "The safe for the jewelry and passports," I said, pointing to it in our shared hotel armoire. "The code is 0881. I figured we'd both re-member that." Our shared birth month and year.

"Before I forget," she said, "I brought you this. My mom gave it to me, and her sister lent it to her. She wore it on her own wedding day to my dad." It was a simple gold bracelet that locked together with a fine gold chain. A piece of Sam to be with me during the hours-long ceremony while she snapped photo after photo from the sideline.

I wanted her to sleep, planned to sneak away to the gym in the morning so she could navigate around the jet lag. Instead, we turned off the lights, crawled into our respective beds and talked through sunbreak.

"Remember the time in Atlanta?" I asked.

"Oh, god, we were dumb. I still can't believe you didn't wake me up when there was lightning over my head!"

"I know, I'm sorry. But maybe it's for the best? Maybe you would have sat up and your head would have exploded."

It didn't matter the distance or the years. We settled together, fit together, no matter what. It was like the first time I'd met her—easy and natural.

We drifted off for an hour, but at eight my body was up. It was looking for its safe routine, its lunges and squats followed by protein. "Where are you going?" she asked, up with my shuffles and small sounds.

"Gym and then breakfast. You wanna come?"

"Yeah."

I walked her through one of my routines, carefully de-signed to bulk just where I wanted. Forty minutes later, both our legs shook like a soufflé about to fall. The breakfast spread was confused, part western and part Indian. We loaded up on meats and vegetables as I tested all the things that she was interested in. "Too spicy for you," for some. "It's okay, you can have this," for others. Afternoons that weren't occupied with shopping, rituals, and eating were spent at the pool. It was just 10:45 in the morning, but screw it, we were on vacation.

"Can we get a cocktail menu?" she asked the young

waiter, who brought us nothing but a snack menu.

"It's 10:45."

"I know what time it is," she said.

"That doesn't start 'til eleven." What magic would happen in fifteen minutes? Then the Big Kahuna arrived.

He was clearly a manager with a strong penchant for Hawaiian shirts. We never saw him wear the same one twice. He came to know us quickly, brought Sam cocktail menus any time of day, and started to let us order off-menu. Naan at noon marinated in garlic and ghee even when the closest thing on the poolside menu was peanuts.

"Ye mere best friend hai, Sam," I said over and over whenever she met someone new. "Just bow to the same people I do, to the same depth," I told her, and they accepted her as my sister.

Victor barely made his flight—it got bumped up during the transit in Seattle and he had to run in his pinching shoes to get through the gate. His hotel was a five-minute walk from ours, and I hadn't even considered how to introduce him. Having a male friend, an unmarried one, who was forty-nine and would trudge halfway across the world for you, was a foreign concept. And homosexuality didn't exist here.

"Why you not married?" everyone asked him, and he would play it off.

"Vic," said one of Chirag's uncles, the youngest who spoke the best English. "I have a friend. She's forty-seven. Very pretty. She'll do?"

"No, no," Victor said. "I don't want to get married." At night, just the three of us as Chirag completed rituals for just his family, Victor told us about his boyfriend. His recent conquests. The nudist fairy festival he was attending as soon as he got back from India. He only mentioned Michelle once, and it was to talk about how good he was at doing her hair.

I wanted them to see it all, and Chirag played host in between balancing family obligations. We whisked them to

Colaba where we walked through the street vendors who nearly wet themselves at the site of three white-ish people. Victor was a six-foot-tall Mexican, but still. He was foreign and too tall and looked like he had money.

The poojas, the rituals, at home were constant. Blessings poured from the priest's fingertips, and I followed along to his gestures. Coconut pieces were stuck to my forehead, and wedding mehendi appointments made. Two days before the wedding, the beautification ceremony was held at Chirag's dad's best friend's house. They were to be my "wedding parents" since I had none of my own. Turmeric and sandalwood blends were rubbed on our faces, and I was wrapped in a green sari with my hair pulled back. Seated on a chair and surrounded by forty people, each came to me, smeared more paste across my skin, and held their fists tight to their temples to draw negative energy away. Then the roles changed. One by one, the women came to me as I dipped my fingers in the cool paste and spread it over their gold skin.

It took nine straight hours to apply the mehendi up to my biceps and to the tops of my calves. Largely a turmeric paste, it's a sacred ritual that's been picked up by tourist shops around the world and now used for temporary tribal tattoos for spring breakers in Hawaii. Still, here, in India it's the ultimate in temporary bodily decoration. The deeper the stain, the more your husband-to-be loves you—and the better your in-laws will treat you. On my left palm, an image of a bride with a nose ring entering her new home. On my right, a groom riding into the ceremony on an elephant. Peacocks, trumpets, and symbols I didn't recognize reached across my forearms. "You want his name?" asked the artist. "Spell for me."

The groom's name is hidden in the mehendi, a sort of foreplay. The C was on my wrist, the H on the swell of my palm. And I on my ring finger, an R on another mound. After the ceremonies, the man hunts for his name, initiating touch. For thousands of years, this was the first time the groom really saw his new wife. The first time he touched her. "Here, C is here already," she said, pointing to the tattoo. But she'd already inked in another.

Sam and I couldn't move after the mehendi without leaving rusty stains in our trail. Chirag and Victor came to the hotel with every vegetarian menu item from McDonald's. "It no spicy!" Chirag told Sam in a faked thick Indian accent. Together, he and Victor fed us, our hands useless. Kitted us out with extra-long straws and made a fuss about how much the room stank. That night, we rolled ourselves up like little burritos and let the excess mehendi flake off into the hotel sheets. By morning, it looked like there had been a killing. It felt like sleeping in dry, flaky mud, but was nothing compared to the scraping. For an hour, we hunched over our bodies, spoons digging into our flesh as we forced off the dried henna. Sam finished quickly—she had none on her feet and it reached only to her elbows. For me, I scraped myself raw. Now, the mehendi was a bright orange but it darkened by the minute, searching for that deep mahogany it needed to be for the wedding.

"Are you nervous?" Sam asked. This time tomorrow the wedding would start. Six hundred people I didn't know would gather and my head would be heavy with gold jewelry.

"No. Not yet," I said, toying with the nose ring. "I want you to take a specific picture as soon as I'm dressed."

"What's that?" Reaching into a suitcase, I pulled out a baby blue garter belt full of crystals and white lace. "I'm wearing this under the sari. I want a photo of it."

"Scandalous," she said about the piece of Americana, my quiet contribution, that would rest under twelve yards of silk and that nobody would know about.

Michelle didn't send a message. Not the night before, not the morning of. Somehow I slept, the stink of the henna permeating from both Sam and me. Chirag began calling at eight in the morning. "Sending a taxi," he said. "My dad will meet you at the venue." My heart began to pick up its pace. I had an appointment at the hotel salon for a blowout—I still wasn't allowed to get the mehendi wet and had to wash my face with gloves on and take baby wipe baths. For days, everyone was telling me how tired I'd be, how overwhelming the whole process was. But that wasn't true. I was alert, I was alive. I was moving towards a life I'd recognized the day it presented to me, as delicious and pull-me-in-sweet as cake.

xxiv.
Rush

THE TIMING was almost freakishly perfect. After Rosa's funeral, Chris and Michelle got into their own two-bedroom unit in Sherwood and I moved in like they'd been expecting me. Chris had sweet-talked his way into an assistant manager role at Best Buy. Michelle was taking one class per term from the same community college where I had graduated high school and worked a $12 per hour job at a childcare center within the VA hospital. For us, that was a lot. She was turning twenty this year, and I lived with them for just one week before she pulled me aside to show me a stick with two clear, fat lines. "I'm pregnant," she said.

"What are you going to do?"

"I don't know," she said, breathing out slowly. "I think … I think I'm gonna keep it."

Scott had disappeared, probably between his manager's thighs—and I was thankful. He'd set up a seamless transition between me and someone else. Only then would he let go. He called me twice. Or, rather, called Michelle. One was to ask when I was coming for my stuff. "But I want the TV," he said. I'd bought it with Papo's money.

"Keep it all," I said. I didn't want those blood items.

Michelle was getting round, forced me to go with her to the Museum of Science and Industry to look at real fetuses preserved in formaldehyde-full mason jars. "It's about this big now," she said, pawing at the glass of an alien curled into itself.

I was floundering. In beauty school, I learned to cut and perm. Roller set. And I was surrounded by people I didn't want to become.

On a whim, I walked into the local university. I knew nothing about it. What a bachelor's degree was, what scholarships were, or what it meant to apply. I just knew I needed to get out.

I don't know why, but I told Scott the second time he called. The new girl he was seeing was still in high school with a preacher father and a sealed vagina. "Couldn't we just have sex sometimes, just for fun?" he asked, and threw a fit when I calmly told him no. Like the old toy was snatched away from him, even though he'd rubbed the nice paint job off it and its hair was falling out.

"College, huh?" he asked. "Good luck with that. I just hope you're not going for the whole 'college experience' bullshit and actually do something useful with your life."

I was the golden child in admissions, but didn't know the right questions to ask. Nobody told me the secret knock. I was considered independent easily with those parental rights reneged, papers signed and notarized. The student loans came flooding in. When Michelle was so big she couldn't get up by herself and ate nothing but Subway peanut butter cookies, I moved out. It was August, four weeks 'til the term started, and I had a single dorm room ten by five feet wide in the old Montgomery building with thick wood trim at the windows. Mysteriously, it had a sink in it but the shared bathrooms were down the hall. It was tiny and perfect.

I didn't just want to go to college, I wanted to *go* to college. When the first week rolled around, I looked at it all. Drama clubs, outdoor clubs, student government, and the newspaper. But it was the sorority open recruitment that drew me in. "Hey!" a girl called, tall and lean with bleached hair. "You with the cute hair." Me? I'd taken to a flippy, ash-colored concoction, dreamt up in beauty school and paid for with a trade. "Take this, you should come to our open house!"

The leaves on the urban campus fell apart under new boots bought on student loans. My sweaters were itchy but trendy, and in a dim room I huddled with sixty other girls to hear about the virtues of sisterhood. "Looking around, it may not seem like it," said a girl with unbelievably straight teeth, "but the Greek system here is highly inclusive. We value diversity, tolerance, and acceptance." The sole Asian girl standing behind her tried to bury a smile. "In fact, that's one of our priorities this year. Diversity. African American, Asian, Latino, even Native American. We're diligently working towards a campus-wide sisterhood that properly reflects our eclectic, urban campus today." There were two girls in the audience who looked not white.

"What a crock," said the tomboy next to me under her breath, her big brown eyes like warm, dark waters. "Hi," she said to me, leaning in. "I'm Sam."

CHAPTER TWENTY-FOUR

I WAS USED TO this taxi driver by now—he'd been picking us up daily to drop us around town. "Good morning!" I said, the excitement falling over my lips. "Morning, madam," he said, touching the Ganesha figurine attached to the dashboard.

Victor had walked over that morning, his wedding kurta and shoes in a plastic zip bag.

I didn't know what to expect. "Small wedding, small," everyone kept saying and I was partially heartbroken. No seven walks around the fire? I knew little about Hindu weddings, and even less about any Jain aspects of it. But the fire I knew. It was kind of like the American ring exchange, although that tradition had been swept up by Indians, too, and now rings were added to the already two-hour Hindu ceremony.

The couple walked around the fire seven times. Each round signified a different aspect of the promises, but also indicated seven lifetimes together. I guess seven lifetimes was enough. After Chirag proposed, I asked him, "So if you're married for seven lifetimes, which one do you think we're on?"

"Well, it's not the last," he said. "But it's not the first. You annoy me *way* too much for it to be the first," he said, laughing.

I'd been lied to. This wasn't a small wedding. The taxi turned into a private driveway that was canopied with white and yellow tents. Flowers weighed down each post, and a few wedding cars had already arrived, the hoods smothered in fresh flowers. "The wedding of Chirag and Jennifer" read the sign outside. Up the red carpeted steps, two stages were already erected. One was a small, ten by ten gazebo of a structure in the center of the room with dozens of chairs circling it. The other was permanent, like a rectangular stage in a school gymnasium with gaudy, gold ornate velvet chairs perched on top. On the other side of the room, waiters hustled from station to station, prepping food and putting out cloth napkins. Flowers, flowers were everywhere. They lit up the room with their sweetness.

Chirag's dad appeared and directed me to one of the private rooms to the side. With every person we passed, he paused to talk and I bowed. He chatted in Gujarati, but every time he said, "She a yoga teacher," in English, like "She's the president!" or "She's a movie star!" Poking his head inside my dressing room to check the size of the bathroom and the coolness of the air conditioning, he said, "This will do," before taking Victor by the elbow to his own private changing room.

Sam and I began unpacking our little bags, but everything had already started. "Chai, madam?" asked a young girl. "Filter coffee? Chaat?" We loved the filter coffee, a way of making Nescafe with boiling milk and brown sugar that made it taste like melted ice cream. No, no chaat. I'd been warned by everyone. Having an empty stomach because the dinner would be intense. That I could do—and I had permission.

"Ready?" asked the only young Indian woman with cropped hair I'd ever seen. The makeup artist and hairstylist, this is all she did. Wedding after wedding, one hair bun and smoky eye after another. She didn't wear a wedding ring. "What style you want?"

"Whatever you think is best," I said.

"I'll do very traditional then. That okay?"

"Whatever you think is best." With her assistant, a silent Nubian-colored woman, they swooped onto us with their creams and powders. The foundation felt an inch thick and the kohl melted into my eyes.

"Thick eyebrows okay?" she asked, and I nodded. The lining, the cat eyes, the eye shadow that dug deep into my creases and fanned up to the brow bone. In thirty minutes, they'd transformed both of us into people we'd never seen. "Your eyes, with your eyes it look so good," she said.

I was unrecognizable. I looked like a woman instead of a little girl. She twisted my hair behind my head and teased it high at the crown. At the top, a sponge roll was wrapped with my auburn hair, my mom's hair, multiple times until it was hidden like a weapon. Pinned and sprayed, she stood me up and began spinning me into the first sari. "This needs to be tight," she said, "really tight or the petticoat won't hold the weight of the fabrics. Suck it in."

She yanked the strings of the petticoat as hard as she could, her assistant holding me still. It cut into my skin, my organs, but it didn't matter. Every fold of the handmade fabric over my hips, accordioned at my side, made me more beautiful. Sam was whipped into her own sari, tan and pink and jeweled, her baby-soft stomach rolling over. "Veil, veil," said the hairstylist, gesturing for her assistant to get the heavy red, beaded cloths. It was pinned into my hair and hung heavily on either side of my face. "Nose ring. What size you want?" she asked, holding up a modest one the size of a nickel.

"Bigger," I said, and she held up a quarter-sized one. "Bigger."

She laughed, "Oh, you want Southie style," and dug a gold and diamond ring the size of the sun from her bag. "Young girls, they don't like this style much anymore." It slid into my nose, brushed against my lips, and hung just below my jawline. "Remember, when you eating, food go through the hoop," she said. "Like a basketball." That's right, I couldn't eat. Couldn't finish my coffee, the china banging against the gold that hung from my nose.

"Oh, my god!" Victor said, sneaking in. "You both look *amazing!*"

"Hey!" said the stylist. "No men."

"No, it's okay," I said. "He's my brother." Victor's peacock blue kurta with gold pants and jeweled shoes with the toes curled up made him look older. In a good way. Like he belonged here, like we all did.

"Hello?" said an Indian woman about my age as she entered. Fake black hair clip-ins hung in ringlets to her waist. "You almost ready?"

"Yeah, almost."

"I'm Priya. I'm your sister for today. Irrfan's daughter." I couldn't remember who Irrfan was. "I will tell you, you know, what all the meaning is. What to do. You don't want to promise something you don't understand!" She was right.

Priya stayed in my ear, at my side, right from the start. "When we walk out now," she said. "We're going all the way outside. Chirag waiting for you there. Don't look up until I tell you. Keep your eyes down, like, how you say … submissive. Modest."

She took me by the crook of my arm and led me outside. Red carpet, red carpet, bottoms of colorful saris and pretty shoes. That's all I saw. Cameras clicked and bright lights. "We're coming to stairs now," she said. "Once we get to the bottom, we'll be outside." I could feel the heat of hundreds of people, the yelling in Hindi. "Almost there," she said, and then there was a small decorated box on the ground before me. "You need to get on," she said.

I recognized Chirag's feet in front of me, standing on his own box. "Okay, you can look up now," Priya shouted from below me.

He was incredible, like the first time we met. Full golden wedding attire and matching gold headdress. A blue marking was over his third eye and golden diamond rings I'd never seen before on his hands. "Here," said Priya, handing red garlands to me. "You get this on him, but don't let him put one on you." Instead of play fighting away like he was supposed to, Chirag lowered his head and let me put the garland on him.

"Aye!" everyone started shouting, pulling his arms down to keep the garland off me. Whoever puts the garland on the other the most easily has the upper hand in the marriage. "Someone lift her!" Priya yelled, but I was too unstable in sweltering silk and five-inch shoes on that shaky box for anyone to brave it. Suddenly big, strong hands grasped my hips and held me high, above them all. I reached back and grabbed the forearms that hoisted me up, trusting blindly that whoever it was wouldn't drop me. As I was set back down, Chirag placed the garland over my head. "Now we go back inside," said Priya. "Come with me."

"Who picked me up?" I asked.

"Your male friend," she said. "I don't know, I just turned around and saw a really big man so I told him to do it. He the strongest one there. Put your head back down." I only saw glimpses of the outside. The seemingly millions of people, the confetti everywhere, and the trumpets. All the trumpets.

Priya took me back to the changing room. "Three minutes," she told the stylist. "Hurry." The second sari was wrapped around me, the red one for the ceremony. It weighed me down like I was drowning. "Put these on," Priya said, pulling 24-karat yellow gold chains and rings from her bag. Two wrapped around my ankles with five chains each for my toes. Two were bracelets with Ganesha idols woven through the chains, four rings for each hand big enough to stack on top of the ones already littering my bony fingers. "See?" she asked. "The designs match the tikka on your forehead." I'd forgotten about the gold chains in my hair, the pendant that hung just below my hairline. "Okay, we go again," she said. "Head down."

This time, my Wedding Father met me on the other side of the doors, held out his elbow and began walking me to the small stage with Priya on the other side. "Slowly, slowly," he said, as if I could run with all the gold.

I picked up the saris in my right hand, my "clean" hand,

while other hands guided me gently up the makeshift stairs to ensure I didn't fall. There was the fire pit. It was here, being tended by a priest and his assistant. Chirag was already seated in one of the plush chairs and I was directed next to him, on his left side. "From now on," Priya whispered as a stool was brought to her so she could sit beside me. "You always sit on his left. Always. It's closest to his heart."

I couldn't understand the Gujarati chants, but Priya stayed in my ear. "This," she said, "this is the, how you say ... vows. You have to take seven, he only takes one. How messed up is that?" She explained my vows to him. How I would treat his parents like my own and not abuse them. Most of the promises were like American ones, about faithfulness and trust. "Now his vow," Priya said. "For him, it's only that he will stay faithful. From now on, it is only you." I saw Sam snapping photos with her pro camera from the sidelines, and I wiped a smile across my face no matter what. There were cameras everywhere. Even as my lips began to twitch. "Okay," said Priya. "Now the fire ritual. You know this one?"

"Kind of," I said.

"Chirag leads first, and you put your right big toe on the stone over there when you reach it," she said. "Stop in front of the chairs. When the priest throw the rice, you sit down first. Whoever sit down first is most dominant in the marriage." Like musical chairs.

The first time around, a garland tying us together, Chirag kept going and didn't wait for me to touch my foot to the stone. The crowds that were milling about and watching laughed, but most were caught up in conversation. Some were eating. It was a party that went on for hours, and we were just part of the entertainment. There was no room for being somber, for being quiet. Standing before the chairs, the priest looked at both of us and then tossed a handful of rice into the fire. Priya shoved me down into the chair, making sure I landed first. "Next time, you sit down faster," she said with a smile.

Sacred sweets were pulled from a decorated cardboard box, and as the priest muttered words over them, Chirag tore off a small piece and slid it through the nose ring between my lips. I did the same. "You want a big piece?" Priya asked. "Yeah, yeah, bigger piece!" all the women began chanting. An elder took three sweets and smashed them in her hand, making one monstrous sweet. "You shove in his mouth," she said.

After ninety minutes of up and down, repeating words, tossed rice and blessings, the priest held a small tin of sindoor—red as blood—to Chirag. With a swipe of his ring finger down the middle of my head, through my hair and onto my forehead, Chirag told me, "Now we're married." The heat from his fingers blazed a trail through the forest of my hair.

On the main stage, Chirag and I were posed and propped by the photographers, shouting the little English they knew to get me to obey. Groups and couples, families and friends in every imaginable combination came up one by one. It went on for two hours, my face frozen in a painful smile. "You so happy!" said one woman to me. "Always smiling. So pretty in these clothes. You look Punjabi with those eyes," and Chirag laughed. She asked him something in Gujarati and all I recognized of his answer was "Native American."

"Eh?" she asked.

He replied in a mess of aspirations I couldn't grasp. "Different kind of Indian," he said, and she wobbled her head—the not-quite-an-answer response.

The crowds had started to disperse. They'd shown face, had their meal, gotten their photo and had completed social obligations. Finally, finally, we were seated at the long tables that formed a big square around the food. A dozen waiters kept making rounds. Spicy rices, the family's favorite chaats, dumplings, parathas, and naan. Chocolate lava cake, eggless, for dessert. "More, madam?" they kept asking and I shook my head. They never let my plate be empty.

Sam was on one side of me, Chirag on the other. Victor

was kitty-corner with the men as they quizzed him about being single. Didn't he want to be married? "No, no. I'm happy," I heard him say.

Priya came for me when the last of the cake was scraped off the white plates. "Now is time for you to leave your parents. You're supposed to cry. Don't laugh!" she led me back to the small stage, now littered with forgotten rites and petals. "Here, this is when the bride leaves her parents for good. Just ... look sad. I know it's not real for you. But for us, now the daughter leaves forever. Your Maa and Papa is Chirag's Maa and Papa now. His brother your brother."

As the cameras readied and the film started to roll, I wanted to do a good job. What would make me cry? I thought about the early days. All those times I'd see Chirag with one woman after another so I drowned myself in whatever lips I could find. About my real dad, and the time I was five and he got so mad at my mom he choked her and lifted her against the wall. She just rolled her eyes and he realized he couldn't hurt her like that, so he stalked over to me, grabbed my toy lion with the real porcelain teeth, and smashed it against the wall. I thought about him dying, about how I didn't go no matter how many times he asked. How incredible it was that now he fit into something the size of a flower vase.

I thought about my mom, how unhappy and scared she must have been her whole life so she dumped her everything into me—the good and the bad. The anorexia, the penchant to drink, the selfishness and the rages. About Michelle, who plugged her eyes and pretended she didn't see my attempts to resuscitate us. About Sam and Victor, the two who trampled across the world to be here with me. Sam, who would make it happen no matter what because that's what we promised each other without a word. Victor, who barely knew me, but placed himself effortlessly into the pinnacle, offering to help any way he could.

I could do it. I could force some tears. "Oh, never mind," Priya said. "They're not going to film this."

"But I got sad," I told her.

"What now?" I asked Chirag.

"Now, nothing," he said. "I'm going home to change, a car will take you all to the hotel."

I'd booked a suite in the same hotel where Sam and I had been staying, the Luxury Suite that was 1,500 square feet of luxury—for our wedding night and a makeshift reception with only friends. It was stuffed with pricey furniture, free cookies and a lacquered bar. A separate bedroom with bookcases that reached the ceiling and a sunken tub you could swim in. Sam and I showered in our shared room, now littered with mehendi droppings, empty sunscreen bottles and makeup everywhere. I'd pre-packed a backpack with a change of clothes, pajamas, Solo cups, and a travel speaker with my iPod.

"I'll meet you in the suite," I told her. Chirag was already there.

"You want a first dance, American style?" he asked. I nodded, my eyes red from too much kohl.

We'd chosen Sarah McLachlan's "Ice Cream," the shortest of songs, and danced to it in the empty suite before everyone else arrived. *Better than chocolate—than anything else that I've tried.*

Friends arrived, beers were cracked, the scotch poured, and Sandeep came bearing Old Monk and Teachers. "There's something wrong with you!" he told me. "You have too much energy! You should be passed out by now."

"It's not even midnight!" I said, the little speaker bursting itself to blast out 90s mashups and desi rap. We ordered Dominos at one, breadsticks and more mixers. It tasted different here, with tikka spices and paneer along with the chicken.

"Hey," Chirag said, cornering me while I made a drink for Sandeep that was ninety percent liquor. "Hey! My mom said—she's demanding a honeymoon. At least three days. We leave tomorrow."

"Where?"

"Agra. The Taj Mahal. And yes, you can ride an elephant."

The Unfolding

I don't know what's coming next,
but god, I can't wait to live it. I told you
years ago,
that I just knew—it wasn't foolish hope
or drunken wishes, but a fact. You and I
are a given, just as my eyes
are green and your hands too big.
What took you so long? The ride's
been idling, chortling exhaust for years
in the waiting for you. And now,
the tickets are punched,
the baggage stowed (it was overweight
and we paid for that, of course). Now we,
clasping hands over *Asks or tells*, bolt
whip fast stupid to the unfolding.